By the same author

Everything but the Truth
Anything You Do Say
No Further Questions
The Evidence Against You

How to Disappear

GILLIAN McALLISTER

PENGUIN BOOKS

PENGUIN BOOKS

UK | USA | Canada | Ireland | Australia
India | New Zealand | South Africa

Penguin Books is part of the Penguin Random House group of companies
whose addresses can be found at global.penguinrandomhouse.com

First published 2020
002

Copyright © Gillian McAllister, 2020

The moral right of the author has been asserted

Set in 12.5/14.75 pt Garamond MT Std
Typeset by Jouve (UK), Milton Keynes
Printed and bound in Great Britain by Clays Ltd, Elcograf S.p.A.

A CIP catalogue record for this book is available from the British Library

ISBN: 978-1-405-94242-3

www.greenpenguin.co.uk

Penguin Random House is committed to a
sustainable future for our business, our readers
and our planet. This book is made from Forest
Stewardship Council® certified paper.

For David, forever

Prologue

During

Lauren ducks into the alleyway without warning. She'll do it here, before she goes inside. She gets out the lipstick. It's a nude shade she's worn for years. Her mirror is old, too. Aidan bought it for her the Christmas before last. She looks at it now, her initials inscribed on the back, and opens it. One blue eye stares back at her.

As she hides in the alleyway, she sees what she assumes is the candidate before her leaving the nursery. *Oh no*, Lauren thinks, as she watches her go. The woman is wearing a skinny trouser suit, burgundy loafers. Good hair. But more than that: she has confidence. It's everywhere. In her walk, in the way she holds her handbag, dangling at the end of a slim arm. Her appearance is neat whereas Lauren, looking back at herself in the mirror, is definitely messy. Her hair has frizzed in the rain, around her temples. The woman glances briefly at her, and Lauren shrinks further back into the alley. *Don't look at me. Don't speak to me.*

She stares out on to the rain-slicked street after the woman has gone. There are people coming and going in winter coats, Christmas shopping in their hands. It's late afternoon, already dark. The light from the shopfronts creates blurred sepia puddles of spilled light on the pavement. It is a totally normal street full of totally normal people. She hopes.

Lauren looks again in the mirror and puts her lipstick on. It feathers at the edges and runs. She wipes around her mouth but smears it further, leaving her skin red and sore-looking. What will they ask? Sweat gathers across her lower back. She doesn't know how to answer interview questions any more. Not even the most basic ones.

She gives up with the lipstick, closes the mirror and slides it back into her handbag. Inside the bag is a Portuguese custard tart from the bakery, which she will eat on the bus home, the paper bag spread across her lap to catch the crumbs. She's also saved a trashy article to read about two celebrities who are rumoured to be having an affair. Five minutes of guilty bliss, just for her, afterwards. What remains of her, anyway.

The handbag, the lipstick and the preference for custard tarts and celebrity gossip are old. The parts of her that she has been permitted to keep. The parts of her that are left. She thinks of everything she can no longer do. Kiss her husband. Post on Instagram.

Tell the truth.

Lauren goes inside. The reception has wooden floors and a branded rug with the nursery's name on it. *High Trees*. They're going to ask her competency questions, she is thinking, as the receptionist slides the glass screen back. 'Can I help?' she says, and Lauren thinks: *no, nobody can. Suddenly, I can't recall a time when I helped a difficult child to develop, or I reported a safeguarding concern*. Perhaps she can just tell them the truth. A half-truth. That she really, really needs this job. That she would be good at it. That she will love the children. That there is nothing better, to her, than seeing a three-year-old late talker say, 'Lauren, look!' out of nowhere, as though somebody just turned on the speech part of their brain overnight.

'I have a four-thirty interview,' she says. As she speaks, she smells it. All nurseries smell the same. Poster paints. The plastic smell of lunchboxes: cucumber and bread. She blinks and glances around her. She is home, home amongst these smells and the little starfish hands and feet of the children she will fall in love with. Lauren forgets her frizzy hair, her smudged lipstick.

'Great,' the woman says. Her nails click on the keyboard. 'Please can you confirm your name?'

'Leonora,' Lauren replies. She glances at her reflection in the glass screen. There is no Lauren any more. Lauren is gone.

Before

I

Zara

Holloway Grammar School, London

August

Zara is fourteen years old when she witnesses the murder.

She is reading a book as she walks from the school football pitch to the surrounding fields. Dry clumps of yellow-green grass litter the lawn like balled-up socks, and she keeps tripping over them. She's reading *Eleanor & Park*. She knows it makes no sense to read and walk, but she can't help it. She's gripped by the love story.

As she narrowly misses walking into a goal post, she puts the book in her bag and thinks, instead. Specifically, Zara begins to think about stationery. She bought new pens today, a pack of three wrapped in cellophane. Blue, black, red. She'll never use the red one – isn't it rude to write in red? – but she likes the collection, the three together in a neat row. Zara likes tidiness, though she thinks maybe she shouldn't. She should like drinking and boys.

But anyway, it is so nice to look forward to things in this way. The past few years have been full of worry. It came from nowhere. One morning when she was eleven, Zara began to worry about everything. What if her mother died, what if she attended a party and felt so panicked she needed to leave, what if the Tube crashed, what if, what if, what if . . . ? It has taken Zara years to learn to manage it. Anxiety. Such a bland name for something so sharp.

Zara has always felt on the sidelines – thinking about books at the school disco when she should be thinking about dancing, apparently – but the anxiety somehow made her more so. An observer of life, not a participator in it. She once said this to her stepsister, Poppy, who said, 'I die, Zara, you're such a mood.'

It's already dusky, at eight o'clock, but the evening stretches out in front of her: tonight is going to be spent in a delicious frenzy of unpacking. Four stiff cardboard folders. Slippery A4 plastic wallets. Sticky tabs. Joy Of Missing Out, is it called? JOMO. Well, that. She'll sort out her folders, and then she'll return to school, to Year Ten, a new woman, she has decided. She doesn't quite know who she will be. Not yet. But it won't be who she was before.

When she first hears the noise, she tells herself it's nothing. An unexplained shout on a hot summer's evening. Her pace is slow and relaxed across the empty field, the sky a high lavender dome above her, little dried tufts of grass sticking to her trainers.

It's only when she hears the second shout, then the third, that she stops, a fine layer of sweat on her lower back slowly evaporating as she turns, scanning the horizon for the noises like an animal looking for its predator.

Her eyes land on the bandstand. It's been having its roof repaired over the summer. Each week, on the way home from her extra literature lessons – not cool, at all,

8

but she loves everything about them – slightly more progress has been made. She squints now in the half-light. That's where the noise is coming from. Two men. One on the stage, another halfway up the steps.

She paces forward, then stops, maybe forty feet away. Something's happening. Zara's anxiety often used to make her think that something bad was happening when it wasn't, but this time she thinks she might be right.

Goosebumps appear on her arms as she moves back across the field to one of the greenhouses nearby. She lets herself in and breathes in its familiar, hot musk tomato smell. She spent so many hours in here over the spring, growing organic and non-organic lettuces for a biology experiment that she found stressful. She would re-pot the lettuces in her break times, moving them from small pots on the window sill to fat Gro-bags outside. She would lie awake, sometimes, worrying about her frilly-leaved lettuces out in the cold, which her mum, Lauren, laughed at. 'But there's no need to worry about that,' she said, a sentence she had uttered often.

Concealed by forgotten, spindly, grey-green plants, she looks carefully through the holes in the leaves and into the bandstand. She can see the figures clearly. Two boys, a couple of years older than her, maybe sixteen. Not men, as she had first thought.

There is no way she can intervene. All of the old feelings rear up. Butterflies in her stomach. Cold hands. A feeling of being watched, being hunted. The old anxiety, but this time with reason. She can't step forward. She is frozen in fear.

She can't leave the safety of the greenhouse. She puts a

hand on the mottled green windowpane, just looking. It is important, if she can't step in, to look. It is the right thing to do, to watch, when something important is unfolding, and Zara so likes to do the right thing.

She watches it unfold, staring, unblinking, so hard her eyes become dry and painful. Something horrendous is happening, but Zara forces herself to keep staring, not glancing away for even a moment. She counts, instead. One second. Two. Three.

It's over in ten. And nothing is ever the same again.

2

Lauren

Islington, London

October, the following year

Lauren watches Zara walk into the kitchen. She's wearing a white blouse and a black skirt. Her legs are long now, somehow gamine, like a deer's or an antelope's. She seems to have grown since witnessing the crime last summer. Taller and more womanly. The way she holds herself, the things she says. 'A Catch 22, isn't it?' she said the other day – her baby daughter!

Lauren considers her, now, just standing there in a patch of October sunlight. She's so beautiful that Lauren feels pride bubbling right up through her like pink lemonade.

'Feeling okay?' she asks. Zara's role in today's trial has become part of their lives this past year. At each meeting, Zara has seemed to mature even further. Speaking up, giving opinions, organizing the family. 'We're at the lawyer's at seven, remember?' she said recently, and Lauren thought: *who are you?* The anxiety that has plagued Zara since she was eleven is still there, sometimes, but so is another Zara, too. A newly brave, bold girl who wants to be a proofreader – 'I'd get to *read books* for a living!' – and who won't eat meat or buy leather. Her daughter, the almost-adult, grown so fully and so beautifully into herself that Lauren wants to call it out of an open window: *I, Lauren Starling, have raised a woman!*

Zara shrugs and Lauren waits. This is what they do. Zara is as circumspect as her absent father, who left before she was born. Or, rather, was never with Lauren enough to call his abandonment leaving. Lauren still marvels at how many of his traits have filtered down to her daughter, even though he never sees her, like how the moon still pulls the tides from afar.

'I mean – it's the right thing,' Zara says now. Zara thinks plenty of things are the right thing. Recycling. Slow fashion. Free-range eggs. And now this, too.

'It is *absolutely* the right thing,' Lauren says to her, wondering if she sounds patronizing, as Aidan walks into the kitchen.

He paces across the tiled floor, dodging the hanging lamps they put up above the table last year. He has one hand in his hair. Shirt untucked. His body is an open bracket, taut with tension. He has wild, dark hair, still thick into his forties, and round brown glasses. He always looks slightly harassed, and more so right now.

'But,' Aidan says, raising his head in a sort of backwards nod at his stepdaughter, 'you don't have to do it. You do not. It's not too late to say no. Say the word,' he brandishes his mobile phone, 'and I'll cancel.'

'She'll be *fine*,' Lauren says, giving him a look.

'I hope so,' Zara says on an exhale. 'I'll look back and be glad I did it. I know I will.'

On the advice of the Crown Prosecution Solicitor, Harry,

an unmarked police car is waiting for them outside. 'More anonymous,' he had said lightly. 'And all three of you in the back is best. Harder to distinguish her that way.'

As they file out down their front path, their neighbour does, too. 'Nice day for October,' he says cordially to Lauren.

She's always liked Ray. He's ninety-three this year and always wears the same jacket, which he repairs in small patches.

'It's been such good weather lately,' she says to him. Aidan rushes past her, throwing her a look. She reluctantly gets into the car. Why can't they chat with Ray, on a stressful day like today, to ease the tension just a little?

Aidan sits pavement side in the car, his back rigid, blocking anybody from seeing in, even though the windows are opaque with frost.

Now they're in the car, she can't prevent herself from thinking about it any longer. That her daughter, who she shielded from swear words on the television and 'scenes of a distressing nature', whose ears she covered during Radio 4 programmes about the Iraq War, was the sole witness of a homeless man being murdered by two footballers.

Today, Zara will enter the courtroom through a back door shown to them last week, and give evidence from behind a screen, known to the jury and the public only as Girl A, her identity protected by the State.

Lauren has been impressed with the justice system's dedication since Zara gave her statement. Not a single slip-up. Zara's identity has been protected by an injunction, redacted documents and the law. The press cannot name her and, if people leak it online, their posts are deleted, and they are arrested.

'Scarf on,' Aidan says as they do a slow loop behind the Old Bailey, ready to be deposited at the back entrance. 'Face covered.'

Zara obliges, wrapping a black scarf around her head, saying nothing, her dark eyes – so like her father's – the only visible feature, scanning the world outside.

'Stop fussing,' Zara says.

'Our little fusspot,' Lauren says affectionately, glancing at Aidan.

He gives her an indulgent, private smile, just for her.

Lauren smiles back, then turns to look at Zara. As she does so, she feels a dropping sensation in her gut, like they have just driven over a low bridge. It's unusual for her. She is the calm one. The optimist. The *it'll be fine*-er.

Lauren explores the unpleasant sensation within her. It's similar to grief. A slow, soft, sad feeling. She looks down at Zara's hand still in hers. It has lost all its childhood chubbiness, around the knuckles, in the past year.

No. It's fine. It's *fine*. It is high-level, and nerve-wracking, but it is fine. Nothing is going to happen. They are here, together, the sunlight on the backs of their necks. Nothing will hurt them, ruin them, destroy them. She tilts her face up to the light. It's not possible.

3

Aidan

The Old Bailey, London

Aidan watches as Zara is led, an animal to the slaughter, into the witness box in the empty courtroom. Her eyes are downcast, head bowed, like somebody about to be executed, not cross-examined. *She's just shy*, he tells himself. *She's just nervous, not properly scared.*

Despite his own reassurances, Aidan is sure that this is not the right thing for Zara to be doing, but his voice has been lost in the crowd. The State does not have her best interests at heart, of that he is certain, no matter what they say. To them, she is a commodity. She has knowledge, and that knowledge is going to be extracted from her, and then she will be discarded. They have placated Aidan with promises of anonymity, with assurances that they are professionals, that what she is doing is important and right. But right for who? For them, that's who. If she angers people, if her identity is accidentally leaked, they won't care. They will have got everything out of her that they wanted, and they will leave Aidan and Lauren to clear up the mess. 'Of course you think that,' Lauren had said recently when he pointed all of this out *again*. 'You're a cynic.' And maybe

that's true. Aidan is drawn to the negative, is forever per-
using horror stories on the internet, has recently taken to
binge-reading articles about leaked identities late at night.
Witch hunts, public sector omnishambles. He works in IT,
and has spent his days recently voraciously reading past
cases instead of working.

The curtain is drawn tightly around Zara by an usher,
secured by Velcro, which Aidan cannot resist reaching out
to check. The usher glances at him, a quick, proprietary
look from behind square glasses. Aidan ignores him, and
keeps checking it along the length of the curtain. If he can
just secure it more tightly . . . make sure nobody at all can
see her . . .

'You'll be in the public gallery,' the solicitor says to them.
Harry's young. Mid-thirties. He drinks matcha lattes that
leave his tongue bright green. Aidan catches glimpses of it
as he speaks to them in meetings and has to try very hard
not to comment on it. Harry gets on especially well with
Lauren, but then everyone does. They're both fast talkers,
gesticulators. Lauren invited him over for a curry she made
from scratch in the summer, bought a load of chickpeas at
the market – way, *way* too many – and Aidan sat and listened to his wife and the CPS solicitor for the evening,
worrying about blurred boundaries.

Harry runs through Zara's account with her quietly
once again. He perches like a flamingo behind the box,
one leg against the wall's wood panelling.

Aidan and Lauren hover in the corner of the courtroom. 'It should be quick,' Lauren says. 'I think.' She
runs a hand through her ashy blonde hair. Aidan's wife is
sometimes beautiful and sometimes less so, though he

would never say that. Aidan finds her fascinating in this way. Her features are slightly irregular somewhere around the nose and mouth. She is 'interesting to look at', he once said while drunk, which he regretted.

'She'll be okay,' he reassures her, though he doesn't mean it, isn't sure. How could he be?

He stares up at the windows above and wishes that they hadn't done *the right thing*. That they had done the wrong thing. The easy thing. That Zara didn't care so much. That she had seen the murder but closed her eyes and walked away. Pretended it had never happened.

4

Zara

The Old Bailey, London

Zara is sitting behind the black curtains, waiting for the questioning to begin. Although nobody will be able to see her, her cheeks are flushed. She tries to calm herself with deep breaths.

All she has to do, she tells herself, is tell the courtroom what she saw.

Except it isn't that simple. Not at all. Zara doesn't find anything simple, not really. She is one of life's over-thinkers, according to the therapist.

But that night changed everything. That night is all about gut instinct, for Zara.

She reaches to take a sip of the water provided in the white plastic cup. This . . . this is different. Right and wrong have become mixed up.

She saw the defendant stab the victim, Jamie, while his friend looked on. She saw the blood leaving Jamie's neck, a cascade on to the floor around him. And Zara is here because of that.

Because she knew Jamie.

She started volunteering in Islington with Waste Not as

part of her anxiety recovery. 'Look, who do you want to be?' the therapist had said, and Zara had thought: *God – who?* What a liberating question.

'I like causes,' she had said eventually. 'Like . . . the environment, and animals, supporting the underdog. I don't know. Homeless people. I feel sorry for them.' It had come out of nowhere, but it had felt like real, authentic Zara who was speaking. Not the one who tried to fit in at the school away weekend – thinking a million disastrous thoughts a minute, instead of cycling – but the real her. And so every other Thursday, at six o'clock in the evening, she'd head to the high street to hand out the food that a few cafés and restaurants had reserved for homeless people. She would wear a hi-vis vest, bright yellow, and carry a stiff paper bag containing hot meals, the steam gently warming her hand. At first, she had to find the homeless people – in shop doorways, in underpasses – but, after a few months, they started coming to her. That's how she had met Jamie, and the rest of them.

And that's how she recognized him when she saw him. When she saw what happened to him.

5

Aidan

The Old Bailey, London

Zara is almost at the end of the questioning.

She has told the jury – from behind the screen – what she saw. About the two teenage youth football team players who killed a homeless man in the bandstand during the school holidays the summer before last. She's told the courtroom in shaking tones that she knew Jamie, the victim. About Waste Not. About the discarded roof tile the second defendant, Mal, picked up and tossed to the first defendant, Luke. Mal is charged with supplying that weapon, Luke with murder. She tells them about how Jamie lay helplessly, blood leaving his body, until he was silent.

Aidan sometimes dreams about what Zara must have seen. A bloodied man and a murderer standing in the twilight. He wakes, itchy with sweat. His stepdaughter doesn't know how much it will affect her, later. He wishes he could take this thing she's seen and absorb it into himself.

'And what did you hear?' the barrister says.

'Not much,' Zara says. 'The defendants shouted something – a phrase? It was in another . . . another language, I . . . Latin, maybe? A club motto?'

'The club's motto is "We Stand Together". In English,' the barrister says icily.

'Not that,' she says. 'Never mind. It was . . . I don't know? A chant?'

'A chant?'

'They said something I didn't understand, alright?'

'But you can't remember anything more about it?'

'No.'

'One final question,' the defence barrister says to the curtains through a sigh. He is irritated by Zara, by her evidence.

He has a pink mark on his nose from pushing his glasses up with his knuckle, which he does every few minutes. 'Can you talk me through the movements of the first defendant, his co-accused the second defendant, and the victim?'

'The movements?' Zara's disembodied voice asks.

'They just walked up to this sleeping, homeless man, did they? And killed him *in situ*?'

'Yes. Mal passed Luke the roof tile, and he stabbed him with the point of it.'

'And the homeless man did nothing? Perhaps he was high on drugs, or drink?'

'No, he wasn't,' Zara says.

'I see,' the barrister says, leaving a drawn-out pause.

Aidan looks across the public gallery. There they are. Holloway FC, the Premier League team, all wearing suits and yellow or blue ties. Club colours. Some key members of the youth team are here, who feed the Premier League team. Five men. Coaches. Managers. A few younger lads, too. Rangy-looking teenagers with tanned foreheads. Aidan saw the latest Premier League match on television two nights ago. The commentators mentioned the upcoming trial, but only briefly.

Luke's parents are here, too. Aidan has a morbid fascination with them. Their child has done something unthinkable. The parents are desperate to believe it isn't true, not their kid. Aidan knows a watered-down version of that feeling. Doesn't every parent? One Christmas, his daughter from his first marriage, Poppy, called him a twat because she didn't get the £500 pair of trainers she wanted. He ate his Christmas dinner alone, heart in his feet, thinking: *I messed it up. She was supposed to grow up to be nice: humble.* That's what children don't realize. They don't realize they are avatars of their parents. It is like Aidan has taken his heart out of his chest and has to watch it walk around outside his body. And the heart doesn't even know. The heart wants Gucci trainers.

'So, Girl A,' the barrister says, 'if this was not an intoxicated person, why would he lie there – and not defend himself at all?'

'I don't know.'

'Perhaps he felt he had nothing to live for?'

'No, he did. He did have things to live for.'

'Did he cry out, or shout? I'm just trying to imagine the scene, here.'

Zara says nothing.

Aidan looks over at Luke in the dock. He used to be tall and slim but, after a year on remand in HMP Wandsworth, he is muscular around the neck and arms, like a swimmer.

The courtroom is completely silent.

Aidan stares at the curtains.

'I don't know.'

'You don't know?'

'It's a . . . a blur.'

'According to your account, Jamie lay silent and still for the *entire attack*, so you say. How sad, that he felt his life wasn't worth anything to even justify rolling over. You're certain he wasn't . . . intoxicated in some way?'

'He didn't do drugs. Didn't drink. Couldn't afford to.'

The barrister lets out a sharp, acidic laugh. 'Surely most sleeping people, if woken by an *attacker*, as you say, would defend themselves, would they not?'

'Yes.'

'But he didn't? He didn't even lift his head? How tragic.'

And then, right before Zara says it, Aidan realizes. The barrister has worked something out, and has set a trap for Zara to walk into.

'He *did* fight,' Zara says. 'He stood up first and he lurched towards them. Don't say that about him. He didn't think his life was futile just because he was homeless. He *didn't*.'

The courtroom is stunned into silence.

Lauren turns to Aidan. She's staring at him, his wife who, at the moment, is in her beautiful guise. She doesn't look away, not even as the barrister starts to speak again.

'Forgive my confusion, Girl A, but you previously said – under oath, I might add – that the victim did nothing. Page three of your witness statement reads: "The two defendants were standing over the victim and the first defendant began to attack him while the victim lay there, motionless." '

'I . . . I . . . I'm sorry.'

And now, like a gun going off, Aidan realizes. Zara has lied. Zara is lying.

23

The courtroom doesn't speak. Nobody moves. Lauren's eyes are boring into the side of Aidan's head.

'So, what is the true version of events?' the barrister asks. 'Who attacked first?'

'Jamie,' Zara says, very quietly.

The courtroom stills.

Only the judge moves, shifting in his chair at the bench, elevated above the courtroom, and speaks. 'Girl A,' he says softly. He's wearing half-red, half-purple robes, a ludicrous court jester. 'I have to say . . .' the judge looks over at the witness box, even though he can't see her. He lowers his glasses down his nose. 'Who attacked first is absolutely crucial in this case.'

'I know,' Zara says, her voice strangled and plaintive from behind the curtain.

Aidan wants to go and undo the Velcro and gather her up. He can tell Lauren feels the same.

'Do you know why?'

Zara says nothing, and Aidan knows she will be staring at the curtains in shock, frozen. She hates to get things wrong. One Christmas, when they were playing Trivial Pursuit, her hands were actually shaking as he asked her a question. She answered incorrectly, but he gave her the wedge anyway.

'For murder to have taken place,' the judge says, 'the defendants need to have *intended to* cause grievous bodily harm or death, and – crucially – *not* to have been acting in self-defence. If you have not told the entire truth, Girl A, about the victim's actions, then the defendants may not have committed murder. So I must ask you: what events took place, and in what order?'

24

'Okay,' Zara says, her voice thick. 'The defendants stood over Jamie. Doing nothing. And then he . . . he attacked them first. And they reacted to that attack.'

Aidan listens intently to the silence, shocked. And then it all unravels.

'I'm sorry,' Zara says from behind the curtains. 'I'm sorry, I lied.'

There's another beat of silence, and then the courtroom comes alive.

The judge shouts, 'Approach the bench,' and the barristers stare at each other. The ushers move around to the back of the witness box and, before Aidan knows what's happening, the jury are dismissed through one door and the public gallery through another. As Aidan waits to leave the courtroom with journalists and other family members, he can feel the blood pounding uncomfortably in his head. Harry nods to Lauren and Aidan. He'll bring Zara to them, the nod says, when the courtroom is empty. When it's safe.

The hairs on the back of Aidan's neck rise up.

They disperse into the foyer and Lauren sits on a bench affixed to the wall. Aidan immediately joins her. 'God,' she says to him, her expression aghast. Eyes wide. Hand to her forehead.

'She lied,' Aidan says.

'They still killed someone,' Lauren says tightly. 'Whatever the detail.'

'It isn't *detail* if they were defending themselves,' Aidan says.

'I'm sure Zara can clear it all up for us,' Lauren says. 'I'm sure she'll explain.'

Aidan isn't so certain. Zara called Lauren right after she phoned an ambulance that night. Aidan had been next to Lauren as she took the call, and, when they had arrived, Zara's hands were covered in dried blood from where she had tried to stem Jamie's bleeding. Aidan watched as Lauren cleaned them up with a wet wipe from a dehydrated packet in the car, remembering sticky summers gone by. When they'd have both the kids in the back, Poppy and Zara, just a couple of months between them, feet kicking the front seats. Lauren had asked her if Jamie had attacked the boys first. If they were actually defending themselves against him. Aidan recalls it now. Zara had looked at Lauren curiously, those beautiful, roving brown eyes of hers focused suddenly on her mother. She had been wearing shorts, a denim jacket and trainers. All bloodstained. 'If so, it was self-defence,' Lauren had continued. 'He could have been threatening them, Zara.'

Aidan rests his head against the wall of the foyer now. But surely Zara wouldn't *lie*? Would she? Why would she do something so foolish – and so unlike her, so misguided? Perjury, for God's sake. Zara's a fucking vegan, a climate change maniac. He thought she was ethical.

'She's in meeting room eighteen,' Harry says as soon as he arrives in front of them a few minutes later. He's holding a drink and looking unconcerned in that languid way of his, one hand in the pocket of his suit trousers. He leads them to the side room. It's up two flights of stairs that turn back on themselves, and down a red-carpeted corridor. It's silent up here, like a museum.

Harry holds the door open for them. Zara is sitting there, just as she appeared in their kitchen this morning.

Harry sits down opposite them. Lauren naturally turns to Aidan, a question mark in her blue eyes.

Zara is absent-mindedly chewing on the inside of her cheek as they sit down, skewing her mouth to the left.

'You said Jamie did nothing,' Lauren says. 'But he did?'

'Yes,' Zara says. Amazingly, she doesn't seem to feel a need to clarify anything further. The mind of the teenager.

'What sort of attack was it?' Harry asks. 'It's very important – *now* – that you tell me the truth, Zara.'

'They stood over him. They roused him, I think. He got up and sort of . . . came at them. He was shouting and stuff . . . but they scared him, they –' Zara stops speaking and turns her hands over on the table, palms up. A small gesture of defeat.

'And what exactly is *stuff*?' Harry says. 'Shouting and –' he taps his pen on the table, '– stuff.'

'Well –' Zara says in a small voice.

'But why would you lie?' Lauren interrupts. 'If he attacked first – I mean – *Zara*.'

Lauren doesn't understand lying. She tells every single person she meets exactly what she is thinking: Tesco cashiers and mechanics and postmen. 'No croissant for me,' she will say in cafés, 'I've got three pounds left to lose!'

'You want to know why?' Zara says.

'Yes,' Lauren says softly.

'After he – Luke – did it, he shouted at Jamie. He said, "You're a waste of space. You're worthless." Right in his face. As he . . . as he died. Those were the last words he heard. And – you know – Jamie wanted to start working for one of the cafés that fed him. He had an interview and everything. And now it's all lost.'

Of course, Aidan thinks, looking at the thoughtful set of her mouth. Zara felt that them killing Jamie – no matter what he did first – was morally reprehensible. Despite the law, Despite everything.

'I need to clarify the actual facts, Zara,' Harry says tightly, glancing briefly at Lauren. 'So the order of events was that Jamie lashed out at them – and Luke and Mal didn't do anything first?'

'That's correct,' Zara says quietly. 'He got up and he was . . . shouting and screaming and kicking out. He was . . . he didn't like people in his spaces. He always slept out of the way. He got frightened when people disturbed him. So he came at them. Lunged. They tried to move – to run away from him. He was coming towards them and they panicked. They used the roof tile to . . . to get him off.'

'Right,' Harry says very quietly, after a brief pause. 'That is quite different.'

'But he didn't *mean it*, I know he didn't,' Zara says passionately. 'He was so scared, he gets like that sometimes because of his PTSD, because of his past, and they were so . . . they were so awful, after they'd done it. They didn't regret it at all.'

'So the footballers were the victims of the attack?' Harry says, writing something down on a legal pad.

'They don't seem to behave much like victims to me, do they?' Zara says, looking directly at Harry.

'This is . . .' Lauren says, and Aidan waits, leaving the punishment to her. 'You shouldn't have done this,' she says eventually.

Harry looks on impassively, ever the lawyer. Gathering the information. Waiting, catlike, for his moment.

'They didn't care at all,' Zara says, and now the tears come. 'They didn't give a shit.' She grips the table. Her hands leave sweaty marks on the Formica. They fade as Aidan looks at them, disappearing to nothing.

'What made you do it?' Harry says.

Zara considers his question for a few seconds. 'The police,' she eventually answers, folding her hands awkwardly in her lap. 'I think the police.'

'What?' Harry says. 'Why?'

'They said, "And Jamie wasn't attacking them, was he?" That's how they said it. *Wasn't*. I thought . . . I thought about self-defence, but I thought. God, it sounds stupid now, but I thought the police wanted me to . . . to leave that bit out. I thought I was being . . . invited to.'

This seems to annoy Harry. He crosses his legs so forcefully under the table that it rises up for a second, and Zara presses down with her hands to steady it.

'How so? Did they say anything else, Zara?'

'Well, I stammered, and then the woman police officer, she said, "And no movement from Jamie?" And then she asked, "And Jamie was just lying there?" and I thought they wanted me to . . . I thought what the boys did was so bad that . . . that we should turn a blind eye to Jamie. Because they still killed him, you know?'

'Right,' Harry says faintly.

Aidan looks at Zara. Teenage logic. There's no nuance to it. No common sense, no understanding of the justice system, of perjury. Just a desire to please, a feeling, instincts.

'Why would the police want you to do that?' Harry adds.

'Because they want convictions, don't they?' Zara says. 'Numbers. I thought . . . I don't know. I saw two boys kill someone and I wasn't . . . I guess I just . . . I got it wrong, didn't I? I did the wrong thing. Clearly.' Her head drops ever so slightly.

'Yes,' Harry says. 'They . . . I mean, he was lunging at them, by your account. They did what any reasonable person would do.'

'I know,' Zara says in a small voice, but there is still something defiant about the set of her jaw.

'Look,' Aidan says. 'What happens now?'

Harry lets a tiny expulsion of air out of his mouth. 'It's pretty unprecedented,' he says. He checks the time. It's an Apple Watch. The screen springs to life as he turns his wrist. Aidan can see he has a waiting text message, too. Lauren leans right over to read it, and Aidan almost smiles. She is always so reliably herself.

'The prosecution will need to take a view,' Harry says. 'Let me consult with my colleagues across the street.' He scoots his chair back and leaves the room in one swift movement.

Aidan looks at Lauren, and they leave the room together.

'I hope he can help us,' Lauren says.

Aidan frowns. Harry isn't going to help them, he thinks sadly. He belongs to the State. He's there to prosecute crimes on their behalf. Crimes like murder and – yeah – crimes like perjury, too.

6

Aidan

Islington, London

In the middle of the night, Aidan is awake for a few moments before he realizes. His eyes are open in the not-quite-darkness of central London. Lauren is sleeping on her side, turned towards him, as she always does, her belly rounded and naked, forming three distinct rolls that she'd like to be two.

A burglar alarm is going off somewhere across the street. Three beeps, then a pause. Aidan taps his foot on the mattress along with it. Beep, beep, beep, pause. Beep, beep, beep, pause. He turns on to his back, an arm above his head, and watches the ceiling light up blue, three times, then dim.

The Crown Prosecution Service reviewed the police tape of Zara's statement in the afternoon, while Aidan, Lauren and Zara waited.

Afterwards, Harry had confirmed that Luke and Mal would be completely exonerated. That they were defending themselves against an attack. He had confirmed, too, that the CPS wouldn't press charges against Zara: the interview footage confirmed her account that the police

31

appeared to ask leading questions. That it would be easy for a teenager to be swayed by such an 'amateur line of questioning'.

Outside, afterwards, Lauren had tilted her face to the sun and said that it didn't matter. That it was over. A quick sweep of fear had travelled up Aidan's back, though he didn't know why.

He reaches for his phone now. Four thirty-two in the morning. On Facebook, he sees that a distant friend of his, somebody he met at a party – a friend of Lauren's? – has made a charitable donation. His heart sinks when he sees the cause it is for.

He needs to steel himself, so he gets out of bed and puts a dressing gown on. Before he leaves, he glances across at Lauren, duvet thrown off her, bottom completely exposed to the air, round and taboo.

He stands in the hallway and peers out of the window. Their Islington street is foggy – big balls of moisture dyed amber by the street lights. Aidan goes into Poppy's room. He wants to be alone. It's empty right now and he gets into her bed. It's a double. She chose sheets from The White Company – if it's not a brand name, Poppy isn't interested – and Aidan has to admit they're very soft. He folds the bottom of the duvet over on itself, creating a kind of envelope, and puts his cold feet inside it.

He bought the bedding after Poppy's mother Natalie's diagnosis. Multiple sclerosis. The post-divorce world they lived in became even more complicated when those words were spoken by the consultant. Poppy's shopping trip was no compensation for it, but he'd taken her anyway. She'd picked out so much stuff. Silk pillows – 'So my hair won't curl so much' – and a brushed cotton sheet. The lot. One hundred and eighty pounds. He'd mentally added up how many hours' work that was on their walk back to his car, a habit he's had since the 2008 recession.

He looks at Facebook now, still lit up on his phone, and back at the donation. It's a Kickstarter. *Help Luke Taylor back on his feet after Girl A's lies.*

Donated £10. Disgraceful, is all his friend's comment says.

He sits up in bed, silk fucking pillows falling around him.

In the half-light of Poppy's empty bedroom, he puts Girl A into Google. He doesn't even have to click the 'news' tab. The internet is awash with his family.

INNOCENT! WRONGED FOOTBALLER WAS ATTACKED BY HOMELESS MAN AND SERVED <u>A YEAR</u> IN A HIGH SECURITY PRISON

SUSPECTED KILLER FOOTBALLER WAS ACTUALLY ACTING IN SELF-DEFENCE — COURTROOM SHOCKER

WHO IS GIRL A? WHAT WE KNOW

YET <u>ANOTHER</u> WOMAN LIES IN THE WITNESS BOX — WHEN WILL THESE FALSE ALLEGATIONS END?

WHAT IS THE FUTURE OF HOLLOWAY FC? LUKE TAYLOR ACCUSED, NOW FREED, BUT WITH HIS CAREER IN TATTERS

Aidan blinks, looking at the headlines about his family. About his stepdaughter's lies.

Aidan cannot understand how this has happened. How they are here.

He clicks on a BBC News article with an accompanying video. It is Luke and Mal, on the court steps of the Old Bailey. He presses 'play', turns the volume down low, and watches.

A news presenter narrates over the footage as the defendants stand posing for photographs.

'Luke Taylor, up-and-coming striker for Holloway FC, was today acquitted at the Old Bailey on a charge of murder, alongside his accomplice, Malcolm Henderson,' the undulating news reporter's voice says. 'While the police suspected Taylor and Henderson of murder, the truth emerged in the courtroom during the dramatic questioning of an anonymous witness known only as Girl A.'

Aidan shudders as the narrator says it. How the fuck has this happened?

'Taylor and Henderson were, in fact, acting in self-defence against an attack by the deceased,' the news presenter says. 'The truth only came to light under fierce cross-examination from Neil Thorne QC. Taylor was released today, free to return to his life, and his career – what is left of it.'

Henderson's representative was contacted for comment, but declined. Taylor's father has told the local news that his son has been robbed of his career.

Aidan lies back in the bed, rubbing his hair back from his forehead with the palm of his hand. Bloody hell. Fucking, *fucking* hell. He knows this is just the beginning.

Aidan wants Lauren's sunny positivity. Her laughter. A wave of her hand. 'Tomorrow's chip paper!' she will say, and he will love her for it. And so, when she arrives downstairs, he knows that he will tell her what he's seen on the internet.

She's wearing leggings, a dressing gown and slippers. She wears odd combinations around the house, adding layers as the day goes on. A T-shirt, a jumper of his, a cardigan. Bed socks and a woolly hat. By the end of the day, she is layered up like a Russian doll.

It's seven o'clock in the morning. The kitchen is half lit by a grey sky and nothing else.

Their dog, Bill, stands solemnly by his bowl. Lauren blows him an unselfconscious kiss as she arrives in the kitchen, as she does most mornings. She refers to him as her 'son' to strangers, and has a photograph of him in her purse, right next to Zara and Poppy.

Lauren falls in love with things. It's a lesson Aidan learnt early on. Bill was a guide dog puppy. Lauren applied to foster him five years ago, without telling Aidan. That was Lauren all over, zany schemes. He wishes he could be more that way. Less uptight. But he can't – not since his father died when Aidan was fifteen, anyway, and he became a man. And so he did the next best thing: he married someone fun.

She said she would be paid to maintain the puppy's training at home and to drop him off at school every day. 'Substitute second baby,' she had said glibly. She'd just turned forty. The baby-making window had closed. And they'd wanted it to, mostly, ready to move on with their blended family: no pushchairs, no nappies, no kids' club holidays.

'I have to hand him over when he's two, though, when

he becomes a proper dog,' she'd explained when she sent the form off. 'When he graduates.'

Bill went everywhere with Lauren. He rode upright in the passenger seat of her car to parks on the outskirts of London – 'Should I put a seat belt on him?' – and slept at her feet while she watched television. Lauren would use 'we' whenever she spoke about him. 'We've been to Hyde Park.' 'We've been playing tug of war all afternoon.'

Aidan could see what was going to happen before Lauren could.

The week before Bill was due to be eligible for guide dog applications, Lauren turned to Aidan and said, 'You know what?'

'What?' Aidan said.

'If I could run away with this dog and not give him back, I would. Be a fugitive on the run from Guide Dogs UK.' And then she gave a laugh, a sort of maniacal laugh that told him she meant every word.

'You want to keep him,' he said flatly.

Lauren shrugged. 'I love him,' she'd said. She self-consciously moved a strand of hair out of her eyes. 'I'm fucking forty,' she'd said with a laugh. 'But I love this stupid dog.'

'But a blind person needs him.'

'I know.'

The next day, while he was working, a text had come through.

Guide Dogs UK said some people do buy back the dog they trained.

That was all it said. Sent exactly at 1.00 p.m. Not a minute earlier or later. Lauren had likely waited all morning for his lunch hour.

What's their price? Aidan had asked, his blood pressure rising.

Lauren had gone silent. Unusual for her.

When he walked in, she said, 'Don't be mad.'

He raised his eyebrows, holding on to the wall as he eased his trainers off. He said nothing; something his wife was joyfully incapable of.

'I asked their price, like you told me to,' she said, like it was all his idea. 'And we could do it.'

'How much?'

'We could do it if we remortgaged.'

'Remortgage? For a *dog*?' Aidan said.

'We could keep him. The funds are used to train loads more . . . that's why it's so expensive. To ease the moral burden!' Bill appeared, then, padding into the hallway. Lauren's hand drifted down to the top of his head and rested there, completely unconsciously. But it wasn't the hand that did it. It was the look on her face. A brief close of her eyes, a smile just beginning as her fingers fanned out across his yellow fur. Love.

Lauren fell in love easily, and she fell hard.

Aidan sent the mortgage form off the next day.

They gave Bill a middle name: Gates. It made them laugh. 'He's the richest dog in the world,' Lauren said, the day the money came through.

'Sleep well?' Lauren says now, though he guesses she knows the answer.

'You should see this,' Aidan says, the anxiety erupting from him without warning. He opens his laptop and tries to pass it to her across the kitchen counter, but it's so messy. She went shopping the other day and overloaded the fruit bowl. It towers between them. She reaches for the computer and stares at the screen as she holds it, standing up.

'What, what?' she says. She reaches over to boil the kettle, balancing the laptop on the palm of her hand. The kettle's blue light comes on, illuminating her face. She looks tired.

'There's a crowd funder, for Luke,' he says.

'Some of the comments,' she says, looking up at him with concern.

'I know,' he says. The crowd funder has been populating with them all morning. Things they'd like to do to his stepdaughter, ways in which they will make her pay for lying. He takes the laptop from her and scrolls through them, reporting each one for violent content.

Lying shit needs to pay.

Think sum1 should find this Girl A and tell her what's what.

She deserves to be hung — isn't it a crime to lie in court x

She deserves worse than hanging, mate.

Make her suffer. Make her realize what it's like to feel pain. Twist her arms behind her back, bag over her head lol. Show her who's boss.

Fuck her I say till she cries out.

*

Two days after the trial, the door closes behind Zara. Aidan watches her go. Lauren is making sweetcorn fritters, swearing at how the batter is clumping together.

'Where's she gone?' Aidan says.

Lauren shrugs, licking her index finger. 'She's gone to speak to the homeless people. I let her go.'

'*What?*'

Lauren looks up at him in exasperation. 'She was anonymous. Nobody will recognize her. And she wants to speak to the . . . to Jamie's friends. To apologize, I think. For letting them down. Look. What time are you going to stop stressing about my child and go to see yours?'

'That crowd funder is vicious.'

'I can't keep her inside for ever, like a prisoner,' Lauren says. 'She wanted to go out, so she's gone. She's almost an adult. Harry said it was fine.'

Aidan stares at Bill, sitting in his bed in the corner of the kitchen, watching the fritters sizzle in the pan.

'I did think about it, alright?' Lauren says to him suddenly. One of the fritters is slowly burning. 'But she has to go to school tomorrow. Ten o'clock on a Sunday morning is a pretty good time to try her being out, don't you think?'

Aidan checks the crowd funder again, as he has many times today. In the comments, somebody has pasted a single link.

Aidan clicks it, and it opens the Facebook app on his phone. It navigates him automatically to a Facebook group.

The group is called Find Girl A. He sits back for just a second, like the beat between a firework being lit and it going off. Fuck.

'There's a Find Girl A Facebook group,' Aidan says quietly, unthinkingly.

'Find Girl A?'

He points to the screen.

Lauren's eyes track across it. She's a quick reader. 'Oh, shit,' she whispers. She looks at him, then points to the screen. 'Zara Starling,' she says.

At first, Aidan thinks she is being superstitious, or reverential. That, by uttering her daughter's name, nothing bad will happen to her. But her lips are white, and he looks at his phone again, searching for an explanation for her terror. There it is, posted by a man with a blank profile photo calling himself Dr NoGood.

News just in on the grapevine, he has written. *Girl A is also known as . . . Zara Starling.* Zara's Facebook profile photo is attached, smiling, happy Zara, taken on holiday this summer, totally unaware.

Aidan's eyes meet Lauren's across the kitchen. His stomach drops. They know who she is.

Lauren's hand is already reaching for her phone, trying to call Zara.

They have found her.

7

Zara

Highbury, London

Zara is on her way back from seeing one of Jamie's friends, and she feels worse, now, not better. She wishes it was possible to remove information from her brain, and store it somewhere else for a while.

Nevertheless, at least she isn't anxious. She is walking in the sunshine in Highbury, thinking how she used to hate to go out. She joked she was a hermit, an introvert, but, specifically, she didn't like the Tube, lifts, wide-open spaces, and exam halls.

From these, she constantly planned escape routes and excuses. If, during an exam, she felt weird, or like she needed to leave, she'd say she was having a nosebleed; no, she'd say she'd got her period unexpectedly. Anything was less embarrassing than anxiety.

She worked through a book about it, with Aidan, *CBT for Dummies*. And then she saw the therapist who said the nice things to her and wasn't weird or whacky – not at all as Zara had expected her to be. She told her that she can do kind stuff for herself. That life doesn't have to be one series of imagined disasters after another. At the first session, Zara said flatly, 'That isn't true,' but then, session by session, she realized that maybe it was. Maybe things didn't need to be risk-assessed, maybe escape routes didn't need to be planned. Maybe a shopping trip could simply be *enjoyed*.

She is better now, she's been better for a year maybe. The summer before she saw the murder, she kept finding herself thinking: *I'm not worried about this any more. I'm out, I'm having fun. I'm myself again. Weird, awkward me.*

Nevertheless, now, Zara isn't anxious, but she can't stop her mind spinning over the lie she told the police. The judge addressing her in the courtroom. Her shame behind those curtains.

Luke and Mal stood over Jamie, and then Jamie reared up, unpredictable, like a monster. Shouting, lashing out. Mal passed Luke the roof tile, and Luke cut Jamie with it, as cold and clinical as a surgeon. And yet, somehow, the law treats Luke and Mal as if they did nothing wrong.

So she lied. And then her lie was exposed. She panicked. That's the truth of it. Cracked under cross-examination. She winces as she recalls it. She wishes she could go back, and hold her own, not rise to the barrister insinuating Jamie didn't value his own life, that he just lay there like a victim. If she had held her own, her evidence wouldn't quite have made sense, but that would be better than this. Two killers released. It's wrong. She just *knows* it, deep inside her. She made out to Harry that she regrets it, but she doesn't. She knows she's right.

It's all bound up with Waste Not, for Zara. She saw the attitude to homeless people all the time. Commuters walking past them, not offering a 'yes' or a 'no' to a *Big Issue* request: just silence. People saying, 'You shouldn't give them money, they'll spend it on drugs.' And some of them would. But Jamie would spend it on something to keep him warm, a hot drink. Anna would spend it on dog food. There is as much variety in homeless people as there is in life. But nobody can see it.

If there is a God who observes who does and doesn't step on paving cracks – one of Zara's very first worries – or think good thoughts, he would recognize that those footballers were in the wrong. Because they *were*. She reached Jamie after Luke and his friend had left. He smelled of blood and urine. The blood didn't smell like iron. It smelled like meat. That sickly-sweet smell of the butcher's. A lime tang of urine underneath that. And at least Luke served some time. At least there is that.

When she told the police that Jamie must have wet himself in fear, they said, 'Yes, or he didn't have access to bathrooms.'

But Jamie never usually smelled. He wasn't an alcoholic and he didn't piss himself, she had said forcefully, but nobody believed her.

This is what she is thinking about as the sunlight dapples the pavement in front of her. That she wasn't in the wrong. She *wasn't.*

And now she knows it.

The high street is cold with frost. The sky blue above her. There is a car idling next to her, coasting along the street. People have started doing their Christmas shopping already. A couple walk along with Starbucks red cups.

The car slows even further. Zara slows, too, looking at it. There is something strange about it. It's not . . . it's not coasting. It's going to stop right next to her. The wheels are aligning with the kerb.

The front passenger's window rolls down slowly. Inch by inch. Zara can't move away. She's frozen. She can't do anything except watch as, little by little, a man in a balaclava is revealed. He reaches a gloved hand towards her right arm and pulls her towards the car. Her side slams against it.

And this is it, and this is it, this is it. She is in true and proper danger. She thinks, suddenly, of her mum and Aidan, of the phone call they will receive.

'So, Girl A,' the man in the balaclava says, his breath hot and physical, both a noise and a sensation, right next to her ear. 'We said we'd make you pay,' he continues. 'Guess how much it cost to get your name? Hardly anything. Just a bit of courtroom incompetence.' He laughs, a cruel laugh, his mouth opening just slightly behind the black wool.

She is sweating and trying to move away, trying to reach into her pocket for her phone, but the man pulls tighter. She tries to reach around her back with the other hand, but he grasps that, too.

'Get in,' he says.

Zara looks into his eyes – brown and cruel – and opens her mouth. 'Help,' she shouts at passers-by, as loudly as she can. 'Help me.'

A woman carrying a paper bag from a bakery starts, shocked, but walks on. A cluster of kids at the bus stop look curiously at her. Everyone has noticed but, for this second, and the next, nobody has decided to step up and help.

'Somebody!' Zara screams. His grip tightens on her. He is going to try and pull her into the car with him. He is going to threaten her. He is going to say he has a knife or a gun and she needs to be quiet and get in the car or he will hurt her. Her entire body is trembling.

He is holding her fast to the car, but she is thrashing around, screaming.

A man straightening a sandwich board outside a café stops and stares. 'Hey,' he says. 'What the fuck are you doing?' He runs towards them, and he is pulling her away from the car, and the man in the balaclava releases her, and she is crying and snot is running out of her nose, and she is saying thank you, over and over, to him, the café man. The car window goes up, and the car revs its engine and speeds away.

'No number plate,' the man says sadly to her. 'They probably wanted your purse. Or your phone. Thieves.'

'Yeah,' Zara says. Her heart is still pounding. But something else is settling around her. After the adrenaline, the fear, and the relief that she is safe. A realization. It was them. The club. They know her. They know what she looks like. Her eyes dart around the street.

'Nobody else did anything,' the man says, looking around them.

Zara looks at him closely. He's wearing a red bobble hat. He has a dark beard. Big cheeks. Looks friendly.

'That's London for you,' he adds. 'Full of cowards.'

'I need to get home,' Zara says. 'Sorry.' Her voice catches, and he reaches to clasp her shoulder, but it makes her flinch.

'You should tell the police. It was a silver Mercedes, the new type,' the man says. 'Let me . . . let me walk you?'

'No, I'll call my mum. Really,' Zara says. Her entire body is trembling like it does in the cold. She needs to go. She needs to go home to safety. They have found her.

8

Lauren

Islington, London

'Where are you?' Lauren says, the second her phone rings and she sees it's Zara. 'You've been ages.'

'Someone just grabbed me,' Zara says.

Blood flashes up Lauren's body, hot and then freezing. 'What?'

'They tried to get me into a car. It was them,' Zara says, her voice full of tears. 'The people. The footballers.'

'Jesus *Christ*,' Lauren says, and her voice must be shrill, because Aidan's head snaps up. 'Where are you? Are you okay?'

'I'm fine, I'm fine,' Zara says. 'But can you come and get me? I'm on the high street. By the bus stops. Please be quick.'

'Coming,' Lauren says, car keys already in her hand. She would send an air ambulance, a police car, the cavalry. 'Are you alone?'

'No, a man – a man helped me. We're outside his café. Please come,' Zara says, her voice watery and scared-sounding.

Still on the phone, she motions to Aidan, who follows.

As she does it, she realizes. This moment, here in the sunlit kitchen with her husband and her dog, this is the moment. Everything has changed. Turned on a dime. She stares at her hand on the door handle, wedding rings catching the sun.

Nothing will ever be the same again.

Lauren has never been so angry in her life.

Zara is home. And they have called Harry, and the police. Aidan didn't have to insist, as he often does. There was no debate over whether it was serious. Lauren stabbed the numbers into the keypad of her phone, her entire arm tense with rage. How fucking *dare* they.

Zara is sitting on one of the bar stools in the kitchen, holding a cup of tea. 'It was awful,' she keeps saying.

Lauren wants to keep reaching over to touch her, to check she's still there. That nobody harmed her, her baby. As she reaches for her, Zara's eyes follow her fingertips.

'I know. We're going to get it sorted,' Lauren says. She shifts closer to her. She needs to tell her about the Find Girl A Facebook group, before the police get here and assume she knows. But she doesn't know how. She doesn't want to crack her, her fragile daughter, not after this.

'Tell me everything you can remember about the man.'

'He was . . .' Zara says, but she can't continue. She hangs her head, looking down into her lap. Her hands shake. Tea splatters the knees of her jeans, darkening them in little navy drops.

Lauren looks away. She can't bear this.

'God, it's so stupid. Almost nothing happened,' Zara says.

'Not nothing,' Lauren says. 'You were almost abducted.'

'He was in a balaclava,' she whispers.

'Oh,' Lauren says. 'Oh, shit.'

'What if I get scared of going out again?' Zara says.

Lauren's stomach folds over in sadness. Even now, in the face of all this, Zara is most frightened of her own anxiety. Maybe Lauren parented her all wrong. Maybe it started with Paris.

Lauren and Aidan had taken Zara and Poppy to Paris when they were six. They'd been together for just over a year. Lauren ordered a glass of wine on the Eurostar and gaily commented on the speed of the train, the things they'd do once they got there, how quick and easy it all was. Zara was curled in on herself. Poppy's eyes were wide, taking it all in. Their two daughters, so opposite. Like each belonged with the other parent.

Almost as soon as they checked into their hotel, Zara started running a fever. She'd had a urinary tract infection the week before – Lauren was forever telling her to drink more, but she wouldn't – so they dosed her up with Calpol and had a quiet evening. She was better the next day. Eyes bright, smile wide.

They were walking along, after lunch, past a shut-up restaurant in Le Marais covered in ivy, worn like a green fur coat in the sweltering August humidity, when Zara stopped walking. Her little hand went to her head.

Lauren must have made a gesture, or a noise, because Aidan stopped and looked at her, lifted his sunglasses up to see her properly.

That's when she saw it. Or perhaps that's when it developed. A kind of pallor. Zara is always swarthy, but she goes sallow when pale, and on that day, she'd gone grey. Lauren had never seen skin that colour before. She crouched down to look at her properly. Little dots of sweat along Zara's upper lip. Eyes drowsy. It came from nowhere.

In the hospital, it was explained to both of them in stilted English that Zara had sepsis. Drugs were pumped intravenously into wires taped to the back of her hand that made Lauren wince.

Zara had opened her eyes after four days sleeping, and began to recover. Lauren stayed in Paris for five more weeks with her. She had no choice. She didn't care about the hospital bills or the fact that all she had brought with her were three T-shirts and a miniature bottle of travel shampoo. Nothing in Lauren's life mattered – because Zara did. She had assumed the mantle willingly, six years before, and she never wanted to give it back.

'We'll sort them out,' Lauren says now. 'Where the fuck are the police?' It feels like her insides are on fire. Those little shits. Those fucking little *shits*. Zara exaggerated their crime in court – their very real crime. And so they go and commit another!

'I just wish . . . I wish we could go back,' Zara says.

'Me, too,' Lauren says. 'And just have you not testify,' she adds, without thinking.

Zara stares at her, a strange expression on her face. 'You wish I hadn't done it?'

'I'm not saying that,' Lauren says, though that is exactly

what she was saying. 'But don't you wish that you'd just looked the other way?'

'*No*,' Zara says. 'That is what *everybody* does to homeless people, Mum. I wish I had stuck to my lie. Not crumbled under questioning.'

Lauren sinks her head into her hands. Teenage principles.

Zara gets to her feet. 'I'm going to get changed,' she says tightly, standing in the doorway.

'Sure,' Lauren says, resisting the urge to follow her up there, to stand watch over her all afternoon, all night.

Aidan fiddles with his phone. 'Look what it's caused,' he says sadly, Lauren's argument with Zara seemingly a permission slip for him to criticize her daughter.

She rounds on him immediately. 'Don't you say that. She did *not* cause this. They may have got off on some technicality – self-defence, yeah, sure – but look what they're doing.'

'But you just said –'

'She's an idealist,' Lauren says. She picks up an orange from the top of the fruit bowl – it looks magnificent, towering goodness right there on the counter for her daughter. She'll feed her up and heal her. Vitamins, minerals, the works. 'The greater good, and all that. If we erode that . . .'

'You just told her you wished she hadn't done it.'

'It's fine for me to say that,' Lauren says. 'Not you.'

He strides away from her, uselessly switching on the coffee machine, then turns back around.

She senses a tension emanating from his body. The difference between their perspectives, where she falls to forgiveness and he to judgement. It reverses if they are talking about Poppy. Of course it does. It's as natural as the orange in her hands.

'This is —' Aidan says. He is rhythmically pulling his hair back from his forehead, elbows on the kitchen counter. 'You know what else I don't understand?'

'What?' Lauren says through a sigh. She is not very interested in the things Aidan does and doesn't understand. It's happening. They need to act, not think. God, she wishes she hadn't let Zara out. Wishes she had been there. She would've pulled that balaclava off. She would've been able to identify him, and get him, this time.

Lauren begins to peel small segments of orange skin off, unable to get a proper purchase, a satisfying whorl. She looks up to the bedroom. Her daughter will be fine. She's up there, now, safe and warm and well. Lauren will protect her.

'Why they're so bothered,' Aidan says. 'They're disgruntled football fans but why would they . . . actually . . . why would they *go* for her?'

'I don't know. Because they're violent,' Lauren says.

'Something's off about it,' he says. 'It doesn't make sense.'

'We need Zara to tell us what the man looked like,' she says. 'His build. Anything she saw. And then we go and find him.'

'Find him? There are a hundred and fifty fans in the group.'

Something folds deep inside Lauren like a popped soufflé. This is bad.

A package is delivered while they're waiting. Lauren wants to distract herself from the roaring terror in her ears, so she opens it. Hannah, Lauren's sister, has sent her a

Korean face mask in a padded envelope. It's a decade-long in-joke between them, their quest to find the product that will stave off ageing. They have tried everything. Retinol-A. Sheet masks. An infused sponge from Spain that made Lauren's eyes sting. A selfie came in from Hannah the other night with a carbonated cleanser frothing around her smile lines. *Thinking of you all!* was all it said.

Lauren, hands still shaking, turns it over then opens it. Inside is a tarry black substance. She presses her fingertip into its surface. It yields, leaving a perfect oval print.

Lauren puts the pot down as Zara arrives back in the kitchen in her yoga wear.

'Will the café man be able to identify him?' Lauren asks her. Maybe he saw more than Zara.

'Like I said, he was in a full head balaclava,' Zara replies. 'Car had no plate.'

'Who were you with? Before?'

'Anna. She knew Jamie well,' Zara says, not meeting Lauren's eyes. 'We had a nice talk. About everything. And then the car . . .'

'Right,' Lauren says. She swallows. She needs to tell her about the group. It's the kindest thing to do, to tell her soon, before she finds out from elsewhere.

Aidan passes her a coffee she didn't ask for; a peace offering between husband and wife. He never holds a grudge against her. Atmospheres are immediately dispelled. 'Oh, forget it,' he will say, minutes after rows. After a lifetime of crap men, Lauren couldn't believe how easy Aidan was.

The mug warms her hands, the smell comforting and toasty as it rises up. She sips it, thinking.

Lauren tries to imagine what she would like in this situation. She would want to be told directly but reassuringly, she decides. Not by the police or a third party: by her mother.

She doesn't hesitate as she turns to Zara, even though her whole body is trembling. The sun has gone in. It's started to drizzle on the windows outside. *No*, she tells herself. *This is all fine. The police are coming, the lawyers. They will crack down on this group and we will all move on with our lives.* But still. Her hand trembles.

Zara looks across at Lauren. 'What?' she says.

As Lauren puts the orange down, she sees that Zara is trembling too. Her hands shaking, just a little, the same as Lauren, almost like they are still connected by an umbilical cord, never severed, after all.

9

Aidan

Islington, London

Aidan lets in an amorphous sea of experts. They stamp the frost from their shoes and fuss with their coats, sparkling on the shoulders with freezing rain.

Aidan offers drinks, exchanges pleasantries about the traffic, a fixed expression on his face. Internally, his mind is spinning. The Facebook group is growing. It is full of vile threats. Rape. Attacks. So much anger.

They won't be able to arrest them all. Friends of friends, disgruntled fans. They have used pseudonyms, aliases. It's full of new accounts. Funny names. Goodbye Mr X. Dr NoGood. The police won't know who they are.

He is standing in the kitchen trying to remember everybody's tea order. There are six mugs in front of him. Lauren's, Zara's. His own. Harry's. And two police officers'. God, who wanted what? He can't think straight. A lynch mob could be outside right now, turning the corner on to their street.

He makes a range of teas. Some white, no sugar. One black. One with three sugars. He mumbles as he sets them down – white no sugar, white three sugars – and lets them choose.

The living-room shutters are closed against the October weather. The lamps are on. Bill is in his bed in the corner of the room, snoozing. Lauren is holding a burgundy throw cushion to her chest, staring at the floor. Zara is pale. She is slumped down next to him, in the dead centre of the sofa, and looking up to gauge his expression. He wishes she wouldn't. She looks to Lauren for most things, but she looks to him when she's in real trouble. When she found horrible Instagram posts about herself when she was thirteen. When a whole site of builders started jeering at her from across the street. It was Aidan she turned to. It's primal. She thinks he can sort it, her stepdad.

He holds eye contact with her, and he's sure something is communicated between them. *Why did you lie?* he asks.

She drops her gaze.

What does he want from her? Screaming regret. The kind of tearful apology he would get from Poppy. Panic. Wanting to put things right. He doesn't quite know, but it isn't this. Silence and the occasional insistence that she made the right choice.

'First things first,' a police officer called Nazir says. 'We are aware of the group. Rest assured, we're monitoring it.' His hand hovers over the teas. Eventually, he chooses one, seemingly at random.

Nazir has the group open on his phone. He clears his throat, then puts his phone away and leans his elbows on his knees, like he's decided to just go off record.

'Why? Why would they go on a crusade against her,

these football fans?' Aidan interrupts. 'I've been thinking about it and . . . I don't know why they would.'

Lauren looks at him sharply, but he can't help asking these people, the people who are supposed to know what's going on. He takes a tea, his fourth of the day, even though he already feels jittery, his mouth bitter and furry.

Luke was going to sign to the Premier League club on his seventeenth birthday. Aidan has been googling him. He'd left school at fourteen and joined Holloway FC as a scholar, playing for their under eighteens and under twenty-threes. Aidan watched a clip of a match, uploaded to YouTube by a zealous fan. He had a good touch.

And now . . . no signing. He lost his fitness while on remand. And Holloway lost their future star striker in his crucial development phase. He might return to form, he might not. He might never reach his potential. The group is focused on this: the loss to the club. The loss of sponsors and money during the year when everybody thought their most high-profile scholar was guilty of murder, his teammate an accomplice. The media storm when the club publicly supported him. Until they stopped.

Their anger makes sense on paper but something about it doesn't sit right with Aidan. He doesn't know a single football fan so committed to their club that they would try to harm a teenage girl. It goes beyond drunken post-match fighting.

'Who knows?' Nazir says. 'Who knows what goes on in their minds.'

'So what are you going to do about it?'

'I was getting to that,' Nazir says crisply to Aidan. His hair is gelled meticulously, almost strand by strand, pointing down to his forehead like a row of teeth.

'The identities are unknown to us – in the group, but also who was responsible for the attempted attack in the car. And so far, the crime they would be convicted of, if we could find them, would attract a non-custodial sentence. So, in some ways, it may be better to watch and wait.' There is a beat of silence, like somebody turned the world off for a second.

'Do nothing?' Aidan says, bewildered.

'Do nothing,' Nazir confirms, misreading Aidan's tone. He's young. No common sense.

'Wait for them to kill her?' Lauren says sharply, and Aidan winces as Zara stiffens next to him.

'Until it dies down,' Nazir says, 'which I'm sure it will. Or until they make themselves known to us. What we can do is offer you police protection. Day and night. At the front of your house,' he says. 'Just in case they know where you live.'

'Right,' Aidan says faintly. 'That's it?'

'It will ensure your safety,' Nazir says.

'Well, you've been a real help,' Lauren says sarcastically.

'When is the police watch starting?' Aidan says, gesturing vaguely to the front of the house.

'Right away,' Nazir says. 'I'll make the call now. Next half-hour, latest.'

Next to him, Zara shifts, leaning her body weight slightly against him. Aidan looks down at the bend of her knees in her lounge wear, the arches of her bare feet. They're exactly like Lauren's. Long, elegant toes.

Something dark settles across his shoulders. He has to do something. Anything. If the police won't, then it's down to him.

10

Zara

Islington, London

Zara has hardly slept for the last week, and last night was the worst of all. It felt like she could hear every sound in London. The creaks of the house, the distant sirens and the shouts as people left the pubs on the high street. They all became menacing. The house creaking was a stranger's feet on the stairs. The sirens were the police, desperately trying to catch up to the men who want to harm her. The shouts were the group. Twice, she got up to check the police presence. True to their word, the Met have installed a man in an unmarked car out the front. He sits there until seven in the morning, and then somebody else takes over. Zara hasn't been to school.

She dreamt last night – when she did sleep – that she had carried out her lie in court. That Luke and Mal were convicted. They'd all be better off. She dreamt, too, of what she could do to retaliate. What she might do.

And now, Zara, her mother and Aidan are walking back from the cinema. It's the late afternoon. Her mother said that they couldn't sit inside all day, that they had to get on with life. It had been almost a week of confinement.

And nothing happened when they left the house. Nothing happened when they turned on to the high street. Zara didn't, as she imagined she might, feel a cold hand on the back of her neck in the cinema. It has been a perfectly normal afternoon. And now, Zara is looking forward to escaping back into *To All the Boys I've Loved Before* on the sofa with a cup of tea. A tame evening, but tame evenings are the best. Escapism is the answer.

The lanes that spread off the high street are made amber by bright shopfronts preparing for Christmas. Zara's breathing is steady. Her pace is slow. She is thinking about the film they saw, a silly action thing, the sort of film her school friends like. It was about bravery and strength. She is thinking, as she walks next to her mother and stepfather, that they will be okay. That they can face anything as long as they're together.

The policeman nods discreetly to them as they walk up their road, towards their house. The autumn leaves line each side of the street like they've been washed there by a tide they can't see. Her mother is laughing at something Aidan said, but Zara isn't listening.

She puts her key in the lock. The house is in darkness, and she doesn't hear Bill come to greet them. He must be sleeping.

They step inside. The hallway is black. Zara flicks the light switch on and Aidan blinks. 'Going to the cinema in the late afternoon always makes me feel weird, especially when it gets dark so soon,' he says, taking his trainers off.

'I like the early dark nights,' Zara says to him. 'Cosy.'

'I'm going straight in the bath,' her mother says. She adores the bath.

Zara pushes the door into the dark living room and stops dead.

A man is standing on their patio, looking in, his face pressed to the glass. Zara's mother reaches for the light switch.

'Stop!' Zara shouts to her. 'Look . . .'

He's looking in, but that isn't what chills Zara. It's his face. He's grinning. A triumphant, cruel grin. He meets her gaze and, with one white finger, points downwards. To Bill, who's sitting by the patio doors, panting excitedly, tail wagging, smiling up at the intruder who he thinks is a friend but is an enemy.

The man then brings his other hand out from behind his back. He is holding a long, silver knife. He brings it up to his throat, making a slitting motion, while staring at her.

11

Lauren

Islington, London

'Bill,' Lauren cries.

Zara reaches for the dog, but Lauren stops her, getting him herself. The man is running down their garden, a black figure barely visible in the darkness. Bill strains against Lauren's grip on his collar, trying to get to the door, trying to see where he goes.

'Get the fuck out,' Lauren hisses. She grabs Zara as quickly as she can, not caring if she's too rough, if she's too frightening. She puts Bill's lead on him. Lauren stares at the brick wall at the bottom of their garden. The man is nowhere to be seen. He could easily have leapt that wall, and now he'll be gone for ever. Untraceable. Vanished.

'I'll kill him,' Aidan says loudly, striding to the back door.

'Don't be ridiculous,' Lauren says. 'He's got a knife. Come on.'

'So I'll get a knife, too.' Aidan turns towards the kitchen.

God, he seriously means that. He starts going through their kitchen drawers. Opening the cutlery drawer, the one containing their best plates, the one with their utensils in.

He's procrastinating. He knows exactly where the knives are. Lauren is relieved to note in the chaos that this behaviour is for show.

'*Aidan.*'

He turns to look at her. For a moment, just a second, she doesn't recognize him. He's puffed up. Angry.

'Come with me outside to the police,' she says.

'Fine.' He slams one of the drawers closed. 'Man,' he says, rubbing a hand across his beard. His expression changes, dropping back to normal. He comes towards her, shoulders slumped.

She grabs his arm and leads him back out into the hallway, to Zara. As they reach the front door, where they stood happily just moments ago, they exchange a glance. Lauren isn't sure what it holds. Only that it is loaded. She will remember this glance, she is thinking, as their eyes meet and part.

They emerge on to the street, which looks exactly the same as it did two minutes ago. Cold, quiet. Unassuming.

Lauren stares at it. Everything is different.

They walk as quickly as they can to the police car, Aidan slightly ahead.

'There's a man in the fucking back garden with a knife,' he says as soon as he reaches the car.

The police officer startles, winding down his window.

'You're supposed to be watching the house,' Aidan shouts.

The officer is out of the car like a shot. Running towards their house. He starts speaking into his radio.

Aidan tries to run after him, and Lauren pulls him back by his arm again. 'Leave them to it,' she says.

63

Bill is sitting, oblivious, and Zara is rhythmically stroking his head, staring into the distance, shivering slightly. Her eyes are wet. Lauren wants to cover her eyes and ears, out here in the freezing cold, hiding from enemies they barely know they have.

She stands next to the unmarked car and pulls Zara to her. She begins to cry into her coat. Aidan stands rhythmically kicking the kerb with the toe of his trainer. The sound thuds like a heartbeat in the night.

Lauren cries, too, on to the top of Zara's head, trying as hard as she can to stifle her tears. *This is it*, she is thinking. They're never going to get away. They're never going to go back to normal. This is it.

Nazir is back. He's in plain clothes – off duty, maybe. Lauren wonders what he was doing, as she rests her hand on Zara's still-trembling leg. Was he out with his wife? Cooking?

They didn't catch the man. *Of course they didn't*, Lauren thinks bitterly. He ran off down their back garden and over the wall.

'There have been two incidents inside a week,' Aidan says, and Lauren's glad he has spoken up for them.

Nazir is clearly waiting to talk. He is holding a white envelope. He keeps touching the long edge of it to their coffee table, but Aidan keeps going. 'I mean, it's time to talk about arrests, isn't it? Surely? Zara got a good look at his face,' he says, looking sideways at Zara, who nods.

'I did,' she says. 'And he did a motion – across his throat. A clear threat. And they know where we live. They

64

know my name and where we live.' She leans forward, folding in on herself. Her teeth are gritted, and Lauren can see she is trying not to cry.

'I know. Look, we are searching for him.' Nazir rubs at his goatee.

Lauren raises her eyes to the ceiling and breathes deeply. She can't bear this. She cannot bear any of it.

'But, first, I need to give you this,' Nazir continues.

'What is it?' Aidan says, taking the envelope.

Nazir waits a beat. 'Do you know what an Osman warning is?' he asks.

'No,' Lauren says. She looks at Aidan, who has an unreadable expression on his face.

'I do,' he says. He slits open the envelope. 'Is this a joke?' He passes the papers to Lauren.

She looks at them, but can't take them in. 'What is it? What is it?' she says. 'What am I reading?'

When Aidan looks at her, his eyes are red-rimmed, as though he's been crying for hours without her having noticed. 'It's a notice . . . of threat to life,' he says.

Nazir takes over. 'It means your lives are under threat,' he says. 'Yes. These two attempts, given the weapon, we believe that . . . if given the opportunity, Zara would be seriously injured or worse.'

'Right,' Lauren says, her mouth completely dry, like she has just woken up with a hangover. 'So . . .'

'Given the anonymous nature of the group, and the careful way they haven't yet committed an offence that would definitely attract a custodial –'

'Apart from murder,' Zara says.

Lauren looks at her in surprise.

'They were defending themselves,' Nazir says. 'Against Jamie.'

Zara laughs – a hard, bitter, adult laugh – and Lauren winces.

'If you find him, what will you charge him with?' Lauren asks.

Nazir looks awkward, his eyebrows going up, his gaze down. 'It would be, basically, trespass,' he says. 'Maybe possession for the knife, if we could find it.'

'Not attempted murder.'

'He hasn't made an attempt.'

'But you have a piece of paper –' Aidan reaches for it again and puts it in front of Nazir on the table, '– that says, given the opportunity, he will. I mean, he had a fucking knife, Nazir. Are we not on the same side here?'

'We in the police,' Nazir says loudly, 'are of the opinion that this group want to seriously harm Zara. But we can't prove that in court. The police and the CPS do not always agree.'

'Great,' Aidan says. 'Fucking great. So . . . what? We're under threat. You can't charge them with anything but trespassing. Carrying a knife at a push. We all know they want to kill us. So, what are you going to do? What. Are. You. Going. To. Do?' He bangs his mug down on the table.

Lauren winces. He's had about eighteen teas today. It makes him rude and hyped up, though today she is thankful for that.

'We are proposing a solution.'

'Go on, then,' Aidan says.

'Based on that . . . on that disconnect,' Nazir says, his hands a few inches apart. 'Between what we think and what we can prove.'

'What is it?' Lauren says, unable to take the tension any longer.

'I am going to recommend that protection is offered.'

'Protection?' Aidan says.

Nazir's eyes meet his levelly in their living room. 'Witness protection,' he says.

Lauren's entire body fizzes, then freezes, every inch of her skin covered in goosebumps.

Witness protection.

Lauren has never really thought about witness protection, and yet here it is, being presented to her as the only solution to a seemingly impossible situation. She stares at Nazir. 'A new . . . a new name? A new location?' she says. 'That?'

He nods. 'I know it's a lot to take in.'

'We can't –' Lauren says, but then she tries to think. Don't get hysterical. Not in front of Zara. She's done that enough lately. She tries to quell the rising panic. They can't move away. They can't leave their lives. Not because of these youths, these thugs, these fucking teenagers.

'I –' she says.

'Is there any other option?' Aidan says, quietly.

Nazir looks at each of them in turn, then speaks. 'No,' he says. 'We think that – if you stay here – they will harm you.'

It begins to rain outside, little patters against the

windows. Lauren can only hear them because the room is completely silent.

'It's protection or our family gets harmed?' she asks.

'Yes.'

Her head drops. All of the fight has gone out of her, like she is doomed, hunted. Like she is already, here in her living room, a condemned woman.

Zara

Islington, London

Zara sits at the centre of the sofa and the centre of the uni-verse, it feels like to her. Everybody is looking at her. Her lie has grown from a single sentence, uttered to two police offi-cers in a shabby room, to this. Weekend meetings of police and lawyers. Witness statements. Conspiracies. Going into hiding.

Zara has always tried to do the right thing. And, today, on this sofa, she takes the truth and anchors herself to it, like a ship out to sea with only this to tether her. She knows that it was right, even though everything fell apart. Nobody can tell her otherwise. Especially not now, not after what Anna told her on Sunday.

'What would that involve?' Aidan now says to the police.

Her mum is rhythmically stroking Bill's ears.

'It would be full protection,' Nazir says. He avoids Zara's gaze.

He goes to the gym, Zara can tell. Swimmer's arms. A tiny waist. His trousers sit low down. He looks like many of the boys she goes to school with, the ones who drink protein shakes out of enormous clear plastic bottles and who Instagram themselves lifting weights. The sort of boys Poppy hangs around with. Full of banter and slang. The sort of people who make Zara feel like an alien.

'New name. New location. New identities. We'll send someone out . . . to discuss it further,' Nazir adds.

Zara's mum is nodding quickly. Zara is queasy, her stomach in tight, guilty knots. This is all her fault.

'The protection service deems you at enough risk that you would be relocated. Now that there have been two attempts.' He catches Zara's eye, this time, and her cheeks colour.

'Like starting a new life?' her mum says. 'From scratch?'

'It's the best solution when violence like this –' Nazir gestures to the phone, '– is attempted.'

'Right,' Zara says, because she feels she should say something. She looks down into her lap, hoping his gaze moves away from her. When she looks up, he's staring at her the same way Jamie looked up at her as he died. A fixed stare. Zara closes her eyes. It's worth it. All of this is worth it. For justice. For Jamie.

'Where would we go?' Lauren says.

'It's best not to disclose that yet. We take you there first. But it's usually far away,' Nazir says.

The enormity of it all seems to step into the room and sit right next to Zara on the sofa. Leaving her school. Her friends. Poppy. Waste Not and the homeless community. Jamie's friends he left behind, who like her just as she is. How she's got her bedroom just so, her many novels arranged by colour, her clothes rolled up like Marie Kondo advises. These may sound like small things, but they are important to Zara.

'There's got to be an alternative to this . . . to this madness,' Aidan says.

'I'm sorry,' Nazir says.

'Why can't the police just keep protecting us?'

'You all need to go to work – and school,' Nazir says. He rubs at his face awkwardly. 'I mean, it's not a long-term solution. To have this –' he gestures outside, '– for ever.'

'But this could blow over!' Aidan says.

Her mother is looking at him thoughtfully, the sort of dark look he receives when he's left wet towels on the bathroom floor. Zara's witnessed it many times.

'We need to be safe,' she says, more to Aidan than to Nazir. 'We'll do whatever it takes.'

'We could hire security guards,' Aidan says.

He sounds so desperate. Zara didn't think it was possible for her to feel worse than she did.

Nazir spreads his hands apart, his elbows resting on his thighs. 'I don't think most families' budgets would stretch to that,' he says. 'You're free to explore alternative arrangements if it would make you happy. But this is what we – the police – are officially advising. Protection.'

'Okay,' her mother says.

'It would be the three of you?' Nazir says, making a note.

'Yes,' Lauren says.

Zara's head snaps up. She immediately looks across at Aidan. The faintest of blushes has stained his cheeks, underneath his glasses.

13

Aidan

Clapham, London

It's six o'clock in the evening. The police have left – save for the three unmarked vehicles that now surround the house – and Aidan has excused himself. He's come out to see his mum, Brenda. And then, later this evening, his daughter.

He shouldn't be out. Lauren and Zara are jumping at every noise, double- and triple-checking locks. But he's so tired, so jaded. So in need of some headspace, of something for *him*.

He sits on a pallet of Carling and looks at his mum. It smells like the past in here. The wood-and-ink scent of newspapers.

'I don't know what to say.' She is bracing herself on the doorframe. Her knees are bad. She's waiting for an operation.

Aidan's mind is spinning over witness protection. If he went with Lauren . . . he'd leave Poppy, and his mother. He shakes his head. This is what he has done since he arrived. Gone over and over what's happened. He wanted, he guesses, to talk to his own parent, while he tried to fathom out a decision about his child. His children. His blended family.

Lauren didn't say anything. When the police left, she sat on one of the stools in the kitchen and sipped her drink. Eyes looking dolefully over the rim at him. But she didn't speak.

He needs to take Poppy with them. He stares at his feet as he tries to think how he could do it.

Brenda hands him a mug. He only drinks coffee with her. They shared a pot in a cheap diner after his father's funeral – she couldn't face the wake, not yet – and it became their ritual. It's sacrosanct, just for them. The cafetière slowly plunging down on the counter in the back room, the black liquid swirling, blond bubbles on top. The two mugs, an inch of milk in each. The click of Brenda's knees as she sits down – she insists on making it.

Aidan pulls at the plastic wrapping between the cans of lager, procrastinating. 'It's not Zara's fault she's not my own.'

'I know,' his mother says, eyes sympathetic.

'How can I make it work? For everyone?' he says, though he knows that's not what it's about. None of those things matter. It's about Poppy, and only Poppy. His beautiful, emotional, complicated child. *Poppy, Poppy, Poppy*, beats his heart.

'You're always trying to make things work,' Brenda says mildly. 'After Dad, and then with Natalie . . .'

'I know.'

'The weight of the world doesn't rest with you,' she says. 'You know?'

'I do,' he says, even though he doesn't. If he hadn't

gone to see his mother four times a week after his father died, he is sure she wouldn't still be here now. If he hadn't tried to make it work with Natalie, Poppy's mother, he is sure Poppy would hate him today. He can't rest. He can't become complacent. He will lose everything.

'But this is serious,' he says.

'Yes. I'm just saying, it isn't your fault. You take it all on yourself.'

'I don't know what to do –' he says tightly, resting the toe of his shoe on the corner of another box.

'Which option,' his mother says, cutting over him and opening a packet of Quavers, 'is the one you definitely cannot live with?'

Aidan pauses for a minute, thinking. And then he recoils from the thought. 'No,' he says. 'No, it's not a straight choice.' He swallows. 'There's no way I can voluntarily leave Poppy,' he adds. It's the sort of truth that feels solid when spoken, like a sad, heavy fact in his stomach. He can't leave Poppy, because he loves her. He can't leave Poppy, because he left her once, already, when he divorced Natalie. She's damaged. He can't leave Poppy alone with her mother, her unwell mother.

But how can he take her? Make her leave her mother, her little life? The cousins on Natalie's side of the family, her friends, her school?

He is thinking of Poppy, of the unwitting carer she's become for Natalie, of the invisible things he tries to do to ease her burden. The shopping trips. Bringing provisions in for Natalie that Poppy doesn't see, so she doesn't feel undermined. He can't leave her to fend for herself. He can't.

Aidan has always known there to be a ranking system within blended families. It's crass to admit, to explore, but there is. Poppy is his. Zara isn't. He loves them equally, but not in the same way.

Aidan looks at his mother, who surely feels the same way about him. She still dyes her hair – a mousey brown – and the effect is that she still looks near to Aidan's age. Her skin is unlined. She uses that Nivea stuff, in the navy and white tub. Her face looks greasy late at night, on the rare occasions he sees it – Christmas Eve, New Year's Eve, birthdays – and the smell transports him back to 1980s London.

'Would you stay with Poppy? Or would you go, and leave Poppy? All things being equal,' his mother says.

Her voice is soft in the dim back room of the shop.

That's it, he realizes: he's got to take Poppy with him.

'I'm going to ask if Natalie can come, too,' he says.

His mother's brow crinkles.

'Would *you* come?' he prompts. 'There's got to be a way . . . a way this can . . . I can . . .'

'Of course I would,' she says. 'You're my baby.' She smiles. 'But, Aidan,' she probes. 'There's got to be a limit to who you can take.'

'Families aren't just neat little sets of four,' he snaps.

'I know.' She holds her hands up.

Of course she knows. He shouldn't have retorted. 'Everybody is connected,' he says, his voice hoarse-sounding in the quiet of the back room. 'I don't know how to . . .'

'What would happen if you . . . if you let them go? To be safe? And stayed here for Poppy.'

'I can't do that,' he says. 'I can't . . . I just . . . it feels like I only just met Lauren.'

'It might not be for ever,' Brenda says. 'Until it blows over. Maybe.'

'I can't leave them.'

'I know.'

'I can't leave Poppy.'

Brenda says nothing.

'I'm going to speak to Natalie, now,' he says.

'Okay,' she says, and there is something funny about her tone.

He realizes what it is as he turns away from her. She is humouring him. She thinks there is no solution, but she is letting him believe that there is. Because he is her baby.

As they part, she stands on one of the tatty old mats they keep outside the back of the shop. 'It'll be okay,' she says. 'Just do your best.' This is the phrase she has always said to him, right from when he was a little boy, and worried about PE lessons and friendships.

As he kisses her goodbye, he feels her cheek quivering, just slightly, like the fluttering heartbeat of a tiny animal.

'That's absurd,' Natalie says to Aidan. She's in bed, propped up against four pillows arranged in a diamond shape behind her. Even though she's ill, currently cradling one limp arm in the other, she is still Natalie. Still his ex. They broke up over a decade ago and, in order to make sense of that, she thinks that he is a twat. It's crass, but it's true.

'It's less absurd than me leaving our daughter.'

'And have you thought about who else *I* would leave?'

Aidan doesn't say anything to that. All of these hurdles are just that. And isn't it better to overcome hurdles than to leave his family for ever?

'You're putting your problem on to me. You don't want to leave your family, so I have to leave mine. Typical you.'

'Jesus,' Aidan says, standing awkwardly in the doorway of her bedroom. It smells old-fashioned in here. Of talcum powder and scented drawer liners. He remembers, suddenly, the first night they slept together. She had a Conservative Party membership card on her bedside table. Traditional talcum powder and traditional views, that had been Natalie. 'One of them was in our fucking back garden, grinning like a mad person.'

Natalie ignores him. 'And my brother? And his kids? And my parents? And Poppy's friends?' Natalie presses. She's always been this way, but the spikes of her personality are more angled, now, with him. 'This isn't just about you, Aidan. You can't take the whole world.'

Aidan walks over and sits on the edge of the bed, his legs too close to hers, really, but he doesn't care. He puts his head in his hands. 'It's an octopus,' he says.

Natalie doesn't acknowledge his apt metaphor. The conversation is over. It has lasted four minutes. His suggestion is too ludicrous to even warrant a proper discussion.

'You won't come,' he adds.

'Have you got any idea what you're asking me to do?'

'I do. But, Natalie. I don't have a choice. You really – actually – won't come?'

'No, I won't come. Some girl I hardly know lied in court,' Natalie says. Her complexion has blanched. He's tired her out.

He is a shitty, shitty person.

'Poppy's half-sister,' he corrects out of loyalty.

'*Step*,' Natalie says immediately.

'If you don't come, I will have to leave Lauren and Zara for ever,' Aidan says. His voice is a cracked vase.

Natalie shrugs then. Not even an outright no. Just a shrug, an argument won. She is the victor, now, over ten years on.

Aidan flushes the toilet and runs the taps in Natalie's bathroom, to cover the noise of what he is about to do. And then he sits on the edge of the 1980s avocado suite, his socked feet sinking into the carpet that's green-black with dirt around the edges, which he knows Poppy religiously hoovers once a week, even though it's never clean.

He concentrates on it. Slowly, his throat seems to open, and, finally, here, alone in the bathroom, he lets it happen. He rests his palms on his knees and lets his body judder. His shoulders tense, his mouth opens in a silent scream. And here they come. The tears.

He has to choose between leaving his wife and leaving his child.

His family. His wife. His poor babies.

14

Poppy

Battersea, London

'It's just wild,' Poppy finds herself saying. She brings a hand to her mouth. She shouldn't say it like that. Sometimes, when it's been a tough day looking after her mother – which, today, it has – she sounds so . . . so *abrasive*.

Her dad has come over to see her. To fill her in properly, rather than through rushed phone calls and cryptic texts. On quite what, she doesn't know. He is behaving like he is about to make an announcement, but isn't making it. He insisted on going upstairs first to see her mum, and then he spent an age in the bathroom, and now he's here, shifting his weight from foot to foot.

He and her mother are cordial, divorced because they no longer loved each other. Nothing more or less than that. It was four years later that her mum developed multiple sclerosis, though her dad worries – constantly – that people think he left her because of it. *Who cares?* both Poppy and Lauren have said in response to this, but the problem is that her dad does care: he cares about absolutely everything.

The kitchen is messy. Poppy can feel her father looking

at it. Seven mugs in the sink, a plate on top of them, a baking tray on top of that, like a tiered cake. She's been meaning to tidy up a bit, but now he's here. There's just a bit of judgement, of concern, but there doesn't need to be. It's just crockery.

'She lied to the police,' she adds.

Poppy is drinking a detox tea by a company that her dad regularly reports on Instagram. He tells her it's non-sense, but she likes the idea of it. She doesn't want to lose weight, or anything. She just saw them as part of a You-Tuber's morning routine, and she thought: *yes*. When her mum is ill, like now, the flare-up affecting her left arm and leg this time, she can open these little pastel sachets and just . . . have a moment.

Poppy means it when she says she never thought Zara would have lied. Good Zara, kind Zara. Poppy is sur-prised. Surprised and, yeah, sort of . . . half pleased. She shouldn't be. But, like all siblings, she wants the heat off herself.

'I know,' her dad says.

The last time he was here, he saw her pass her mum a drink to sip with a straw. When they were alone, he said, 'She can't sip a drink now?'

'Sometimes she can, sometimes she can't,' Poppy had said shortly, rinsing out a jar of curry sauce and upending it in the dishwasher. 'It depends,' she added. 'It changes, you know. Some weeks are much worse than others.' Her voice was clipped. She didn't want it to be, but it came out that way, like she was a bored, harassed old housewife.

Her dad took the plate she had started rinsing and ran

it under the tap himself. His cheeks were red. 'Maybe we should sort some outside help.'

'She doesn't want carers,' Poppy said in a low voice. She sounded stoic but, inside, her heart was singing. He had noticed. He had noticed.

When she went to lock up after he left, she found a handwritten note pushed through the letter box. *Anytime you need a day off, an evening off, a weekend off, you call me, and I'll sort it for you*, it had said. Poppy had sat on the doormat and had read it, over and over.

'But this is the situation,' he says now, 'and we need to –'

'I mean, are they just going to ... what? Start new lives?' She leans her elbows on the kitchen counter, staring up at him.

He doesn't look irritated by her reaction, or like she is being a nuisance, or he is tired of explaining things to her, as he sometimes does. He looks ... he looks bewildered. Lost, as though he's arrived in totally the wrong house.

'They say we'll never see them again,' he says eventually, and he can't keep the tears out of his voice.

Poppy stares down at her swamp-coloured tea, horrified. 'That's ... I can't imagine. God.' That's all she can say. She can't fix it for him. She can't fix either of them. She stares at her bare feet, jeans carefully rolled up after she watched a how-to video on YouTube, and feels her own emotions, right after his. Her stepmother. Bubbly Lauren, who says things like, 'We all need daily treats *and* lovely eye make-up.' And Zara, too. Quiet, calm, bookish Zara, who is clearly waiting to meet a boy out of a novel rather than from the real world.

'Imagine leaving everything?' Poppy says. 'If that was

me, I'd have to say no to the art foundation!' Her mouth falls open in horror.

'Yeah,' he says. 'None of it is easy. Or ideal.'

He says it in the tone of voice of somebody who is trying to teach her something. But she already knows it, of course. Life isn't fair. That much is clear to Poppy. She remembers the moment her mum was diagnosed. She had gone with her, on the bus, the number 344.

By then, even though her mum's eyesight had temporarily gone, Poppy hadn't expected the diagnosis. Nobody had prepared her. And then the consultant neurologist said 'multiple sclerosis', and Poppy's brain remembered whenever she'd heard those words: conjuring images of monstrous, uncontrolled people in wheelchairs. That famous woman who went to Dignitas to end it all. Poppy sometimes looks on Instagram at the #MSStrong hashtags. *That's better*, she thinks. People hiking. Shopping. Walking with a stick, but still walking.

Her dad fiddles now with the zip of her make-up bag, which is lying on the counter. She's got it out to practise doing liquid liner, but that doesn't seem to matter now.

'Do you think . . . are they really going to *go*?' she asks.

'They tried to grab her in the street, Pops,' he reminds her.

'I know.' Poppy picks up the tea again and takes a sip, then grimaces.

'That tea work, anyway?' he adds.

'No detoxing that I can see, yet,' she says. 'Unless detoxing is just having the shits, instead?'

He laughs. 'Oh, come here,' he adds. There is something off about his tone.

Poppy puts the tea down and crosses the kitchen to

him. His arms are around her shoulders just like they've always been, on and off, for fifteen years. He smells of dads. Imperial Leather soap. Outside. New car smell.

And that's when she realizes. What is he trying to tell her, exactly? 'Are *you* going to go?' she says, filled with horror.

She feels his body tense as they stay embraced, together.

'I don't suppose . . .' he says into her hair. 'I don't suppose, if I went, you'd ever come?'

She pulls her head back quickly, stumbling away from his embrace. Surprise ratchets up to alarm as she catches his serious expression. Has he just asked her this? Is he *going*? She looks upwards, at the ceiling where her mum's bed rests. The universe is out to get her.

'What?' she says. 'Are you going?'

He doesn't say anything.

She thinks of her friends and her school and going off to do the art foundation next year in Chiswick. The beacon on her horizon. And after that: fashion school, she hopes. And, always, caring for her mum, as long as she needs it, just as her mum once cared for Poppy, too.

Jesus fucking Christ. *What* has he just asked? She feels light-headed.

'I can't leave my life!' she says.

'Don't worry,' he says quickly. 'I don't mean that. I would never ask that. No, I'm not going.'

She looks up at him, wanting to believe him. 'Really?'

'Yes. Absolutely,' he says earnestly.

She sighs, relief unspooling on the exhale. *Thank you*, she thinks. *Thank you*. She steps back into his arms and hugs him for a while longer. 'I'm sorry,' she says. 'I'm sorry, but – God.'

His embrace is stiff. The relief disappears immediately. How could he? *Does* he mean it? She thinks of her parents' divorce, and her mother's illness, and now this. She tries to slow her breathing in her father's arms. She can't carry on being so angry all the time. It can't be good for her. She'll get frown lines, for starters.

'Don't worry,' he says, so softly into her hair. 'Don't you worry.'

It feels awkward after another minute, and he must think so, too, because he adds, 'That diet tea stinks,' even though it doesn't.

She laughs loudly, her hoop earrings pulling at her ears as she throws her head back. 'It's detox, not diet,' she says. 'Though I take your point.'

He pulls her close again and says, so softly she wonders if she might be imagining it, 'Never, never, never. I will never leave you.'

It's only later that she thinks: *so what is he going to do?*

15

Lauren

Islington, London

Aidan is sitting in their tiny garden, apparently waiting to speak to Lauren, who has been in the bath. The bath is always where she goes. In times of happiness, in times of sadness. There isn't much the hot water can't cure.

It smells of wood smoke and autumn peat, out here in the cold.

Aidan had wanted to move to the suburbs a few years ago. Kent. Sussex. He'd wanted a big garden. 'But it's my soulmate, London,' Lauren had said plaintively to Aidan.

'Your soul is overly mated,' he had said with a half-smile. 'Remember the Mulberry handbag?'

She'd bought the handbag with Hannah, her sister and biggest enabler. They'd gone up to Bicester for the day from London one February, and then into Oxford afterwards, the sky white and the stone brown, like they'd stepped into the pages of a Victorian novel. 'I'll get lunch,' Hannah had said wryly. 'You've just spent half a grand on a bag.'

'God, don't tell Aidan,' Lauren had laughed.

They'd eaten lunch together, not speaking much, in

that comfortable, intimate way that siblings can. Lauren had looked at her sister's features and enjoyed seeing her deceased parents reflected there, like a small holiday from the grief of being an orphan. As they waited for the train back to London, Hannah had said, out of nowhere, 'You look so much like Mum,' and Lauren had told Hannah she'd been thinking the exact same thing over lunch. They had laughed while standing there in the bleak winter mist, against the brown stone station, waiting for the train.

So they stayed in London, Lauren and Aidan, in the end. Three parents, all dead before they were sixty-five. Three early inheritances. The only way to buy in London. Aidan's father had been a saver, just like Aidan tried to be, and they'd almost paid off the flats' mortgages with the inheritances in one go. They saved the rent from their buy-to-let, and bought the Islington house with the garden. They kept her old flat in Shepherd's Bush. They rented it out until recently. Now, it lies empty, and they never quite got to the suburbs with the big garden, though this'll do.

Aidan is in their very small garden, wearing sweatpants and a navy T-shirt, even though it's freezing. In front of him is a cup of peppermint tea. Lauren gets her packet of Marlboro Lights out of the drawer in the kitchen. She brings them out, lighting up as she crosses the cool paving slabs, the end of the cigarette an orange dot in the night. She is a casual smoker, a few times a year, though Aidan hates it. The last time she smoked was in the summer when they went to a beer garden. *Cigarettes should only be smoked in summer,* she finds herself thinking as she sits down, the smell evocative of gin and tonics and of cut grass as she taps the end to dislodge the ash. She won't smoke again in the winter fug. It's too depressing, like she is a widow or something.

'Look,' Aidan says. It's a conversation opener, not a command. He stretches his legs out under the table.

They've come outside to talk in privacy, at his insistence. Zara's room is at the front of the house. They won't be overheard.

Lauren is wearing a dressing gown, socks that come up to her knees, and a scarf. She's perfectly warm out here in the cold, like a skier in full gear.

'What?' she says.

'I've got a plan,' he says. 'We should sell the house and hire our own security guards.'

'*What?* Aidan, Nazir dismissed that out of hand.'

'He did not! He said we are free to explore it.'

'It's farcical. What are we supposed to do – sit in the house, forever under watch?'

Aidan looks at her. 'Isn't that less farcical than going into witness protection?'

Lauren says nothing, staring into the distance, smoking. 'If we were to have any sort of life, we'd need three,' she says eventually.

'Then let's not have a life,' he says, and Lauren is surprised by the desperation in his voice. 'And be together.'

'What?'

'I've worked it out. We'd need fifty grand a year. If we sold the house and lived in the Shepherd's Bush flat . . .'

'Which has two bedrooms.'

'Yes.'

'And we'd never be able to go out.'

'Yes.'

'And Zara would never go to school.'

Aidan sighs, an angry exhale. One of the many things Lauren loves about Aidan is his sense of responsibility. He takes on seemingly endless tasks, never moaning, never saying he feels pressurized. At various times over the past ten years, she has guiltily caught herself thinking: *Aidan will sort it.* About birthday parties, MOTs, life admin. But this is . . . this is extreme, even for him. God, she thinks, staring down at her cigarette packet. He sounds like – well, he sounds like *her*, saying the sorts of fanciful things she would usually say.

'Why are you trying to do something they haven't even advised we do?' she says to Aidan, meeting his eyes. 'They dismissed security. Witness protection is their solution. It's a threat to her *life*.'

'I know,' Aidan says quickly. 'I know.'

The moon is out, full and bright. London is usually too bleached with light pollution to see the moonlight, but tonight, Lauren can. It creates shadows as vivid as a flood-light on their patio. Lauren stares at the silhouettes of spindly trees and rooftops on their paving slabs like a light show. Neither of them speaks for several minutes.

'I can't imagine leaving everything, either,' Lauren says eventually, her breath clouding the night air in front of her with warmth and moisture and cigarette smoke. 'But we have to. We can't sell the house and hire . . . that's . . . that's ludicrous.'

'Lauren,' Aidan says.

She looks up in surprise. 'Yes?' she says blankly. She finishes the cigarette and lights up another. A new job.

A new town. God, a new school. It is all she is thinking about. New things close in like the autumn cold. She doesn't want them. She wants her life – exactly as it is now. She takes a deep, steadying drag on the cigarette. No. They can make this work. There has to be a way. They will build a life together. They're strong enough. She reaches across the table for his hand. 'We'll be okay,' she says. 'We'll be okay, won't we? Wherever we end up.'

'How can I come with you?' Aidan says quietly, in the tone of voice of somebody who feels that they are not being heard.

There is no sound. Lauren breathes smoke into the night. It hangs suspended in the air for just a second. She watches it, a slow-motion disappearing act. 'What do you mean?' she says eventually, though she has grasped his meaning immediately.

'Lauren, I . . .' Aidan says. His voice is sore-sounding, ragged at the edges. He reaches, to her surprise, for a cigarette and lights up. It takes him three rasps of the lighter. His hands are shaking.

'How can I leave Poppy?' he says.

'No,' she says, shaking her head. 'No.'

But even as she denies what he is saying, she understands it. Of course she does. Their children are more important than each other. Zara is the love of Lauren's life, and Poppy of Aidan's. She just hadn't . . . she just hadn't thought it through. Her first thought is that she has been so selfish and single-minded. The second is that she is going to lose him.

No. That can't happen. She understands it now. The talk of security guards. Desperation. And she's desperate

89

too, but she's got to follow the advice of the police. If she stayed, and something happened to Zara . . .

She stares at the table, his steaming peppermint tea.

'I can't see a way out. You have to go,' he says. 'And I . . . Natalie won't.'

'Natalie?'

'I asked if she could come. I can't . . . I can't rip up Poppy's family, I just can't.'

'I know,' Lauren says. 'I *know*.'

'I'd rather rip up mine than hers.'

Stoic Aidan. He has only told her now. He let her prattle away to the police about them all going. She is glad of it, that the conversation – and the heartbreak – is here, in their garden, while they're totally alone, like a controlled explosion. He always knows how to do things the right way.

'You have to go,' he says. His cheeks hollow as he drags on the cigarette. 'She's not safe. That fucking Osman notice.'

'I can't start a life without you,' she says through tears. 'I can't.'

'I don't know what to do,' he says.

They sit in silence for several moments.

'It's impossible,' Lauren says eventually.

'Yep. My mum basically said the same.'

Despite everything, Lauren feels a shard of jealousy lodge inside her chest. Oh, to have a mother. Her own mother would never have given advice. She would say that she didn't know. Honest and straightforward and totally unable to emotionally connect, that was Lauren's mother. Even now, sometimes, when Lauren cries, she feels embarrassed that she's doing it. 'If Brenda doesn't know, then we're truly fucked,' Lauren says.

Aidan throws her a half-smile. 'I know.'

'There's got to be a middle ground,' she says.

He puffs on the cigarette again. She wishes he wouldn't. That poisonous cigarette.

'Now it's you who wants to hire security guards,' he says dryly.

'I still think that's ludicrous,' she says softly.

'What if it blew over?' he says, a funny expression on his face.

'Huh?'

'What if you go – we'll try it for a bit . . . and hopefully it'll blow over? We'll give it a time limit?' he says.

'A time limit?'

'A year or two.'

'The idea is they give you a new identity for life. The protection service wouldn't do it for someone who intended to come back,' Lauren says.

'So don't tell them that,' Aidan says, looking directly at her. Brown eyes behind glasses. 'The group will die down, surely? It's fucking kids.'

'I can't go,' she says, but she knows that she can. That she must. 'I wish I met you in 2004 and Zara was yours,' she says suddenly, emotionally, panic mounting up inside her.

Aidan smiles a kind of wan smile around the cigarette. 'Then she wouldn't be Zara,' he says simply.

Lauren closes her eyes and sees her beautiful daughter in all of her guises. She opens her eyes and looks at Aidan. His strong jaw. How much he cares. She loves him so completely, her life partner, her best friend, her lover.

But she loves him slightly less than she loves Zara. She always will. And he will always love Poppy more than he loves her. It is what makes their choice impossible. There is no way for him to come with her.

The confirmatory thought chokes her. They're going to be parted. The sadness is so deep she feels it cracking her, and so she turns it to anger, instead. Aidan is fucking right. Her soul *is* overly mated. She loves too many people too much, and look where it's got her. Maybe her mother's way made more sense, after all.

'Try it,' he says. 'Two years, say. I'll be here, waiting.'

She reaches across the table for his hand. He holds on to it, but despondently so, their hands trailing low, between their chairs. Eventually, he pulls away. Goosebumps have formed on his arm. *He must be cold, after all,* Lauren thinks, *but not showing it.*

Jon, their assigned case worker from the protection service, is standing in their living room by nine the next morning. Zara is upstairs. Lauren thinks that for the best. Jon cautioned against Zara being present, because she is a minor. Lauren could filter out the appropriate bits and tell them to Zara later, he said, a beat of judgement behind his words about the conversations Zara has already been privy to. Lauren is too tired to think properly about what's best.

Everything has happened so quickly, like a fast-tracked health referral for something sinister. Lauren is existing in a different world to last week, and it is getting worse and worse as more people get involved.

Jon has just informed her that they are leaving tomorrow.

Tomorrow.

He is tall, with strawberry-blond hair, good teeth, the front ones slightly larger than normal, and a long, straight nose. He pauses just slightly before answering questions, which Lauren likes. She always answers right away, and is often bullshitting. She is in safe hands with him.

He sits on the armchair in the bay window. Lauren hesitates, then sits on the sofa. They're slightly too far apart, but it's better than being too close together.

It's sleeting outside. Lauren looks out at it as she tells Jon that Aidan does not intend to go into protection. He shows no emotion, no surprise, except when Lauren looks at him closely. Something around the eyes. A slight narrowing. Just a tiny bit of sympathy. A squint of understanding.

'He has a child from a previous relationship,' Lauren explains needlessly. 'Zara isn't his.'

'I see,' Jon says carefully. 'Well, I will need to brief you on . . . the implications of that.'

'Okay,' Lauren says.

'Is Aidan here now?'

'He's upstairs.'

Jon inclines his head just slightly towards the ceiling. Lauren swallows. She ascends the stairs. The striped runner she fell in love with last year is soft against her feet.

'They need to see you,' she says to Aidan at the door of his office. He must surely have heard her coming, but he hasn't turned around. He sits with one foot tucked up underneath him, the other resting on the light wood floor. 'Hello?' she adds. 'The protection guy wants to talk to you.'

He closes the Kickstarter page down. 'What about?'

'Implications.'

He looks at her for a second. Something seems to cross his features, like a shadow from a nearby window moving over them. 'Okay, sure,' he says easily.

When they arrive back downstairs, Jon is holding a different leaflet. *Contact with Past Family*. 'Right, then,' he says.

Lauren and Aidan sit on the sofa at exactly the same moment.

'You have made the decision not to join your wife in protection,' he says to Aidan. His tone is that of a police officer cautioning a suspect.

'Yes,' Aidan says, though she hears the subtext loud and clear: *I didn't decide anything. It has happened to us.*

She reaches for his hand, warm and leathery in hers.

'Needless to say, there is to be no contact with your wife once she leaves. You will not be told her new address, her new name, or Zara's new name.'

'No,' Aidan says softly. He rubs his other hand over his beard, which bristles like sandpaper.

'We therefore have to ask if you're sure?' Jon says. He looks down at the leaflet, giving Aidan space to think.

Lauren is cradling yet another mug of coffee. How many coffees has she drunk with professionals since this whole thing began? It must be hundreds, maybe thousands. She stares at the sleet outside. She wants a bath.

She wasn't a bath convert until she had Zara. Everything had become so functional since having a baby – meals eaten quickly, make-up applied in a hurry while jiggling a bouncy chair with one foot – so when Zara was finally asleep, Lauren wanted a treat, but something that was still necessary. *Well, I've got to wash*, she'd think as she guiltily ran the taps, as though she wasn't supposed to be doing anything nice for herself. Those mad baby years. As Zara grew older and more settled, the baths became more decadent. A candle, a single almond-shaped flame lit up at the end of the bath. Face masks. In the hot water, naked, alone, Lauren was completely herself.

'Yes,' Aidan says now. The word is firm but the tone behind it is weak and reedy.

Lauren has an arrow right in the centre of her chest. The life is spiralling out of her, right here in the living room as the sleet rushes down outside. The protection service think they will never contact each other again. Lauren can't comprehend the word. Never. She's just found him.

She told Aidan she loved him after their third date. She had been overcome by it, a sort of effervescent madness.

Afterwards – she did it by text – she paced around her flat in Shepherd's Bush. In the end, she put her phone on a high shelf in the bathroom and had a bath, paying her dues to the gods of text messages by not checking it for an hour.

When she checked again, he had replied four times, only one minute into her bath.

First text: *Wow!*

Second text: *Me, too.*

Third: *I feel the same.*

Fourth: *x.*

And here they are, a decade on, and they still feel the same.

Lauren looks sideways at Aidan. *Two years*, she thinks, and he seems to understand.

'So, in terms of you, Aidan, remaining here, in London. We ask that you be vigilant against any threats, both to you and . . . your child.'

'Okay.'

'And report anything suspicious to the police.'

'Okay.' Aidan pauses. 'On, like . . . a designated number or anything?'

'Dial 999. Or log it with 101, if non-urgent.'

'Right,' Aidan says, and Lauren can hear that his words are laced with his displeasure. If he's not coming with them, he's on his own. Not even the mobile phone number of a helpful police officer to call.

'How many people know the identity of Girl A?' Jon says to both of them.

Lauren counts on her fingers, looking at Aidan. 'Well, us, Poppy, Natalie, a few trusted officials at the school where she saw the crime?'

'Yes,' Aidan says. 'Lauren's sister and her husband. My mum. The lawyers. And the group. Of course.'

'Right, okay. Anyone else? That you know personally?'

'No,' Lauren says, though it has pained her to keep it private this past year. Colleagues pushed away, concerned friends ignored. She has offloaded everything on to Hannah and Aidan, instead. And soon she will be without them. She turns her head to the window and stares outside. Wood smoke puffs out from a nearby chimney. The sleet is turning to snow. It looks like a Christmas scene, little cotton-fluff snowflakes being hurried along the roads by the winds.

'Right.' Jon looks at Aidan. 'You will explain to anyone who knows about Girl A, when they inevitably ask, that Lauren and Zara have been removed for their safety. They will put it together anyway.' He consults a notebook tucked into a zipped pocket inside his briefcase.

'You have an injunction in place so that, even though her name has been leaked online, the press can never report that Zara was the Girl A who gave evidence, is that right?'

Lauren nods. An application made by Harry under the Youth Justice and Criminal Evidence Act 1999. An application that cost the State £30,000. 'You could get a really great guide dog for that,' Aidan had said dryly to Lauren in the meeting.

She stares at a flake that has landed on the window. It is crystalline and fluffy. She watches it quickly melt, the heat from their house making it disappear to nothing.

'So when anyone else asks, our advice is to say they moved away for a time. Make up any credible reason you like. Schools. An ill distant relative. Divorce. Affairs. Decide on one together, tonight, then stick to it, okay?'

Lauren thinks of these people Aidan will have to tell. The mums from the school gates. Her colleagues. The Chinese takeaway delivery guy, Ed, who always brings a bottle of Coke. Their neighbours. Her cousins. Friends. Aidan's colleagues. People with big and small roles in their life who, together, like the stars above them, form a galaxy, mini constellations.

'Okay,' Aidan says, moving his head in a nod that turns into a drop, staring at his feet.

'Let us know what you agree. People will press you, but stick to the same story, then say you don't want to discuss it. Eventually, people will get the message. If they believe you, they're less likely to dig or report her missing, so be convincing,' Jon says.

'Lauren would never leave me, though,' Aidan says

plaintively. He covers her bare foot with his. Warm and heavy and comforting.

Jon says nothing, but makes a funny kind of gesture.

Lauren understands it immediately. It says: *but she is.*

Aidan has had to go out for Lauren's private briefing.

When he's gone, Jon continues seamlessly. 'Before I give you the background, please be assured that everything is in hand. The identities were organized yesterday afternoon,' he says. He pulls out two plastic wallets, fastened with a popper. A third remains in his briefcase. Aidan's identity, cast away. They'll never know him.

'So, I mean . . . you just give me somebody's identity?' Lauren says.

Jon blinks – a flutter of apricot-coloured lashes – then fixes his gaze on her. His eyes are a mid-blue, unremarkable, his lashline pink.

'It is a fictitious identity,' Jon says.

Lauren crosses and uncrosses her legs, then sits forward. She can't deal with this formality. This man is orchestrating the destruction of her life. She has to *understand* this. And him.

'From where, though?' she says. She sees there is a passport in the plastic wallet. God, already.

'No laws are broken in the procuring of identities.'

'But –'

'I'm here to brief you on your protection,' he says, a slight tinge of irritation in his voice, as though he has lost control of the meeting. He finds a pen in his jacket pocket. 'And I will be your point of contact through your first year.'

'Okay. What's your background?'

'I've worked for the protection service for five years.'

'So you do this . . . what, how often do you set up new people?' She tries to catch his gaze, but he avoids it.

He puffs air into his cheeks. 'I understand you've had the Osman warning?' he says, as though she hasn't asked her question.

'How bad is that?' she says. She wants a connection. She wants Jon to grab her shoulders and say: *I know! Isn't it horrendous?*

'Well,' Jon says, 'it means the police believe there is a serious threat to your lives.'

'Right,' Lauren says, swallowing.

'Okay,' he says, clicking the pen on and off and looking at her thoughtfully. 'This is for the best,' he says. 'Given the situation.'

'I know,' she says quietly.

'Then let's get going.' He bites his bottom lip. 'Let's start from the beginning, now that the business with Aidan is sorted. I work for the department of person protection services. We look after a . . . a wide range of those in need of protection. Not just witnesses. Released offenders. Victims. I assure you, I am experienced enough,' he says, misinterpreting Lauren's earlier nosiness.

'Okay.'

'We are happy to offer lifelong protection, but we expect that you assist us in keeping yours and Zara's new identities private. That is to say, as I have explained to Aidan, you are not permitted to tell anybody who you really are.' He produces an information sheet. Typical public sector fare. Made using WordArt.

'Witness protection is a pact made between the service and you – your family. You agree to adhere to these rules.' He shows her the information sheet. *A Quick Guide to Protection*. Lauren scans it quickly.

1. *SILENCE – you must not make contact with anyone with whom you were previously affiliated.*
2. *SECRECY – you must not inform anyone you meet of your past identity.*
3. *STORY – you must strictly adhere to the background information provided to you regarding your new identity.*
4. *STRAIGHT AND NARROW – you must not engage in any criminal activity.*

Breaches of any of the above rules can lead to immediate cessation of the protected person scheme.

Lauren wishes there was somebody else here. Somebody to take notes and pay proper attention. Somebody like Aidan. Her mind is spinning. He'll just be outside, walking aimlessly in the snow . . .

'Historically, the service has found it helpful if service users think of it like a line that cannot be crossed. The before,' he gestures expansively to her living room, 'and the after,' to the folders and passports.

The words. *Service users*. The body language. It's like a corporate presentation. And, in a way, she supposes it is.

'It can never be crossed,' he says.

'I know,' Lauren says.

'And it can never be undone.'

Lauren stares down at the floor.

'Nobody from your past can know where you are. Nobody you know now will be permitted to contact you, nor you them. We do understand,' Jon says, bringing the leaflet to his chest, 'how hard this is. How it is not what you would choose to happen.'

'No, I know you do,' she says, though she doesn't know why. People pleasing, she guesses. There is no evidence that Jon really does understand.

'You'll be relocated and given rented accommodation for six months while you set up your life. We'll give you matching, but invented, school and university results. A fictional job history that resembles your own.'

'Right,' Lauren says, thinking of the fabric of her identity, ripped apart. No longer a student from Mary Magdalene's School For Girls. Five GCSEs. Fell into being a nursery key worker. Fell in love. Would the substance of that remain, behind the lies?

She won't be a stepmother. She won't be a wife. Will she still be a sister? An orphan? A woman whose mother was difficult? A woman who finds solace in the bath? A woman who can't resist the bakery section of the supermarket? Who is she, if not Lauren? What will remain?

Her eyes are wet. She can't say this to him. She'll sound mad. She shakes her head from side to side. It is overwhelming.

'I know it's a lot to take in,' Jon says. 'I tell you, I don't think I would be very good at it.'

And that's all it takes, that window into him, the real him. Who is Jon? Who is anyone?

'Yeah?'

'Definitely,' he says.

Fuck it. It won't be the first or last time she over-shares. Besides, soon, she won't have anybody left to confide in – except him, it seems.

'But . . .' she says, venturing in.

Jon's eyes flick to hers, like a dog chasing a ball.

'I feel like I can't leave everybody,' she says plaintively. Something about real, tangible Jon here in front of her – talking logistics and passports and names – has made it seem concrete in a way it wasn't before.

'I know,' he says, in the careful manner of a professional who has seen this reaction countless times.

'Who would you have to leave?'

'I don't think that's relevant.'

'I just mean . . . I'm a person, you know?'

'I know.'

'So how the fuck am I supposed to actually do it? You know? In this day and age, when you can just text at any time . . .'

Jon says nothing for a few seconds, evidently thinking. 'Your lives are at stake,' he says simply. 'You can't afford to do that.'

'Right,' Lauren whispers. 'Okay. Got it.'

'So, the next steps are to issue your new identity. There are some things to sign, here . . . then I will be able to get you bank cards and your provisional driving licence.'

'I don't need to drive.'

'You'll want to learn where we're going.'

'Okay,' she says quietly. She reaches to sign the form where he's put a messy X. The name says Lindsey Smith.

'That's . . . I'm Lindsey?'

'Yes. Same initials. Results in fewer breaches, if you keep your initials, we find. I'll give you your entire identity when we're in the new location.'

'I ... I see,' she says. She scrawls her new name thoughtlessly.

'And for Zara. You can sign for her,' he says. 'As her parent.' He holds out the paperwork and she sees Sienna.

'Not a Z?' she says.

'No. It was too identifying, we thought. Not too many Z names. We went with an S.'

Lauren considers it. Lindsey and Sienna Smith. How strange it is to be named by the department for protection. Christened by them. Not lovingly, with baby books, as she did for Zara.

'The bills and rent will go in Lindsey's name. Don't tell anybody this name before you leave, even Zara. We need it to be watertight. If I didn't need you to sign, I wouldn't have told you. Okay?' he says, holding her gaze.

'Okay.'

'So, packing.'

'Yes?'

'No mobile phone, obviously. We'll get you a new one. You'll give us your old one. We'll wipe it. No laptop. No photographs.'

'Photographs.' The room feels suddenly airless. Aidan. Bill Gates. Poppy. Hannah. Her parents. Her wedding photographs. Her iPhone photographs. All gone. How will she remember what they all look like?

'No particularly identifying items of clothing – if you have a bright pink coat, that sort of thing.'

'Okay.'

'No personal items with your name on.'

She can take the mirror that Aidan bought her, with LS engraved on the back. Same initials. She'll treasure it.

'Will I need to disguise myself?'

'No,' Jon says, his smile more a flex in the muscle of his cheek. 'Everyone thinks that. But, no, you don't need to dye your hair for ever and get glasses.'

'Okay.'

'And, anyway, you'd be surprised how easy it is to hide in plain sight. Nobody will suspect you're in witness protection.'

'Really?'

He pauses, looking at her. 'Well, have you ever suspected anybody is?'

'No,' Lauren says with a nervous laugh.

He rises to his feet.

She stands by the door while he fumbles with his coat. So that's it. That's how you change your identity. He reaches for the door handle. He smells of cut grass, an expensive aftershave. She wishes she hadn't asked him who he would have to leave behind, hadn't tried to force him to confide in her. The feeling isn't alien to Lauren: she thinks it on the way home from most parties. 'Maybe don't do it next time, then?' Aidan sometimes says kindly, but she always does. The effect of a distant mother, she supposes, is a daughter who shares too much. Perhaps Zara will end up somewhere in the middle.

'Two suitcases. Four o'clock tomorrow afternoon. Aidan should be out,' he says, sending her another apologetic smile.

'We're not leaving at night?'

'No, long drive,' he says. 'It's good that it's dark, but we don't want to arrive too late and attract attention. Two suitcases. Zara's allowed the same.'

'Okay,' she says. 'Is there, you know . . . is there a time limit on all of this? Say if the threat disappears tomorrow . . .'

'What?' Jon says, looking shocked for the first time, his eyebrows raised, mouth open. 'No, Lauren. This is for life. All the stuff we said earlier . . . you can't go back. Were you not . . . were you not listening?'

'I know. I was. But, I just wondered.'

'It's a last resort. You understand that, right?'

'Right. Okay. Forget I asked,' she says.

He holds her gaze for a moment too long.

She watches the paperwork go into a folder and the folder go into a box file, and the box file into a briefcase she didn't realize was standing up next to her sofa, and all the while, she is thinking: *Lauren is dead.* She is no longer Lauren. She will be wiped. Disappear from Islington, from the electoral roll, from her GP's surgery patient list, from the dinner table at Hannah's house, from Facebook. From all the places people leave a digital or analogue footprint.

She watches the identities get packed away like Russian dolls and thinks: she is no longer Lauren, and she is not yet Lindsey, either. So who is she? She is identity-less. Nobody.

16

Aidan

Islington, London

Tomorrow, Aidan's wife is leaving him.

Witness protection. Something he was aware of from TV shows. Something that might happen to a tiny fraction of the population. Something like homelessness, house fires, asylum seeking. He can hardly believe it.

Aidan watches Lauren pack. Her movements are as familiar to him as his own.

They met at a wedding, but it was the dates that followed that he really remembers. The day after the wedding. Breakfast at the hotel, was it? They ate croissants – Lauren put cheese in hers, which Aidan told her was wrong. They spoke about weird combinations of food – he's sure that's all they spoke about – but when they looked up, they realized that everybody had gone, and hours had passed. They veered from topic to topic. He was an only child. She had a sister. His dad was dead, so were her parents. Both of their fathers had had heart attacks. Her mother had had pancreatic cancer. A swift death, Lauren had said, ripping another croissant in half. They covered the basics but the basics were intimate, for them. Grief, loss, love. She missed her mother, even though she'd been 'difficult to really like', Lauren said, looking him straight in the eye.

And now, here. Ten years later. Nine years of marriage – they married quickly, so sure of each other. And now he's watching her leave him.

His chest is full of panic. It feels like there is something trapped inside him that is fighting to get out. He sits on the edge of the bed while Lauren packs around him. In twenty-four hours, she is going to be taken from him for ever. And he's not permitted to know where she will be. Already, she has pulled away from him. There are things she cannot tell him.

He sits there, watching her try to decide between two pairs of jeans, then put them both in, and he wonders if he has made the right decision.

He sits on the bed, facing her, so she can't see his phone, and logs on to his Facebook profile. Within a few minutes, he has deleted all of his friends. Next, he edits his profile, changes his name to something anodyne: James Thomas. Then he removes his photos – anything identifying – but leaves a couple of shots of sunsets and shared posts, just to look like he's not a brand-new account.

He gives his profile a once over. He's sure he's caught most of it. That there is nothing there that he's missed. He is now James Thomas who likes REM and Tom Hanks and Marvel. Mainstream, unidentifying, popular stuff that everybody likes. It is a kind of witness protection, he concedes. His own new identity. His own way through.

He heads to the bathroom and looks at himself in the mirror. He's pretty nondescript. Forty-something. Lines across his forehead. Clean-shaven. Round glasses. Mid-brown hair. Tall. He looks at himself. He hopes nobody will connect James Thomas to the man who sat in the public gallery. The injunction prevented the press from running any photographs, but if he meets these people . . . they might know him. He finds some old sample contact lenses he got and never wore in an old wash bag, and puts them in. He puts his razor away. He'll grow a beard, too.

Next, he strides into the kitchen and gets out the small black plastic phone he purchased yesterday evening from a market stall in Camden. He places it in the kitchen drawer.

Untraceable.

Undetectable.

Private.

'The group has now been made private. Aidan doesn't know why, but his eye through the keyhole is now blocked up.'

He looks at James Thomas's profile photo – Aidan himself wearing a Hallowe'en costume complete with mask – and navigates to the closed Find Girl A group. After a second's hesitation, he presses 'request to join'.

Because that is Aidan's plan.

He's going to infiltrate them.

Why do you want to #FindGirlA?

It's a message from somebody calling himself Kevin Green.

Aidan goes to Kevin's profile. It's clearly a fake, a brand-new account set up, created just a few days ago, no friends.

Aidan navigates to Messenger and taps out a reply.

Because I want her to get what she deserves! he types.

A second later, a new notification pops up.

What skills do you have to help find her?

Aidan sits on the bed, thinking. All he knows is computers. How do people find people? He takes a few seconds more to think before replying.

I can build you a scraper, he types. *To comb the internet, to find her.*

Sold to the man in the mask, Kevin says.

And then I can join? he writes.

We'll see if you pass first.

Later, he comes out of the shower and stops on the landing after hearing Lauren's voice. He showered after overhearing her say goodbye to Poppy on the phone.

'It isn't that I don't love you,' she is saying. She's sitting on the bottom step, next to the radiator.

He stops, unseen, at the top, just looking.

'It's just that sometimes in life –' she wipes at her nose, '– you just have to do the things you don't want to do. Sometimes, adulthood is rocks and hard places. And I know how much you love to chew rocks, but . . .'

Aidan shifts on his feet, and sees: she is talking to Bill. His head is in her lap, and she is bent over him, her tears drip, drip, dripping on to his fur.

17

Lauren

Islington, London

Her things are packed. Two black rectangles sitting on her bed containing everything *Lindsey* will ever know. She's always been a bad packer, will take eight tops on a weekend break. Hannah used to pack for her. She is ruthlessly organized, overtook Lauren quickly in 'being an adult'. She cleans a different room every day of the week in her house and has a capsule wardrobe. Lauren needs to ask Hannah how to pack, but she hasn't even told her she's going. Lauren can't find the headspace. She's lost everything in a single weekend.

There is nothing identifying in Lauren's cases now. She left her leopard-print Converse trainers in the wardrobe. Photographs of Aidan remain here, on the iPhone she will soon give up to the protection service.

She shakes her head as she struggles to do up the zips.

'There's nothing identifiable in there?' Aidan says.

'It's all bland stuff,' Lauren says. 'They've told me I can't take anything too personal. No crazy shoes . . . no zebra-print jumpers.'

Aidan's mouth twists into a sort of smile. She is sure he

remembers the zebra-print jumper she first saw across the street in a shop window while they were on holiday in Devon. The next morning he woke to an empty bed and texted Lauren.

You're out buying that bloody jumper, aren't you?

She was, yes, but she was also purchasing his reaction: incredulous, a wide smile, a spotlight on only her.

Her eyes fill with tears as she thinks of all of those memories. The time she went to IKEA and couldn't fit her shopping in the car. She had sent him a text.

I bought a spontaneous bookcase and it won't fit.

He'd left work early to come. They'd jostled with the flatpacks, trying to push them into Aidan's car. Halfway through, he'd said, 'What even is a spontaneous bookcase?' and they'd doubled over, laughing.

Lauren walks upstairs to check how Zara's getting on. As she stands in her doorway, her heart breaks as she watches Zara carefully packing an entire suitcase with library books. 'I can't leave them here,' she says.

'They've got your name on them,' Lauren says gently.

Zara shrugs. 'But . . .'

'You can bring the ones you own,' Lauren says.

'But I've not finished this one,' Zara says, brandishing a pale blue book with a clear plastic library cover.

'I know,' Lauren says. 'Anyone you want to call – before we go?' she says lightly.

Zara sits on the bed, her hands around her forehead like blinkers. 'It's just a bit . . . it's all a bit massive, isn't it?'

'I know. I haven't even told Auntie Hannah.'

Zara throws her an understanding smile. 'I'm sorry,' she says sincerely. She looks at her for a second.

'We can join a new library.'

'I'm halfway through *To All the Boys I've Loved Before*.'

Lauren raises her shoulders to her ears. She doesn't say any more than that. Doesn't need to.

'Fine.' Zara sets the book down. 'Let's bounce, as Poppy would say.' Zara smiles, which makes Lauren laugh.

'She was trying to take library books,' Lauren says when she arrives back in the living room.

'I wish she hadn't lied,' Aidan says. Here, now. Of all the things to say. 'If she hadn't lied, this wouldn't be happening,' he adds, as though that is an explanation.

Aidan said goodbye to Zara earlier. Lauren doesn't know what took place in that conversation, but she hopes it wasn't this.

'It might. She would have . . . they would have been angry with her even if she told the truth,' Lauren says.

'The CPS wouldn't have prosecuted,' Aidan says with the resigned tone of somebody who is seven steps ahead.

'Yeah,' Lauren says softly.

'I don't know what to say,' he admits, and she loves him for that.

They're parting ways. But there's no divorce, no affair, no death. No illicit text message discovered on a lit-up iPhone. No condom found in a wallet. No traffic accident, no sudden-onset chest pain in the shower. But this is a divorce. This is a death bed. Make no mistake.

'What about everyone?' she says. Her brain throws up different problems she is not able to deal with. Poppy was so nice about it, but will she privately think her stepmother has abandoned her? What about Hannah? God, Hannah. Hannah and her baby-making. Years and years of IVF behind her, their latest attempt commenced a few weeks ago. What if it works? What if it *doesn't*?

'I'm going to tell Hannah the truth,' Aidan says.

'Yes.'

'And the rest . . . I think I'm going to say –'

'Say what?' Lauren says sharply.

He is blushing across his cheekbones. 'Say we've split up.'

Her eyes widen.

'Well, what am I supposed to tell them?' Aidan asks. 'That you've gone on a fucking holiday?'

'Don't swear at me,' she says, sinking into the armchair, her legs weak. 'I don't know.'

'It'll result in the least questions,' he says.

'They'll think I'm an ignorant cow, never saying goodbye. My colleagues . . .'

'I'll say I had an affair.'

She looks up sharply. 'Don't say that. Don't taint us.' Her eyes are wet. Aidan blurs as she looks at him.

'We've got to let that go,' he says. 'We can't care what they think. We need to keep you safe.'

Lauren says nothing, staring at the two suitcases. 'We haven't split up,' she says.

'No.'

'Have we?'

'No.'

Neither of them says anything for a few minutes.

'Two years,' Aidan says.

She raises her eyes to him.

He's looking straight at her.

'They said yesterday that it's supposed to be for ever,' she says softly.

'Okay . . . well, I'm not going anywhere.' He puts his hands on his hips. 'Am I?'

'No.'

'I'll be faithful. Waiting here for you. I will see you again, I know I will.'

Lauren closes her eyes. 'I know,' she says. 'Okay. Two years. If you don't hear from me . . . move on.'

'I think I will hear from you,' he says.

As she looks curiously at him, a signal passes between them. She's not sure what, but it's more than just chemistry. It is . . . *something*.

'Stay safe.' He holds her gaze. He reaches behind him for the doorknob, still looking at her. He opens the door a few inches, letting the cool winter air in. 'Well,' he says.

They don't embrace or kiss. It would be too loaded. The final kiss, the final touch. Instead, he does something far more intimate. He reaches over and ruffles her hair, just the ends of it, mussing them up, tangling the ends, his touch on her shoulder light. He retreats through the door, after that. She watches him go down the street, the sunlight behind him, leaving him in shadow.

She reaches for her suitcase and thinks she won't brush her hair, not ever again. Those strands tangled by her husband will intertwine for ever.

After

18

Aidan

Islington, London
One day gone

The first sound Aidan hears in his first morning in the afterworld is the ping of Facebook Messenger. It's Kevin.

Your task: build us a tool to scrape for new social media profiles appearing online that match Girl A's interests. We stood outside her house last night. It's all shut up. Neighbours said they've gone away. Reckon the police have taken her into protection. Comb for new images too that match this.

Kevin sends over a photograph of Zara, taken from her Facebook profile. Smiling, nervous Zara. Aidan's heart turns over as he downloads it. He is a double agent. What is he doing?

Sorted, Aidan types, his hands shaking.

They were at the house. Thank God he was at his mother's. Thank God. He has to move, in case they're still monitoring the house.

Aidan spends the morning coding a bot that will scrape the internet for any new Facebook, Twitter or Instagram profiles within Zara's age range and with her hobbies. He sends a video of it working over to Kevin. He scrolls down the results page, presses 'scrape', and the links are added to a spreadsheet of viables.

Kevin writes back immediately.

Thanks.

A notification on Facebook then appears.

Your request to join the group Find Girl A has been approved.

Of course, Aidan is going to run the scraper himself and never give anybody the results. He will give the group fake results. Fabrications.

He sits up in bed, where he's been working, and puts his feet down on to the bare wood floor. They stripped the boards two years after they moved in, using a rented machine to varnish them which Lauren rode around on, her eyes scrunched up in laughter. 'I want to commute to work on this thing!' she'd said. God, she was fucking fun.

He opens the blinds. Grey skies. Silence. He closes his eyes. Lauren is just at work, he pretends. She always got up earlier than him, was forever busy. Cleaning with that stuff she loved – Zoflora. Buying 'oven bags' and dissolving the contents of their oven, holding up a disgusting bag full of rust-coloured slop. That time she made a rainbow cake and enjoyed using the food colouring so much that she later made him a purple stew. 'Blue mashed potato tomorrow,' she'd said.

He is going to move into Lauren's old flat in Shepherd's Bush soon. He phoned 101 last night, for advice, alone in bed, where he's wanted to be ever since she left. 'Lie low, wherever you think they're least likely to discover you,' they said, the language deliberately distanced, as though the decision was for Aidan only.

Aidan used to play chess with his father before he died.

Every Friday night. In the garden during summer, by the fire in the winter. His mum would make the drinks. His father was excellent and would often win in a handful of moves. 'Five steps ahead,' he would say wryly as he moved so Aidan's king was in check, tapping the board with his index finger.

Aidan thinks now of the chess matches and his dead father. He never got even remotely good, but maybe now he can. Maybe he can stay five steps ahead.

First, he thinks, looking at the bay window where Lauren used to sit, he will infiltrate them. Become one of them.

Second, he will work out who they are.

Third, he will wait until they're ready to commit a crime and gather the evidence. He'll do it so much better than the police. They're public sector. They would google the group once a week.

And then, fourth, before they do it, he will entrap them. Hand them over to the police.

Timing will be everything.

Fifth, his wife and child will come home.

Five steps ahead. Check.

He starts to pack. He takes more than just a bag, more than just a few clothes. He packs jumpers and T-shirts and shorts, too: he can't come back here. Two suitcases, just like Lauren did. Thank God. Thank God their rental flat is empty. Thank God they procrastinated over re-letting it.

He looks around the house before he leaves. Bill Gates's lead is in his hand. Bill trots faithfully after him down the street, following him wherever he will go. Trusting that he is doing the right thing. That he is keeping them both safe.

When he gets to the flat, Lauren's old flat, full of memories of her, he checks the group, but it's gone. He messages Kevin, who writes back immediately.

Group's been shut down. Club only now.

I can be club, Aidan writes, without thinking.

No ur not.

Aidan's face twists into a smile. Text speak. Fucking teenage yobs. Fans.

You need this scraper. The internet is the fastest way to find someone, Aidan writes. He googles missing people quickly, then types again to Kevin. *Search for skip tracing. I know about it,* he lies. He can learn. Aidan is a fast learner. *My services are for hire.*

Kevin types on and off for ten minutes. *Okay,* he says eventually. *We need your services. Come to Warehouse 6B, South Croydon, Tomorrow. 7.30 a.m.*

A second message arrives.

Tell no one.

19

Lauren

The M40, northbound

One day gone

Here they are, just Lauren, Jon and Zara in the car, in awkward silence.

When was the last time they were this far north? They went to Cambridge last year, maybe then? It was just after Zara had turned fourteen. This is how Lauren pinpoints dates: using Zara's age. She has done so ever since she was born. *Zara was three, so it was twelve years ago.* She doesn't work in years any more. She works in Zaras.

Lauren sighs as Jon indicates to change back into the slowest lane. He is doing dead on seventy miles per hour. Zara is staring out of the window in the back. They surrendered their iPhones to Jon, but haven't yet been given new ones. Zara hasn't complained. She's not bothered by the smartphone like Lauren is. Zara will probably enjoy being temporarily 'off grid'.

'What were you, before?' Lauren asks him spontaneously. She can't sit here in silence as her life changes up the motorway. It is too strange. He knows everything about her. He *invented* her.

'Before?' he says blankly.

'You said you've worked in witness protection for five years.'

'It's not witness protection. It's person's,' he says automatically.

She says nothing. Aidan taught her the value of a loaded pause. People always fill them. Jon's cheeks blush. Lauren is used to that. 'Oh, it's because I've had too much coffee, it gave me the shits!' she would say at a party and then, at home in bed, she would lie there and think: *why did I say that?*

They pass the rest of the journey in silence. M1, M6. M62 past Liverpool. Further and further up. Finally, she sees the sign that prompts Jon to indicate left, a soft flick of the stick, three clicks, the car moving over carefully. Coniston. The Lake District.

'Police,' he says quietly, when they pull off the motorway. 'I was police. Before.'

Coniston Water is to the left, but Jon drives right. The streets angle back on themselves, hairpin turns as they snake their way up a hill. It's completely dark. No street lights. Lauren misses their amber hues: the night-time is black and white without them. She squints out of the car window. It's raining steadily. Tap, tap, tap on the roof of the car.

John swings into a driveway, checks the rear-view mirror, waits, and then turns the engine off. Zara is asleep.

'This one,' he says, indicating a terraced house in front of them.

It's made of flat, grey bricks. Like a drystone wall. The effect is a sort of brindled colour, like an animal. Lauren studies it. She gets out of the car and stands on the gravel driveway.

Silence.

Zara stirs inside the car and gets out, too. 'Wow,' she says drowsily, rubbing her eyes. She's wearing pale jeans, a pretty white top with frilly arms, and a light grey cardigan with a big, rust-coloured scarf. She looks so adult. Always neat, not a hair out of place.

Lauren hides a smile. Her daughter has no idea what a knock-out she'll be.

Jon is getting a set of keys out of a plastic wallet and standing by the door. They're number two. Both houses next door, numbers one and three, have no lights on. It's a safe haven, flanked by two empty properties. They are uniform, identical, plain. Net curtains across every window. Metal handrails by the steps. There is something of the public sector about them. Social housing. Army housing. Care homes. Something like that.

Lauren stands awkwardly, staring at the ghoulish black windows. She hopes she can fall in love with this house. She has to be able to fall in love with this house. It has to become hers. But where are the shined wooden floors of her London house? Where are the deep bay windows, the twenty-four-hour shops, the art galleries?

It smells up here. Freshwater on stone, the air misty and thick. It's so isolated. The street is unlit, and Lauren can only see a hundred yards or so into the distance. Then it is blackness. She shudders. Anything could happen here.

'Come on in and we'll talk properly,' Jon says, catching her hesitation.

He unlocks the front door and it opens straight into a

living room painted grey. It's furnished. A cream sofa with fluffy cushions. An empty bookcase. A lamp in the corner. Jon ushers them in and closes the door behind them.

'Three beds. Same as in London. We place you in like-for-like conditions. No Ferraris and unlimited funds here, I'm afraid,' he says, standing right in the centre of the living room and staring out of the window. His posture is rigid, like a guard's.

He leads them down a beige hallway and into a small kitchen with oak worktops. 'Kitchen. Basic appliances here. Anything you need within reason, we get it for you. Okay?'

'Okay,' she says. The house has that cold feeling peculiar to buildings that have been unoccupied for more than a few days. A dead fly lies on its back on the window sill, legs in the air. She can see little chains of dirty droplets, like tidemarks, where somebody has hastily cleaned. She looks up at the ceiling. Artex.

'Do I own this?' she says. 'This house?'

'No.'

'Does the State?' she asks.

He blinks, surprised at her inquisitiveness, as people often are. 'You can't ask people how they vote!' Aidan once said as they were walking home from a party. But she could. She would tell people how she voted. What she earned. Regularly did.

Jon turns his mouth down, nods his head slightly to the left. 'Yeah,' he says, though it sounds like no.

She would've laughed with glee if somebody had given her a free house a year or two ago. No bills to pay. Everything taken care of. But what she wouldn't have realized is that it feels artificial. Sterile. A life being constructed around her is not her life. She has stepped into somebody else's. Lindsey's, she supposes.

'When you're settled here, six months or so, we'll liaise with Aidan to sell the Islington house and get your half. Then you can buy here.'

She closes her eyes against these words. Zara is standing next to her, holding a paperback. *The Hunger Games.* She started it in the car, shutting Jon out by reading it, escaping somewhere else. Lauren doesn't blame her. She could never do denial, closing her mind to terrible things, but fair play to Zara if she can. It's a privilege afforded to kids. One Lauren wishes she still had.

'Boiler – gas, combi,' Jon says, morphing from chauffeur to bodyguard to estate agent.

'Good for your baths,' Zara says immediately to Lauren.

'Is it?' she says.

'Yes – no water tank, right?' Zara says to Jon.

'You're so smart,' Lauren says sincerely to her daughter, who makes a face. Somehow, somewhere along the line – probably because of some shitty boy – Zara has come to believe that being smart is a bad thing. Lauren wishes she could undo it. Study hard. Know about boilers. Read three novels a week, if you want to.

'Small utility,' he says, opening a wooden door off the kitchen – it's split horizontally, like a barn door, and the two halves clack together. *That will be good for Bill*, she thinks. No. It won't. Her mind hasn't yet adjusted to her new reality, and she doesn't know how to make it happen. Bill's gone for now. Consigned to the past, like everyone. She misses his ears already, so soft, like stroking a silk collar.

Jon leads her back into the hallway and up the stairs. The master bedroom is to the left – bed, chest of drawers, empty wardrobe, four coat hangers. Zara's, Lauren supposes, is to the right.

Zara walks in and runs her hand along the coat hangers. She looks cagey. The body language of somebody who has followed through on a dare.

As Jon descends the stairs, Lauren reaches for her. 'Feeling okay?' she says.

Zara shrugs, not saying anything, but when she looks up at Lauren, her eyes are wet. Lauren can practically feel the anxiety coming off her daughter in vibrations. 'I . . . I don't know if I should say this –' she starts, but Jon calls up to them.

'Shall we do the identities before it gets too far into the evening?' he says.

Lauren looks downstairs. He is standing in the hallway, holding a pink plastic wallet. When they reach him, he leads them through and lays it out on the kitchen table. 'Passports. Lindsey and Sienna.' He hands them out.

Zara turns hers over in her hands. It looks stiff and new. They took their photos from their old passports. Zara is so young in hers: a relic from a past life. She stares at it. Lauren has been able to bring baby photos of Zara – was encouraged to. Just no other photos.

'Tea?' she says artificially to everybody, searching in the cupboards. Eventually, she finds a blue-and-white striped tin containing tea bags. She makes three cups and sits back at the kitchen table.

'You're going for an interview here,' Jon says to her. He pushes two pieces of paper over, printed out from the internet. She scans them. Nursery key worker. All new colleagues. All new kids. But the same job. The same little toddler feet. The same fat hands inexpertly holding paint brushes. It is a tiny consolation prize.

'Did I apply?' she says.

'Don't worry about that.'

'What about references?'

'Don't worry about those, either,' he says. He runs a hand through his hair, not breaking eye contact as he does so. 'That's all in hand.'

'But is my . . . my employment history must be fabricated, right?'

'Look, Lindsey,' he says, using her new name totally unironically.

Lauren stares at him. She isn't Lindsey. Not here, not behind closed doors.

'In some ways,' he continues, 'the less you know about how this operates, the better.'

'Why?' she says shrilly. She shouldn't be asking this in front of Zara, showing, behind the curtain, her mother's own human fallibility, but she can't help herself.

'Because then you can't give anything away.' His eyes – dark blue in the dimness – look directly at her. 'You have to live it. Become Lindsey. Don't be thinking about where your references come from. You applied. You were a nursery nurse before, in Bristol, remember. Become it. Become *her*.'

Lauren turns away from him. No. No. In two years, she'll go back. Somehow. Does Jon not have any idea of the magnitude of what he's asking her to do?

'Next up, driving lessons. You'll need to drive to get

around up here. On Thursday, someone called Janey is coming at eleven for a five-hour lesson. An intensive course is the best.'

'But I don't want to know how to drive,' Lauren says. *Not* doing it has become part of her identity. She hates chips, Prosecco, and will never learn to drive, doesn't need to, likes the Tube, doesn't want to become the designated driver. So she always thought, but here she is, an ex-Londoner, exiled to the Lake District. Pour the Prosecco. Pour the whole fucking bottle.

'It's for the best,' Jon says. He takes a sip of his tea. The steam leaves his nose damp.

Lauren is struck by how little he moves. He doesn't fidget or mess with anything on the table, doesn't blow his nose or rub at his eyes. All the way up here, he had his hands at ten and two, driving slowly, eyes scanning the road. Everything measured, calm, robotic.

'Background, then,' he continues.

'Just give it to us,' Zara says tightly, which surprises Lauren. She's drawn the sleeves of her cardigan down over her hands.

Outside, the wind blusters around their row of houses. The heating clicks on, and Lauren rests her arm along the kitchen radiator, waiting for it to heat up. 'Okay.'

Jon addresses Lauren directly. 'You're Lindsey Smith. The most common breach is signing the wrong name. So watch that. Only child. Different parents' names – they're noted down here.' He slides a family tree over to her. 'They're ex-pats, in Spain. Costa Del Sol. Dead parents make people suspicious. Estranged is better.' He tells her this like he is confirming an order back to her. *So that's the soup, the roast chicken and the parfait.* Her parents, resurrected, just like that. Back from the fucking dead.

She looks at the family tree. There is no fanfare about it at all, no branding. Done on Microsoft Word in Times New Roman, clip art arrows connecting the people.

Her mother went to choir and voted for the Green Party for her entire life, never travelled by plane because of the environment. Her father hated the sun. And yet, 'Sue and Gerry', her parents, are resident in Estepona, Spain. Lauren stares at the table and tries not to cry. She shakes her head and looks across at Zara, whose body is trembling.

'You were born and raised in Bristol.'

'But I've never even been to Bristol,' Lauren says. 'And my accent . . .'

'Your accent is neutral,' he says tightly. 'Your medical records have been moved over into Lindsey's name, too. But,' he holds a hand up, 'only the main events. Vaccinations. Allergy to penicillin. Glandular fever. Appendicitis.'

'I've never had glandular fever,' Lauren says after a second's pause. But, inside, she is thinking it all sounds so irreversible. So final.

'Oh, really?' Jon says, a pen in hand. He slices a clean line through the words. 'We'll get that altered.' He doesn't apologize, or say there's been an error. He simply says nothing, which makes it worse. Some poor other woman whose life has been uprooted has probably been confused with her.

'Okay,' she says, in a small voice.

'And finally, here's your mobile. The other's been wiped now.'

Lauren blinks, looking down at the table. All those old text messages. All those photographs. All those memories . . . gone.

'New number,' Jon says. 'Memorize it, because everyone knows their number these days.'

Lauren's had the same number since she got her first phone in her mid-twenties. She can trot it out without thought, the numbers falling rhythmically off her tongue. She picks the iPhone up and scrolls to the top of the contacts. She'll never memorize it. There's no rhythm to this one. 07912 . . .

She opens the apps. All blank. All waiting for logins.

'So, social media,' Jon says. He leans forward, more engaged, his elbows on the table, his forearms parallel to each other.

'Right.'

'You can use it. In fact, it's better to. Because somebody with no obvious family who's also not on socials might raise questions.'

'Right.'

'I'd stay off Facebook because people will see that you have no network, which is unusual.'

'Okay.'

'But Twitter and Instagram are good. Make your profiles private. Follow celebrities and brands. Just look normal. Okay?'

'Yep,' Lauren says, her tone sounding clipped and efficient, though she is feeling anything but.

'No selfies.'

'I'm not really much of a selfie taker.'

'Zara will be.' A sidelong glance at her.

She shrugs.

She's really not, Lauren thinks. She's so beautiful, but she couldn't be less vain.

'We don't want photos of either of you online. It's so easy to stumble across these things, now, and one person tells another . . . and there are computer programs that can scan faces for matches these days.'

'Okay.' Lauren places her hands back on the radiator. It's hot, now, and she shifts closer to it. At least they're safe, she tries to tell herself. At least they're warm.

'And so that leads us nicely on to breaches.'

'Yes.'

'Needless to say, no contact with anyone back home.'

'Right.'

'We try to be understanding of breaches,' he says. 'Of the need to . . . reach out. But they make life hard for us. If you're not cooperating with the protection we give then we can choose not to give it.'

He's making too much eye contact and Lauren feels her cheeks heat up. How is that being 'understanding of breaches'? It doesn't sound understanding to her. It sounds like a threat.

Zara's life is at stake. She's got to make this work. She stares down at her hands, at her bare ring finger. Maybe she can wait out the two years. Maybe it *will* blow over.

Lauren looks at the small collection of papers on the pine table between them. A new passport containing a tiny photograph of herself, Lindsey Smith. New medical records. An interview. A driving lesson booked. So that's a life, according to the department for protection.

She thinks of all of the things that really comprise a life.

A real, authentic life. An identity. Possessions. Preferences. The purple leather purse Aidan got her one year for Christmas with the three sets of pockets inside that was so special to her because he had *seen* her: seen her fumbling with multiple sets of loyalty cards, and cash and lipsticks, and solved a problem. The bedspread she bought them that had llamas on. 'Which is your favourite llama?' Aidan had asked at night, and she had said, 'The prancing one.' The baking tray with the crimped edges that she used to make lemon tarts during the summer. How much she loves the bath. Her name, her job, the way she cuts her hair. The thoughts she has. Her mannerisms, the way she holds herself. Where she chose to live, in cool-as-fuck Islington. That her parents are dead. That she married a man called Aidan Madison who takes the piss out of her shopping habit.

'Are you going to give Zara her history now?' she says, her voice cracked.

'Sienna. Yes.'

Sienna again. She would never have chosen it.

She gulps as she sees Zara's date of birth. 23rd October. Six days out. Different star sign. It shouldn't matter, but it does.

'She has had all of her immunizations and the sepsis is on her record, but in the UK.'

'No.' She can't help but say it. Don't erase that. Not that.

'It's too distinctive, that five weeks in Paris,' Jon says. 'A doctor might mention it to a friend of a friend, they happen to recall Zara's history, they tell someone they think they know where you are . . . it wouldn't be right.'

'Six degrees of separation,' Lauren says bitterly. Her

eyes seem to mist over, even though she isn't crying. Whatever identity is, that experience is part of it. 'But she was . . . they treated her differently in France,' she tries. 'It's important that any doctor is aware of it.' Even as she says it, she knows it to be irrational. There's nothing wrong with Zara now. But she's . . . somehow vulnerable. Always has been. The sepsis was a symptom of it, but there are others, too. She gets every cold, flu and stomach bug going. Has always been too thin. Bookish. Left behind sometimes, extra-confident and athletic friends striding in front of her at nursery. She would fall over at sports days, over-think, lose friends easily, confident girls moving on to new groups.

'Rest assured, our medical experts have reviewed the notes and taken any salient points over,' Jon says.

'It's fine, Mum,' Zara says, looking tired around her eyes.

'Give me the rest,' Lauren says.

Zara's left hand is wrapped around her mug. It must be burning her. Her hands are adult size, the exact same as Lauren's. Slim fingers, short nails.

'You'll start school the day after tomorrow,' Jon says, directing his gaze to Zara. 'Millfield. Comprehensive. But we'll pop over tomorrow afternoon. Sure you'll have questions, after your first night. Anyway.' He puts his suit jacket back on. 'Time,' Jon says. He raises his eyes to the window, and Lauren sees another car passing by. The beam of the headlights is refracted in the rain into a blurred, imperfect diamond. 'Practise filling in the gaps tonight. This is just the start – you need to work out your own stories.'

'That's it?' Zara says shrilly.

Lauren looks at her in surprise.

'What about the rest? Who am I supposed to *be*?'

'You can be yourself, just with a different name,' Lauren says quickly, but she feels sad as she looks at her daughter, who has always seemed ashamed of herself anyway, without this.

'If you stick to the rules, you'll be fine,' Jon says as he scrapes his chair back.

Lauren sees him into the hallway.

'And just so you know,' Jon says to her when they're alone, 'we have installed this.' He opens the front door and points above the threshold. 'A doorbell camera. So you can monitor who comes and goes. Anything unusual, you call me, alright?'

'Okay,' Lauren says, looking into the eye of the CCTV camera. Aidan always wanted one of these, but she held off, knowing he'd obsess over it. She looks out into the blackness beyond them. The wind sounds so full-bodied, so loud. She draws her jacket around her more tightly, and looks at the camera again. She's glad of it, that tiny piece of security, here, where they're so totally isolated.

Jon shows her the app, then turns again, on the threshold of the door. 'And in general safety terms,' he says, 'we don't brief kids about these things – don't want to scare them – but don't walk places in a straight line. Always check if someone is following you by varying your route. Don't be too open or too guarded. Don't answer the phone or the door to anybody you don't know, and if a car pulls over next to you, go and get somebody's attention. Anybody's. Okay?'

'Yes,' Lauren says, blinking, overwhelmed by the

deluge of information. 'Don't walk places in straight lines. Don't talk to strangers.'

'Right . . .' Jon pauses. 'And I know your husband decided to stay in London . . .'

For the first time, Lauren sees a flash of something human cross his features. A brief flicker of his strawberry-blond eyebrows, like a poorly tuned television momentarily picking up a different channel.

'He has another child. Zara isn't his child,' Lauren says.

'I know,' Jon says. 'You said.' And, even if she hadn't already told him, he would know. He must know all sorts of things about her. How many smear tests she's had. Her grade D in GCSE home economics.

'I'll stick to the rules,' she says.

He pauses, hand on the doorknob. 'Nobody's ever been seriously harmed or killed in witness protection in the UK,' he says.

'Oh. I see.'

'Nobody who has obeyed the rules, anyway.' He leaves right after he's said it, as though it is the only sentence he really wanted to utter to her. Or, at least, the most important one.

20

Zara

Coniston, the Lake District

One day gone

The bedsheets don't feel right. They're stiff and starched-feeling, the duvet crunchy against Zara's chin. She can hear her mother turning over in the bedroom next door. Just a slim wall divides them.

Zara tries to think what would make her happy. What would Poppy do? Buy make-up samples and experiment. Maybe she will do that.

Zara has been ripped from her life. Parts of it – things she took for granted – are hanging loose, like torn threads. That she would often go down for a bowl of cereal at night, and pass Aidan, who had the same habit. They'd stand there chatting, bare legs lit by the light of the fridge, she eating Cornflakes, he Weetabix.

And now, here she is, in the Lake District with a secret. One she can't even bring herself to think about, to turn to face and look at.

She misses the noise of London. The silence of the Lake District keeps her awake. It is punctuated by strong winds that seem to shake their row of terraces, by geese flying overhead, and by an occasional passing car. She listens each time she hears one, her whole body tensed. Is this the car that contains the Find Girl A group? But no. Each car becomes louder and then fades, driving away, and each time, her body relaxes.

She misses her school friends, Kelly and Hattie. She wonders what they've been told.

She rolls on to her side and thinks about Jamie, and the homeless community. Richie, Anna and the rest. They are Islington's subculture. They know all about each other, but nobody knows about them. It is so wrong that there is a whole section of society ignored by everybody. God, she wishes she hadn't caved in in the witness box. She's let them all down.

In the end, she gets up and goes to shower, even though it's late. She enjoys standing there in the steam, the water searing against the back of her neck.

She's made her decision now. She's here. And now she has to follow through with it. And there are things to follow through with.

Back in her bedroom, Zara checks her new phone. She is ready.

When she finally sleeps, she dreams of school photo day. The flash of the bulb. Her fixed smile. Her photograph getting into the wrong hands, ending up online, them coming for her, an amorphous group of men in hoodies. She wakes up with a start, her back sweating, and doesn't sleep afterwards.

21

Lauren

Coniston, the Lake District
One day gone

Aidan often used to make an envelope at the bottom of the bed, folding the duvet over itself. Lauren used to say it annoyed her, but now she does it herself, because it feels like he's in the bed next to her.

The Lake District is completely silent. Lauren sits there, listening to the quiet, imagining the Find Girl A group closing in. A mechanical whirring rings out in the night, and Lauren feels adrenaline flash across her body.

No. That's just the shower turning on. Zara mustn't be able to sleep, either. She reaches for the iPhone sitting on the bedside table. She logs on to Amazon and she does what she always does best when stressed: she shops. She orders all sorts of rubbish. A heated airer to dry the clothes on. A pack of fancy vanilla-flavoured coffee beans. The witness protection service have provided them with a monthly budget of a thousand pounds, until they're 'up and running' with their new lives, but Lauren isn't really thinking of that. She is just acting. She spends £150. Candles. Nice cleaning stuff from Method. A cake tin.

Once the basket is checked out and her new debit card details have been typed in, she feels sated. She will look forward to the packages arriving. Little treats in the wasteland of her life.

She opens Instagram and signs up under her new name, which she has to think twice about. Lauren Starling is typed so effortlessly, her fingers knowing which keys to push without her thinking. Lindsey Smith is stilted, unfamiliar.

She browses who to follow. Beyoncé. Mac Cosmetics. She finds a few stock photographs of sunsets and cups of coffee but can't work out how to backdate them. Should she just ask Jon the next time he comes over? What a banal query. Aidan would know how to do it.

She wants to look him up.

But she can't.

Instead, she closes her eyes, and imagines his last Instagram photo.

It was the sunset in his computer room, two and a half weeks ago, before the trial began. Their blond floorboards. Their slatted white blinds that almost bankrupted them but they were too far down the ordering process when they realized the full cost. 'Morning view' was the caption.

It would be so easy to go on to the app and like that photograph. He'd realize, she thinks. He's smart. Lindsey Smith. Signed up today. Blank profile photo. She could easily tell him who she is. Put up some secret sign or other: they have thousands of shared words for things, in-jokes, history, memes he has shown her and laughed at. It would be so easy to contact him. She's amazed he's not been blocked for her, this man that she loves. The trust the protection service has placed in her.

Tears leak out of the side of her eyes and catch in her ears, forming hot, itchy pools. She scratches at them, irritated. She ought to pull herself together. She was a single parent for years. She was fine alone, just fine.

But she wasn't in love with somebody then. Her mouth opens in a silent scream and more tears come. Two years. And then what? Life stretches out in front of her without him. It isn't loneliness, it isn't starting over, it is heartbreak.

Early in their relationship, they went to Tuscany. They got a villa, their own pool. Self-catered, though they went out to eat some nights, wanting to save on the washing up, wanting to walk and talk and eat outside, summer air on their skin. The kids – both six – had adjusted easily to the later evenings, and had been well behaved in the restaurants. They'd draw together, wax crayons melting in their little hands in the heat. 'Are they twins?' a kindly Italian waiter had asked one night, and Aidan had laughed, not saying yes or no. They'd stayed out too late, gone ten, and Aidan had picked both of them up and carried them, a sleeping child over each shoulder. Lauren had walked the few hundred yards home with him, the sound of crickets at their ankles, dust and sand kicking up miniature clouds between them, and she'd felt that nobody would look after Zara as carefully as him. He'd laid her down in her bed, fully clothed, safe, and smoothed the hair from her forehead, and Lauren had thought: *we've made it*. A blended family.

Lauren picks her phone back up and stares at the Instagram logo.

She types in Aidan's name, then backspaces. She hasn't done anything, but, nevertheless, it's a risk, a line already stepped over. An invisible line.

22

Aidan

Shepherd's Bush, London
Two days gone

'Yeah, but life is crap sometimes,' Poppy says down the phone to Aidan, whose heart breaks right there and then. His poor baby, made into a pessimist by the hand she's been dealt.

'Are you really fine?' he says to her.

He glances at his bag across the hallway. Everything reminds him of Lauren. 'That fucking rucksack,' she sometimes said to him. 'Nobody has a rucksack in their forties,' she'd add, but she would be smiling. It's brown leather, with two red stripes down the centre. Perfectly inoffensive. He needs it, doesn't understand how most men live without one. It contains his wallet, spare coins, a bottle of water, his iPad, a charging case. Normal stuff.

And his burner phone. Ready to communicate with the members of the Find Girl A group.

'Look, I'm a hundy-p.'

'Hundy-p, she says.'

He can hear her roll her eyes down the phone to him. 'A hundred per cent,' she says. 'You know.'

'Right.' Aidan laughs quietly.

'I've spent a ton on H&M online,' Poppy says.

Aidan gives a wan half-smile. His daughter's dedication to shopping knows no bounds. She could almost be Lauren's child.

'I'll transfer you some money.' He makes a note to write something funny on the internet banking reference. 'I'll come over soon,' he adds.

'Do. I bet it's quiet over there.'

He sighs as he thinks of it. Like planets with moons, families come as a set. When a member leaves, the balance is upset: seas flood land, ice ages start, fires rage. He felt it when his father died, and Brenda didn't have colour in her cheeks for a full year. And he feels it now, too. Zara and Lauren have gone into the void. Some black hole in space – or it may as well be. Aidan tries not to let the thoughts show in his voice. 'It is,' he says.

'When I'm lonely I leave the radio on,' she says.

'Maybe I will.'

'You'll be fine, I can just feel it,' she says emphatically, and he doesn't disagree. He can't bear to. His little moon, in perpetual orbit of him, her father.

'Hundy-p,' he says softly.

Aidan is outside the first Find Girl A meeting.

It is in a warehouse near South Croydon station, next to a banner that says Christ Embassy, Croydon. It was dark when Aidan got on the overground train, his feet making impressions in the frost. Now, outside the warehouse, it's only just getting light, the sky a parchment colour, a sepia backdrop behind the buildings. Apparently, it's less suspicious meeting in the morning.

He puts his phone in the front pocket of his rucksack. The burner phone is in the main section of the bag, deep inside, in an inner pocket that he made by ripping and sewing it himself. His hands are frozen, his fingers struggling to do his zip back up.

The warehouse has *Dooper Distribution* written along the top in amateur-looking bubble lettering. A few pallets are leaning against the wall, evidently unused, covered in splatters of November leaves.

The silver roller shutter door is down but a red door is ajar. The paint has become mottled in places, faded pink and bright red, intermingled like a rash. He waits outside it, listening, hoping he's disguised enough, then lets himself in. His heart speeds up. His stomach curls into a tight knot.

The first thing he sees inside the warehouse is a forklift truck abandoned in one corner. He walks past it and the unlabelled stock, wrapped in so much clear plastic it's opaque. At the back is a meeting room, and he can see from a small, rectangular window that they're in there. A man in a brown beanie. A woman with long dark hair standing by the door.

He pushes it open. The door sticks, then gives, and he almost falls in.

'The final person!' the man in the brown beanie says. He glances at Aidan, whose fingers instinctively reach to push his glasses up his nose, but he manages to stop himself.

'Welcome,' the man says. He extends his hand. 'Brian.'

143

Aidan looks at him closely, then releases his hand in shock. The man heading up the vigilante justice group isn't a child. He isn't a football fan. A yob. An angry teenager.

He is Luke's father.

He was in the public gallery that day. He will almost certainly recognize Aidan.

Panic rises up through him, a rushing sound in his ears like running water.

'Nice to see you here,' Brian says. He's short, with a dark beard and gold-framed old-fashioned glasses.

'And you,' Aidan says neutrally, trying to cover the shock on his face. He looks around him. It is more than just members only. Other than Brian, it is only footballers. A couple of lower-profile players. Two people who are clearly coaches – their jackets say so. And the youth team. All sixteen or seventeen. Thirty or so young, strapping men. Aidan swallows. What the fuck is going on?

He looks to the left of him. And there he is: Luke.

God, Aidan has been a fool. He thought there would be more people here, that he would be able to hide in plain sight. Not just this. A tiny core.

'James is here to help us with IT,' Brian says.

Aidan turns his head immediately. He must become James Thomas. He works in South London. He's lived there all his life. An ex-wife, a kid. Family around the corner. He practised it on the way over, under his breath on the Tube. He, too, has changed his identity for protection.

'Where are the rest?' Aidan says. 'The Find Girl A group?'

'This is private business,' Brian says, shutting the door behind them. 'First, a warning.'

'Right,' Aidan says, his mouth dry.

'You're here because of your brilliant scraper.'

'Yes, yes,' Aidan prattles. 'I can build as many as you want. To search for the mother, too. They can be designed to capture any new starters on all websites – which we can look through, too, if we can find out what she does for a living.'

Brian is holding a hand up, and Aidan stops. He is glad to stop talking about his wife in this way.

'Alan is also here,' Brian says, gesturing to a man in a parka in the corner of the room, 'because of his access to a CCTV database.'

'Okay,' Aidan replies.

'If you talk about anything that goes on in here,' Brian says to both of them, his tone icy, 'we will make your life a living hell.'

Aidan feels his jaw slacken in shock.

'Okay?' Brian says. 'We wouldn't want that, would we?'

For the first time, Aidan notices Brian's muscles. 'Okay,' he echoes, thinking only that something very bad is happening. Something worse than he had first thought. Only he doesn't yet know what.

'Right. To business,' Brian says.

Luke shifts his weight against the desk he's leaning on. He looks uncomfortable. Arms folded. The room is dimly lit, a single bulb in the centre of the ceiling. Some of the men are in the circle of light but most, around the edges of the room, are in shadow, like a sinister congregation, the murderer, Luke, at the near-centre.

'Luke was . . .' Brian glances at his son. 'This time eighteen months ago, Luke was . . . well, what were you?' he addresses Luke directly.

'Fit,' Luke barks. He still has his prisoner's pallor. His dark hair contrasts with it. 'About to sign for the Premier League team,' Luke says bitterly, his lip curling up with the memory of it. 'Full of . . . I don't know –' he drags a hand over his chin and mouth. 'Potential.'

'Exactly,' Brian says in a nurturing tone. '*Exactly*. And then, you defended yourself against a homeless man.'

'Yes.'

'And now what?'

Luke clears his throat. 'A year on remand. Bad food. Limited exercise. Lost my touch. No clubs will take me on, because of "reputational damage".' He brings his hands in front of him and clasps them together. The effect makes his shoulder muscles rise up. His eyes look dead.

'Right,' Brian says, nodding. 'No wonder we're angry. And the sponsors pulled out, didn't they? The club's reputation has plummeted, because two of their players went through a murder trial.'

'It's true,' Luke says. He shifts his weight on his feet. 'Yeah.'

'So what're we going to do?'

'Find her,' Luke says.

'And then what? Petrol through the letter box?' Brian says.

Aidan's stomach drops fifty floors in an elevator.

'Or worse,' Luke sneers.

'Good. Good.' Brian is pacing. 'Yes. We'll find her.'

'We will,' Luke says.

'On to the crux of the issue.' Brian sips his drink.

Aidan watches the exchange. Terror courses through him.

Brian walks the room like a caged lion, slow and sinister. 'Zara – Girl A,' Brian says, 'knows about *ex nihilo nihil fit*.'

Aidan's eyes are on Brian. *Ex nihilo* . . . ?

Brian steps into the light. It glints off his glasses. 'The weekend after the trial, she met with a local homeless person, Anna. We had just discovered her identity, thanks to a stupid court usher. All we had to do was ask. Said we were a paralegal, needed the name of the list of witnesses. And there it was. The day's line-up. And then we followed her.'

Aidan stares, his gaze fixed. What? When? It slowly sinks in. That Sunday . . . that Sunday when she went out to see Jamie's friends.

'Anna told her that Holloway was connected to another homeless person's death – Bertha. Two of our players urinated on Bertha for the initiation, she lashed out, they hit back and left her bleeding on the pavement. It was a game gone wrong, is all. But Anna told Zara that when Bertha was urinated on, our slogan was shouted. And Zara can now connect us to it, because they shouted it when they initiated with Jamie. She is the only person who can do this. She's smart, so she remembered it, used it in the court testimony. And she now knows it was shouted when Bertha died, too. She knows. She knows about the initiations, and she knows about *ex nihilo nihil fit*.'

He finishes, having just shouted out Aidan's stepdaughter's death warrant, and Aidan sits there, winded, sweating, almost crying.

Hazing.

Jamie lashed out because of an initiation. He was provoked after all. The club have been doing this for years. And Zara knows it. That is the missing piece.

That is what didn't make sense.

This is why this group wants to harm his stepdaughter, destroy his family. This is why they want to find her. She has information. She is valuable. And she is vulnerable.

Brian picks up a polystyrene cup of builder's tea and takes a sip. His fingers are holding it so tightly the polystyrene yields, little scored fingernail marks appearing. They're talking about next steps. 'For me . . . well, it's affected everyone. The mood at Holloway – I was there last night – and it's so sombre. Isn't it, Luke?' He clicks his fingers. 'Look at me.'

Luke starts, glancing up at his father in the dim light. 'I was set for the Premier League. Now, I'll be lucky to play again at all,' he says obediently.

'Exactly,' Brian says. His tone is off. Almost mock-sad, a parody, like he is acting. He is riling the group up. Trying to incite something. This is a speech.

This is propaganda, Aidan finds himself thinking. 'I know,' he says. He can't be a wallflower here, despite what he's just learnt. He can't just observe, watch and wait. He has to be tight with them. Be involved, so that they tell him things, so that they don't suspect an informant. And then, when they find Lauren and Zara, he will find them, too, and warn them.

Aidan is putting the pieces together silently in his mind. That Sunday morning, when Zara was uncontactable. Shit, shit, shit. He adds it all up. The case was dismissed. She went to see a friend of Jamie, to apologize, to explain maybe. That was when they told her about *ex nihilo nihil fit*. About another death connected to Holloway. Imagine if she'd been told before the trial. It might all have been different.

She must have been too afraid to tell them. That she knew information that would make everything worse for their family because she is valuable, now. She must have felt like it was all her fault for going to meet the second homeless person. She'll have been terrified.

Another piece of the puzzle falls into place: Jamie apparently smelled of urine when Zara discovered him. And nobody had listened to her – they all told her it was how homeless people smelled. But it wasn't his urine. It was Luke's. Initiation. Hazing gone wrong.

This is why the group was made private. Club only. It is no longer a viral group intent on justice. It is the opposite. A cover-up.

'The most important thing is to stop her talking,' one of the players says. 'By whatever means necessary.'

Aidan stares at his trainers. He's got to ask what they intend to do. Now that he knows what's really going on. 'So when we find her,' he says tentatively, rubbing a hand self-consciously over his face, glad he is standing in half-darkness, 'we . . . silence her?'

Brian looks straight at Aidan. His gold glasses catch the light above. He turns his mouth down instead of answering.

Aidan waits.

'Yeah. Make sure she stays quiet,' he says eventually.

'Warn her off?' Aidan prompts.

'And warn her not to tell anybody we warned her off,' Brian adds.

'And if she doesn't listen?'

Brian raises his shoulders in a shrug, holding eye contact, saying no more.

Aidan's heart is a hailstorm in his chest. 'If we hurt her, though . . .' he says, then pauses. 'Won't that just make it all worse? An eye for an eye, and all that.'

'I don't need your input on my strategy,' Brian says coldly. He turns away from Aidan.

Aidan stares at the ground, blushing and thinking. The violence is worth the risk. Because they'll all go down for this one, he guesses. Not just Luke and Mal. But . . . every last one of them.

'So,' Brian says to the rest of the group, changing the subject easily. 'She's likely been given a new identity.' He shifts his weight against the table.

Aidan moves slightly away from him, his bowels loose. He might be sick. He closes his eyes, sweat forming on his forehead. It's for the best. It's for the best. It's for the best. He's doing it for the right reasons.

'On the fucking taxpayer, too,' Brian adds. 'But the most important thing is: how are we going to find her?'

'Six degrees of separation,' a young man who hasn't yet spoken says. He is tall, pale and sinewy. Ash-coloured hair shorn close at the sides, longer on top. 'My cousin's wife is a police officer,' he says. 'And she once said they always move people more than three hundred miles away.'

Aidan's throat fizzes. Yes. Yes, yes, yes: information. This is what he is here for. He memorizes it. There aren't many places to go other than the north, except maybe Cornwall. Otherwise: Yorkshire, Newcastle, Northumbria, Scotland? He will look at a map later.

'Great. That's a start,' Brian says nicely. 'Anyone else for justice for my son?' There is something frightening about his tone. An insistence to it.

Aidan suddenly imagines meeting him as a real, true enemy, and shudders.

'We'll get James's scraper going,' somebody adds.

Brian turns to Aidan. His eyes are blank, like a shark's. Emotionless. 'Yes, how long until you find somebody matching the facial features?' he says. 'For the photo I sent you.'

'Not long,' Aidan says, swallowing hard.

His mind whirs over it. He needs to come up with false information. Find a similar-looking girl. But then what – lead them to her, an innocent girl?

He almost starts to cry, right there and then. This was a mistake. He hasn't thought it through.

'I wouldn't want you to take too long over it,' Brian says softly.

Aidan's entire body breaks out in goosebumps.

'She has a sister she left behind,' Luke says. The tips of his fingers are nicotine-stained, a bright kind of bronze around the nails and across his index finger, which surprises Aidan. 'Not sure of her name.'

Aidan tries to manage his body language. The instinctive urge to question Luke, to correct him – *step*sister – and to stop everyone asking about Poppy is physical, animalistic.

'I don't know why she didn't go, either,' Luke continues. He fiddles with the navy zip of his coat. 'But she's still here. They were local to Islington, otherwise Zara wouldn't have seen the hazing. So I guess that's where she is . . .'

Aidan shifts his weight on his feet. Good. They think Poppy lives in Islington. Good.

'She might be a good place to start. School children around Islington. She will have told her friends her sister's moved away, surely? Anyone have kids who go to school around there?' Brian says.

'My sister's kids are in Holloway,' the sinewy man says.

Aidan looks at him, and he gives Aidan a slow, cruel smile. Conspiratorial and sinister, his lips blood red.

Aidan is trying to resist the urge to get out his phone and remind Poppy right away: *don't tell anybody anything.*

His poor baby. She will have to confide in him, and only him.

'How long for the scrapers to work, did you say?' Brian says, turning to Aidan and looking at him.

Aidan meets his gaze and feels exposed, naked. His disguise of a slow-growing beard and losing his glasses seems so amateur. What was he thinking? He brings a hand to wipe at the sweat from his forehead. His fingers are trembling. He forms a fist and holds his hands by his sides.

'A couple of weeks.'

'Maybe you could give us an update then? And then we'll pay you,' he says. 'If you're the real deal.'

Aidan's mouth dries up so fast it feels like he's been burnt. He swallows, but his tongue sticks to the roof of his mouth and he starts sweating again, water in all the wrong places. Sweat on his forehead, no saliva in his mouth, tears – always, always, always – at the back of his eyes, since they left.

'I'll check in with you . . . next time,' Brian says. He holds eye contact for a moment too long, then flashes a false, wolfish smile at Aidan.

He jumps as the burner phone vibrates in his bag as he's walking to the overground. He stops to fish it out, and sees Kevin – Brian – has messaged him.

What date shall we agree you will get the scraper information by?

The hairs on the back of Aidan's neck rise up. He is being managed. Brian's repeated questions are designed to spur Aidan into action.

Give me a few weeks, Aidan writes, the longest period he can possibly stretch it out for. He exhales, his hot breath vaporizing in the frigid London atmosphere.

As he's walking along the street to South Croydon station, Aidan sees the sinewy man just up ahead. He's wearing skinny jeans, black boxers visible just above them. He pats the shin of his trousers with his right hand as he turns the corner. Aidan stares at the shape. Something long and thin sits in that pocket of his jeans, close to his skin. Something like a knife.

When Aidan gets home, he googles Bertha. She was a German homeless woman who bled to death two years ago. There were, according to a local news article, several wounds to her head. She'd been self-harming on her arms, and had likely hit her head on something deliberately, the article says. But Aidan knows differently now. It's abuse. Hazing. Games played by the strong in an attempt to bait the weak. He feels sick.

He looks into initiation, and the case against Luke. There is a reason the murder took place on Luke's seventeenth birthday: that is the day he became eligible to sign for the Premier League club. And so that is the day of the initiation. It's their version of a celebration.

And so the other murder must have taken place on another player's birthday.

Next, he googles the motto. *Ex nihilo nihil fit.* He pales as

153

he reads it. It is a phrase only the elite would use. Ostensibly inspirational, but when applied to weak people, social outliers, it becomes sinister.

Ex nihilo nihil fit.

From nothing comes nothing.

Aidan paces the living room. He is on the phone to 101.

He has told them everything he knows.

A very patient woman is repeating some of it back to him. 'So you believe your daughter, in witness protection, may know something about a wider conspiracy?' she is saying.

'Yes. A series of attacks on homeless people,' Aidan says. 'As part of Holloway FC's initiations.'

Eventually, she puts him through to a police officer.

'If your daughter is Girl A, then she is a discredited witness,' the police officer, Daniel, says crisply. 'I followed the trial. Nobody would be interested in hearing more from her. In the nicest possible way,' he adds. 'There won't be a second investigation. Your family should get on with their new –' he clears his throat, like he doesn't believe Aidan, '– their new identities.'

'But if she gave the police that information, they could all be arrested,' Aidan says.

They argue for a while longer, until Aidan hangs up in frustration. He marches down the street with Bill, sweat moving down his back like a slithering river, dampening his T-shirt.

He travels to his old local police station that he's walked past countless times, in the City. He takes the Tube to Moorgate, going with Bill down the backstairs instead of the escalators. It'll be his walk for the day with Bill, his city dog. He feels guilty about it.

At this time – the morning rush hour – it is full of suits. A woman in baggy, long trousers is eating a croissant, miniature leaves of pastry landing on the lapels of her jacket. She's holding on to the red pole. Her nails are bitten. There is something of Natalie, his first wife, about her. The way her shoulders round as she stands there, her head dipped, short hair exposing her neck.

He met Natalie in his late twenties. At a tech event, when he was still ten minutes late every morning, cup of takeaway tea in hand. When he was young. Before mortgages and kids.

He had liked the idea of her more than the reality. He can see that now. When he was away from her, he would try to reason it through. No, no, she was super organized and made great tea and she liked cool music and he liked her laugh, a throaty, dirty laugh. She was perfectly normal: she liked guitar music and planning ahead. What was the issue, again? But then he would see her, and she would say something unfunny, something slightly judgemental-sounding, a joke about an Irishman or something with a bawdy punchline about an ugly woman, and a very specific sad and aching feeling would unbutton inside him, expelling a truth. Something he knew, but didn't want to.

She was pregnant within three months. He had assumed she would be as regimented about contraception as she was about the order of the mugs in her cupboards, but she hadn't been. He'd been a typical man, an idiot. They'd married when Poppy was four months old and they were both so tired the floor felt like it was moving underneath them during the ceremony. They had divorced eight months later when, in the middle of the night – isn't it always the middle of the night? – Aidan had finally listened to that voice.

Four years later, he had met Lauren at a wedding, who said to him, across the dance floor, 'I've only got one contact lens in, and it's *wild*,' and that was that. Something happy, instead of sad, opened up inside him. He wanted to marry her then. Life would be forever interesting, with her, the woman who put slices of Dairylea inside croissants and called it breakfast.

It's raining when he emerges at Moorgate and his hair is wet within seconds. Cold rainwater dribbles down his neck. Bill shivers and shakes it off. The buildings of London that he's grown up with his entire life seem imposing to Aidan this morning. He arrives at the police station a few minutes later. He ties Bill up outside. As he turns away from him, his heart wrenches. Their little guide dog. He's so good. He deserves a long walk in Hyde Park, not this.

Rain drips off the end of Aidan's nose and on to the floor of the foyer, leaving clear inkblots on the concrete floor.

The foyer is official in appearance, a government building. Paranoia creeps up the back of his neck. This thing they're in. It's bigger than all of them. They're out of their depth. Witness fucking protection. He shakes his head. It still seems unreal.

Maybe he shouldn't be telling so many people that they're in protection? But no, these are police he is telling, for God's sake.

He approaches a metal desk and introduces himself.

He asks to see a police officer, but doesn't provide the reason why.

He sits on a bench affixed to the wall for half an hour before somebody comes out. A woman in full police uniform. He tries not to look disappointed: he needs someone else. Someone powerful. CID. Plain-clothes officers.

She has black hair, dyed, he thinks. She's too young. Mid-twenties, if that. She introduces herself as Lottie, then leads him into a meeting room. It doesn't look like a usual police station. It looks corporate. Metal, glass, angular. It gets shabbier the further in they get. Eventually, they reach a carpeted corridor with a meeting room just off it. She doesn't offer him a drink or invite him to tell her what's happened. She just takes a chair at the Formica table with the peeling top. He can't help but pick at the corner of it. When he looks up, her eyes are on his fingers.

He explains it all to her. Bertha, Jamie, the motto. How Zara connects it all. He sees a flicker of recognition when he says Girl A, but she hides it well. He sounds like a mad conspiracy theorist, but he isn't. He's the sanest, most clear thinking he has ever been. He omits that they are in witness protection. He needs her to be on board first.

Lottie listens better than Daniel from 101, but, when he's finished, she says, 'I have to ask – sorry – do you have a crime reference number with us?'

'Not yet,' Aidan says. He likes that apology. That apology that tells him she doesn't go by the book. 'The man on 101 was no help but, please, will you be?' he says. He says it to get her onside.

'What exactly are the nature of the threats?' she says. She has curious eyes. A very pale blue.

'They're saying they will put petrol through her letter box.'

'And they're identifiable. The people?'

'I can identify them.'

'Is there any evidence? Have they said this in writing?'

'I could get it,' he says.

She leaves a beat, a significant beat, then says, 'I see.'

'Could you help me if I did?'

Lottie pauses. 'Maybe.'

'Can you reopen the file into Bertha's death? It was December – two years ago. It's a cold case, maybe closed. They thought it was like . . . misadventure. Self-harm. It will coincide with one of the football players' seventeenth birthdays. I'm certain of it. There's your corroboration,' he says excitedly.

'You've got an uphill struggle there,' Lottie says thoughtfully. 'You've got a discredited witness.'

'I know.'

'And once a trial has collapsed, it is very tough to reopen it. The first killing has been deemed suicide, the second self-defence. And your stepdaughter is the only witness that this is not the case. That Bertha was murdered. That Jamie was provoked.'

'Look –' Aidan says. 'These people know they've moved. They're threatening all sorts.'

'The protection service will be closely monitoring this. I'm afraid I shouldn't have let you believe I could help you.' He can see a line of ashy roots at her parting. Lauren's hair colour. 'The protection service will be monitoring the threat.'

'But I don't know anyone there. I don't have a contact.'

'Your wife will,' she says firmly.

But Aidan doesn't even know where his wife is. He looks up, and can tell by her expression that there's no point pushing her further. She has moved away from the table, has her hands on the sides of the plastic chair, ready to go.

'Right,' Aidan says. 'How will I know, though . . . that they're okay?'

'They will have it in hand,' she says, standing up. 'You need to trust them.'

'Can I just . . . if I monitor it, can I just have a contact here? Someone to call if . . .'

He expects to receive the usual spiel. Dial 999 for a threat to life. Or 101 to report a crime.

She stops and looks at him properly.

'It's my family,' he says. 'I'm so fucking scared I'm going to lose my family.' He says it barely above a whisper in the cold, corporate lighting.

Something in Lottie's expression changes. 'I know,' she says softly.

'You're too young for kids,' Aidan says. 'But trust me – it changes everything.'

'I have two. Twin babies. Just off maternity leave,' Lottie says.

'You're young.'

'Got pregnant too early in my career, everyone thinks,' she says. Her expression becomes neutral again as she looks at him. She knows she's revealed too much.

But Aidan likes that. This is what he wants. 'Never too soon to start a family,' he says. 'Best years of your life.'

Lottie rubs at her face and he sees the tiredness, now.

A subtle layer of make-up under her eyes. 'Maybe so,' she says. 'I'd certainly do anything for them.'

'Exactly,' Aidan says.

'Here,' she says, seemingly spontaneously, passing a card to him taken from a box on a shelf in the meeting room.

Aidan takes it. 'Should I call if it escalates?'

Lottie is still standing, waiting to go. 'Yes. Look. Focus on the now. On what they intend to do to your family. That is what we'll be able to get them on most easily. Those shits.' Aidan appreciates the returned swear word. A collaboration of language. They're on the same side.

'The now.' Aidan looks at her. 'Okay. What if I . . . what if I kept an eye on the group? And passed you the information?'

Lottie blinks slowly, staring at him thoughtfully. There is a hesitation. Something she is not saying to him. 'I could never advise that you do that,' she says quietly. But she holds eye contact for just a second longer than is necessary.

He collects Bill and walks home. On their way, Aidan texts Poppy to remind her to keep quiet. After, he replays Lottie's parting words over and over in his mind. I could never *advise* you to do that.

But who's to stop him? He's got nothing to lose.

He's lost everything.

23

Poppy

Battersea, London

Two days gone

Poppy has broken up her family. That is what she is thinking as she pulls her school tights on in the darkness of the morning. Dawn is just beginning, outside her window, grey and colourless, and she is thinking of the way her father used to look at Lauren. He never looked at her mother that way, not that Poppy can remember, anyway. Eyes crinkled up, head tilted, as he watched her.

And now Lauren's gone. *They've* gone. And, if Poppy had made a different decision, she would have gone, too. Suddenly, she wishes she was asked properly. Not out of the blue, in her kitchen.

This morning, the reasons why she stayed – her mother, this house, her school – all seem tainted, loaded. Like she has to enjoy them twice the amount, because of what they have cost her father.

She finds her school skirt and pulls it on, then her shirt. The clothes are cold against her skin.

She sits on the side of her bed in the semi-darkness and sips her strawberry tea. She has a new Teasmade, and it's brilliant. The tea was there waiting for her this morning when her alarm went off. The cup is warm in her hands and the steam mists her nose as she sips and thinks.

But it's too late. It's all done. They've gone, and now her father is alone. She looks at the dawn beyond her window. The first Tube rattles by. Where are her stepsister and stepmother now? Out there, somewhere in the wilderness.

Poppy has boarded the Tube and is currently wondering if her hairstyle is ill advised.

She would be able to tell from Zara's facial expression what suited her and what didn't. Poppy would emerge on to the landing wearing a pair of peg trousers and Zara's brow would crinkle.

Just a few days after the murder, Poppy was at her dad's for the weekend, and dithering between two pairs of trainers, when Zara appeared at her bedroom doorway. One hand on the frame, one on the door handle, eyebrows raised. Poppy gestured to the pillow at the top of the bed and Zara sat there cross-legged, watching her get ready, poised to offer up opinions.

Poppy looked at her in the mirror as she redid her mascara. Zara was so pretty. She didn't know it, but she was. Never pale or spotty or tired-looking. The arch of her bare feet, her slender arms clasped around her knees. It was all elegance with Zara. Like a ballerina. She didn't have to try at all.

Poppy looked at herself. Bags under her eyes. She was beginning to look old, she was sure of it, and it had happened basically since her mum's illness had progressed. Immediately, tears started in the back of her throat.

She looked back at Zara, who was staring straight at her in the glass. 'Sorry,' Poppy said. 'I was thinking about my mum.'

'Oh,' Zara said immediately, her eyebrows drawing together. 'I . . . what about her?'

Poppy spun around to look properly at Zara and sat down heavily next to her.

'Do you know if multiple sclerosis is hereditary?' she said.

'Wow,' Zara said, swallowing. She laced her fingers in with her toes, which Poppy found vaguely disgusting, and looked down. 'Shall I do a danger google for you?' she said.

'A danger . . . ?' Poppy asked.

'When you google something scary for someone. I wish I had someone to do it for me.'

'Okay,' Poppy said, smiling gratefully. Outside, early September, a couple of yellow leaves were clinging on by just a thread or two against the bright blue sky.

Zara typed away, then started reading. 'MS is not an inherited disease,' she said.

Poppy's shoulders sagged. She trusted Zara. She was so smart. She'd have gone to a reputable website. Read a conclusion of a peer-reviewed study, probably.

'Do you have . . . are you . . . why are you worried? Do you think you've got it?'

'No,' Poppy said. 'It's not that.'

Zara said nothing, waiting. Even though she wasn't her dad's child, Poppy was sure she got that from him. The loaded pause. He was good at that.

'I wouldn't want any child of mine to be my carer,'

Poppy said, and the tears came properly this time. 'It's so . . . God, it's so shit at times. I made her a packed lunch for today because I didn't think she could make a sandwich.'

'Is she in a relapse?' Zara whispered, her eyes round and surprised-looking.

'She's always in a relapse. And I'm just . . . I'm snappy and I'm like a fucking grumpy old woman all the time. I'm so fucking angry with the whole . . . the whole thing.'

Zara said nothing, gazing at Poppy. 'Are you trying to decide between those?' she said, pointing at the two pairs of trainers at the foot of Poppy's mirror.

Poppy liked the seamless way they shifted topic, the way only family can. From the serious to the mundane, their boundaries as open as the bathroom doors they never locked. 'Yeah,' she said.

'Definitely the white. The others look so nineties.'

'That's the point.'

Zara laughed softly. Poppy sat on the bed next to her.

'You're so good for caring for your mum,' Zara said. And then she added, in a way that was intended to look like an afterthought, but Poppy knew wasn't, 'A nicer person than me.'

'Thank you,' Poppy said.

'And it isn't fair. It shouldn't have happened. Your mum should let you get a carer. My mum said she won't . . .'

'I know,' Poppy said. She shrugged. 'But carers are an admission, apparently.'

'Well, I think you're a hero,' Zara said.

And that had helped. It didn't solve the situation, or the fire of anger that still burned in Poppy. But it did help.

They sat in silence for a few minutes. 'You're a way better person than me,' Zara said again.

'Why do you say that?'

Zara paused. And then she said it. 'I lied.' She looked up at Poppy. 'Those lads . . . the homeless man . . .'

'*What?*'

'Jamie went after them.'

'Oh,' Poppy said, her mouth forming a perfect 'O' that she hoped even though she should be thinking of more important things – made her plain face look momentarily beautiful.

'You know what, though?' Zara said in the quiet of Poppy's bedroom.

'What?' Poppy said warily, not knowing what to do with what she had just been told.

'I think he just felt so vulnerable, lying there, two lads looming over him – I'm sure he got up to defend himself. He was covered in his own urine. Wet himself in fear, I guess.'

'Oh . . . that's . . . that's heartbreaking,' Poppy said, thinking of the one and only time her mother had done the same, just a few feet from the toilet, the flies of her jeans undone, her bladder not able to last the distance. Poppy had helped her, and they'd ignored it all afternoon. In the evening, Poppy had said, 'You know, you used to help me, too. When I was small. It's no different.' Her mum had smiled, but Poppy thought the joke had been too painful for her mother just then, and her cheeks had heated up later, when she had relived it. She was so insensitive.

'Yeah. But I still lied,' Zara said, her face resting on her knee.

'Do you know what?' Poppy said. 'Fuck it.'

'Yeah?'

'Like you say, you know you're right, don't you? They're thugs. Whatever the sequence of events was.'

'Yeah,' Zara said, smiling, finally.

As she left Poppy's room later, her walk was more buoyant somehow. Poppy was glad she'd lifted her up a bit. Her beautiful stepsister could be so insecure, so worried all the time.

Today, getting the Tube into school, standing on the Victoria Line at rush hour, nails still wet from a hasty paint – coral – this morning, Poppy's wondering what Zara would make of her Heidi braids, plaits that go right across her head. And she's wondering, if she had told her father that Zara had lied, whether they would have avoided all this. And so she is also thinking that it is mostly her fault.

She gets off at Green Park. Her friend Emily is waiting at the top of the steps. It's a bright autumn day, and Emily's bare legs are in a slice of sun, the rest of her in shadow. Concern is written across her brow, which comes into focus as Poppy mounts the stairs.

Emily has dark hair, with baby hair at the temples that she once tried – disastrously – to shave off. She smells of lemon shower gel, though she swears she doesn't use it. It must just be her mum's fabric conditioner. Emily's mother is a mother who has the energy and mental space to care about fabric conditioner.

'Nice nails,' Emily says.

It's an unspoken rule of their friendship: compliments. No jealousy. No dragging someone when you feel bad about yourself. Just raising someone up, and trying to say the same things to yourself.

'Thanks. Still wet,' Poppy says. She touches her index finger lightly. The polish yields, viscous and not yet set, like putty. She's left part of her fingerprint behind in it. Damn. She always checks too soon.

'Were you okay yesterday?' Emily says. 'Where were you?'

'I was just sick,' Poppy says. That's her story and she's sticking to it. 'Vomiting thing. Twenty-four hours. Horrible.'

'My mum had that,' Emily exclaims.

Usually, Poppy enjoys her friend's enthusiasm to discuss all things with *zeal*, as they recently learnt in English class, but not today. Today, there is a sick, sad snake curled up in her stomach, and it is all she can do to get through the day without disturbing it.

Poppy looks down at her feet as they walk. She has on new pink Stan Smiths. She will have to take them off the second she is inside the school gates, but they're worth carrying around all day for the joy she gets on this, her walk to school. She watches the salmon-pink laces bouncing as she walks, and breathes deeply, trying to calm the voice that says, repeatedly, that her stepmother and stepsister have disappeared, and that she can't even tell anybody.

Everything happened so quickly. There was talk of witness protection and then, like a rocket going off, it was actually happening, too fast and powerful for anybody to be able to stop it. Her eyes are wet, and she keeps them trained to the ground.

'What's the matter?' Emily says.

'Nothing,' she says. 'It's just the cold air.' She tries to blink them away.

'That's bullshit,' Emily says.

Poppy likes it when she swears so well. Exactly like an adult. The punctuation of it is perfect. Everyone except her dad would appreciate that – only a few weeks ago, he told her off so badly for swearing.

'That sounds so crass coming from your mouth,' he had said, raising his eyebrows to her over his iPad.

'Didn't you swear as a teenager?' she'd said.

'That's totally different.'

'Don't you swear now?'

'That's also different.'

'Why?' she'd said to him, muting the television, ready for an argument.

'Because I am not pure and sweet and kind,' he had said.

That had shut her up.

'Shade thrown,' she'd said.

'You're *cancelled*,' her dad replied, laughing.

'Really,' Poppy says now to Emily. 'It's just cold.'

Emily's mouth parts, just a little bit. She has on brick-red matte lipstick. It's gorgeous. 'Okay,' she says with a shrug. And it's that simple understanding that does it. Emily knows Poppy is lying, but is respectful enough to not probe any further.

Real tears come now for Poppy. They're hot and satisfying and they spill down the sides of her nose. She's not a pretty crier, but she doesn't care, not in front of Emily.

'Oh, no, no,' Emily says. They stop in the crowded street while she puts her thumbs under Poppy's eyes, skimming the tears away while still more come.

'I'm sorry. I'm exhausted,' Poppy says.

Emily stares at her, blue eyes concerned, still saying nothing.

Commuters in suits, men with briefcases, women in heels, keep jostling them, so they duck into an alley without really meaning to, like they have been moved seamlessly in by a tide. Two industrial blue bins with black lids stand next to them. They smell hot and filthy.

'God, sorry,' Poppy says.

Emily hands her a wet wipe from a packet and Poppy gratefully uses it to swipe away her mascara. Black tears. She uses the camera of her iPhone to look. 'Ever the image-conscious,' her dad will mock, but she doesn't see it that way. Looking nice is self-care, as Instagram will tell you. It's as important, to Poppy, as food and drink and sleep and time with Netflix and showers and downtime. On bad days, like lately, it's a treat. Last year, when her mum's sight went, Poppy fell asleep, thinking: *tomorrow, I will wear the full-coverage Mac foundation with the Hourglass blusher, the pale pink one. I'll do an English rose look.* It had helped her.

'Can I do anything?' Emily says. So simple. So supportive. There's no ego involved, no indignation that Poppy is choosing not to confide in her.

Poppy clutches the baby wipe in her hand. It's warm and wet and comforting and leaves a greasy smear on her fingertips. 'No,' she says. 'It's not even about me.' She pushes her hair back. 'It's so selfish of me to be upset about it.'

Emily's eyebrows draw together. 'Is it about your mum?'

'For once, no.'

'Dad?'

Poppy raises her shoulders and drops them. It's not about her dad, not directly, anyway. It's about all of them. Lauren, Zara, her dad, Bill. Poppy's been browsing dog walkers on the internet. Her dad isn't walking Bill enough, and he's whining. She's hired one, and she'll tell him soon, and make him pay them. He won't mind. He'll be thankful.

She sighs out of her nose. The tears have stopped now, but nothing else has changed.

'Well, whatever it is, remember, this too shall pass!' Emily says.

She opens her arms and Poppy steps into them, head against the fur collar of Emily's parka – it's beautiful, from Barbour – and lets herself cry.

'I hate this,' Emily says. 'Whatever it is, I'm sorry. I'm so sorry it's happened to you.'

Poppy pulls back and – honestly – she doesn't even really think about it. She could say she does it because of the power of friendship, of unconditional love, of support, or because everybody has told her what *not* to say, but really, she does it because, in that moment, it feels like the exact right thing to do. And Poppy trusts gut feelings.

'Zara and Lauren have gone into witness protection,' she says, the words sounding implausible, even to her. In the cool, blue shadow of the alleyway, she sees the shock in Emily's eyes. She sees the whites of them, like a frightened dog's.

'Jesus,' she says. 'What? Why? Is this about the trial?'

Poppy rubs at her forehead, baby wipe still in her hand.

Of course she told Emily about the trial. What else was she supposed to do? Continue to suffer completely in silence through divorces, brain lesions and murder trials? 'Yeah.'

'Oh,' Emily says, nodding quickly.

'Now there's this . . . this weird vendetta against her. And she's been taken into protection. She's literally moved out. Disappeared.' Poppy makes a hopeless sort of gesture, hands rising by her sides, then falling again. 'Just like that. New name, everything.'

'Oh my God,' Emily says.

'Yes.'

'Let's walk and talk,' Emily says.

They step out again into the low winter sunlight and walk down the high street. It's set to snow later today, apparently, but for now, the sky is a bright blue dome above them.

'They've just . . . gone,' Poppy says softly. 'And I'm not supposed to be telling anyone. Nobody knew she was Girl A, but then this Facebook group . . . they just leaked her name, so she had to go.'

Emily nods. She steps past a *Big Issue* seller with a dog who she usually always pats but this time ignores.

They round a corner and cross a green in the shade from a cluster of tower blocks.

Emily's face goes from a sunlit bronze to a dim greyish blue. 'When did they go?' she says.

'Two days ago.'

'God. No vomiting bug yesterday, then.'

'No,' Poppy says. 'No vomiting. But still as horrible. Dad wanted me to go, too, and I wouldn't.'

'Wow.'

'I know. He just sprang it on me, and I said no because of the art foundation. I am a selfish twat.'

'Oh, you're not at all,' Emily says sincerely. 'I promise.'

They reach the school gates.

'I need to take this off,' Emily says, gesturing to her lips. 'Mrs Mitchell will go mad.' She pauses. 'You've got my last baby wipe.'

Poppy smiles and passes it to Emily, who starts scrubbing. She wipes at the cinnamon colour, and it blurs and feathers around her lips.

'Will you never see them again?' she says.

'I don't know.' Poppy slips her trainers off and takes her sensible black school shoes out of her bag. 'That's what they say.'

'I can't believe they've just gone.'

'I know.' Poppy has no idea what to say. She hears her phone go off and checks it.

Her dad. Always worrying: this time reminding her *again* not to tell anyone. Shame and guilt flush her cheeks.

'I'm not supposed to be telling anyone,' Poppy says obediently to Emily, as though the act of confessing will ward off the punishment.

'Don't worry,' Emily says.

And it does help. Poppy's shoulders relax.

Emily balls up the baby wipe, its grease making her fingers look oily. 'I won't talk about it to anyone.'

They walk past a bin and Emily tosses the wipe upwards. It is bright white against the blue sky, momentarily, a thick red smear at its centre like a wound. Poppy blinks, and it's gone.

*

Poppy likes it when it gets dark while she's still at school. They're coming into winter, and the snow has begun. Fat, infrequent flakes like cotton-wool balls drift down outside.

She rests her head in the palm of her hand and tunes out the fractions and the equations and the algebra. The moon is up, a reflective disc in the sky. The twilight clouds are shifting, their forms blurring with the classroom's reflection. Maths wall hangings and strip lights mingle with skies and street lamps.

As she stares, she sees a form appear in the gloom. She blinks, thinking she's imagining it, but she isn't. A man is standing outside the classroom, his eyes only just visible above the window sill, hands cupped around them, looking in, hardly noticeable at first until she concentrates on him, like a magic eye picture.

She starts, chair scraping back noisily in the quiet classroom, and he ducks down. She looks around the classroom. Should she say something? No. She'll look mad. Or worse, she'll have to reveal everything. Who her family are. The vendetta against them. The things she's been warned and warned again to keep secret.

She keeps watching, and he lopes across the school grounds. One, two, three steps. Then runs. He has on baggy jeans, boxers visible above them. No coat. Short, greyish hair that catches the street light as he moves towards the road.

And then he's gone.

It was nothing, she tells herself. Some weird bloke just being nosey. Nothing.

Later, at home, she drags the dustbin down the drive.

Her mum isn't well. She got stressed about her dad, and the MS is worse again. The bin is wet with snow and bumps the back of her legs. It's completely dark, the air a wall of cold, the frost on the streets yellowed by the cast of the street lamps. She stands for a second, looking at the neat rows of bins. Without warning, the hairs on the back of her neck stand up. She looks around her. Nothing. As she turns back towards the house, she feels it again, and sprints up the driveway, her shoes wet and slippery on the frost. She slams the front door behind her, out of breath.

It's only later, after stacking the dishwasher, her mum in bed, that she sees it. Her front door handle, moving down. She blinks, staring. Has somebody just tried the door? Surely not, she thinks, her heart racing. No.

24

Lauren

Coniston, the Lake District

Two days gone

It's the evening of their second day in the Lake District. Lauren's second day as Lindsey, Zara's second day as Sienna. The sun sets earlier here, up north, just a couple of minutes. It's weird to think of herself in darkness and Aidan still in light.

The washing machine beeps, signalling it's done, and she jumps. She double-checks the doors and windows are locked, and takes the laundry up to the landing where the airer is. Zara appears and starts to help her hang it out. She would never usually help with this, but, like a holiday, witness protection has rejigged their routine. Her always tanned arms, with their fine blonde hairs, stretch to hang up a white T-shirt. She straightens it carefully, and Lauren watches, remembering hanging up all of Zara's sleep suits before she was born. She'd bought them from Marks & Spencer, even though she couldn't afford to, and washed them all while she was pregnant, her belly nudging the edge of the airer so it teetered. Lauren didn't mind, by then, that she was hanging them up alone. She was a wild animal, left to raise her child solo, the way it's always been.

'You know,' Zara says, her eyes focused on a white cotton hoody. She reaches in and unfolds one of the arms. 'He was alive when I found him.'

'Jamie?' Lauren says, concentrating on a pair of socks, not looking at Zara, even though she wants to push the airer out of the way and embrace her.

'Yeah. On his side. He had a pulse.'

'I see.'

'Yeah. He was looking at me.' Zara finishes hanging the hoody up and looks at Lauren.

Those eyes. Lauren only ever had two encounters with Zara's father. The one-night stand – Lauren had never had one, but it had seemed like the right thing to do on that night in the Spanish bar, full of cocktails and wearing a floor-skimming dress – and the day she told him she was pregnant. And now Zara has those eyes for life. Two brown orbs, those Disney eyes.

Zara puts her hands on her hips and looks at Lauren. 'Do you think he knew it was me?' The question is a throwback to the days when Zara's anxiety led her to asking question after question. 'Will it definitely be fine on the Tube? What if I feel weird?'

It makes Lauren wince. '*Yes*, undoubtedly,' she says, though it is a white lie: a necessary lie. Parenthood is full of them. 'I bet he was so glad somebody he knew was there with him.'

Zara makes the tiniest movement. An open-hands gesture. A step towards her mum. She wants cuddling, and Lauren obliges.

'Hope so,' Zara murmurs into Lauren's hair. 'He died while I was holding him.'

Lauren says nothing, Zara's hair tickling her ear, just standing there, in their new house, in their new lives, alone, together.

'You did everything you could.'

'I dream about him.'

Zara withdraws from Lauren and she sees that her eyes are bottom-heavy with tears.

'And . . . you know,' Zara says, 'he stunk of wee. And they just . . . after it was done, they just stood over him like he didn't matter at all . . .' She pauses, staring at Lauren. 'Do you . . . I'm sorry I lied. It just . . .' She takes a shuddering breath. 'It felt like the right thing to do. I know how bizarre that sounds.'

'You did exactly the right thing. I would have done the same.' Lauren says 'Of *course* I don't blame you.'

'Don't you?'

'No,' Lauren says. 'You're my baby. I don't blame you for anything.'

She looks just beyond Zara, to the textured wallpaper, the shabby stairs. Another white lie. Lauren does blame Zara. She is only human. If Zara had told the truth, had cared less about social justice and more about their family, or even herself, they wouldn't be here, and Lauren would be in her old life. It doesn't stop her loving Zara – but it doesn't mean she doesn't blame her, either. The complicated cocktail of parenthood. Loving and liking not always aligning.

'Good,' Zara says, exhaling with what seems like relief.

'So. Tomorrow . . .' Lauren says. 'First day of school.'

'I'm Sienna Smith,' Zara says. 'From Bristol, escaped the accent somehow.'

'Good, good. Birthday?'

Zara smiles as she recites it all. She's always been a conscientious student. It's Lauren the protection service should be worried about. She can't memorize anything, has no idea of her new birthday without looking in the folders.

'Best not to have any friends around this side of Christmas,' Lauren reminds her. 'Until we've got some photos up. It's all a bit . . .' she looks around. 'It's all a bit obvious to me.'

'Yeah.'

'Just say you'll go to their house, if it comes up. Okay?'

'Okay,' Zara says. 'Yes. But what if they insist?'

'Say we're having work done, or something. I think.'

'Okay,' Zara says. She reaches for the final sock and hangs it up, then pats Lauren's hand. 'Thank you,' she says sincerely.

A car backfires on the street outside, and they both jump.

Lauren is up late waiting for a delivery. She's ordered food on an app. An old vice of hers. Sneaky Deliveroos when she was home alone. There is not much finer than an illicit food drop-off.

A cake is coming. She knows it's mad, the kind of behaviour Aidan would shake his head at, a half-smile hidden as he looks down, but it is Lauren. Vintage Lauren.

She waits by the window for her extra-large chocolate ganache cake. She will eat it, still hot, in the bath.

The whole thing, all £20 worth. Fuck it. Fuck behaving herself. An app is safe, isn't it? The delivery drivers are vetted.

A November frost has settled outside on the Coniston street. She is imagining walking Bill through it. Fat paws in the frost. A sheen to his coat as they arrive back, a warm towel around his body. She misses him so much she can almost feel his fur against her hand.

Zara went to bed at nine. She's bored, and lonely, Lauren knows it. She hasn't been able to act normally.

Lauren has been trying to get the boiler to run a bath while waiting for her cake. It fires up enough for a shower, but gradually fades to cold water after ten minutes. She needs to ask the protection service. It's on her list.

The window is lit up by the delivery motorbike. Lauren rushes to the door. She pays him two £10 notes, and takes the cake, warm in a white box.

But, in a way, it isn't the cake she ordered. It's the company. 'Got a busy night planned?' she says desperately to the driver.

'Always,' he says, putting his helmet back on. 'Have a good night.'

That's it. Her interaction for the day.

She opens the cake in the kitchen, intent on calories, but jumps as a gentle buzzing noise interrupts her thoughts. It's coming from upstairs. A soft, flaring sound. It stops, then starts again. The unmistakeable noise of a mobile phone vibrating against something. Lauren looks at her iPhone, on the kitchen counter, its black surface glossy with one globule of water from the kettle. She reaches to wipe it with the sleeve of her jumper.

She looks up at the ceiling above her. It must be Zara's. Who could she be texting? Who could be calling her? Neither of them has a single friend. *Yet.* A single relative they are permitted to contact. They are satellites, alone in space, together, mother and daughter.

She reaches the landing and stands outside Zara's room. There is silence. A pure silence that seems to throb around her ears in a way London never permitted. She presses lightly on the door and it opens, the catch cheap and flimsy, and she sees Zara lying on her back, completely asleep. She is sleeping in the exact position she used to. Legs splayed outwards like a frog – Lauren can see the outlines of her knees in the bed – one arm behind her on the pillow, palm up, fingers curled. Her little cricket baby. And, ah, there's that feeling. That fat, happy/sad feeling, the blessing of a child, the mourning of the passing of time, the impermanence of it all. It's nice that that feeling is still here with them, in the north, where the sun sets earlier.

Zara's phone is resting on the duvet by her right hand, a few inches away from her. There's no way Lauren would have heard that downstairs. And there's no way Zara was awake just a few minutes ago. Lauren knows the many moods, emotions and states of her daughter and this one is called deep sleep. She used to watch it overtake her baby as she lay across her lap, little chest panting, mouth relaxing, lips sticking together until they released and parted, like a slow goodbye. Watching her baby daughter fall asleep was one of her favourite things to do. Still is.

She glances at the window looking to the back of the house, suddenly fearful. That this is something. A trick.

A warning. The phone has stopped now, but she starts searching for it in her bedroom anyway.

Just as she's thinking she'll never be able to place where it came from, it begins again. A rhythmic beeping. Three sounds, then a pause. Three sounds, then a pause. She can feel her heart pulsing in her throat. What is it? *Who* is it?

The wardrobe. That's where the noise is coming from. She ransacks it, pulling out the clothes she has reluctantly unpacked. No, it's not coming from here. It's coming from down below. She knows it might stop again soon, so she bends down and frantically feels around on the tattered carpet. There's a burn from what looks like a pair of hair straighteners. The carpet has congealed into two lines, thick and plasticky. The only thing remaining is her suitcase. She pulls it out of the space on the floor and puts it on the bed. The sound moves with it.

She opens it, even though she knows it to be empty. She feels around inside it. It's a shell case, made of hard material, and maybe that would have amplified the noise of a phone vibrating. Maybe she accidentally brought her old phone with her, she is thinking, as she palms her way around it, even though she knows that isn't true. She knows exactly what she is about to find.

A small object sits behind the lining. She unzips it, and there it is. A Samsung flip-phone. A charger and cable bound up around it. She opens it and it's on. *Alarm 1*, it says. *Stop. Snooze.* She stops it.

A low battery warning flashes up, which she dismisses.

The phone is blank. No apps. No messages. She goes to the contact. There's one.

In Case of Emergency.

A number she doesn't recognize.

Her hands are shaking. She sits on the flattened carpet, her back against the cold wardrobe, and closes her eyes. Jon said nobody's ever been seriously harmed or killed in witness protection in the UK who has obeyed the rules. *I know your husband didn't come . . .*

She studies the suitcase, thinking.

As she's handling the phone, the alarm now a few minutes ago, a text comes through from In Case of Emergency.

It's me. Did you find it? A.

25

Zara

Coniston, the Lake District

Three days gone

Bill always acted as Zara's alarm clock back in Islington. He knew she had to get up at seven, and he always arrived at exactly then. Her room this morning felt empty and sterile.

Her mother offered her chocolate cake for breakfast, and she gladly ate it. 'Everything is better with cake,' she said, and Zara agreed, raising her fork in a toast. She has a plan, and it began with that cake salute. Internally, she is going to pretend she's Poppy. Breezy, laid-back, confident Poppy. Poppy is the kind of girl who would toast somebody with a fork, not caring how she looked, and so Zara adopted it, too. She's going to show up at her new school and . . . just be cool. No angst. No bookishness.

It is her first day and Zara is so nervous her hands have gone cold. As she approaches the school gates, a slow-moving car passes her. She holds her breath, waiting. Waiting for that gloved hand, that balaclava, that knife. But it's just a parent, dropping their child off. Of course it is.

She wishes there wasn't such a persistent alarm system in her head. That everything new didn't make her nervous. She is trying to ignore it, the hyper-vigilance, but perhaps anybody would be afraid in this situation. Perhaps it isn't only anxiety.

A girl is standing outside the grey reception building – all of the buildings in Coniston are grey – holding a pale pink bag.

Zara walks into the reception and the girl follows her, smiling self-consciously as Zara holds the door open for her. There's a dark brown rug, wrinkled up, the very end of it folded over like a duvet cover, exposing the rubbery underside. It smells like schools. Pencil shavings. Trainers. Industrial floor polish. Overcooked dinners. Sweat. Zara likes that they all smell the same. She and the girl sit on two green chairs, side by side. The seats are made of cheap foam, and it yields too much underneath her.

'That's disgusting,' the girl with the pink bag suddenly says, gesturing to the upturned rug and the dirt, fluff and crumbs underneath it. 'They never even lift it to hoover?'

Zara can't help but smile. 'It gives me hives to look at,' she says, thinking of her always ordered bedroom, her new stationery, the chaos of her mum's messiness. She might be Sienna now, but she still wants to wipe up under the rug. So much for new Sienna. It's funny how hard it is to change. She wishes she could say something funny. Something original or cool.

Jamie used to say the same thing to her about change being hard. He'd been in the army. Served in Afghanistan, so he said, and she believed him, because he knew things about it that you couldn't make up. How the ground beneath him would shake with tremors during explosions. He described it so well to her once, both hands coming out in front of him and trembling. 'Sounds like an engine starting up, couple of streets away,' he once said. 'It's hard to change my mindset back to safety.'

She can't forget the wound. A ragged line across his neck, still feebly leaking, like a faulty tap rhythmically spurting mouthfuls of water, a betrayal, his heart unknowingly pumping blood out of him instead of around inside him. She'd rolled him on to his side and tried to stem it with her denim jacket, later taken away by the police for forensics. They offered it back to her, months later, pale denim in a clear plastic bag, a stain across the collar like a huge red flower. Zara had just looked at them, and her mum had said, 'Please dispose of that for us,' in an incredulous voice.

She's glad she had a shot at getting Luke and Mal sent where they belong, that's the truth of it. Jamie didn't deserve it. She did it for a subculture of people who are ignored and marginalized. She did it for people who are only ever offered leftovers, both literal and metaphorical.

And now she's paying the price. Their family divided, because of her. And it isn't over yet. She thinks of the motto . . . and the rest of it.

'Reckon we can sweep it up while we wait for them?' the girl says, interrupting Zara's thoughts.

'Probably not,' Zara says.

'I'm Phoebe.'

Zara waits just one beat. This is it. Her rehearsals in front of the dingy mirror in their new bathroom. The chanting in her head as she walked into the school gates today. 'Sienna,' she says. She feels as though she has a gun to her temple. God, why is she like this?

'What a nice name. Where have you moved from?' Phoebe says.

Zara swallows, trying to remember her story. It's written in a note on her phone – locked down, password protected, like Jon told them to do – but there, just in case she forgets.

'Bath – no, Bristol! It's Bristol,' Zara says. Her hands are sweating. She is so bad at this. 'Lost my mind for a second there,' she says, with a forced laugh. 'You?'

'I'm only local.'

'Oh, right,' Zara says, but, instead, her mind is racing. Already, she's slipped up. She glances towards the window. How long before it gets out, and they come for her? The gloved hands, the tight grips? Anxiety clutches at her chest again like an old enemy. Her entire body is tense, like she is made of wood.

She stares down at her feet, trying to breathe deeply the way the therapist told her to, thinking of the people she has left behind. Poppy and Aidan. And Bill.

'Must be so weird to move miles and miles away,' Phoebe says, and Zara feels her whole body start. She *knows*?

No. She doesn't know. Bristol *is* miles away. It's fine. It's fine. 'It's okay,' she says. And then she adds, 'Must be kind of weird to move locally.'

Zara watches as Phoebe turns to the window. It is frosted, toughened glass, with metal threads running through it like graph paper.

'Yeah. It is. But necessary.'

'Same for me.'

Phoebe leans her head back against the wall and sighs. 'I don't know if I should have moved, or stuck it out,' she says.

'Bullies?' Zara says immediately.

Phoebe waits a second before answering. 'Yeah, I guess they were,' she says eventually. 'Group of vicious girls. Used to be my friends.'

'Oh,' Zara says, and her heart seems to expand painfully for her. Maybe she could make a real friend up here.

'How come you moved?' asks Phoebe.

'Mum's work,' Zara says faithfully. Panic moves up her body, the exact way it used to. She needs to escape. She can't do this. She's going to mess it up.

Phoebe is looking at her closely, can see she is struggling.

But Zara can't say. She takes a deep breath as she thinks of the witness protection rule sheet. She likes rules.

She's got to be convincing. She can't let on that there is even a secret to conceal. She's got to keep people at arm's length.

'Well, sorry you were bullied,' Zara says. 'I hope it's better here for you – it's going to be good for me. I'm sure we'll see each other around.' She turns away from Phoebe.

Phoebe's expression opens like a wound, then closes down. She's been given the brush-off.

Zara stares at her hands.

A middle-aged man strides into the reception. 'Sienna and Phoebe? Today's new starters.'

*

Later, much later, Zara is walking home, alone, the mountains in the distance, the pavements sparkling at her feet, thinking of how soon she can sign up to the nearest library.

She is totally alone out here, tonight. Goosebumps cover her back, nevertheless. She wonders if she will ever stop being terrified.

She gets her phone out and trudges along, ruminating. She walks for five minutes, now thinking about Phoebe, then stops suddenly when she hears something. Other footsteps. She turns around in a slow circle. She's on a residential street. It's deepest, darkest winter, the grasses spiked with frost, air vents pumping out steam into the evening air. She can't see anybody, so she keeps walking, her skin freezing in the cold, her eyes darting around her.

How is she going to make any friends when she can't tell the truth? A heavy weight sits in her stomach as she thinks of it. How is it ever going to work for them, here?

The footsteps again. She stops. And, this time, she sees him. A tall man in a black coat, his face completely obscured by the shadow of his hood and the darkness. He's a few hundred yards behind her, emerging from an old-fashioned wooden bus stop. He stands and watches her for a beat, then resumes walking towards her.

Her heart rate quickens. She's all alone out here. What should she do? Phone somebody? She gets her mobile out and taps a text out to her mother that she doesn't send. *Prospect Road, come find me.* It's there, just in case. She watches the man catching up to her. She can't turn her back to him. She can't keep walking. She is frozen, out here on the winter street, waiting for him to get to her.

As he approaches, she sees his face. He's wearing glasses. She can just make out the white trail of a pair of headphones down the front of his hoody. He's almost reached her, now. Her entire body is trembling.

He walks past her, jostling her arm slightly. 'What you looking at?' he says accusatorily.

Zara's shoulders sag with relief. Thank God, thank God, he's just a regular yob.

She deletes the emergency text to her mother, but adds one into the keyboard shortcuts. If she types *SOS*, her phone changes it to *Please help me, they've found me.* It makes her feel better.

She carries on walking, more slowly this time, letting the man recede into the distance. She resumes her worrying, as Zara often does, about how to make friends in protection.

After a while, she begins to talk. To nobody. To herself. She is walking an imaginary Bill, an imaginary lead in her hand.

'I am worried they'll find me. I regret lying. I miss Aidan and Poppy. I miss London. I'm never going to have a single true friend ever again,' she is saying. Tears are collecting in her eyes and her nose is streaming and her mouth is full of sticky, sad saliva. 'I'm sad, I'm scared, and I'm lonely,' she says to the night air. 'I'm so lonely. So lonely and so frightened.'

26

Aidan

Shepherd's Bush, London
Four days gone

Aidan hasn't seen Lauren for four days. The longest they have ever been apart. He doesn't know if she got his text. She hasn't replied yet. He thought setting the alarm to go off on the second night made logical sense. She'd be alone by then – especially at eleven at night – and he calculated it would be before the battery ran dead. He is surprised she didn't text him right away. She's the impulsive one, he the considered over-thinker, but maybe their roles are reversing. Or maybe she didn't get it. Or maybe he got her into trouble. Maybe, maybe, maybe.

The truth is, he needs a line to her. An open method of communication. Not because he misses her – though he does – but because he needs to be able to warn her. If the group find Zara. That's why he's taken this risk. Because not taking it is worse than taking it.

He can't tell Lauren about Zara and the cover-up, even if he could get hold of her. He weighed it up this morning in the shower. If he told her, what would it achieve? It would frighten her. She's in protection anyway. Everything that can be done is being done.

And, deep down, he knows she might tell somebody. That's the truth. She could go nuclear.

And information is harmful.

He is standing in central London as he re-justifies this decision to himself, waiting for Lauren's sister, Hannah, underneath a dripping awning, Bill sniffing at a wrapper of something. Thinking about when he might see her again. He watches a glassy raindrop fill and bulge, then fall to the ground, shattering to nothing. Still thinking.

He checks his map and sends Hannah the street he's on. He wouldn't meet her at hers, in case her house is being watched.

The Find Girl A meeting pops into his mind while he is staring out at the street. Nobody has mentioned Malcolm, the second defendant, who doesn't appear to be in the group and wasn't at the meeting. Where's he at, then? Is he holding a grudge? Or . . . ?

Hannah is late, just like Lauren would be. He texts her again.

Am walking now, call when you're here.

It doesn't deliver. So she's on the Tube. He starts walking with Bill, who falls easily into step beside him. He feels safer in backstreets, his thoughts racing like hamsters in wheels.

He walks through Leicester Square and Piccadilly. He buys a cup of tea from a cheap café in a plastic white cup that burns his hand. The rain becomes heavier, and water begins to run down Aidan's neck. Bill shakes it off his cream fur. A church looms up above him. He looks at the sign outside it. *The Church of Notre-Dame de France*. It's a huge, ugly building, grey-brown stone – 'A lovely greige,' Poppy would say – with navy-blue gates either side. But it looks open, and it will be dry, and there won't be anybody in there from a Facebook group that might want to harm him.

He ascends the stone steps and slips inside. If anybody wants to throw Bill out, they can, but he's not leaving him in the rain again. He tugs him up the steps and he follows Aidan faithfully. It smells of smoky incense. There's a confessional box just on the right.

It's silent in the way that places of worship are. Wooden pews, a huge oval window up ahead. Six stone pillars in front of him. He wishes he was religious, that he found comfort in crosses nailed to pillars and hymn books and cushions for kneeling on. But nevertheless, the air is quiet and still and calm, like he is looking at his own reflection in a pond.

He sits on one of the pews, cold underneath him, his back to the entrance, feeling safe for the first time since he left the flat. He extends his legs, his jeans damp with raindrops, and exhales. Relaxes his shoulders, the way Lauren told him to when he gets like this. He sips his tea. Despite it costing 89p, it's nice tea. Rich and smooth. Steam curls out of the little hole in the lid, and he covers it with his fingertip.

What is he going to do about giving the group the information from the scrapers? He'll have to stall. Get the evidence and give it to the police, and quickly. That's the plan.

He opens his burner phone.

There's a text from Kevin.

Download Telegram app, OK?

Aidan knows exactly what Telegram is. An encrypted, self-destructing underground messenger service where texts disappear at will. Untraceable. Banned in Russia and used by radicalists, Aidan has never downloaded it, but he's not afraid to. It isn't illegal, not of itself.

He circles around the church, phone in hand, and stops by a statue labelled *Saint Anthony of Padua*.

It downloads over 4G – anachronistic, next to a statue of a patron saint, but still true – and he's in. He sets his profile photo to a bland cartoon version of himself – brown hair, no glasses, beard – and, within a few moments, he's added to a group: *Find Girl A – Underground.* A self-destruct timer is set for one day. The messages will disappear after that. Aidan makes a diary reminder to screenshot each evening before bed. There are thirteen members. Already, information has been gathered.

Here is a list of Girl A's old interests, from Facebook: Bookish Box, Anxiety and Me (Recovery Stories Only!), Shelter, Golden Retriever Owners, Smart Girl Problems.

They also have two new photographs of her. One Aidan recognizes – Zara by their Christmas tree with Bill – and one he doesn't, a selfie taken with Zara's friend Hattie. Both are good resemblances to her, and his heart sinks.

At the top is a pinned message by Kevin.

Now, we really can plan.

Underneath it is a sticker: a little cartoon with black gloved hands, a dark cape, holding a cross up. A *Scream* mask over his features.

The grim reaper.

*

'I just can't understand it,' Hannah says to Aidan for the third time.

He closes the door to the pub behind them, heading out into the frigid, damp air. Leaves line the gutters of the streets like litter. Bill crunches through them, oblivious to the dark tone the conversation has taken, to the danger they are in.

Aidan told Hannah everything he feels able to share while she listened, wide-eyed. They'd found a deserted pub and sat right at the back, able to whisper in private over a pot of horrible tea made with UHT milk that curdled in the cups. It is the only time they have ever been together, one-to-one. Afterwards, he tried to ask her about work and her husband, Conrad, but she kept circling back to witness protection, to her missing sister, and still does now. Aidan understands: he is the same.

'Everyone thinks I know what the fuck's happened, but I'm as clueless as you, Han,' he says now in the cold.

'They can't mean it,' she says, her breath vaporizing in the air in front of them.

It's freezing. The cold seems to wrap itself around Aidan's legs. They turn towards the Tube and descend. The steps are slick with dirt and rain, a brown city watercolour at their feet.

'Why would they want to harm a girl who annoyed a football club?'

Aidan winces. He can't tell her the truth. Instead, he says nothing.

'It can't be for ever,' she says, and Aidan says nothing.

She's going west and he's heading north, so they part in the artificially warm Tube tunnel. A brief hug. She pats

Bill's head. He found an old tennis ball in the pub under a table, left by another dog, and has been squeezing it all the way home.

As Aidan walks to his platform, he feels his torso is littered with bullets, one for each question she asked him. 'It's for ever?' 'How could it be?' 'Why didn't you stop her?' 'How did you say goodbye?'

So he does what anybody would do in this situation: he calls his mother. He's been hiding, deliberately not updating her, in the way that people do sometimes when they can't face those closest to them in a crisis. But now he wants to reach out. Now that Hannah is relying on him for answers. He needs his own safety net. His mother.

'How are you all?' she says, instead of hello.

He stands on the platform, his breath misting the air in front of him, the phone warm to his ear, and lets tears collect in his eyes. They leak out, and he tries to not let them affect his voice. 'Yeah, alright. Keeping on,' he says. His sadness is a wound deep inside him that he can't expose, not even to her. Aidan doesn't know why he is like this, but he is. Really, it is since his father died. He became the successor, the next Mr Madison, the man of the house.

'They went,' he says simply.

His mother inhales quickly. He can tell she is casting about for something to say.

'I'm so sorry,' she settles on eventually.

'Me too,' Aidan says. 'But I'll be fine.' He looks into the distance. The lights of his train are two pinpricks on their way to him in the freezing mist.

'Sure you will,' Brenda says. 'You will.'

Aidan says nothing, letting the tears fall and freeze on his face as he waits, with Bill, for his train. 'Anyway. How're you?' he says. He can't tell her about the group, about what he's started. She would be so disappointed.

'All fine here,' she says.

He boards the train, grateful for the rush of artificial warmth. He sits right by a heater.

'You should come over soon,' she says.

'Yeah,' he says. 'I will.'

His mother says nothing for a few seconds, and Aidan waits, tears running down his face.

'You got a tissue there with you?' she says quietly, listening to him cry, as she has a hundred times before.

He wakes in the night and thinks again of Mal, the other defendant. He looks him up on Facebook – Malcolm Henderson – and finds him immediately. Aidan sets up a new account, as Mr A, and adds him.

Even though it is three o'clock in the morning, Mal accepts almost immediately.

Aidan opens the message box and writes and deletes and writes and deletes, thinking. Eventually, he doesn't send anything, but the message box is there waiting. For when he's thought it through.

27

Lauren

Coniston, the Lake District

Five days gone

At the moment, all of Lauren's concentration is taken up with a black handle she has discovered on the side of the combi boiler, in search of generating enough hot water for a bath. Lauren is going to fix it, tonight. She is determined.

She has changed into her favourite pyjamas – striped almost-cashmere, some cheap variation, as soft as Bill's tummy fur. She's glad she could bring them with her.

She has not touched the burner phone.

How can she justify replying to Aidan? She can't. That's the truth.

She's been told not to contact anybody.

She's promised she won't.

They will withdraw protection – for her daughter, grabbed by a man in a car in London, just days ago – if she does.

But she's glad she's got it. A line to him. If she needs him. And if he needs her.

She is sure that is why he has sent it.

So, to distract herself, she's sitting on the floor of the kitchen in front of the boiler, thinking about today and working out how to turn the black handle, which won't budge. She's had a driving lesson today, and thinks back to her job interview yesterday. The rebuilding of it all, the ingredients for a life.

'So you were a nursery nurse in Bristol, born and bred,' her interviewer said.

Lauren had nodded, thinking: *Lindsey, Bristol, Sienna, Sienna's father estranged.* That last part, at least, was true. 'Yes,' she said.

After she was given a tour of the nursery, the interviewer said she would be in touch. That was all. Perfectly normal. Except who would she be in touch with? The references are fabricated. Not real people. Would the people at the nursery not know that? Would they not google the fake nursery on her fake CV? Lauren can't work it out. Aidan would know. He's smarter than her.

She's not sure the black handle on the boiler is a handle. It could just be a fixed part. She stares at it. Zara has gone for coffee with 'a new friend'. Just like that. Kids. They moved house when Zara was six, to Islington with Aidan, and Zara said, 'What old house?' just two weeks later. She'd forgotten all of it. They adapt so easily, even anxious types like Zara, still forming themselves, like a seedling that can withstand regular replanting.

The handle doesn't turn either way and Lauren has no tools. She fiddles with it uselessly. Is it a wrench she needs? Pliers?

She gets a tea towel. She pauses as she grabs it. What's that outside the window? She stands completely still, imagining the worst. A gang, a lynch mob, people in hoods, masks, carrying flaming torches. But it's nothing. There's nothing there. She checks and double-checks, standing in front of the window, a blurred reflection of herself looking back, terrified. It must have been the wind moving a tree, is all.

She grips the handle of the boiler with the tea towel. She'll have a fucking bath soon, even if she has to hire a plumber herself.

Something happens. Just something. The handle shifts a millimetre or so. She puts her weight behind it this time, but nothing. No more movement.

Tears threaten at the back of her eyes. It's so quiet here. She is so displaced, stuck in the Lake District, with nobody she can call to confide in. It's been four days and a lifetime.

Despondent, lonely, a pit of sadness in her stomach, she reaches for her phone, just a couple of feet away on the carpet, and opens her apps one by one.

Instagram. She looks at her feed – anodyne posts from brands – and then Twitter, which has more of the same.

Sobs catch in her throat as she tries to turn the fucking black handle on the boiler, but it doesn't budge. God, maybe she should ask Zara. She'd probably work it out quicker than Lauren. But no. How humiliating that would be. She can't let Zara see how hopeless her mother is. What a useless custodian she is.

'What would you do?' she asks an imaginary Aidan, pretending he is just behind her.

'Give it some elbow grease,' he replies.

So she does.

The boiler makes a gentle hissing noise. A red arrow moves along a pressure gauge. Lauren watches it in astonishment, waiting for it to turn all the way up. 'We did it,' she says aloud to Aidan.

She dashes to the bathroom and runs the tap. It's hotter than it was, and she lets it rush over her fingertips, the water parting softly around them. There's an inch of water in the bath. An inch of glorious hot water. She checks the tap again, just to be sure, but it's gone cold.

Lauren sits on the carpeted bathroom floor – she always hated carpet in bathrooms – and stretches her legs out in front of her. Fuck this. Fuck everything.

She still has her old pedicure on. Pink, from the last time she got her toenails done, at the end of October. The last of the summer colours. She looks at the grown-out varnish and thinks she might never take it off, this relic from her life with the man she loved and Bill Gates and her daughter and her stepdaughter and her sister and her bath and the Chinese takeaway round the corner where they knew her name and her order without her having to say anything. She misses so many things about her old life, she doesn't know where to start.

She cries until her throat is sore, until her cheeks are wet, until her legs are quivering on the carpeted floor. She cries for Aidan and for Poppy and for Hannah and Bill, and for everyone she's been forced to leave behind. Most of all, she cries for Zara, and the crime she witnessed, and the lies she felt she had to tell because of a failing system and a dose of misguided teenage idealism. She tries to tell herself she's not angry about it, but she is. She backed her daughter doing the right thing, encouraged her, protected her, but, all along, Zara was actually doing the wrong thing, committing a crime of her own, perjuring herself in the witness box, for nothing. Jamie was already dead. What good did it do?

She calls Jon's mobile when she has composed herself. 'Sorry,' she says, when he picks up. 'I just wanted a bath, and this boiler . . . it just doesn't run enough hot water.'

'Oh, yes,' Jon says easily, coolly. 'I know. We'll get someone out. Soon. Sorry, I did know. I should have fixed it sooner. It's been busy.'

Busy, Lauren thinks. Busy like shops are busy. Like the pre-Christmas period is busy in offices. Like the nursery in the early autumn. She knows it is just a job to him, and yet it feels wrong that it is, too.

'I can call someone now,' Lauren says. Her monthly protection budget will cover it.

'No, it's best if we do,' he says.

Lauren sighs. She never thought she'd miss the autonomy of running a house, but she does. She thanks Jon curtly and hangs up, then leans her head against the wall and tries not to cry again.

The urge to pick up the burner phone and text Aidan is physical. It rises up through her, a toxic combination of temptation, guilt and love.

She uses her iPhone instead of the burner phone to google plumbers. Some misdemeanours are less than others.

She chooses the first one that comes up, an expensive, sponsored ad, an 0345 number. She'll charge it back to the protection service. Fuck them.

'Emergency Assist plumbers, how can I help?' a detached voice says.

Lauren explains the problem.

They'll dispatch somebody tomorrow morning, they tell her. 'Can we take some details in order to pop you on the system?' the woman says. She has a London accent, which makes Lauren miss home.

'Fine,' Lauren says.

'Full name?'

'Lindsey Anne Smith.'

'Date of birth?'

'Oh, hang on,' Lauren says. Wait, is it February – the fifteenth? She has to check. Everything anybody normal would usually know, be able to recite without thought, without meaning. 'February the twelfth.'

'Mother's maiden name? To set up your security questions for your account?'

'Oh, God,' Lauren says thickly. She doesn't know it. She doesn't know herself. She hangs up the phone in a hurry, then leans her head against the side of the bath and sobs.

After a while she goes back to Instagram and hesitates on the search bar.

Nobody will know.

She types in her sister's name, then clicks and looks at her bio.

Hannah Starling. East London. Photos of dogs, nieces, skincare. #IVFWarrior.

Lauren swallows. They used to text all the time. Lauren scrutinized every single negative pregnancy test Hannah sent a photo of, sometimes filtering them through apps to make them clearer. She has had two failed cycles of IVF. She and Conrad were on their third when Lauren left. They'd spent all their savings on that and private fertility consultants. She'd cried about it a few months back, in Lauren's kitchen. 'Fucking twenty thousand pounds,' Hannah had said.

'That's a lot of sheet masks,' Lauren had said with a wry smile, hoping it was the right thing to say, that the joke wouldn't sink.

Luckily, Hannah had smiled back.

'How many more goes have you got?' Lauren said.

'Just this one, but . . . you know. We said we'd only do two, then three. Who knows?'

Her sister – younger, by three years – is almost forty. They hadn't started trying until she was thirty-five. They'd been ambivalent. Conrad worked long hours in the City. Hannah worked at a jeweller's. They'd had four holidays a year. Easy lives. But then they'd got a puppy, and Lauren had thought: *it won't be long.* Sure enough, the folic acid supplements appeared on Hannah's immaculate kitchen counter. But then one year became two, and then she started taking Clomid – 'It makes me fucking mad!' Hannah had said – and then the IVF had begun. They really wanted it by then. 'I don't *just* want a baby,' Hannah had said passionately one night during the interval at a comedy evening. Lauren had strained to hear her over the chatter. They should never go out to things, she had thought privately. They liked to chat, a thousand words a minute: they should stay in and do just that. 'I want to be a *mother* myself,' Hannah had said. She'd grinned, then, her gap-toothed smile making a rare appearance, but it wasn't a nice grin. It was one of disbelief. That she had articulated so perfectly what she wanted – something she didn't even know herself to be true until she had said it, there in a blue-lit comedy club in Soho – and the universe still would not give it to her.

She scrolls through Hannah's feed now, even though she's seen it all. A waiting room. Lauren knows exactly which one it is, the Nuffield in Chiswick. *Two weeks before #transferday health check*, Hannah has written.

Nothing since.

The next day, Lauren sees the red lanyard around the man's neck through the glass and immediately opens the door. Outside smells of wood smoke; a specific, ashy sort of smell that reminds her of a winter break she once took with her mother and Zara to the Cotswolds. It was six months before she would meet Aidan. She'd walked next to her mother in awkward silence and wondered when she'd find her place in the world.

She looks at the man with the utility company's name emblazoned on his lanyard standing outside her door. 'You're a repairman?' she says hopefully. She abandoned her phone call about the boiler. The protection service must have sent him.

'That's me,' he says, after a beat. He's wearing big boots, and is tall and broad, with hair that is neither brown nor blond but some nondescript shade in the middle. He blocks out the weak winter sunlight momentarily as he moves in through the doorway.

'In here,' Lauren says to him, leading him through to the kitchen.

'Great,' he says. 'Kitchen taps, is it?'

The briefest of shivers travels up Lauren's spine. Shouldn't he know the problem? Her eyes scan to the lanyard. *Utility Co.* Is that who the protection service have sent? Are they legitimate? Her mind races. The man stares at her, eyebrows raised, expectant. He's about twenty-five. He could easily be a football fan. What has she done?

'It's the boiler . . . the hot water runs out,' she says, her eyes frantically scanning him for tools, any evidence he is who he says he is. Maybe he misunderstood what he was told. Hot water running out. Taps. An easy mistake to make.

'I'll . . . I need to make a call. You okay here?' she says.

'Oh, wait – I need to ask you some things first,' he says, gesturing to the boiler.

Panic fills Lauren's body. She's not normally like this. But she's so vulnerable here, alone, being kept away from an amorphous mass of strangers. She stares up at the man. Say if he pulls a weapon out of his coat, right now? Or he fixes the boiler, and disappears, but then Jon confirms they didn't send anybody over, and Lauren and Zara are moved, a man having cased the joint, ready to bring the group back to harm her daughter . . .

'I can't,' she says. She turns and flees the house, leaving the front door standing open, and calls Jon on the driveway.

'Did you send a man over to repair the boiler?' she says. 'But I like your vigilance.'

'Yes,' he replies.

Lauren seems to deflate, right there on the drive. 'Oh, you didn't say.'

'Sorry – thought it was self-explanatory,' he says. 'But I like your vigilance.'

'Right.' Lauren looks back at the house from the driveway, a hand to her forehead, taking in the confused man inside the kitchen, the way the sunlight catches the window, thinking: *another bullet dodged*. But how long can they keep dodging them for?

28

Poppy

Battersea, London

One week gone

Poppy is on a school trip to the National Portrait Gallery. Unlike other trips – to visit old coal mines, or to see musicals she doesn't care about – Poppy has been looking forward to this. It is early, half past nine, and she is in the Rubens section. She'd never heard of him, but she is looking at his Baroque paintings, alone, away from her friends. They're going to be studying them after Christmas. She's excited about them because they're almost all portraits, and she loves the clothes they wear. Total vintage gear. A portrait at the end of the room catches her eye. She sits on a bench and stares up at it.

It's a nude. No clothes, but that fascinates Poppy more, not less, today. The skin is pale, the colour of off-milk. The breasts are uneven, one nipple pointing slightly to the left. There are three little rolls of fat running down her side. Her stomach is a dome, rounded out like a fruit bowl. Poppy is fascinated. The nude woman in front of her does not look like somebody off *Love Island*, or Instagram, and Poppy can't stop staring. Not because of the imperfections, exactly, but because it is a body. A body that does what it is supposed to. A body that can walk, and run, and climb, and sleep when it is supposed to. Her mother's body looks like this one, right in front of her, but it isn't healthy. Poppy swears to herself, right there in the National Portrait Gallery, that so long as she stays healthy, she will never take it for granted, never complain about cellulite or uneven teeth or grey hairs. Never.

'Pops,' a voice says, and Poppy turns.

It's Emily. She has a clipboard in hand, a half-finished sketch on it. 'Wow.' She looks at the painting. 'Send nudes.'

A laugh escapes from Poppy's mouth.

'Look,' Emily whispers. 'I just spoke to Ryan. His cousin goes to your sister's school.'

Poppy and Emily move away from the handful of people in the room with them. The carpet muffles their steps.

'Right?'

'It's all over there, you know?'

Poppy looks furtively around them. Suddenly, it seems ludicrous to be here, talking seriously, surrounded by boobs and bums. 'What – Girl A?' she says in a low voice.

'Yep. The school's issued an email to stop people speculating that Zara was Girl A.'

'Jesus. If they . . .' Poppy looks down at her hands. 'If they talk about Zara too much, the group could find out a lot about her, couldn't they?'

'Don't worry,' Emily says.

'It's like trying to stop an earthquake, isn't it?' Poppy says in the dim, quiet sanctuary of the gallery.

'I know,' Emily says. 'I know.'

Emily sits down and Poppy leans her head on her shoulder, the way she wishes she could do with her mother. She's tried to ask her mum so many times how worried she should be about Zara, but she just can't do it to her. She'd ask, and her mum would worry and – like clockwork – three days later, her health would fail. And whatever that relapse was, it would have Poppy's name on it. Poppy read online once that there are only a finite number of relapses in front of them before . . .

'It'll be okay,' Emily says, brushing Poppy's hair back from her face.

Poppy cries again. She doesn't have to hold it all in here, with her friend. She finds the emotion comes out truthfully. It's not anger or frustration or slamming the dishwasher shut because, once again, the housework has taken over her evening. It is just what she feels. Sadness. Sadness and guilt at not going. And hopelessness, too. Like, if she could find a way to put it right, she would. But she can't. She just can't figure it out.

As they turn to leave, a tall man, not unlike the one outside her school, emerges from behind a statue, then walks away, too. For just a second, Poppy is sure he has been eavesdropping.

29

Aidan

Aidan hears the noise of the Telegram app while he is brushing his teeth. The burner phone is on the side of the sink. It keeps sliding slowly off the ceramic, but he doesn't want to be parted from it, in case she rings, in case she needs him.

The message is from somebody who calls himself *Dr NoGood*. His profile photo is a man in a balaclava.

How're the scrapers going @James Thomas? he's written.

All up and running, Aidan lies. He scrolls up. There's a little notification in the group.

Goodbye Mr X has left the group, it says, at 4.00 a.m.

Aidan stares at it, then navigates to his profile on Telegram. It's blank. Why would he leave? Could he ask?

Kevin has answered him in the group. *Great – we know the mother is a nursery worker.*

Aidan types back. *Where has Goodbye Mr X gone?* he says.

Aidan sits on the side of the bath, waiting, his toes in the soft bath mat. The windowsill is littered with Lauren's old bathtime candles. Winter spice. Walk in the Woods.

Home Baking. He reaches out to touch one of them, lifting it to his nose to smell.

He wasn't in line with the ethos of the group, Kevin writes after a few moments. *Wasn't willing to go the whole hog. Promised things he didn't deliver.*

Sorry to hear that, Aidan writes. He thinks, his brain whirring.

Hopefully the arm teaches him a lesson.

The arm? Aidan asks.

He's got a bit of a bad arm now ;-).

Aidan's heart is in his feet. Concentrate. Don't get frightened.

Okay, Aidan writes. *Well, I'll start pulling all newly hired nursery nurses off the internet for you to review.*

Shit. He tries to rationalize his thoughts, still sitting on the side of the bath. Lauren used to sit in this exact spot while the bath ran.

Another message appears on the Telegram group from Brian.

Making a list of Zara's acquaintances. Got a mind map going. Can your scrapers monitor them to see if she gets in touch with anybody left behind? Also, both the mother and Girl A were members of a load of golden retriever Facebook groups, so can you comb those too for new likes?

Sure, Aidan lies.

I've got all my friends looking. Friends of friends. Been circulating her photo. We have Omar reviewing CCTV too – some CCTV has facial recognition. We'll get there. My boy deserves the best efforts. Who agrees?? Brian writes. Then adds: *We were going to be rich.*

Aidan stares at the phone. So that's what it's about.

Money. No wonder. No wonder he is intent on justice. He feels he has nothing left to lose. He's hard because he is at rock bottom.

Three people reply positively.

Anyone else?

Definitely, Aidan writes. *Girl A deserves to pay.*

Jesus. He can't take knowing this. That they're closing in. That they're violent. But it's worth it. This heartache, this hyper-vigilance. This collecting of information. All this thinking. To keep them safe.

His family.

The next morning, his phone rings with a withheld number. He immediately thinks of Kevin, of mysterious injuries, people whipped into line.

He answers, and is surprised to find Lottie the police officer on the end of the line.

'I wanted to update you and see how you're getting on,' she says. 'Check you're being sensible.'

Aidan can't help but smile at that.

'As you know, the Facebook group has been made private. So we've lost our eye through the spyhole,' she says.

Aidan pauses for just a second. 'They've taken it on to Telegram,' he says.

Lottie pauses – shocked, Aidan guesses. 'Right.' He can hear a smile in her voice.

'So I've joined it,' he adds.

'I see,' Lottie says, but Aidan hears: *I see who I am dealing with here.* She exhales slowly. A staticky noise fills the line. 'Okay,' she says. 'I don't have to tell you how risky that is.'

'You don't. But won't it be useful?'

'Yes . . .' Lottie pauses. 'Yes, it will.'

'Right, do you need to go and report this now? Fill in a risk assessment form?' Aidan says.

'No,' Lottie says, but she says it thoughtfully. 'You know, Aidan, there are people here who would do that, one hundred per cent,' she says. 'You're not wrong. But I'm not one of them.'

'Why?'

He imagines her shrugging and thinking. She's closer to Poppy's age than his. He's surprised she didn't say *hundy-p.*

'I believe in a different way of policing,' she says eventually.

'Yeah?'

'Yeah,' she says, without elaborating.

'What would you do? In my shoes?'

Lottie pauses again, and Aidan waits. 'I would do what you're doing,' she says finally. 'Because of my twins.'

'Would you have – before?'

'I don't remember what my brain was like before them,' she says honestly, which Aidan appreciates.

Parenthood changes you so completely. Aidan can't remember what he even used to do. 'Good. If you went after Brian – the leader – now, what would you charge him with?'

Lottie utters a thoughtful *mmm.* 'Maybe something under malicious communications,' she says.

'What would you need in order to arrest them for more?'

Lottie is silent. Aidan waits.

'Not for this homeless person stuff,' she says.

'No,' Aidan says, knowing whatever Zara knows is a lost cause.

'If you wanted – hypothetically – for them to be arrested and convicted, you're looking for the offence of conspiracy,' Lottie says eventually, her voice low. 'Two or more people agreeing to carry out a crime. Their crime being, by the sounds of it, murder or grievous bodily harm.'

'Right.'

'They would need to have reached an agreement to commit that offence. And you would need to have evidence of that. Together with their identities.'

Would. Those *woulds*. Making something real sound hypothetical. *She could never advise him to do that*. Become an informant. A spy.

'Somebody intimated that they injured somebody else in the group who wasn't complying,' Aidan says.

'Who?'

Aidan thinks of the message he sent, asking where Goodbye Mr X went. He can't send the police round now. He just can't. They'd know there was a mole in the group. 'I . . . I can't say,' he says. He can only double-cross them once. When absolutely everything is lined up for them to get arrested and go to prison.

Lottie is silent in response. 'Okay,' she says, with a sigh. 'Yes, I see. Right,' she says. 'You'll continue to monitor the Telegram group for evidence of conspiracy?'

'Yes.'

'Talk of weapons, dates, and so on. Firm plans.'

'Okay,' he says.

'Send everything you have to me.'

'Great.'

'And I'll be ready to act, here, when you have enough.'

'Will you have to disclose it to someone there?' he says.

'Don't worry about that,' she says.

The weight on his chest is lifted by her tacit agreement to help him. There's two of them now. The burden is shared. Their own conspiracy.

'What if I got them to meet in one place? Like a sort of . . . I don't know. A formal strategy meeting. And I made sure they would have their burner phones there, with all the evidence on them.'

'Yes . . .'

'Would that be enough? For you to arrest them for conspiracy?'

'Yes. If they had the phones with the Telegram app on them,' she confirms.

Aidan's heart seems to sing. His Gen-Z police officer, on his side, willing to break the rules and let him infiltrate encrypted groups. 'Okay,' he says, thinking. He's sure he can engineer that. He thinks, next, of the scrapers. Of his wife and stepchild, vulnerable, waiting to be found. He needs to end this. And soon. He's running out of time. 'If I get you a date of that meeting, would that be . . . would you act on that information? Would you be there?'

'If you have a date and time where you know they will be . . . we can arrange ourselves for then, too.'

'Thank you. Will you . . . will it just be you?'

'It's in hand here. You don't need to worry. I'll alert the team when the time is right.'

'I'll suggest a few weeks' time,' Aidan says. That'll be

enough time to collect the evidence, but not enough time for them to find Lauren and Zara. He hopes. 'Before Christmas? Maybe?'

'Okay then,' Lottie says. 'Let me know when you've set the meeting up. And when you feel able, do send us what you have.'

Aidan thanks her before hanging up, feeling hopeful for the first time in weeks.

Buzzing, he opens up the message thread to Mal.

Don't you want to #FindGirlA? Aidan writes, then closes it.

He will see what Mal says to that. Next, Aidan opens the Telegram app and scrolls up. He will just screenshot everything. His fingers are poised to do it, but then he stops. His cheeks heat up and he races over to his computer. *Of course, of course,* he thinks, as he googles Telegram app screenshots.

Telegram monitors screenshots depending on the settings of the group. If the group is set to secret, it will prohibit screenshots or tell the members of the group that a user has taken a screenshot (and name the user).

Aidan puffs air into his cheeks. He has dodged a bullet. Sweat blooms across his forehead.

He gets his usual phone out and begins taking photographs of the screen of his burner phone. He sends them to the burner phone and saves them in a file called 'evidence'.

30

Zara

Millfield School, the Lake District

One week gone

Zara's smile is fixed as Phoebe takes the selfie. She tries to make it seem more natural, to smile how Poppy does, both rows of teeth on show, but she looks ridiculous, rigid, instead. Despite her brush-off, Phoebe has latched firmly on. Zara is glad of it, in a way. It's nice to have an ally, even a fake one.

They are on their way back from school. Nothing special, but her mind is racing. It always is. She checks the witness protection list of rules every morning and still she can't remember them all. No, that's not quite true. It isn't that she can't remember them. It is that she requires clarity. What does 'no contact with anyone with whom you were previously affiliated' really mean? What is contact? Is looking at a photograph okay? And what does 'you must strictly adhere to the background information provided to you regarding your identity' mean? A girl called Sienna from Bristol is a different person to Zara from London. She just *is*.

'Am tagging you,' Phoebe says. She shows the phone to Zara as she types *Sienna Smith* into the search bar.

'That one,' Zara says, pointing to the third name down. *SiennaSmith99*.

'Your initials are SS,' Phoebe says, with a dimpled smile. 'How cool.'

So they are, thinks Zara, for the first time. And then she thinks. And thinks again. *Social media, but no selfies.* It's listed in the witness protection rule sheet.

'Wait, actually, I look awful in that,' Zara says. She grabs Phoebe's phone from her. 'Let me delete it and take a nice one of you.' She gestures vaguely to the roadside. 'Stand there.'

Phoebe blinks, surprised, then smiles for the photo. She takes the phone back and looks at it. 'No, you look lovely,' she says. 'I'll put both up.'

'No,' Zara says. 'No. I don't want you to.'

'Oh. Okay.' Phoebe says. She widens her eyes as she looks down at her phone. 'Sure.'

Zara stares into the distance. She hates this. She hates the lies, the constructed, fake personality. She's not vain. The selfie *is* nice.

Phoebe is so much cooler than Zara. Her hair is not straight or curly. It's unruly, but it looks good, tucked behind her ears like that. The sort of mess Zara is afraid to make. Sometimes, Zara wishes she could let her hair down, and set herself free. Wear odd socks and zany clothes and stop giving so much of a shit what everybody thinks.

They start walking home.

'I've followed you, even if you won't let me put your photo up!' Phoebe says. 'You have five hundred followers – wow! But no posts?'

'Oh,' Zara says, biting her lip. She reaches for her phone and looks. 'Must be bots,' she says. Bots organized by the protection service. Bots arranged to follow her in order to legitimize her profile. She hopes it's that. Rather than . . . anything sinister. The group members. The people who know she knows about the motto. The people who know what she might do about that.

'I deleted all my posts. I wanted a digital purge, you know?' Zara says, though she would never care about such a thing. Or would she? She doesn't know any more. Who is she? Sienna, or Zara? Panic rises up through her.

'You have to like the photo of me,' Phoebe says as they round a corner. There are mountains up ahead of them, a backdrop that hardly shifts, no matter how far they walk. The sky is a darkening royal blue, the mountains beige and grey. Zara can't stop looking at them. Her legs ache from the undulating hill roads she has to walk to school on.

'It's the algorithm,' Phoebe says. 'More people see it if it gets lots of likes in those first few minutes.'

'Sure,' Zara says as she looks down and watches their feet walk in perfect sync along the road together. Imagine wanting more people to find you, and not fewer?

'I think I like it here,' Phoebe says.

Zara feels so bitter, suddenly, next to her contemporary who wants Instagram likes and who has never seen somebody be murdered. 'Great,' she says.

'Do you?'

No, Zara screams internally. *I miss absolutely everything. I miss bookshops with late-night openings and being able to buy stationery at eight o'clock on a Saturday night.*

'I don't really think about that stuff,' Zara says with a shrug. She stares at the mountains, still in sunlight, though they are in the encroaching dusk. She lets a sigh out, and allows her true feelings to pass. It's for the best. It *is*. Phoebe says goodbye to her as her mother arrives in a Volvo and waves to Zara through the window. As Phoebe gets in, she hears her say 'sleepover at the weekend' to her mother. Phoebe closes the door behind her, and the rest of the sentence is lost. But then Phoebe opens the door again, to dislodge a seat belt, and she hears the rest of it.

'Not your new friend Sienna?'

'No,' Phoebe says, fiddling with a seat belt that's become stuck in the door. 'She's a total ice queen.'

Later, lying on her bed, trying to concentrate on a boring geography textbook on globalization, Zara gets a text from Phoebe.

You didn't like the photo!

Zara rolls on to her stomach, dropping the book on the floor, and opens Instagram.

Ice queen. Zara has been called many things that are mean but correct – nerdy, overly earnest, awkward – but never, ever, ever an ice queen.

She finds the photo and scrutinizes Phoebe. All that hair. She's gorgeous. She presses 'like', then looks to see who else has. Names and names, nobody she knows. People from Phoebe's old school, she guesses. Forty-one likes. Zara would get none from anybody real.

She stares at the geography textbook on the floor next to her bed and wishes school taught other things. How to report a crime. How to stem a wound. How to liaise with the police . . . and the rest.

She reaches down for the herbal tea she made herself after school. It's camomile. Nice stuff. Her mum is forever trying to treat her — 'Nice things are the backbone of life,' she will say — and she cradles it between her hands, lying on her front, the phone on the bed next to her. She holds the mug with one hand and types with the other. Nobody will ever know, she reasons, thinking of the rule sheet. She can just take a look. It's harmless.

She types Hannah's handle into Instagram and watches it populate. She's updated her Instagram stories, but Zara can't watch those: it tells the user the viewers' usernames.

She looks at the latest photograph, taken in a waiting room, and pinches to zoom in on it. As she does, her mug wobbles on the bed. She reaches out to grab it, in haste, and double taps the photo. She puts the mug back down on the floor and stares in horror. She double taps again, to undo the 'like'. Her upper lip is sweating. Will Hannah be told?

Zara sits up, hands shaking. And there's nobody she can ask. No well-meaning friend to whom she can say, 'Hey, would you mind just letting me know if Instagram tells you something, if I go and like and unlike your photo?'

It's not like she can ask her mother. It would be another thing she has done wrong. Another disaster in a whole line of them.

31

Aidan

Shepherd's Bush, London

One week gone

It's three o'clock in the morning when Aidan wakes. 3.02 a.m. precisely. He's woken at this time since Lauren left. He can predict the time before he has even opened his eyes.

Bill is sleeping on Lauren's side of the bed. 'This is a sham marriage,' Aidan says to him.

The dog opens his eyes sleepily, then huffs, his jowls quivering.

He gets up, just like the NHS website says to do if you're suffering from insomnia, and sits at his computer, staring out at the street below. They're opposite a twenty-four-hour shop in Shepherd's Bush. It has a yellow sign. *Food and Booze*. Did Lauren ever shop there?

He wiggles the mouse and his computer wakes up.

He's going to provide the group with fake information.

He types *private investigators, skip tracing* into Google. He clicks an article entitled *Finding People Who've Skipped Town*. He just needs to be one step ahead of them, is all. His eyes blur as he reads it.

1. Reverse image searching – scan the photograph of them to search for similar images.
2. Social media research – have they contacted anyone from the past?
3. Put up a fake job advertisement they would be interested in and see if anybody applies.
4. Monitor any niche or specific hobbies they had, Facebook groups, etc.
5. Good old word of mouth, especially if a photograph of their old identity is in their possession. Unless they never leave their house, somebody will find them. Eventually.

If you need any assistance with skip tracing, do call us on . . .

He closes the website down and starts his scraper but, instead of an image of Lauren, he uses a stock image of a blonde woman. Similar enough to yield results that the group will chase up.

Next, he messages the group.

What's the plan, when we find her? He says.

He's trying to elicit 'a conspiracy to harm' for Lottie.

What do you think? Kevin writes back now.

The defendant's father, also awake in the middle of the night. For different reasons to Aidan, but similar, too.

Are we prepared? Aidan writes. *Do we need weapons?*

Leave that to me, Kevin says.

Aidan stares at it for a while. It's almost enough. Almost.

But look at this, Kevin types.

A photo appears. It's Luke, a younger Luke, in the

Holloway blue and yellow. Neat football socks pulled up over his shins. Muscle definition in his arms, across his chest, visible even underneath the kit. Pink cheeks. The world ahead of him: that is what Kevin is trying to say.

Lies ruined this for us, he says.

Too fucking right, Dr NoGood writes back. *I'm angry all over again.*

Aidan looks at the messages for a second. Is it about justice for his kid, or is it about protecting himself from a prosecution? Both, Aidan thinks sadly. The duality of parenthood. Aidan's actions aren't solely in protection of Zara, after all. He wants his wife back. For himself.

He goes back to bed and, as sleep comes for him, the neuroses of the day seem to fall away. The hyper-vigilance, the information gathering, keeping all the plates spinning. And he's left with what he's avoiding: loneliness. A loneliness so potent it feels like a physical pain, deep in his stomach. He rolls on to his side and draws his knees up to his chest and clutches them, letting the sobs out. Tears fall sideways, running across the bridge of his nose and into his ears, and still more come. Stupid sobs. They sound wrong, coming from a man. Deep, husky shrieks of pain.

He misses her, he misses her, he misses her. He found her so late in life, and he's lost her so fast.

Bill rolls over and huffs a warm jet of air into Aidan's ear. He reaches behind him to stroke Bill's ears, and they fall asleep like that, together. A man and the dog that belongs to the woman he loves.

32

Lauren

Coniston, the Lake District

One week gone

'And that's it, now just ease the car into third,' Lauren's driving instructor, Janey, says. She's not at all like how Lauren thought she might be. She's tall, blonde, glamorous in a sort of undone way, and has a ring on each finger, including her thumbs.

'It won't go into third,' Lauren says, wrenching the clutch.

The car lurches forward, a jack rabbit jump, and Janey uses her brake.

'Okay, let's start again, in first gear,' she says nicely.

Lauren knows the protection service arranged these lessons, knows this instructor has been checked, and yet, she is still tense and terrified, alone in a car with a stranger.

There are tears in Lauren's throat. She tries to swallow them down. Restart the engine, okay, now clutch down . . . she pulls away.

'And now second gear,' Janey says.

Lauren slides the gear stick down.

'And now – slowly – up to third as we pick up speed,' Janey says.

'I'm pretty sure this car doesn't have a third gear,' Lauren says, with a strained laugh. 'It won't go in!'

'It will,' Janey says.

Lauren looks out in front of them at the Lake District rain, the grey stone buildings. Two men are standing at the bottom of the street, and, of course, it crosses Lauren's mind that they might want to kill her daughter. She stalls the car.

'Everything okay?' Janey says.

'Just need to get used to driving, I guess,' Lauren says.

'Maybe somebody could take you out for extra practice,' Janey says.

'Maybe,' Lauren echoes. Her loneliness may as well have come and sat in the car between them. Somebody to take her out for extra lessons. A small favour, half an hour, an hour. But she has nobody who could do it. Not a single person. No relatives. No friends. No Facebook acquaintances. No colleagues she can call on.

'I'm a rubbish driver,' Lauren says, and the tears that are constantly threatening behind her eyes spill over. 'God, sorry.'

'Learning to drive brings everyone down to the same level,' Janey says sympathetically. 'I've seen the full range of emotions in this car. But you *will* get there. Everyone does.'

'I can't even change gear!'

'You can,' Janey says.

'Sorry,' Lauren says again, rubbing at her nose. 'Been a tough week.'

'Yeah?' Janey says.

There is something confessional about a quiet car in the late afternoon in the winter. The heating is on. The headlights make the frost sparkle. And here is a stranger, next to her, who could become a friend.

'Yeah,' Lauren says. 'I . . .' And then the hands of the protection service grab her, and pull her back, back out of danger. 'I mean, I . . . had a bad bereavement,' she lies.

'Oh, I'm so sorry to hear that,' Janey says, her cheeks reddening.

Lauren sighs and looks out of the window, the silence feeling too loaded to interrupt. The truth is, the advice for the bereaved doesn't apply when the person you're grieving is yourself.

God, she wants to shop. She wants to go home and buy something ostentatious. A gingerbread house for Christmas. A stack of hotel fluffy towels that cost £50 each. She stares into the distance as she fantasizes.

'Look, let's stop for today,' Janey says kindly. 'Your friend booked the crash course, didn't he?'

'Oh, yes,' Lauren says, thinking that Jon is no friend of hers.

'So let me give you my number so you can come direct – if you have any problems, or need to reschedule.' Janey gestures and Lauren passes her phone over. Janey navigates to the contacts.

And that's when it happens. Just a flash, a blink, something flitting across Janey's expression as she sees the contacts list. Jon. Sienna. And nobody else. Utterly empty.

'New phone,' Lauren says pathetically.

'Sure,' Janey says.

*

226

Jon pays them a cursory visit that evening. Lauren hides the burner phone in the back of the wardrobe. She almost laughs as she does it. As if he is going to strip search her, go through her handbag. Hardly. He asks them a handful of questions about how they're getting on before he stands up to leave.

At the door, Lauren says to him, 'Do most people find it as hard as I am?'

In the November air, she draws her cardigan more tightly around her waist.

Jon motions outside, and she grabs a coat, follows him and closes the door behind them. His shoes crunch on the gravel driveway as he steps back. They are alone, together, his car keys in his hand, his dinner likely waiting on a table somewhere, wherever he comes from. His breath smokes the air as he exhales.

'It's an upheaval,' he says. 'All change is tough. Would you say you're coping – or wanting to do things that would jeopardize you?'

Lauren's body fizzes in the cold air. She so wants to tell him about the burner phone, suddenly, in the manner of a child confessing to their parent. Attention seeking, rebelling. This is how badly I am coping, she would say, leading him upstairs and showing him the cheap, untraceable flip phone. But she won't. She's starting her job at the nursery tomorrow. She's got to keep it together.

'I can't imagine,' Jon says. He nods to her. 'Let's go round the block.' He pockets his car keys and sets off towards the left. It must be safe, mustn't it, to head out into the night, to leave Zara inside, if he, an ex-cop, thinks so? She falls into step beside him, torn between wanting to confide in him, wanting him to hold her unhappiness outside of her for a while, and wanting to distance herself and her secrets.

'I'm scared all the time,' she says to him, in the end. She'll confide, she'll cry, he'll console her, but she won't tell him about the phone. Intimacy is easy for Lauren. Secrets pour from her like a river that's burst its banks. Indiscriminate sharing. Everyone gets the same thing. Ray next door knows as much about her life as her closest friends. 'That I'll make a mistake.'

'But if you live it, you'll get used to it,' Jon says.

Jon is one of those people whose message never changes, no matter the different tactics somebody like Lauren tries. He is never going to tell her she can go back to London, or that one slip-up won't hurt. Lauren bends, but he doesn't yield.

'Maybe.'

'Definitely,' he says.

They walk past a row of cottages. Inside the first, a woman is serving what looks like soup. Steaming bowls held in oven gloves. Lauren's heart wrenches as she stares in. Lit-up windows always remind her of Christmas.

They take a Christmas Eve walk each year. Nothing special. Four o'clock, or thereabouts, around Islington, when it's just getting dark. It's usually frosty underfoot. Every house has its windows lit up, a miniature play taking place inside each one. Christmas trees. Dogs on sofas. Stacks of presents sometimes visible, people opening ovens, couples on sofas with their legs tangled up. One time, they looked into somebody's dining room and saw a whole row of friends and family lining up holding paper plates, taking food from a buffet. Lauren had cried with the magic of it, and Aidan had laughed at her.

'I'll look back on this and laugh,' Lauren says to Jon, though she knows it isn't true. It's beyond farce.

Jon says nothing, unyielding again.

'You know the most damaging thing to witness protection?' he says.

'What?'

'A lack of commitment.' He puts his hands into his pockets.

The air is cold on Lauren's bare neck.

'If you're half in, half out, you won't last.'

'Why?'

'Because you can't begin over again if you're not willing to start,' he says simply.

Lauren stares into the next house – an empty living room with a football match on the television – and speaks without thinking. 'Aidan wanted me to agree to two years,' she says quietly.

Jon sighs, a small, sad sigh. 'I see.'

'Yeah.' She shouldn't have said it. She regrets it immediately. She hopes she hasn't got him in trouble. When will she learn?

'I looked after this bloke, once. In protection because he whistle-blew on his gang. He went home for his mother's funeral, just that one event, and got murdered. They knew he'd go back. *I* knew he'd go back, and told him not to. But he did it anyway. And now it's all over for him.'

'That's so sad,' Lauren says. 'It's all so unfair. We didn't do anything. I didn't join a gang. She –' Lauren deliberately disguises Zara's name, as natural to her now as looking before she crosses the road, '– just witnessed something.'

'I know,' Jon says.

They round a corner and the mountains pop up, a consistent, benevolent backdrop to Lauren's stagnant misery.

'She was in the wrong place, wrong time,' Lauren says, though she knows it is more complicated than that.

The air smells of burning wood, of real fires. Chimneys on nearby houses puff out smoke into the night. Her mind scans back over what Jon said earlier. Something isn't sitting right, but she can't put her finger on what.

'Look,' Jon says, gesturing in front of him. 'This is the hand that you have been dealt. So you can either cling on to the past – or move on. Trust me when I say one will make you happier than the other.'

'Yeah,' Lauren says.

'Give it a shot, really,' he says. 'Any connections. Sever them.'

Lauren realizes as they turn the corner and her house looms back into view that this conversation is off the record.

As they arrive back at his car, he turns to her. 'My sister died,' he says. 'Five years ago. I remember it – it felt like I had woken up in a totally new world. But you . . . eventually, I had to move on. So, this is just to say . . . I shouldn't divulge personal stuff. But I want to. To let you know that I do understand.'

Lauren takes this nugget of Jon's truth – and empathy – and holds it close to her.

He nods as she reaches her front door. Her security light pops on.

'Thank you for telling me,' she says.

'But I mean,' he says softly, as she turns to open the door, 'Sacha would've given anything to be alive. Even living like this,' he says, gesturing up to the house.

He turns to leave, pressing a button on his keys, which flashes his car's headlights. They light up the road amber, two quick blinks. *If you're half in, half out, you won't last.* That's the thing that wasn't sitting right with her. What does he mean? That she won't be happy? Or . . . worse? But it's too late to ask – he's in his car now, easing it slowly off her driveway.

As he leaves, Lauren watches, thinking. And that's when she sees it, lit up by her security light. It's tucked away slightly, on the parcel shelf, but it's clear. A sports shirt. A football shirt. She might be mistaken, but she is sure the colours match Holloway FC.

Lauren closes the front door in a panic. What if Jon isn't who he says he is? Has she ever seen anybody else from the protection service? What if he isn't the protection service?

Her entire body is covered in sweat. This can't be happening. This can't be real. She needs help. From Aidan. Maybe she's gone mad.

She goes into the downstairs toilet and closes the door, then looks at herself in the mirror. Her hair is snarled, her face off-white and clammy-looking.

She sits on the toilet lid. She needs to think this through.

No. Nazir put her in touch with Jon. And Nazir is the police. Jon *is* who he says he is. He must be.

He's had multiple opportunities alone with them. And he hasn't done anything.

The football shirt is a coincidence. Or she was seeing things. She tries to anchor herself to this logic, but she can't. She can't stop seeing that kit. Blue and canary yellow.

She lets herself out of the toilet and breathes. She will watch and wait. That's what she'll do. And not be alone with him again.

One of the houses next door has become occupied, and Lauren jumps as the bang of their front door wakes her from sleep.

She lies in bed, thinking of Jon. She rolls over on to her side. She feels calmer now she has some distance from it. It was just a football shirt. She was mad earlier. A woman who has begun to mistrust everyone, even the police.

The night hours creep by heavily, like a slow-moving black river. When she dozes, she dreams of angry football fans. When she wakes, she thinks of the shirt again, going back and forth over what it could mean.

She googles how many kits have those colours on her phone. Somebody has asked that exact question on a site called Quora. She wonders why they were asking. Not for the same reasons as her, surely. The answer is four. Four clubs have those colours. So the risk that he is a Holloway fan is one in four.

She wouldn't bet money on those odds. Or her life.

*

It's Lauren's first day of work, and it's a dream that does it. The dream, the colleague, the drink and the boiler.

It is cold when she wakes again in the morning, this time after only an hour's sleep. That is the first thing she notices. A draught in the duvet. It's colder in the Lake District. Gales seem to blow between the hills: no skyscrapers, no buildings, no concrete to buffer them. A blue air vent in the very top of the bedroom kept her awake all night, flapping. She's not tall enough to reach it. She'll get a chair from downstairs and try to tape over it. She needs to buy tape. She needs to buy scissors. She rolls over in frustration. There is so much admin involved in building a life.

She dreamt about sex. That's all. Simple, messy, beautiful sex with Aidan. He had been kneeling up in bed, she braced against his thighs. She doesn't remember much except an unnameable but specific feeling that seems to wash over her, the waves getting weaker and weaker the more she tries to recall it, until she feels completely alone again. The ghost of Aidan visited her in the night, but now he's gone. It's a fiction. A neurological spark born out of missing him, of sleeping on one side of the bed, her body still expecting him to fill the other.

Zara is in the bathroom. The extractor fan hums, the light a thick orange stripe underneath the door. She emerges in a fog of shower steam, glances at Lauren, then walks past her without saying anything, rolling her eyes as she goes past.

'Sorry?' Lauren says to Zara.

'What?' Zara says, still walking, not turning around.

Something about it – the morning routine, Zara's

tiresome teenage body language – sparks anger in Lauren. She can't do it. She just cannot do it. Another miserable fucking day in witness protection. Another day spent jumping at all the noises the house makes. And now, too, spent questioning whether the person charged with keeping them safe is even on their side. Another day of bearing it all on her shoulders, alone.

'All okay?' Lauren says through gritted teeth.

'Fine,' Zara says shortly, closing the door behind her.

Lauren goes in after her. 'What's up?' she says, bewildered. Zara's room is immaculate. The bed made perfectly, a white fluffy throw along the end of it, a splayed novel – *The Hate U Give* – on her pillow.

'What's up?' Zara says. 'Oh, my whole life's over?' She smells squeaky clean, hot and soapy. Something about it is nostalgic to Lauren.

Lauren's jaw sets, then she nods. Of course. Of course. But that isn't Lauren's fault. In fact, a small voice speaks up inside Lauren, it's Zara's fault.

'Can you leave now?' Zara says, her eyes looking just past Lauren to the door.

Lauren looks at her daughter's angular shoulders, at the tiny pinch of fat appearing over the towel held tightly around her. Her caramel-coloured skin.

'Quickly?' Zara says.

Lauren says nothing in response. Her daughter has very rarely spoken to her like this. Rude, aggressive. No, the worst is that it is dismissive. As though Lauren doesn't matter at all. Happy first day at work for her, she thinks bitterly.

She leaves without saying goodbye, even though she

knows that is childish. She stands and waits for the bus in the cold, dense cloud. It arrives twenty-five minutes late and takes cash only, which she has to dig around in her bag to get. It isn't a London bus. No vibrancy. Just a few tired old silent commuters. No phones playing music. No teenagers who look like they need a mother, all low-slung jeans and attitude.

The first morning passes slowly in a fug of loneliness and the unfamiliarity with the nursery systems. She eats lunch alone, taking exactly the sixty minutes' allotted break, and thinks about Jon. *Let's say he is a Holloway fan*, she thinks, while eating a cheese sandwich that's still cold from the fridge. Why wouldn't he have harmed them yet? And how would a football fan have secured fake passports? It's just not possible.

God, she wants a friend. Somebody to discuss this stuff with.

'I'm being mad, just tell me I'm being mad,' she would say to a girlfriend.

'Totally,' the friend would say.

She loses herself in the children in the afternoon. She's in charge of the babies. Her favourites. Six months up. Fat bottoms rounded with nappies. Gummy smiles. Naptime and milky-smelling skin and warm little hands on her collarbones as she soothes them to sleep.

If Lauren could have just raised babies for all her adult life, she really thinks she would have. Babies and dogs and keeping a house. She knows it's unfashionable to admit it, but she used to love hoovering the living room, cooking a pie, lighting a candle, putting popcorn in bowls ready to watch movies. Catering to everybody's needs.

There was something loaded about it, home-making, like it had been passed down through generations of women. The soft, wet sorting of laundry, the burn of bleach on her hands as she scrubbed floors. Something primal.

But her new house . . . it is not a home yet. It is not capable of being tidied, cleaned, loved. Not yet. She is thinking this as she is changing one of the babies' nappies. The baby has dark eyes, so like Poppy's and Aidan's that Lauren almost cries.

She is preparing to go home, at dead on five, when a colleague called Pippa approaches her. 'Smile,' she says, holding an iPhone up.

'Oh – no,' Lauren says immediately, but the photo's been taken. 'No, that'll be rubbish,' she says, thinking quickly of a reason why she can't agree to a photograph.

'It's fine. We like them candid,' Pippa says, showing her.

It's a nice photo, actually. Lauren is surprised. She doesn't usually take a good photo. Always looks misshapen, somehow. Distinctive, Aidan once called her, while trying to dig himself out of insulting her.

But she's looking up towards the camera in this one, a neutral expression on her face, one hand blurred, moving up to stop the photo being taken. 'It's better to be surprised, or you'll look too formal.'

'Right,' Lauren says, thinking. Oh, fuck it. She has no energy to fight systems today. The photo will just have to go online. Sod Jon. Dodgy Jon. It's just a single fucking photo.

'Fancy a drink?' Pippa says. 'There's a pub just . . .'

'Sure,' Lauren answers. A spark of something ignites

within her. Here it is: a building block of a life being presented to her. A drink with somebody who may become a friend.

Lauren took a full four decades to handpick her friends. Her twenties were spent enduring friendships with people who said things like, 'You did *not* just admit to that!' and, 'Sometimes, we do let the kids watch television – but only when they're ill.'

But, in her thirties and forties, she found them. Oversharers. Drama queens. Women like her. Women who lived without shame or pretension, who cried messy tears on her in restaurants over the division of chores, who would WhatsApp photographs of cracked nipples, suspicious moles, filthy kitchens. Her tribe.

She wants to speak to Hannah. She wants to speak to her friends. It thuds in her chest, every moment of every day, like a second heartbeat.

She heads to the nearby pub with Pippa. They sit at the bar, on high, rickety stools. Zara is at the after-school drama club. Lauren lets a breath out. She could even confide in Pippa about Zara. About the struggle of parenting her.

'So, is Cumbria very different to Bristol?' Pippa says to Lauren.

'Um, quite similar . . . both old. Bristol is bigger,' Lauren says. She glumly sips at her cocktail. All of the booze – rum, vodka – is in the bottom, and she can feel it rushing pleasantly to her head. Shit. She can't get drunk at five o'fucking clock.

'Is Bristol quite upmarket?' her colleague asks. On the way here, Pippa had called herself frugal, said she had a coupon for this pub, and Lauren had thought sheepishly about how expensive Bill Gates was, and wondered if they could really, truly be friends. Probably not.

'Yeah, a bit,' she says now to Pippa. She stares into the distance of the room, past the dark wood bar, past the stained-glass window – it's the oldest pub in the Lakes, apparently.

What's the point? She stirs her drink miserably. It's empty. It's so empty to be making small talk about a city she has never lived in. To be answering to Lindsey and not Lauren. To be telling lie after lie after lie.

'And you have a daughter?' Pippa goes on. She is tall and blonde, with a fringe that is slightly too short. Lauren can't quite work out if it is stylish or strange. Poppy would know, and Lauren wishes she could ask her.

'That's right,' Lauren says. A lump in her throat. She downs her drink and orders another round for them. Pippa is surprised, eyebrows disappearing up under that fringe. Fuck it, it *is* weird, not fashionable, she decides. Lauren knows she's drunk already, but she doesn't care. 'She's struggling, actually.'

'Oh, what with?'

'New school, and stuff.' *Lies and court cases and murders – you know, teenage moodiness. The usual,* Lauren thinks.

'She'll soon settle,' Pippa says, but the advice is so inadequate, because Lauren can't begin to tell the whole truth.

She hands over a £10 note – at least the drinks are cheap up here – and leans back on the bar stool. 'She's just turned sixteen,' Lauren says.

'Sienna, right? Did you say?'

No, Lauren is thinking. *She is not Sienna. She is Zara.*

'That's right,' Lauren says.

'Single mum?' Pippa says.

She's got a sympathetic expression on her face, and no wedding ring, so Lauren knows the question comes from a good place, but nevertheless, it does her in. It is the undoing of her. She sips her drink down, the alcohol swirling in her stomach, and nods again.

'Single as fuck,' she says, much to Pippa's surprise. 'Sorry,' she says, smoothing her hair back from her face, trying to collect herself.

No. She can't. She can't do it. The bar tilts in front of her, like it is a see-saw and somebody has sat on the other end. She blinks.

'Sorry, I have to get off now,' she says, downing the rest of her cocktail and grabbing her coat and bag from by Pippa's feet. Pippa is saying something, but Lauren can't work out what. She is underwater, drowning in a swamp made of alcohol, and she has to leave to tell somebody the truth, because, if she doesn't, that person will be Pippa.

'Sorry,' she says again.

On the bus, she pulls the burner phone out of her bag where it always sits. She stares and stares at In Case of Emergency, right until she arrives back at the stop near her house. She trudges up the frosted driveway and lets herself in.

Zara isn't back, and Lauren dials her number. 'Where are you?' she says.

'Out.'

'Yes, obviously. Where?'

'Do I have to tell you everywhere I am now?'

'Sorry?' Lauren says, not to admonish Zara but, really, because she is genuinely shocked.

'I said . . . do I have to tell you where I am?'

'Well . . .' Lauren prevaricates. She doesn't want to be the bad cop, the nag. It doesn't come naturally to her. She thought they'd got away with it. Over half way through the teenage years with hardly any rebellion.

Zara takes advantage of the pause. 'Good,' she says crisply.

And then, to Lauren's shock, she hangs up.

Tears clog Lauren's throat.

She goes to sit by the boiler. The repairman said he wasn't sure what was wrong the other day, that he'd come back with some 'things to try', but she fiddles with the pressure gauge handle anyway, twiddling knobs uselessly. She wants a fucking bath. She wants a bath so hot her skin steams when she gets out of it. She wants a Belgian bun. And she wants her husband.

She's reaching out. Not to Hannah. Not to Poppy, but to the person whose presence she feels next to her even when he's not here. Whose presence she can almost conjure up. Aidan's.

She flips open the burner phone and finds him.

And so it's the combination of the dream that does it. The dream, the colleague and the drink. And the boiler.

And her daughter. Her sedate, easy daughter, speaking to her like she is trash. Lauren buries her head in her hands, then begins to type.

I got it, she sends to In Case of Emergency, before she can stop herself.

Lauren relishes doing something she regrets. Something she wants to do. She always says to Aidan, 'God, just do it already, and then get on with regretting it.'

I'm here, she writes. A second text.

She goes into the menu and finds her credit. Aidan's put £50 on it: not the behaviour of somebody wanting a back-up plan, a contingency, something 'just in case'.

A new message fires back from him. *You found me.*

Yep.

I love you, he writes.

She smiles through tears. She could ask him about Jon now, her husband who she is supposed to never contact again, but she doesn't. It would worry him too much. He'd go into overdrive, call Jon up himself, probably, and wreck the precarious foundations Lauren's tried to build.

Z was so rude to me earlier, she types.

She lets a breath out. Finally. Somebody to confide in.

I'm sorry. Give it time x

She treated me like a piece of shit.

Aidan seems to be waiting, not typing back, and Lauren can imagine his solemn, understanding gaze. She can say anything to him. Anything at all, and she will be accepted by him.

And so she says it. The thing she's been thinking. The thing she could only admit to him.

I love her, but I don't like her right now. I hate so much what she's done to us. It makes me feel ashamed x

You're perfect. Anyone would feel as you do. Don't sweat it x

She pauses, looking up at the boiler. She doesn't need to be held in the bathwater now, like a big, hot hug. She doesn't need that, because she has him.

33

Aidan

Shepherd's Bush, London
One week gone

Lauren has texted him. Their relationship has always been wordy, tens of texts a day. And now, here they are, linked by two illicit burner phones, only it doesn't feel illicit: it feels right. He's sure it's safe. They're untraceable, and nobody knows about them.

He taps out a rundown of things she shouldn't be doing. Website photos, hobbies, make sure she's not being followed. Everything he's learnt since she's been gone.

Of course, she dismisses him. *Thanks for the info*, she says, with a detective emoji.

Miss you, he writes.

More than I can say, she writes.

She doesn't return the sentiment explicitly. She doesn't have to: they are one person. Split in two.

The phone may be safe, but he shouldn't have texted about personal stuff. He is thinking this as he strips the bed in the Shepherd's Bush flat. That is not what they're for, and the slope is so slippery.

'Already, everything is covered in your fur,' he says to Bill, then looks around. It's Lauren's flat, from her life before him. He unbuttons the duvet cover that he sweated in last night.

His burner phone makes a sound as he's removing the pillow cases. He tries to resist it, to relax, instead. He's got to learn how to relax. His smartwatch keeps telling him his heart rate is too high, and he can feel it sometimes at night, blood pounding in his ears, a whoosh, whoosh, whoosh, as he tries to sleep. But it's no use. He sits on the bare mattress and reads the message.

@James Thomas, Kevin has written. *Scraper yielding any results?*

Aidan leans forwards on to the pillows, his breath hot and shallow.

Shit, shit, shit. He's always being chased. Never being proactive. He needs to get ahead of them, or they'll figure him out. Hurt his arm, too. Or worse.

He doesn't appreciate the entire group knowing. He types a reply.

A few more hours, then will have first batch.

He makes the bed using Lauren's sheets. Perfect white seersucker duvet cover. Soft grey pillows. A pink throw. He makes it the way she would, neat and tidy at the edges. It still smells of the fabric softener she always used. He hasn't been able to find it, spent half an hour in Sainsbury's smelling them all last time he was there, but ended up leaving without any.

Bill immediately jumps on to the made bed, the duvet coated again in seconds with his fur.

Keep us posted, Kevin writes back. *Please.*

Aidan stands, looking at the bed. The two pillows in the exact centre. Something catches his eye on the street outside. There's a woman below who resembles Lauren. Blonde hair. Thinner. But something about the way she holds herself. Something about the arm reaching to touch the bag strap across her shoulder.

The phone goes off again.

Firm lead, Jackman3 has written. His avatar is a skull. *More soon. Narrowing things down.*

Aidan's hands shake as he types.

Great, what have we got? he writes.

Nobody answers him, despite seven people having read his message. He's still on the outside of this damn group. He has to know what they know.

In a frenzy, he adds: *Was thinking we should have a group-wide meet up. Next month? To share info.*

It's too early to suggest it. He shouldn't have. He doesn't yet have their trust. But there is a firm lead. They've never said that before. He panicked.

@James Thomas u concentrate on those scrapers, Kevin says.

Aidan drops the phone on to the bed like it has burnt his hands, like he has been branded.

34

Lauren

Coniston, the Lake District

One and a half weeks gone

Lauren bought a packet of cigarettes last night and smoked them all, one after the other, out in the garden. She hasn't done such a decadent thing for years. To literally set fire to eleven pounds in less than an hour.

And now she is on the bus again, thinking about London. She misses so many things about it, but part of it is the shopping. It was always so easy to shop there. Little treats. Crêpes on the way home. Pic 'n' mix from the stall in the Tube station. A bunch of daffodils from a street vendor for £1, just because. Sod it, three bunches. They would brighten up the hallway and the lounge. A Costa coffee to take home and finish on the sofa.

There is nothing along the road here except Coniston-grey houses, square and neatly spaced like they are on a Monopoly board. There is nobody around as the bus pulls away, like it is some post-apocalyptic playground. It's hard to believe it's only just after five.

She is trying to forget her altercation with Zara. It is

just a difficult period, she is telling herself. Zara will come back to her. Open up. Be *nice* again.

She mists up the black window with her breathing. Outside, it's frosty. The coldest November on record, apparently. The bus lurches to a stop, its suspension sighing loudly. A teenager gets on with a blast of frozen air. The hairs on Lauren's arms rise immediately. He's tall, rangy, and glances at her twice. The first look is curiosity, the second something else.

She opens her phone and tries to distract herself.

She types Hannah's username into Instagram. It won't harm anyone if she looks up her sister most days privately, will it? Just to see how she's getting on?

As she lands on her account, goosebumps break out across Lauren's shoulders. *Account is private. Request to follow?* She's made it private. Why? Are the Find Girl A group monitoring her?

She's got to know what Hannah's up to: if the IVF transfer worked. She just has to.

Without thinking, Lauren presses 'log out' on her account, and logs in as Aidan: *AidanMadison5*. Password: *th1sis3ncrypted*.

She's in. She navigates immediately to Hannah's post.

35

Aidan

Central London

One and a half weeks gone

'Look, I'm sorry,' Hannah says to Aidan as he kisses her on the cheek. One of her curls attaches to his beard, and she laughs awkwardly.

They duck into a nearby restaurant.

'I'm sorry about last time. I gave you the third degree.' She smiles up at him, revealing the gap between her front teeth.

They're seated, and Aidan finds that he likes, despite himself, to see a poor facsimile of his wife. Different smiles, different hair – Hannah's is dark and curly – but definitely a resemblance. Something around the brow bones. The mannerisms, too.

'How's it going?' Hannah says, looking directly at Aidan. She glances down at the drinks menu.

He is envious of her, for just a second. She has only lost her sister. Her grief is simple.

'You know, it's tough,' Aidan says, trying to ignore the ghostly presence of his wife at the empty seat next to him. She'd be on the wine. She is almost here with him, his beguiling wife. He knows her so well he can construct her out of nothing, like she is a work of art he sculpts into being.

A waiter approaches and Aidan orders a beer, Hannah a lemonade instead of her usual vodka and Coke.

He knows then. His head drops. He should be feeling pleased for her, but the consequences of it stretch out in front of him like a straight railroad. Hannah fusses with the menus while Aidan's heart strains in his chest.

When their drinks have arrived, Aidan sips his beer, enjoying its malty coldness, watching her, wondering when she will tell him. He knows the Starling sisters well, and, sure enough, she does it immediately.

'Look, I just told Insta, literally two seconds ago, so now I want to tell you. The embryo took,' she says.

Despite the sombre dinner of just the two of them, and despite the fact that Aidan keeps watching the window in case somebody is watching him, his chest feels full of hope, for just a second or two.

'One beautiful baby, inside me.' Hannah smiles. She looks disbelieving as she says it.

'Oh, congratulations, Han,' he says sincerely.

Hannah raises her lemonade to him. 'Hard won, right?'

'Just a bit,' Aidan says. His face is hot. He's smiling at her – he hopes nicely – but, inside, thoughts are going off like fireworks. He grips the edge of the table. He needs to sort this out. Work it through. What it means for them, that their blended family is growing. Growing across a wound where Lauren once was.

He stares at the menu, thinking. *Sea bream with winter greens* looms up at him as he tries to think. *Corn-fed chicken . . .*

Right. What should he do?

Hannah has been trying to get pregnant for four years. She's never managed it, she once told Lauren while he ironed awkwardly in their living room, within earshot but probably not supposed to be listening. 'Not a chemical pregnancy, not a period a day late, nothing,' Hannah had said.

'But you ovulate. So I'm sure . . . God, I know it's tough. But I bet it is just a matter of time,' Lauren had said.

'How much time, though?' Hannah had said.

'A year, tops.'

It has taken three more. The IVF started a few years ago. Hannah never spoke to Aidan directly about it, but, as things go sometimes in families, she expected that he would be told, had once shown Lauren a row of injection marks across her stomach in front of him.

It feels so wrong to hide this from Lauren. She's been there through all of it. A hundred pregnancy tests, at least. Hannah used to order them in bulk off Amazon.

But then what will Lauren do, if she finds out?

Squid ink pasta with a parmesan crumb. He can't think here. He excuses himself and goes to the toilet. He stares at the mirror. His shirt is rumpled. He doesn't suit a beard. He looks like a professor or something. He leans over the sink, his head near to the taps, thinking. He blinks, looking at the reflection of one eye in the polished metal.

In the quiet of the bathroom, it comes to him: if she finds out, Lauren will contact Hannah. She'd do it immediately. She'd breach protection. That is what she would do. He knows it as easily as he recognizes his reflection in these taps. He knows his wife.

Zara is her priority, but Lauren is hot-headed, makes decisions based on heart, not head. She would risk everything, as she would for Aidan if he asked her to, as she did for Bill. There is consistency in her wildness, once you know the rules. And Aidan does.

So she mustn't know. He stands upright again. He will have to keep it from her. His poor wife. He is tasked with shielding her from the happiest moment of the past ten years. And all in the name of protection. *Protection.* He fucking hates it.

'Will Lauren find out?' he says later, once their food has come.

Hannah shakes her head. 'No. I don't think so . . .'

'But the internet.'

'It's on lock down – I'm not accepting anyone new on Insta. I decided, the other day. Just in case . . . you can learn a lot about me from that account.'

'Right,' Aidan says, thinking. 'That's good. But . . . it's such a small world. Could you take it down?' he says. 'Your post? Just for a bit? Just . . . while Lauren is still so . . . it's all so new. Breaches always happen sooner, before the people in protection are properly settled in.'

'Maybe. Yeah,' Hannah says. 'Yeah, you're right.' She gets her phone out and fiddles with it for a few minutes. 'Done,' she says, looking back up at him. She stares out of the window for a few minutes, sipping her lemonade and thinking.

Aidan gazes at her profile, half in the restaurant's light, half in shade. There's so much Lauren in her. Yes, yes, the forehead, the hairline. He is mesmerized.

'Weird for you to know, and not her,' Hannah says eventually, biting her lip and looking down into her lap.

Aidan is still staring at her, still trying to find the features of his wife hidden amongst hers, so says nothing in return.

When he gets back to the flat, he sees that the dog walker Poppy hired has been, and taken the money he left out for her. Bill is tired, sleeping in his basket in the bedroom. Aidan reaches to stroke his head. He lets out a little, low whine, a sad whine.

'I miss them, too,' Aidan says to Bill. 'I miss them so much.'

36

Lauren

Coniston, the Lake District

One and a half weeks gone

It's a positive pregnancy test. Hannah has put a positive pregnancy test on Instagram.

Lauren's eyes race over the caption.

I would be doing you a disservice if I kept this private. I have faithfully chronicled every step of my #IVFJourney here. Every injection, every egg harvest, every failure, every false hope. And now, here we are. Transfer day has been and gone, and – right now, right this second – I am #pregnant. #FourYearsInTheMaking #48PeriodsLater #Perseverance #NeverGiveUp.

Lauren's eyes are hot and wet. Not just the pregnancy. Not just the years and years and years of toil, but the fact that – right now – a brand-new relative of Lauren's is growing in her sister's womb.

She logs out as Aidan and back in as herself. Hannah must have gone private because of the group. She must be saying no to all new follower requests, despite wanting to grow her following. It's all for Lauren.

The strip lights of the bus seem too bright as they move through the Cumbrian darkness, the seat patterns garish.

She and Aidan wouldn't be speaking, if he were here with her. They wouldn't need to be. They had infinite days ahead of them in which to talk, so they would be wasting it, time's passing, on this bus, not bothering to engage. She likes to think of it. Of them: old, complacent, in love, with nothing at all to worry about, not really.

It's just her and the teenager, who has put on big headphones over his ears, his feet on the seat opposite him. She stares at him. He looks at her just briefly, one glance over his shoulder, but that's all it takes. In Lauren's mind, he is checking for his weapon, then putting a knife to the driver's throat, and killing Lauren, too.

Google Maps tells her she is one stop away from her house – she still doesn't know exactly where she lives – and so she presses the 'stop' button and dismounts in a panic. She just can't risk it. Bravery means nothing if you're wrong.

She stands and watches the bus pull away. Lauren is left on the dark street alone. She begins to walk in the direction of home, when she sees it. A lit-up shop with a little red postbox outside it. The light casts a golden glow over the pavement. Shopping. That will make her feel better.

She's entranced by it. She's tried to explain it to Aidan before. She loves all shops equally. Tesco. Service stations. Shopping malls. Designer outlets. Museum gift shops. It is the warmth. The yellow lighting. The quiet aisles to browse. The permission to buy something special, something nice to cheer her up – a pick-me-up. The paper bag handed over at the till. The new possession brought home, unearthed, placed somewhere. It's a drug to Lauren.

She is alone up here in the wilderness, missing the magic of seeing her sister's body do what she always knew it could. She's pregnant! She's actually, finally pregnant. The baby will stick. Lauren just knows it will.

And she's fucking missing it.

She lets herself into the shop. It smells of newspapers and the hot, synthetic puff of electric heaters. It's quiet, brightly lit. Polish, Lauren thinks. There are aisles and aisles to browse and hide in. Ah. This is better, she thinks, as she wanders up the biscuit aisle. Polish biscuits lie before her. Her breathing slows. It's just her, the shopkeeper – reading a magazine – and an aisle full of treats. She takes her time getting to know this shop near her house. She buys a pint of milk, a mint Aero and some Radox – wishful thinking – then stops at the counter as the shopkeeper scans them. Her hands still.

There's a display next to her. At first, she thought it was a tourist-style stand of postcards. But it isn't. It's skincare.

She reaches to finger a slippery packet. It's a Polish sheet mask. She's never seen one before. She turns it over, the plastic cool between her fingertips. An alarm sounds as the door opens and another customer walks in, but she doesn't look up. A sheet mask. What are the chances? It's a sign.

She passes it to the shopkeeper and adds a large brown envelope, a book of stamps, then pays for everything. Ten pounds, cash, part of the set-up fund from the department of protection. The receipt is binned right outside. She is deliberately obscuring her motives, her plans, from herself, not willing to look at them until it is done. And she is deliberately covering her tracks, too. She checks for CCTV: none.

Next, she googles postmarks. They're no longer used. Only for small letters according to a forum, which she chooses to believe. If the envelope is above a standard size, then she's safe. The only thing that will be marked on the envelope is a code which Royal Mail employees alone have access to.

She's safe.

She leans against the postbox outside the shop. She finds an old pen in her handbag – she was allowed to keep her fucking pens – and scribbles the address on the envelope, peeling off the 59p sticker and sticking a couple of stamps in its place. Hannah Starling. She has written this address so many hundreds of times.

She puts the face mask in and, on the inside flap of the envelope, across the seal, in scrawling handwriting, writes: *Congratulations*. And then, in case there's any doubt, given that she is supposed to be missing, she signs it off, *L xxx*.

Nobody will know. Nobody except Hannah. And Hannah won't tell anybody. She can trust Hannah. Of course she can. She's her sister.

Lauren places it in the mouth of the postbox and holds it there for just a second. But she must send it, because this is her sister, her niece or nephew, and she can't let witness protection mar the occasion, leave it unmarked.

The postbox is freezing against the palm of her hand as she stands there, the envelope dangling inside it like a tongue.

Fuck it, she thinks, letting it drop, that love letter from sister to sister. That letter that says 'I'm so pleased for you' and 'I miss you' and 'please take care of yourself' and 'use this face mask, from me to you'.

What harm could come from that?

*

Zara is home when Lauren gets there. 'Good day?' Lauren says, putting her handbag down where a hall table would be, except there is nothing there, and it thumps to the floor unexpectedly. She doesn't pick it up. She is not at home here, and so it doesn't matter.

Zara shrugs. She is sitting on the kitchen chair, her knees drawn up to her chest like she is about to tip straight off.

'Hey?' Lauren says.

Zara looks straight at Lauren. 'I fucking hate this,' she says.

'Zara!'

'What? You swear all the time. You said "cunt" to Aidan once.'

'God, Zara. What's the matter with you?' Lauren says. She puts the milk away in the fridge, turning away from her daughter. She meant to get her a library card today, on her lunch hour, and she plain forgot. Maybe this is why she's being like this. Inadequate parenting.

'I can't do this . . . here,' Zara says. 'I fucking hate it. I *fucking* hate it. All the lies.'

Lauren looks at her, not saying what she wants to say, which is: *so why did you lie, then, and land us all here?*

Instead, she says nothing, reaching out to Zara, a squeeze of a hand.

She waits for a second, feeling Zara's hot fingers in hers. 'I know,' she says softly. 'I hate it, too,' she adds, though she shouldn't, she shouldn't confide her own problems in her daughter. She should be better than that.

'It sucks,' Zara says softly.

As Lauren crosses behind her to go upstairs, later, she

sees her daughter googling something that makes her stomach drop: *how to make friends*, it says.

Lauren cries properly as she walks upstairs. *Oh, my baby girl*, she is thinking. But the internet is not the answer. The internet is loneliness. The internet is separateness. *No wonder you were rude to me.*

She can't do this, she thinks, walking along the landing alone. She can't parent alone. She doesn't know how to do it. Aidan drew boundaries and Lauren and Zara crossed them, that's always how it's been. She reaches for the burner phone. She catches something. Just a whiff of it. The scent of Aidan on the phone. She sniffs and sniffs, but she can't catch it again.

The scent of Aidan.

Of home.

37

Aidan

Shepherd's Bush, London

One and a half weeks gone

Eleven o'clock. Three rings on the burner phone. He can see exactly who it is, and he answers, his throat constricting. This is it. They've found her. That *firm lead.*

'Hello?' he says. He's been walking, trying to tire himself out, and he takes his coat and scarf off, his hands stiff and cold.

'Oh, crap.'

'What?' he says, but already, the bubble of anxiety in his chest is popped with relief. It's *Lauren.*

'I was looking at your contact. I didn't mean to ring.'

'You were looking at me,' he says.

She laughs.

There's an awkward pause. A fork in the road. They could go this way or that way. But, now she's here, on the line, how can he leave her?

'What else are you up to?' he says.

Lauren waits a beat. They both acknowledge it. The path he's chosen.

'Rowing with Zara. I just want a hot bath and to forget about it.'

'Have one,' he says.

'I can't. This boiler,' she says. She lets a sigh out, a sort of sexy sigh, and he closes his eyes. 'This *fucking* boiler.'

'You're calling me for plumbing support?' he says.

'I miss you,' she says.

She says it loudly, boldly, and Bill must hear her voice, because he stands straight up and barks at the phone.

'Bill!' she says.

'He misses you.'

'Will you put him on?'

'What?' Aidan says.

'Put him on.'

'He's a busy man, Lauren. He owns a computer empire,' Aidan says, smiling the first true smile he's felt in months.

'Tell his secretary it's Lauren Starling,' she says, with a laugh.

Aidan dutifully places the phone next to Bill's ear. He can hear Lauren cooing to him. Bill barks back.

When he puts the phone back to his ear, she says, 'I just want a bath and it won't let me.'

He lies down on the bed. It's warm in the bedroom, the heating on full, and the linen still smells like her. A low bass thrum of pleasure fills him up just like it did in the early days when he wanted her so badly and had to play it cool on their calls.

'What's it doing?' he says, a smile in his voice. He can just imagine her. Vintage Lauren, up late, manically trying to have a bath she probably doesn't even want any more.

'The hot water lasts exactly five minutes. You can time it.'

'Pressure alright?'

'I turned a tap. It's at full pressure.'

'Are you running the bath taps on full?'

'Yes.'

'Don't,' he says, rubbing his feet together absent-mindedly. 'Run them so they're a dribble. See if that works better. Sometimes the water runs cold because it runs past the pipes too fast.'

Guilt is nagging at his stomach. She's safe. He shouldn't be taking her calls. This is the very top of the slippery slope. But he can't bring himself to say goodbye. He can't bring himself to leave her, not again.

'Everything is . . . I just want a bath.'

'I know,' he says softly to her, thinking of the space at the table with Hannah, thinking, too, of what he knows about Zara. Meeting homeless people. Knowing valuable information.

Aidan isn't going to tell her either of these things. It won't end well. It's not the right thing to do. Neither piece of information will benefit Lauren.

'It's no warmer, even when dribbling out,' Lauren says to him, interrupting his thoughts.

He swallows. 'Give it a few minutes,' he says.

'It's cold.'

'Cold – or lukewarm?'

'Totally cold.'

'Has the boiler locked out?'

'God, I don't know. I don't know. I just want a hot fucking bath.'

'I know,' he says.

'You try to do the right thing always, and you end up sent away, away from everyone, and they act like it's a crime to even want to be in touch with anyone. It's a joke.'

Aidan knows to try and address the symptom, not the cause. That's the best way, with Lauren. She won't know that she is homesick. She will only know that she wants a bath.

'Okay,' he says. 'Does the boiler switch off when the water gets cold, or does it stay running?'

'Let me see,' she says. 'I need to be quiet. I'm going to tell Zara you're the protection service.'

'Right.'

There's a beat. A comedic beat, where they almost both laugh at the absurdity of it. It throbs down the phone.

He glances towards the window. Victorian sash windows. They used to open them right up in the summer, hot, spicy London smells rushing in. Now, they're closed tight against the cold air, the blood-orange street lights. Anybody could be out there. He swallows, tongue dry against the roof of his mouth.

'You okay?' she says.

She knows him. She may as well be here next to him. She would see the duvet tucked protectively around him, his wild eyes, and she would know.

'I'm just worried about you,' he says.

'I know. But we're miles away. Nobody is going to find us,' Lauren says.

'Okay,' Aidan says. 'Okay.' He swallows, then. *Miles away*. He stares at the sash windows, thinking. *Miles away*. Already, she's revealing things, without even meaning to.

38

Poppy

Battersea, London

Two weeks gone

Poppy is keeping her mother company. Her mother is on a new drug, and symptoms are milder, a nuisance, like summer flies in the heat, rather than a catastrophe.

'I don't feel perfect today, you know,' her mum said this morning, 'but the symptoms are so much more predictable on this drug. Does that even make sense?'

Poppy tells her it does, even though it doesn't, not really. Her mother seeks reassurance from Poppy, and Poppy can completely understand why, and so she gives it.

Anyway. Her mum looks better in a sort of intangible way. There is colour in her cheeks, a powdery pink. Poppy hopes it lasts. That she gets stronger and stronger and . . .

They've brought the spare duvet down, the one they usually keep in the airing cupboard. It's November, and it hardly ever gets light. It may as well be the evening, Poppy thinks, as she channel hops. Her ankles are just touching her mother's, and she likes it. The warmth of another body next to hers.

'*Escape to the Country*? I like that one,' her mum says.

Poppy nods. 'Though they never actually buy a house.'

'No, I know,' her mum says, tipping her head back as she laughs. It's funny. Everyone – even people Poppy knows well – thinks of her mother as ill. Sometimes she walks with sticks. She doesn't drive. But Poppy only sees this, here. Slightly crooked teeth. Shiny dark hair that hasn't gone grey yet. Her laugh. The way she says things like, 'Sod what people think, Pops,' smiling naughtily. Her father doesn't like that attitude of her mother's, but Poppy does.

Escape to the Country begins and her mother settles back against the sofa cushions. Poppy brings out her phone and starts scrolling through it. It's packed full, like a box of treats. Instagram, Twitter, Facebook.

'You'll miss their budget,' her mum says, but she doesn't mind the phone use. Her dad does – ironically enough, because he's always on his.

'Shame,' Poppy says. She opens Instagram. Eight new followers. She follows them back without thinking, browses the feed for a while. She begins to feel relaxed and numb, the scrolling bright images a kind of kaleidoscope in front of her.

Now Facebook. She prefers Instagram: she likes the selfies and the make-up items listed underneath. And the art of it – though, if she ever told anybody that, they'd laugh.

She has four friend requests. She accepts them all, too. She doesn't put much on there anyway.

39

Zara

Coniston, the Lake District

Two weeks gone

'Where have you been?' Lauren says.

'Nowhere,' Zara says, which is true. She's been around the block. What's it to her mother what she's been doing? She can't tell anyone that.

She feels so . . . so pent up. Like the tension she has always carried with her, inexplicably, at times, has begun to boil. She wants to join the after-school literature club but she is worried she will have no friends if she does. If she does the things she wants to do, her school friends will reject her. If she tells white lies in court, her family gets destroyed. There must be something wrong within herself, she is thinking, as she stares at her mother's bewildered expression. She must be rotten to the core.

There is a civil war raging inside her. Who she wants to be. Who she should be. And who she will be accepted as. None of them match up. They never have, and witness protection has made it all worse.

In doing the right thing for Jamie, what did Zara get in return? Absolutely nothing. She grits her teeth as she thinks about it. She has, instead, been robbed. Of her family, her friends, her dog. She had no idea how much she would miss Bill. The rhythmic slosh of him drinking from his water bowl. The way he was terrified of the vacuum cleaner. The way he didn't understand the dishwasher and used to look at her, like, 'The plates live in the wall?' every single time she opened it.

'You can't just be half an hour late and not tell me,' her mum says. Her eyebrows are raised in exasperation.

'I can,' Zara says. Fuck it. Let her be unlovable.

'It's dangerous. Don't you understand that we're here because . . . because it's dangerous?'

'If you fucking speak to me like that again,' Zara says, feeling empowered suddenly, adult, 'I'll make your life miserable.'

Her mother steps back in shock.

Zara has never shocked Lauren, but it feels good. The anger has been a stopped bottle, and Zara has pulled the top off.

40

Lauren

Coniston, the Lake District

Two weeks gone

Lauren is baking cookies.

It's her day off from the nursery and she has tried every-thing today to stop the heartache. She's tried a hot-water bottle, chocolate bars, and crying. She downloaded a stupid app where you tell people your secrets, anonymous people, but she deleted it because she couldn't type hers in the little box. She ordered an entire sticky toffee pudding to the house and ate it in one sitting, her stomach fat and distended afterwards.

It didn't work. She didn't feel anything.

She's losing her daughter.

Her bookish, moral daughter, always composed – she blew up. Lauren loves her, but she's so angry with her, too. How dare Zara be so rude to her? The only person in the world ostensibly on her side.

And so now here she is, self-soothing via the medium of baking cookies, even though she will feel too sick to eat them. They're called abbey biscuits, Hannah's recipe, though Lauren can't remember it. Oats, syrup, butter, flour. Was there something else? These biscuits that she's made hundreds of times with her sister aren't coming together in her kitchen. The mixture feels like cement, so dry, not combining. The cookies crumble as she scatters them on a baking tray and tries not to cry. She added too much flour, maybe. Or was there an egg? Fuck it. She kicks the oven door closed. Fuck the witness protection service. They've taken everything from her, and now she's losing her daughter, too. She sits on the kitchen floor, the tiles cool underneath her, and cries.

She doesn't miss her family and friends today: she misses herself. The Lauren she used to be. Part of her identity was the people in her life, the location in which she lived, the job she did. The kind of parent she was. The daughter she had: anxious, but biddable. Not ever hard work, even when she was little.

She takes a shower and the water cools to freezing as she races to wash the conditioner out. As the icy rivulets track down her spine, she lets out a moan of frustration.

In her bedroom, she opens the burner phone. She stands there for a second, then dials.

But he doesn't take her call. She shivers, freezing shower water on her skin, rejected by the man she loves. She reaches for a towel, warm from the brass radiator, and wraps it around her, pretending it is him. That is what Lauren does, these days: pretends. All of her intimacy is artificial. She cuddles up to a row of pillows in bed. She informs an imaginary friend, Aidan Madison, of all her news.

And so she tells him, now, for real, on text message, about Hannah, because she knows he will call her. It's manipulative, it's wrong, she knows. But she does it anyway. She has lost her life, and now she feels like she is losing her daughter to some teenage rebellion. She just wants a dose of normality, just one, swallowed down like medicine.

I sent something to Hannah.

Aidan rings her immediately.

'It's finally happened for them,' Lauren says. 'So I had to send something.'

'How did you know?'

'I used your Instagram login.'

'*Jesus*, Lauren.'

'Are they pleased?'

'Yes. Very.'

Lauren's entire body relaxes. They could almost be brushing their teeth together, bodies in each other's way, debriefing. They have had hundreds of conversations like this about Lauren's sister.

Hand in hand on New Year's Day, at two o'clock in the morning, coming home from a party at Hannah's. 'Did they kiss at midnight?' Lauren had said.

Aidan had rubbed a hand over his face. 'You were supposed to be kissing me, not monitoring them,' he'd said. 'You big gossip.'

'I wonder . . . is she anxious? Will she have extra scans?' Lauren asks now.

'I don't know,' Aidan says.

'Was Conrad pleased? Or worried? I always wondered if he was as up for it as she was.'

'You can't be doing that,' Aidan says. 'Posting things to them.'

'Is she well?' Lauren says.

'I think so?' Aidan says distractedly. 'Look –'

'I got the *worst* sickness, in the first trimester. I was admitted twice for fluids.' Lauren is gabbling just to keep him on the phone. She misses him so much.

'I think she's fine. Where did you post from?'

'Outside a convenience store with no CCTV,' Lauren says proudly.

'Aren't parcels postmarked?'

'No, I checked,' Lauren says. Admittedly on a forum. 'Look, she won't tell anybody.'

'Lauren. They are watching everyone who used to be connected with Zara. Hannah's her aunt. They'll probably go through her rubbish. What did it say?'

'She won't throw that out,' Lauren says.

'I'm just worried,' he says. 'I'm just . . . I'm trying so fucking hard to keep you safe. What did it say?'

'It's fine,' Lauren says sadly, not wanting to spend this precious time fighting. 'I wrote congratulations on it. That's it.'

'Right.'

'And an "L".'

'Lauren!'

'Tell me something good. Zara shouted at me earlier.' She says it even though she doesn't want to, doesn't want to wallow in the swamp waters of this topic.

'*Zara?*'

'I know. Wouldn't tell me where she'd been. I don't even know if she's made any new friends.'

'What's going on?'

'Oh, just more rebellion, I'm sure. She's just angry. And I can barely even comfort her . . .'

Aidan sighs, a soft, sad sigh for her. 'What fabric soft-ener do you use?' he says. Distraction. He knows her so well. 'I can't get it smelling the same.'

Lauren smiles as she tells him the brand.

He's smiling too. She can't see it, but she can hear it in his voice. She closes her eyes and conjures it up. That smile. Like a crack of thunder, like a downpour after a drought. She is drowning in it, that wide, white, bright smile of his.

The next time she calls, exactly a week later, he answers first go. She knew he would. He would have observed that nothing bad has happened as a result of their last call. He will have rationalized it, drawn a new boundary. Lauren knows it is wrong to capitalize on this nature of his, but she does it anyway. She's so lonely. She's so lonely it has made her desperate.

'It can be our thing,' she says to him. 'A Friday-night little chat.'

'You've not sent any more letters?'

'No.'

'You've not over-shared to anybody?'

'*No*. We're safe,' she says, without thinking. 'Zara has gone bowling with a new friend from school.' And they are safe, even if they're not exactly harmoniously living together. When was the last time she jumped at a noise? At least a few days ago, she thinks. Hard times always ebb away slowly, until you wake up one day and realize you don't feel worried, or fearful, at all.

'Good,' he says. His signal is bad.

'Where are you?' she asks.

'The flat.'

'Oh, yeah – terrible signal there.'

'Yeah. Thought it was best to be here, though.'

'Are people harassing you?'

'Don't worry about it. I'm fine. Tell me about today,' he says.

Lauren chatters. About this and that. 'Speaking of which, I might lose signal downstairs. We're between hills and . . .' The words seem to die on her lips, but it's too late, and they are out. And she can't take them back, no matter how hard she tries.

41

Aidan

Shepherd's Bush, London

Three weeks gone

Aidan waits a beat. He should resist – oh, he should resist – but, surely, if he knows where they are, it's better? If he knows, then if the Find Girl A group guesses their location, he'll know whether or not they're right.

At least three hundred miles away.

In between hills.

'Are you near lakes?' Aidan says.

'Yes,' she whispers.

The hairs on the back of his neck rise up slowly, one by one, until his entire back feels shivery. He tightens the duvet around his shoulders like there's a draught. The Lake District.

Aidan cannot imagine Lauren in the Lake District. She is a city girl. A shopper. She can't even drive. She does not appreciate stark beauty and bleak landscapes and bodies of water. She likes Westfield shopping centre, late-night corner shops and Yo! Sushi.

'God, bet you're loving that,' he says.

Lauren laughs softly, sadly. 'So now you know,' she says.

'Now I know.'

'You can't come looking.'

'I won't,' he says. He pauses. 'Bill would love it.'

'He would. But you *can't* come.'

'I know.'

That's where he will draw the line. He can call her on this phone he knows to be safe. He'll only ever do it here, inside a locked flat, late at night. But he won't go there. He won't visit her.

Those are his new rules. Written and rewritten, the lines in the sand moving constantly, a tide moving further and further out, but these are the absolutes. The tide can only go out so far. If he isn't careful, they will both drown.

They talk some more, with him lying in bed on his back. And on the other end of the phone – in his hand, a device containing his wife – Lauren is listening to him as she has a hundred times before.

42

Lauren

Coniston, the Lake District

Three weeks gone

Saw this and thought of you, Lauren sends to Aidan, with a photograph of a man wearing a backpack in the street.

She has both of her phones in her hands, but she doesn't care. Nobody is looking at her, Lindsey Smith, a perfectly normal middle-aged woman.

Amazingly, another backpack man exists! she adds.

My backpack makes perfect sense. But his is nicer x, Aidan replies immediately.

He must have his phone out with him, too. It's a weekday afternoon.

Yours is nicest because it is on you x

You old flirt.

Lauren: This is apparently a Cumberland Tatie Pie. Picture coming . . .

Aidan: This is the face of a confused man.

Lauren tops up the phone the next day. Credit from a market stall.

Another £10. No, make it £50.

274

43

Aidan

Shepherd's Bush, London

Three and a half weeks gone

Lauren: Thinking of you. In this naff bar by myself. With col-leagues. Pre-Christmas thing.
   Aidan: It's November.
   Lauren: I know. They have empty lives.
   Aidan: I am walking to running club. Put your burner phone away!
   Lauren: Everyone is completely self-involved. We are safe. Any-way, yours is out in public. Shock horror.
   Aidan: . . . true.
   Lauren: I think we're fine.

Hannah has had an early scan, and she wants to show Aidan the photograph. She suggests meeting outside his work, but he can't do that, though he doesn't let on why. The group probably know where he works, but he would sound like a maniac, a paranoid person, to say that he thinks it's likely he'll be followed. To admit that he leaves in a baseball cap from his work's back entrance.

   Instead, he tells her that he is only free on his commute,

so that he can lose anybody who might be following him from work, take some backstreets, and get to the Tube alone. She joins him at Green Park. He waits at the station for her.

Hannah looks different as she emerges. Her gait has changed, more cautious somehow, as she boards the Tube, as though she is injured.

He's glad of the packed rush-hour Tube. The rattle of the open windows, the lights flickering on and off. It is anonymous. It is public and safe. And, when they get off it, he will walk a circuitous route with her, and they can talk then.

'So busy you have to see me on your commute?' Hannah says archly to him.

Her face looks different. Lauren always said she could tell when somebody was pregnant. She would always make the same gesture, a one-handed wash of the face. 'Something around the . . .' she would say. It had become a joke between them, but actually, he can see exactly what she means. There *is* something around the . . . the eyes? Tired, but happy.

'Sorry,' he says, not elaborating.

Hannah huffs in a very Lauren way. She's annoyed because he rang her up the week before last and told her to burn the envelope Lauren sent. She insisted she'd keep it safe. That she wouldn't throw it out. But she wouldn't burn it, either. He hung up on her. He's not proud of it.

Hannah looks out of the window of the Tube, waiting, Aidan guesses, to be asked how she is.

'How are you feeling?'

'Good,' she says. 'Weird, though. Feels like there's a balloon in my stomach. I'm so gassy.'

They lapse into silence until they get off at Holland Park.

'Lauren said she got really bad sickness,' Aidan says, once they're on the stairs, catching Hannah's eyes. Her dark curls are obscuring one of them. 'In her pregnancy. She told me ages ago,' he adds quickly. God, how amateur. He may as well have said: *we haven't been speaking on burner phones.*

'That's okay so far,' she says. 'Early days, though.'

Aidan directs them into an alley, walking in the opposite direction to his flat. The street is slick with rainwater. A chip shop pushes fried smells out into the air.

Hannah reaches into her pocket and opens the NHS piece of cardboard, the scan inside. It looks exactly like all scan photos he's seen. Black, white, pixellated. Something resembling an alien in the centre. Aidan could send Lauren any scan off the internet and she'd never know the difference. But, nevertheless, he takes a photo of it on his phone, smiles briefly at Hannah, and passes it back to her.

'Fingers crossed,' he says, because it seems churlish not to acknowledge her anxiety.

She winces, and he guesses he said the wrong thing. They emerge on to a side street, passing behind a set of sixties office blocks. It begins to spit rain again, and Hannah wipes at her face. She bites her bottom lip with those gappy front teeth and nods.

'Where is the envelope Lauren wrote on?' he says quietly.

'It's safe, don't worry. I told you I'd keep it safe.' She gives him the exact same wounded look Lauren would. An indignant sort of expression.

Aidan can't help but smile at it, mostly because it reminds him of all the times he has been on the receiving end of it. In a simpler, past life, when his errors related to saying no to rescue cats and elaborate holidays.

'It wasn't postmarked, anyway.'

'But if they know you're in touch, Hannah, they will come to find you and make you tell them.'

'Will they?' she says.

In her eyes, he sees his own former doubts echoed there: *why would a bunch of football fans care this much?*

'Did you tell anyone?' he says. 'About the envelope?'

They're walking quickly in the November cold. In between two office blocks and out on to a high street with a Pret on the corner.

Hannah's eyes avoid his. 'Conrad,' she says.

Aidan nods.

'And a friend,' she says.

'*What?*' Aidan says. It comes out too loud, and Hannah winces, moving away from him. It's okay, it's okay, he tells himself, though he doesn't believe it. He is the captain of the *Titanic*. The orchestra is starting up, the lower decks are filling with water, and he's listening to a fucking violin concerto.

'It's *hard*, this,' she says. She gestures vaguely to, Aidan guesses, her own baby, and then to him. 'My sister is . . .'

'I know,' Aidan says, thinking, selfishly: *it's harder for me.* Not only missing Lauren, but trying to keep everything taped together. Plasters over wounds that are lacerating faster than he can cover them. 'Who's the friend?'

'She's called Molly.'

Aidan waits, looking at her.

'She isn't going to tell anyone,' Hannah adds.

Her breath clouds up the air in front of her. They walk past a Costa and she is silhouetted against it and, once again, he sees Lauren. The slightly crooked nose.

'How do you know? *You* weren't going to tell anyone,' Aidan says.

'We spent the day together on Sunday. We went walking. Bushy Park. I don't know. I just told her. Look, I told her to not tell anybody. I'll make sure.'

Aidan looks beyond her, into the Costa full of Christmas drinks. They walk on, past a bank. Hannah looks up at him in the gloom, those tired, happy eyes.

They part ways and Aidan gets the Tube two stops one way, two the next, just to confuse anybody who might be trying to follow him. The lights flicker and go out halfway back home, and he enjoys sitting in the dimness, thinking. Lauren tells one person. Hannah tells one person. Molly tells one person. Each of those people tells another. *Promise you won't say anything, but . . .*

That's the age they live in: information is gathered and disseminated to those who care about it. If everybody tells just one person, how long will it be before they're found?

Not long at all, he thinks. The Tube lights come back on, but Aidan still feels like he is in the darkness.

That blackness follows Aidan home. Not home. To his flat. The place he is now forced to call home. Bill greets him, but he hardly sees him. He sends the group the latest results from his scraper, all faked. A blonde woman working at a nursery in Fife. The woman doesn't exist, and everyone who works at that nursery has dark hair, so nobody will be harmed.

He'll get found out, soon, when all of his results are deemed bogus, but all he needs is a bit more time.

His iPhone is ringing and he answers it without looking who it is. It won't be Lauren, and the rest doesn't seem to matter.

'The envelope has gone.'

It's Hannah. Aidan sits on the uncomfortable, cheap old sofa.

'What do you mean?'

'Conrad put the envelope in the recycling. I'm sorry. He's a neat freak. It was on top of the microwave. He thought it was rubbish.'

'Well, get it out, then,' Aidan says, his palms slick with sweat. More moisture in the wrong places. The phone slides against his hand.

'They collected it – he always does it dead early . . . the recycling.'

'Great,' Aidan says flatly.

'Look, it's fine,' she says. 'It'll be in some recycling centre somewhere, now. Best place for it. Only . . .'

'Only what?'

'Well. Look. It's probably nothing . . .'

Aidan closes his eyes. There is a furnace in his chest, the heat turning up and up and up. This can't be happening. 'What?'

'Well, it's the sort of thing I would never . . . I'd never have noticed, before.'

'Yes . . .'

Aidan has to pace. His body is a home for his worries,

and he can feel them in every inch of him. He can't raise his voice with her. He can't get cross with her. She is fragile.

'There was a man. Just . . . a man. The other day. I should've said earlier, but I thought it was . . . just nothing.'

'A man?'

'I don't know. Hanging around near my house. Enough for me to remember him, you know? He seemed out of place.'

'In what way?'

'He looked like he didn't want to be seen,' Hannah says. 'Just on the corner, at the end of our terraces. The other evening. I don't know.'

'How was he dressed?'

'Dark clothes?' she says, as vaguely as Lauren would.

Aidan cannot understand how they are not scanning and memorizing the faces of everybody they meet, at the moment. He rises and crosses the room to sit at a makeshift desk. A pine table in front of the window. He picks up a pen and clicks it against his teeth.

Is this a risk? A missing envelope. *Congratulations* and *L* written on it. No postmark. And a suspicious man. He clicks the pen once, twice. Hannah isn't speaking. She is waiting – as everybody seems to – for him to make a decision.

His hairline has started receding.

He puffs air out of his cheeks and decides. Yes. It is a risk. Anything tiny is a risk, or rather, the stakes are too high. They'll know exactly who *L* is. And, if they know Lauren is in touch with Hannah, they will try to get information out of Hannah.

And they will assume she is in touch with other people, too . . . him.

And, if they monitor him, they will find out that James Thomas is Aidan Madison.

He has to tell Lauren. He rings off and runs a bath because he misses the sound of her regular baths. Sometimes quick and functional. Sometimes elaborate. But daily, at a minimum.

His hands are shaking as he squirts shower gel into the running water – Lauren would baulk at that – and gets in. He thinks about all of the text messages. All of the little breaches. Texting in public with a second phone. Taking her calls. Finding out her location. Her sending the little parcel to Hannah. And the rest. The things he doesn't know about. The *firm lead* the group has on Zara. He still doesn't know what it is. He'll out himself if he insists they tell him.

They've made too many mistakes. And the parcel to Hannah has confirmed that. A warning sign.

He calls Lauren and she answers. 'A *weekly* call?' she says.

'Two things,' he says.

'Are you in the bathroom?' she asks.

'I'm in the bath,' he says.

'Nice!'

'Look, the envelope you sent to Hannah has gone missing,' he says. 'I think you should tell the protection service. Hannah saw someone hanging around, too, and . . . well, you can never be too careful with this stuff.'

'Nothing's going to happen,' she says drily, sounding tired, suddenly, of his concerns. 'It's an envelope, Aidan, not an identity card. It had an L on it. It could have been anyone.'

Aidan stares at his toes surrounded by a crown of cheap bubbles that are popping quickly. The water is already becoming tepid.

'And they only postmark small letters. It was risk-free, which is why I did it,' she goes on.

'You don't know what they're like,' he says quietly.

'Neither do you.'

He thinks about telling her, then, but he doesn't. 'When I was looking at the Facebook group before it got taken down,' he lies, 'they said they would watch the people left behind.'

'For how long?'

'Look, just tell the service, will you?'

Lauren pauses. 'I am not going to tell them I sent that parcel, Aidan. What's the second thing?'

'The phones,' he says. 'They were for emergencies only. These phones.'

'No,' she says softly, her tone completely different. 'You're the only person I know. Please don't. I made these fucking cookies the other week and –'

'Can't you see?' He tries to be gentle with her. 'We're going to end up slipping up. Already we've gone from texts to calls to this – I was half-cut, texting you the other night – in plain sight.'

'Nobody is looking,' she says. 'Please don't leave me. Zara is – she's being a nightmare, and I . . . I need you.'

'I love you too much,' he says.

'Please.'

'We can't. We can't,' he says. 'We can't.'

'We *can*.'

'Every call we make, it endangers Zara. You have no idea how badly they want to find her.'

She pauses. A loaded pause, a pregnant pause. 'Aidan, what do you know?' she says.

Her tone chills him. He has frightened her. He gazes at his shadowy form in the frosted window. He is changing. He looks menacing, his features drawn. He looks away from himself.

He says nothing, hundreds of miles apart, their ears just inches away from each other. 'I know things I shouldn't,' he says softly. God, what is he doing? He is telling her things. More things he said he wouldn't. Reasonable, logical Aidan: he crumbles around her. 'Keep the phone charged. But don't ring me,' he says. 'We have to obey the system. Or we're going to get caught.'

'But —'

'For Zara,' he says.

Her silence is her agreement.

'I'll contact you if there's anything you need to know,' he says.

When he gets out of the bath, he still has too much energy. He starts doing push-ups, feeling his biceps strain. It's for the best. It's for the best if he gets fitter. It's for the best if he gets bigger. Stronger. Able to defend himself against anybody.

Aidan wakes in the night.

Daytime Aidan tells himself that he's ahead of the group, that he's controlling the situation. But, right now, as the dawn is just breaking and the rain is falling on the roof of the flat, he can feel it: they're coming for him, too. It's all going to fall apart.

So he does what most people would do in this situation, living in fear for themselves and for their children: he travels to see his mother.

She's sorting a delivery of stock when he gets there at seven thirty. He's hardly ever seen his mother sleep. She seems to be on the go for eighteen hours a day. Always up before him when he was a child.

'I knew you'd be here,' he says to her as he approaches the shop.

The sky has lightened from navy blue to grey beyond the row of shops – a pharmacy, a takeaway and his mother's shop. She is checking items off a list as a delivery driver waits, his van idling on the leaf-strewn road at the front.

She catches his eye. 'It's nice to see you,' she says in a considered, slow way. She is wondering how he is.

And there it is: his safety net.

That thought is all it takes. Everything Aidan is trying to keep aloft falls down around him. His jaw shudders and his mouth opens against his will and he's crying, right out here on the street, in front of the delivery man, in front of his mother for the first time as an adult.

Brenda glances at him, then says quickly to the delivery driver, 'Just leave the stuff – just leave it.'

'Okay,' the delivery driver says, having not noticed Aidan. 'We do just have to do the check –'

'Just tick them all off,' Brenda says. 'I'll just sign it.'

She holds Aidan's arm and leads him inside, through the shop and into the back room. She silently makes a pot of coffee and gestures for him to sit on one of the delivery pallets. It yields underneath him.

'It's just juice,' Brenda says. 'Burst it if you want to.'

Aidan gives a wan smile and rubs at his face, then lets the tears keep coming. 'God, sorry,' he says, while Brenda plunges the coffee. 'I miss them,' he says. 'I miss them and I don't know what to do.' He takes a deep breath. The back room is warm and is filled with the nutty smell of the coffee. He feels each muscle relaxing in his back, one by one.

The pallet of juice depresses as Brenda sits next to him. It isn't big enough for both of them, but she squeezes on anyway and suddenly, he is young again, Aidan the child, in the safety of his mother's presence.

'I know,' she says. 'You must. I do, too.'

Aidan nods quickly. Lauren always got on with Brenda. She gets on with everyone, which is actually part of the problem.

'You know, after she met you, Lauren only shopped here,' she says, gesturing to the shelves around them. 'She had a shop right outside her flat, and never went there. She was loyal only to here.'

Aidan stares at his lap, his hands shaking. He had no idea. He had no idea of all the ways his wife had privately loved him. 'Wow,' he says.

'And she bought tons of stuff.'

'I can imagine,' Aidan says wryly.

They don't speak for a few minutes.

And then Aidan looks sideways at his mother, blinking so the tears clear in his vision. 'What do I do?' he asks.

'You know,' she says, 'I used to be a night owl.'

'Did you?'

'Yes. I made sure to be in bed by two, before work, that was my rule. Before I had the shop,' she says.

Aidan nods. She worked in a laundrette for years, evening shifts. He remembers her telling him about it when they walked past it one day. 'Your father came to wash his sheets and we got talking,' she had said, pointing to a red laundrette in Clapham. She used to come home when he was a child smelling of detergent, the white powdery kind with the blue flecks in it.

'Wow,' Aidan says.

'And you changed it all.'

She sips her coffee and he does the same. It's bitter, tarry, like liquorice. Something in the way she dips her head, the bend of her neck, reminds him just of Poppy. He's never seen that before. Families are so funny, the way the genes thread seamlessly through the generations.

'I was a bad sleeper?' he says.

'Not bad, no,' Brenda says, her mouth turned down. 'You just had a very set body clock. You wanted to be in your cot, on your own, by seven. Up the next day by six. I learnt to appreciate the mornings, you know? The fresh breeze, the pretty colours in the sky. You taught me that. And then, when we bought this place –' she gestures around them to the canned goods and the newspapers, '– we were set. I was used to it. Haven't had a lie-in since. Wouldn't want one.'

Aidan says nothing, enjoying sitting next to his mother and letting his tears fall, his nose running unchecked on to his top lip. He leans back, his shoulders touching the hot radiator.

'You never regret what you do for your kids,' Brenda says. 'It's always the right thing to do.'

Aidan grasps her meaning immediately. 'You do your best,' he says. 'I'm doing my best.'

'You'd feel a lot worse if you had gone,' she says, with a small, sad shrug.

And it's true. Both options available to him were poor. That's all. It's as simple and as difficult as that.

Aidan begins to cry again, in earnest this time, and his mother wraps an arm around him, the way she has done for over forty years, and he cries against her collarbone. And that's all he needed. His problem hasn't gone away. Nothing is solved. But he feels better. Because he has seen his mother, and because he knows that he is doing the right thing. He's been dealt a bad hand, and all he can do is make the best of it. It's all anybody would do. It's not his fault that this has happened to him. He looks into his mother's eyes, so like his own, and he feels whole.

He takes a deep breath, here in the back room, his own confessional, and tells her what's really going on.

'I'm trying to get them arrested,' he says. 'The footballers. The group. I've . . . I've joined it.'

He expects his mother to be shocked, to advise against it, to be disappointed, even, but she doesn't. 'You always did whatever you wanted to,' she says, with a wan kind of smile on her face.

'Did I?'

'All the time,' she says, though she doesn't supply a memory of him, and he wishes she would.

'It's all a complete mess,' he says. 'They think I'm someone else.'

288

'Aidan,' she says softly.

'Please help me,' he says in a small, sad voice, even though he, a father himself, knows that parents don't always have the answers. 'Tell me what to do.'

'What made you do it?' she says, finally being drawn now that he has asked explicitly for her advice. He should be more this way with Poppy. Less dictatorial. Brenda turns and looks him square in the eye.

'I wanted to help,' he says.

She breathes in deeply, then lets it out slowly through her nose, like a smoker. Perhaps she wishes he hadn't told her, as he sometimes does with Poppy. Parenthood, for Aidan, has been a series of worries, one resolving as another is created, year after year, and he supposes it must be the same for Brenda.

'I think you should stop it,' she says softly. 'Leave it to the police. The protection people. Sometimes life is about acceptance, not battles,' she says, and Aidan knows that they are both thinking of their father, who spent his whole life gripped by hypochondria, and then died anyway. 'You know?'

'I'm going to end it,' he says to her.

She nods once, sucks her lips in, and pats his knee. He deliberately lets her misunderstand him. She thinks he is going to stop. He means he is going to end it all. The protection arrangements. The group. He is going to save them.

On his way home, he gets a message from Kevin on Telegram. He still hasn't sent the scrapers. Has given excuse after excuse.

Ordering a few bits n bobs, if you know what I mean — who needs any? — message me privately.

Aidan stares at it for a second. Weapons. It's all he needs. Evidence of intent.

He messages Kevin: *What sort of bits n bobs?*

You know.

I need a knife, Aidan writes.

He holds his breath as he waits for a response.

Consider it done.

Bingo.

When he gets home, he finds a central London warehouse online and books a slot.

Then he sends a message to the main group.

Things aren't moving fast enough for my liking, he writes. *Let's meet. 7.00 p.m., 20th December. Find Girl A massive – anyone who's anyone. Strategize. Compile knowledge. Bring everything you know. Defeat.*

The messages start coming in.

U r on, Kevin writes eventually, and Aidan lets his breath out.

Three weeks from now.

That's when it'll end. But he won't tell Lauren. The hope would kill both of them.

Later that morning, he tells the police. Lottie. She picks up, listens, and tells him she'll prepare to be there. With a team. Ready to arrest.

44

Poppy

Battersea, London

Twenty days to go

Poppy says goodbye to Emily at her road. Auckland Road. They hug goodbye because it makes them feel like adults. Their fuzzy winter coats catch on each other.

They have been learning about Jesus in religious education. Poppy didn't expect to enjoy it, but she did. The tragic figure of the man on the cross who sacrificed himself for the world. She doesn't believe it, but she likes learning about it. She likes thinking that there is ... something else. Beyond all this.

She looks around her. It's completely dark. She cuts down Cairns Road, a small shortcut. She takes it often. Usually when she's cold or rushing. She's less than five minutes from home. The cemetery is on her left, houses to the right. She takes her purple gloves off and runs a hand along the black railings. They're cold, wet with raindrops. It's been the coldest November Poppy can remember. The air so fresh and blue and misty as she steps into it each morning, like walking into a huge freezer.

Her nails hit each railing and the sound rings out like chiming bells in the evening air.

Her phone buzzes in her pocket and Poppy picks up the call.

'You on your way home?' her mum says. She doesn't usually ask.

'Yes,' Poppy says. 'Less than five minutes.'

'It's been a good day today.'

'I'm glad,' Poppy says sincerely. It's the first time she's said that in years. She's still on the new drug and, the longer she's on it, the better it seems to be working. Poppy fizzes with joy to think of it. Maybe her mum will become . . . what *could* she become? Imagine. Hiking in the mountains. Working. Giving TED talks on how to get your life back from multiple sclerosis.

Poppy went to Emily's house recently when they had a snow day – they got to school and it was closed. Her mother made them chicken soup with actual real noodles swimming at the bottom like eels, and she told Poppy her blusher looked lovely (and it did). Then she started tidying, but not in a harassed way. Just in a sort of calm, methodical way, stacking up two pots of fair trade coffee and putting them neatly away in the cupboard, leaving the work surface completely free. Just . . . being a mum. A little like Lauren.

'I'll be home soon and you can tell me about what you've done,' Poppy says.

'I will,' her mum says, and her voice seems higher and lighter.

Poppy hangs up, puts the phone in her pocket and resumes her trilling of the railings with her nails. She hears an Instagram message tone on her phone, but she doesn't check. Not because she is enjoying being 'off grid' or anything, but because she enjoys saving up the notifications and feasting on them, later, seeing a whole screen of messages queued up. She once told her dad this, and he said, 'I know *exactly* what you mean.'

It is under way before she realizes anything is happening at all.

A man all in black. Tall, lanky, like a big spider. Eyes just visible. They're dark, with long lashes. *He would look great with some mascara on*, she finds herself thinking, absolutely completely nonsensically.

He grabs her.

And the thing with crises – she learns, while it all unfolds – is that you might worry and worry and worry about them happening, but actually it is so totally different when they do. A basement in her mind opens up, revealing new strengths, new resources. A calmness descends. She is not thinking *shit* or *fuck* or *call 999* as the man pulls her towards the railings. She is merely thinking: *I am not currently dead, yet, and that is good*. Poppy is Zen, there in the small street, being dragged by a man in a balaclava.

'You say anything, I hurt you,' the man says to her.

The railings are digging into her back. The man has one hand across her chest like a seat belt.

'Your sister is Girl A,' he says. He has a West Country accent, maybe Bristol. 'Zara Starling.'

She's glad she just had a call with her mum. Whoever finds her phone will be able to find her mother, fast. And, anyway, she's glad she . . . she's glad they spoke, and that it was nice. If that's the last thing she has done. Well. That would be okay.

'You know where she is,' he says.

The small opening in the balaclava is parting as he speaks, revealing a pink mouth like a hamster's. Poppy stares at it, trying not to move. She breathes shallowly. 'No,' she says. 'They disappeared.'

'She hasn't got in touch with you?'

'No.'

'You know where your dad's wife is?'

'No.'

'She's with Girl A.'

'Yes, I guess so.'

'You know who *does* know where she is? Girl A?'

'No.'

'Your dad.'

He says it like a punchline, the red line of his mouth curling up slowly as he delivers it.

'I don't know that,' she says. 'I didn't know that.'

'Well, do you know what? That's your job.'

He stares at her. They're still joined together like two jigsaw pieces. Poppy struggles against him but his arm tightens across her. It's effortless, his power over her.

'Her mum is in touch with your dad.'

She says nothing to him, just looking.

'Your job,' he says, louder this time, 'is to find out from your dad where they are. Alright?'

'He doesn't know,' she says, thinking of him and the weight he's lost from his face already this week. The way his hair has gone white at the temples. How, suddenly, she can see how he will look as an old man.

'He fucking does,' the man in the balaclava says, spittle collecting on his bottom lip.

Poppy stares at him, horrified.

'What's your job?' he shouts.

She says nothing.

'What's your job?'

'To find . . . to find out where they are.'

'And then what?' He's still yelling.

Poppy doesn't know the answer. She's trembling.

'You tell us. Or it'll be much worse for you next time,' he says.

He makes an impatient sort of gesture, beckoning abruptly with his fingers.

Poppy looks at him blankly.

'Phone,' he says.

She passes it to him wordlessly, and thinks about that Instagram message. He throws it to the ground. She sees it crack like a lightning bolt across the screen. The sort of thing that would have devastated her before a man grabbed her in the street.

'Not your phone, you little fucker,' he says. 'What's your number?'

Poppy reads it out to him and he enters it into a cheap, old Nokia. 'So I can keep in touch,' he says. He kicks her iPhone a few feet away. 'When shall I check in with my new penpal?'

'I don't know.'

'When are you next seeing your dad?'

'I don't know. Weekends, sometimes.'

'Monday, then. Who's going to call you?'

'You,' Poppy whispers.

'You tell nobody,' he says. 'Five o'clock, Monday.'

'Yes,' she says again. And then he's gone. The grip across her chest lifted. She breathes slowly in and out.

She blinks up at the houses in front of her, the windows that remain blank like heavy-lidded eyes. The people who didn't even look out as a crime was committed. She walks, jelly-legged, across the street and retrieves her iPhone. The unread Instagram message, splintered into two across the broken screen. She wonders what to do. Who to call. They might still be looking at her. She'd be foolish to call 999 now. To call her dad, her mum.

She hurries home, little steps becoming bigger strides becoming a jog and then a run. Poppy hates running – hates getting sweaty – and she's amazed she can even think these thoughts from a past life, but she can, and she is.

She reaches the busy road with the church just opposite and she crosses it, so pleased to see shopkeepers with propped-open doors, and kebab houses and cars and lights and people and noise. She stops running, her breathing shallow, and tries to think.

Telling will make her mum more ill. That's the truth of it. Poppy is used to thinking, and then thinking again, about her mum's illness.

But she can tell her dad.

'Please, help me,' Poppy says on the phone to her father.

He will sort it. That is what Poppy is thinking. He can't help her with everything. He can't help her care for her mother. She is slowly seeing the chinks of bright light in his armour. But she still thinks he can help her now.

'What?' Aidan says, his voice immediately alert.

'Please come and get me.'

'Where are you? Are you alright?'

'Near Mum's.'

'Okay, I'll come to Mum's. Be half an hour. Traffic –'

'No, come here. Right where I am now,' Poppy says. She can't go home. She can't let her mum hear her. She stands outside a phone case shop and next to a shoe repair place, staring up at the church.

'Um, okay. Send me a pin, a location pin thing. You *are* okay?'

'I'm okay.'

Her dad arrives after only twenty minutes, which must mean he was speeding. His face, even his too-thin face, fills her with a rush of safety as he winds his window down. She gets into the passenger seat. The heat is up, Radio 4 playing soft night-time murmurs. She unfolds her legs, drops her broken phone into her father's lap, and cries. She so rarely cries on him. She didn't cry on him when her mother was diagnosed, or the first time Poppy needed to wipe her mouth for her, or the time she got an F in maths because her mother kept her up all night before an exam and she couldn't concentrate on the questions. But now she does.

And when she's told him, he says nothing for ninety seconds. She counts them. He stares out at the wintry sky, completely black, looking across at the little lake in Wandsworth Common where they've parked up, evidently thinking.

'Monday,' he says.

'Yeah.'

'You come to me Monday. I'll meet you. I'll take that call. I'll sort it,' he says, as though it's simple.

'Okay,' Poppy whispers. And she doesn't ask him what he'll say. And she doesn't ask him if the balaclava man is correct. She doesn't ask him anything. Instead, she thinks again of the 'Jesus classes', as Emily calls them. She is happy to be handing this over to her dad, her saviour. She is giving him this impossible task, this poisoned chalice, this crown of thorns.

45

Aidan

The edge of Wandsworth Common, London

Twenty days to go

Aidan's heart is three times the size it normally is. He's looking out at Wandsworth Common, trying to cry without tears. To release his feelings, somehow, without showing her. He fakes a yawn, and that helps a little bit. He is opening the void, here in South London. His poor baby girl. His poor, innocent baby, so angry already by what life has dealt her, caught up in his shit.

Aidan has no idea what he's going to do when this call from the man comes, so, instead, he watches a group of youths play basketball, envious of their braying masculinity, their games, their child's play.

The common is brown, like the world has turned sepia. Dark spindly trees. He hopes the spring buds are in there somewhere, waiting to come out.

On Monday at five o'clock, Aidan sits in the car in the under-building garage, while Poppy watches TV in the flat upstairs. For an entire minute, Aidan thinks the man isn't going to call. But he does, a few seconds after the display ticks over to 5:01 p.m.

'Thought I'd leave you hanging,' a voice says.

Aidan strains to recognize it. He turns the car's interior light off and leans back in the seat, eyes closed, mentally going through everyone he's seen at the group meet-up. It might be the sinewy man with the brown-grey hair.

'I thought I'd deal direct,' Aidan says crisply. 'Rather than involve my daughter.'

'Well, hello there, Mr Madison. Been having a nice time liaising with the old ball 'n' chain in protection, have you?'

'No,' Aidan says.

'No?'

Aidan stares at the blackness of the car park. The neat demarcations of each bay. The sandblasted side of the building. The security gate, accessible only with a fob.

'Where is your wife?'

'I don't know . . . I don't know where she is.' He tries to play it down. If he didn't know, he doesn't think he would cry, or beg. He tries to be his two selves, the Aidan who knows and the Aidan who didn't ever plant that burner phone.

'You don't ring her – little marital chats? Little missives sent?'

'No.'

'You don't know where she lies awake, missing you?'

'No.'

'I'm giving you one last shot . . .'

'I don't know,' Aidan says tightly.

'Okay, then,' the voice says, suddenly jolly. A sort of gung-ho cheerfulness.

300

He rings off before Aidan can say any more. Aidan sits there, under the cover of the garage, watching the cars come and go, watching the moon rise. Watching the world, from darkness. Anxiety floods his body. What the fuck is he doing? He's dicing with death, endangering his daughter. His mother, the person he trusts most in the world, advised him to stop, and he did the exact opposite. And now he can't even tell her how much worse he's made it all. He's too ashamed.

He lies the seat back, flat, in the car, and puts his hands over his face, and cries.

Later, when Poppy asks him what he said to the man, before she heads home to her mum, he tells her the truth.

But when she asks him if he is in touch with Lauren, he lies.

Aidan leaves work unusually late for somebody in IT, at almost seven o'clock. He puts his headphones in and the radio on as he leaves out the back. It helps the loneliness. There's something about the voices directly in his ear that makes him feel as though he's with people. He sleeps with it on, too, through the night. The shipping forecast. The soft hum of the news.

The stars are out already. It's been raining, and the puddles are smeared with the red of traffic lights and the reflections of the London buses passing by.

Earlier today, during the work day, he checked the burner phone. *Fuck it*, he thought, as he did it. He's all in now. This plan has to work.

The group have found more photos of Zara. They have twenty-five images now. They're combing CCTV for her.

They are talking to her friends. It's all to the good, for Aidan. The more witnesses, the more evidence. He is noting down the names of the people they're in contact with, and sending them nightly to Lottie, who always seems to be on her email.

Somebody is walking too closely behind him. Aidan turns, hoping to startle them, but they are reaching to clasp his shoulder. It's a colleague, in HR, somebody who believed him when he said his wife had left him. 'See you in the morning,' the man says to Aidan, who lets him pass before saying, 'Sure.'

'Chin up, okay?' the HR man says.

Aidan ignores him. He will fall asleep on the Tube, he thinks. He gets more sleep on the Central Line than in his bed. It's the only place he feels safe, half listening to Radio 4's *The Pin*, the warm air around him, the safety of strangers. He's looking forward to it.

Later, as he gets off, something cold presses into his back. He thrashes immediately, turning around. Hands encase his own, drawing them together effortlessly behind his back, like he is under arrest. A voice in his ear. 'Don't say a word or Poppy's dead.'

Aidan's body becomes limp, immediately compliant. He walks where the man leads him: towards an alley between two buildings. You'd never look twice at it. It's grey, dirty, a forgotten, rusted ladder leaning against the wall.

He's been foolish, wearing his glasses, his work pass. Hasn't varied his route home.

He turns around and sees there are two men, both wearing black balaclavas. Neither from the group. They're hires,

Aidan presumes. The group don't want their hands dirty. The realization gives him momentary relief, like somebody who's been given their favourite meal on death row. At least they won't connect him to James Thomas.

'You say you're not texting Lauren,' one says to him. A heavy London accent. They can't be over twenty. Just kids, really. But that's worse: kids don't think actions through.

'No,' Aidan says. They're leading him further up the alleyway. The buildings are getting closer together, like they're in *Alice in Wonderland*. Something is still pressing into his back, and he is trying to commit to memory any identifying features of the men who are about to kill him.

'In there,' the first says to him, pointing to a fire door with the torch of his phone.

The light hurts Aidan's eyes and leaves bright zigzags in his vision. He squints at his assailant before they go in. He's mixed race. Dark eyes. That's all Aidan can work out.

'Your phone to us.' He holds a palm out with one hand, and wrenches hard on the metal door handle to open the door with the other.

It's a warehouse. Clearly long abandoned. It's tomb-like in its temperature and smell. A layer of plaster dust kicks up a cloud as they walk through it. The first man releases Aidan and throws him to the floor. He scoots back towards the door, but the other man closes it. They're in semi-darkness, the only light coming from their torches, two bright beams, two suns in the night sky.

'Phone,' the first man says again.

Aidan hands it over. There's nothing on it. The burner phone is safe in the lining of his rucksack.

The man holds it up. 'Passcode?' he says.

'It's fingerprint,' Aidan says, holding his thumb out.

The man unlocks it then begins scrolling. 'Your texts with Lauren stop,' he says.

'Yes.'

'We know this is bullshit.' He throws the phone on the floor, where it lands and skids away from him.

The second man grabs Aidan's bag and rifles through it. He throws out a couple of receipts, Aidan's Oyster card. Any minute now, he's going to find the phone. He's going to find it and they're going to work out that Aidan is James Thomas and he and his family will be dead.

Sweat blooms across Aidan's chest. He tries to keep his face impassive. His hands are wet, skidding through the plaster dust on the floor.

The burner phone is light in weight. It's concealed well. He's prepared for this exact eventuality, he tells himself. But this inner monologue is pointless. They're either going to find it or they're not.

The second man throws Aidan's wallet on to the floor, then holds the bag up. An efficient hand into each corner of it, like a security guard. Aidan stares at it. He hasn't found it.

He throws it to the floor in anger. 'Remember, you tell the police about this – we take Poppy,' he says to Aidan.

Aidan swallows, then nods. Of course they will. They almost already did. They are setting out to be violent. And so, of course they will be violent.

'Where's the second phone?' the first man says.

Aidan thought the group members would be cold when inflicting violence. But those eyes aren't cold. They're something worse: hyped up. Angry.

'What second phone?' Aidan says, trying to buy time. He's thinking about Poppy, Lauren and Zara. If these men kill him, he needs to make sure they will be safe. Quick. Think. He closes his eyes for just a second. He needs to get the phone and tell them to run. Go abroad. Do anything to minimize the risk.

'Your wife sent a little fucking parcel,' the first man says.

The letter. His mind races ahead. A congratulations message, signed by L. They have assumed only one person could have told Lauren Hannah's news: Aidan.

Why didn't he tell Hannah to make the Instagram post public, reinstate it – and then the information could have come from Instagram and not Aidan? That would have solved this. Idiot. Idiot. Idiot.

Or maybe they are going after every single person Lauren left behind. The thought chills him.

'So we need to find the line of communication, you see?' the other says.

He's too close to Aidan. He can smell coffee on his breath.

'So, you going to tell us?' the first says.

Aidan can't think of a solution. There isn't one. It's impossible. 'No,' he says. 'No.'

'Okay, then.'

The second man grabs him and holds him down.

Aidan braces for impact. The first punch is a sunburst of pain right in his chest.

Each time he thinks they've stopped – the kicks to his head, the punches to his gut – they continue.

'We'll come back for more, soon. Every week, until you tell us,' one of the men says. Aidan doesn't know which. He can't look up. It's too painful.

When they finally leave him, three of his teeth are on the warehouse floor, in a deep splash of red.

46

Zara

Coniston, the Lake District

Five weeks gone

Some things have changed that Zara didn't even think about. They're studying different novels in English literature, novels she has had to speed-read over the weekends. This school is doing *An Inspector Calls* and *Of Mice and Men*. Her mother has read the latter, but told her it's about farm workers, which it doesn't seem to be.

Zara finds her jaw is set constantly. Clenched into a horrible shape. There's still yet more things to come, more things to steel herself for. She concentrates, instead, on making friends. She overheard Phoebe talking about another sleepover with a popular girl called Olivia earlier, and now she is going to invite herself, while Olivia is enjoying a lunchtime detention for standing and talking too much in PE.

Zara and Phoebe are sitting on a wall that is slightly too high to get up on gracefully. Zara thinks they ought to be reading the scene of *An Inspector Calls* they have a class on after lunch, but Phoebe doesn't want to. 'It'll be fine,' she said, with a wave of her hand, and Zara isn't yet in a position to be herself. She can't talk too earnestly about Shakespeare and lettuces. She needs to be liked.

'What are you getting for Christmas?' Zara says.

'God, look at him,' Phoebe says, pointing down to a boy she likes. 'Has no idea I exist.'

Zara's cheeks colour as the shameful feeling of having been ignored descends on her. It happens all the time. If she speaks up – in group situations, or one on one – she is very often ignored. Sometimes, she wonders if she is wearing an invisibility cloak, like Harry Potter. But the reality is that she's just irrelevant. Plain, bookish Zara. Not even worth listening to.

Last night, Zara walked in on her mother with the television paused on live music. The National. Her mother and Aidan had always joked about how much the lead singer looked like Aidan, and there she was, staring at it, on pause, her eyes wet. Zara couldn't help but say something. She told her mother to get her shit together. She can blush with the shame of the memory now. It just came out. This temper, it's come from nowhere.

'Do you think he'd meet me, if I asked him?' Phoebe says.

'Maybe,' Zara says.

'Maybe next week.'

This is her moment. She should ask about the sleepover. The words are fully formed in Zara's mouth, but she can't say them. She just can't.

Phoebe puts her lunchbox back in her rucksack and jumps down from the wall. 'Should make a move,' she says. 'I need to go and find Olivia before class. I said I'd sit with her.'

'Right,' Zara says. She follows Phoebe, deflated. The moment has been and gone. She's not going to be invited to the sleepover. Instead, she is going to have to make her own evening. A shower, a novel. Something to pass the time. Maybe she'll reread *The Hate U Give*.

'What're you doing this weekend?' she says to Phoebe.

'Oh, this and that,' Phoebe says.

Zara's heart hurts. They don't even want her there. Why would she want to invite herself somewhere she isn't even welcome? They walk through a drift of autumn leaves.

'I love these crunchy piles,' Phoebe says.

'Want to do something Friday?' Zara says suddenly.

Phoebe hesitates, looking at the school building in front of them. She seems to think for five seconds, ten.

Zara holds her breath.

'Come to mine,' Phoebe says eventually. 'I'll have a sleepover.'

Zara closes her eyes in relief. Not because of the invite, but because she said *I'll have*, not *I'm having*. She was sparing Zara's feelings, like throwing her a bone, a pitying bone. Zara takes it, only because she has nothing else.

47

Aidan

Central London

Sixteen days to go

'We've all had months like this, Aidan,' Aidan's HR manager is saying to him in the meeting room.

Aidan is nodding.

'When one thing goes wrong, and then another, and another.'

'Yes,' Aidan says. He can't tell the truth. What would happen? He would say: *actually, my wife is in witness protection with my stepdaughter – but please don't tell anyone. And the people looking to hurt them beat me up – but please don't tell the police, or they will harm my daughter.*

'After my divorce I had all sorts happen. Car got clamped and then I kicked the clamp and broke my toe.'

'I'm sorry,' Aidan says.

'But, nevertheless, a few comments have been made recently about your work ethic. And now, in the light of this . . . brawl . . . we're just wondering if you need to take some time off?'

This is his cover story. Lauren left him. His life has spiralled out of control and, last night, he hit somebody in a pub in a moment of frustration, who hit him back even more forcefully. Of course, Aidan wanted to say he was attacked. That he was the victim. But he needs it to be completely believable. A double bluff. And nobody who was lying would say they landed the first punch. So that is what he did. Stalemate.

'No,' Aidan says, rubbing a hand across his stubble. He couldn't give less of a shit about work.

He's got a dentist appointment in the morning. They're going to fit him three false teeth for the princely sum of £1,000.

'I just need to get the teeth sorted, and then I'll be fine.' He lisps on the *s*. 'I'll take tomorrow.'

'Take as much time as you need. We've all lamped someone once. Or wanted to.' His manager raises his eyebrows.

Aidan drops his head. As much time as he needs. Is that a dismissal, or a hint at one? HR never say what they mean, after all, do they?

'It'll get better, mate,' the man says. A friendly clap on the shoulder, and they leave together.

Since the attack, Aidan has a new plan. He has shaved his beard off, and replaced his smashed glasses. And, now – just for today – he is going to leave out of the front, and do his normal commute to Islington.

Hannah has collected Bill from the flat this afternoon.

Aidan is going to sort it out. As Aidan, not as James.

It takes only a day for them to follow him when he leaves the office. They're tracking his movements. He makes it easy for them. Leaving work and going straight to Islington. He even wears a name badge from a work event on his coat.

They are the same two men: the group must have hired them, just as Aidan suspected. The thought gives him shivers. They have the ability to hire people. To blame those people for a killing, and get away with it themselves. There must be conversations in the group that he is not privy to. Maybe the group knows exactly who he is, what his plan is, and are exacting revenge right this second.

When he's sure they're watching, at the Buy and Collect Tickets machine next to a flower vendor, he pulls a piece of paper out of his bag. He scrutinizes it carefully, then types *Truro*, on the big screen, in full view of them. He looks around him surreptitiously. They're watching. Just in case they haven't got it, he flags down a TfL worker and asks loudly if this is the right way to buy a ticket to Truro. He practically shouts it.

When he's bought it, he places the ticket in his rucksack. Then he lightly screws up the piece of paper, and puts it in an overflowing bin, just outside the station.

On that piece of paper is an address: 5 School Road.

It took him a long time to find the right combination of addresses. He needed something that would throw up multiple results: a common street name within the vicinity of Truro. And he needed, obviously, nobody to live at any of them. It had to be far away. To be credible, and to buy him time.

There are three streets called School Road near to Truro. It should be enough to keep them busy: 5 School Road, Bodmin; 5 School Road, Truro; 5 School Road, Redruth. None of them is the address of a house. Two are schools, one is an eye hospital. It took Aidan hours.

And they will be on their way soon. To the addresses in

Cornwall. And then, by the time they arrive back – newly angry, no doubt – he will be ready.

For the meeting, and for the police.

You added me ages ago and just wondering y?

That's the message that is displayed on Aidan's phone as he stands on the roof terrace of his flat in Shepherd's Bush. He's smoking, roll-ups, from the corner shop. Cigarette after cigarette after cigarette. Already, his fingers smell, his cheeks feel hollowed, his teeth fuzzed. He looks out over London in the darkness. Tiny little model houses beneath him. Yellow windows. The clouds above are luminescent, even in the darkness, lit up by all of London.

He's almost there. It's almost over.

The message is from the second defendant, Mal. He considers it before replying.

Aidan finishes his cigarette, breathing the chalky clouds out into the winter air, then types back a reply.

I'm trying to Find Girl A, he writes.

Mal reads it, but doesn't reply.

So Aidan types: *I know about the initiations.*

A few seconds later, Mal has blocked and deleted Aidan, Mr A, from Facebook.

48

Poppy

Shepherd's Bush, London
Fourteen days to go

Her father has been beaten up.

Poppy is sure of it as she watches him move around his flat's tiny kitchen. Bruises. Strange teeth, his jawline odd, jutting forward. He told her he walked into a lamp post. Isn't that the oldest story in the book? Like something from a bad play.

And so it isn't what her dad pulls out of his rucksack, rips up and puts in the bin that makes Poppy pay attention. It's the bruises. Her father is up to something.

Poppy rinses the plates before stacking the dishwasher, as she always does at this time of the evening, whichever house she's in, and waits for him to be elsewhere.

As soon as he's in the shower, late, ten-ish – he seems to let her stay up these days without any argument – she has her hand inside the kitchen bin. Old tea bags and mouldering vegetables touch her arm, but she digs further anyway. Her merino wool sweater gets wet, but for once she doesn't care. All she can think about is what the balaclava man said about her dad being in touch with

Lauren. She knows exactly what she's looking for. That distinctive orange-and-white stripe of a train ticket. She's sure that's what he ripped up.

She finds five pieces of six and takes them into her bedroom. Before she looks at them, she lights a Diptyque candle her dad bought her two weeks ago. It was £40, and only tiny. She just couldn't resist the smoky fig scent, the weight of the votive in her hand. So far, she has burned three millimetres of it. She'll allow herself one more millimetre, tonight, while it's on the windowsill, a lit-up beacon right in the middle of London. Something to relax her, to steel her nerves as she looks at the ticket.

It's easy to piece them together. Straight edges around the outsides, torn edges inwards.

It's a return to Truro. For Saturday. Poppy sits back on her bed, stunned. They don't know anybody in Truro.

Unless they do.

Unless her dad has lied to her.

Poppy is walking to school with Emily, after filling her in on the discovery of the train tickets, when Emily says it. 'I think we should look at your dad's phone.'

Poppy isn't surprised by this, only humbled that Emily has taken the time to think it through since she told her about the balaclava man.

The sad snake is back in her belly. What if her father has lied to her? He left her and her mother, her mother became ill, and now he might have lied to her. She is so *mad* about it, she could kick something.

She looks across the street, trying to distract herself, and that's when she spots it. She grabs Emily's arm, a desperate, unconscious sort of grab. The kind people make when they're choking or trying to stop somebody walking into traffic. Emily looks at Poppy, then follows her gaze to the Perspex newspaper stand catching the sunlight on the high street.

Truro pensioners threatened at knife point in own home by balaclava youths.

'What?' Emily says.

'Look,' Poppy says.

Emily stares at the sign.

'Truro. In balaclavas,' Poppy says.

Emily heads decisively towards the news stand and Poppy follows her.

Emily scans the article. Poppy can't look. She's going to be sick. She wipes at her eyes – tears have come from nowhere – and her fingertips come away chimney-black, stained by her supposedly waterproof new mascara.

'It doesn't say.' Emily puts the newspaper back. 'They don't know who it was.' She looks at Poppy.

Emily pulls her into the foyer of McDonald's where they stand amongst the people waiting for sausage and egg McMuffins. 'They went in – two men in balaclavas. They took a knife. When they realized it was two pensioners, they left. The people reported it.' Emily's bony shoulders that Poppy has long admired rise up and then down again. 'They didn't steal anything,' she says softly.

'It's them, Em,' Poppy says tearfully. 'Isn't it?'

'Possibly,' Emily says quietly. 'Probably. But, look, they got the wrong address. They don't know for sure.'

Emily picks up a straw and rips the paper casing off it. Poppy watches her. Emily tugs on her arm and they go and sit in a plastic booth. There's a half-finished cup of coffee on the table, scummy tidemarks of cappuccino foam around the rim. Emily puts the paper straw wrapper in it and it becomes brown and saturated.

'I need a milkshake,' Emily says. 'Then we can strategize.' She cracks a wry smile. 'You want one?'

'No. Can't stomach it,' Poppy says.

'Okay,' Emily says, with a patient smile.

Her beautiful friend. Poppy shouldn't have led her into this mess. She sits for a few minutes in one of the cream plastic booths.

Emily arrives back with her milkshake and sips it, no straw. Strawberry. Same thing she always has. She gets a milk moustache, like a small child. She smiles as she wipes it off with a stiff napkin.

'We'll sort it out,' Emily says. 'I mean . . . if he is . . .' she invites Poppy to say the unsayable.

Poppy looks around her desperately, tears budding in her throat. 'Em, I was reading about witness protection online. They literally present you with a sheet of rules and you have to sign it. You know, don't lead a life of crime, don't contact family members from the past, because it messes it up. I need to . . . I need to tell someone. The witness protection people. If he's in touch with them. Pensioners are getting threatened. It'll be Lauren and Zara next.' The thought makes her chest bloom with anxiety.

Emily bites her bottom lip. Her two front teeth come away covered in MAC's Ruby Woo lipstick. 'If it was them.'

'Exactly,' Poppy says.

She fiddles with the lid of Emily's cup. Emily reaches over the table and holds on to her hand. It's cold and damp from the drink, doesn't feel like a hand at all.

'We'll look at Dad's phone, soon,' Poppy says.

'And in the meantime . . .'

'If balaclava man rings me back,' Poppy finishes. 'Which he will . . .'

'Well, then you need to lie and tell him they're not actually in Truro,' Emily says.

49

Zara

Coniston, the Lake District

Six weeks gone

It's ten past five in the afternoon. Phoebe is sitting opposite Zara. She's double-jointed, kneeling with her feet splayed out to the side. The undersides of her heels are completely smooth, her toes painted a perfect pastel blue.

Zara is sitting rigidly next to her. Here she is, at the fabled sleepover. This is her moment, and she is trying, in her own awkward way, to seize it.

'Yeah, definitely,' Zara is saying to Olivia in response to whether or not she is going to go to university. And she is. She'll study English.

Olivia is the oldest of the year, born on the third of September, and her entire identity seems to have been constructed around that. She seems to know about things before they become *things*. Tortoiseshell nails. Calling people 'a mood'. Zara naturally shrinks into herself as she encounters her, and becomes somebody she isn't. The yin to Olivia's yang.

But maybe soon they will be friends, and Zara won't need to sit on her bed and have imaginary conversations with Poppy, with old friends. Or to replay old memories late at night on her bed.

'Sienna is such a nice name,' Phoebe says. She is softer than Olivia. She concentrates avidly in all lessons except maths, which she ignores. 'I'll just fail it,' she said sadly, a few days ago. 'I haven't got a clue what's going on. I've decided I'll just be one of those adults who's crap at maths.' Zara had laughed at that, and wished she could have that sort of perspective. The high-level view. Zara's entire self-worth is predicated on passing her GCSEs. She doesn't know where she gets it from. Her mum treats exams with derision – 'Far more important things in life,' she will say. Zara sometimes wonders if she gets it from her father, her real father, but now they will really never know.

Sienna. Zara turns her head immediately. She has trained herself to. She thought she would find it difficult to answer to a new name, but she doesn't. *Sienna* is a smoke signal to her. An alarm. A warning sound.

Phoebe's bedroom is enormous, an old bedroom in the eaves of the house. There's something shabby about it, but Zara likes that. Cobwebs across the beams. The pale blue carpet, darker at its edges where it meets the skirting boards. Old, shapely radiators that hiss and creak.

There are two skylights above the huge bed. Steady December rain runs down the glass. It rains a lot here, so much more than in London. It's cold with it, too. In London, the rain formed a kind of steamy closeness, especially on the Tube and in school. Out here, the rain is wild. Cold and free, being blown through valleys and across the lakes. It smells salty and clean. Zara likes it, but she isn't used to it.

'So. Truth or dare,' Olivia says. She raises her glass of squash. It's cheap stuff. Orange. The colour of butter.

Zara is surprised: she thought it would be alcohol and cigarettes at sleepovers – she came steeled to try things – but it isn't. There is something charmingly wholesome about Phoebe and her ancient house and the row of teddy bears that still sits along the end of her bed, faded and dusty.

'Truth,' Phoebe says, shifting ever so slightly closer to Olivia.

Zara is unnerved by Phoebe's eagerness. She guesses it comes from having been bullied. But it gives Zara the uneasy sensation that, if necessary, Phoebe would say something about her. Something private, secret, to get close to Olivia. Zara closes her eyes, just briefly, and imagines she is thirty-five, that this phase of her life is over. She will have been Sienna for longer than she was Zara. The lies won't matter, because they are so far back, a dot on the horizon behind them.

'Number one fear,' Olivia says.

'Spiders,' Phoebe immediately says.

Zara made friends with so many spiders during the spring/summer she spent growing those lettuces that she hated. The spring/summer she saw the murder from that same greenhouse, and after which everything changed. People shouldn't be afraid of spiders: they should be afraid of football fans, of entitled men, of criminals, of the justice system, and of the police. *That's what is to be feared*, Zara thinks. She closes her eyes again, and wishes she could go back. Back to fears of spiders and snakes and the dark. Of flying and heights and vaccinations and public speaking. But she can't go back. And she can't go forward.

'We get so many spiders here,' Phoebe adds, gesturing to the old, uneven walls of her bedroom. 'It's a thing with period properties. Nightmare.'

'Exactly what I was thinking,' Zara lies. 'We used to get loads . . .' She pauses, for just a second. 'In Bristol.'

'Really? City spiders?'

'Yeah, there was a certain type,' Zara says. 'Um, black widows, or something.' Her mind is racing, trying to inhabit this new person. There aren't black widows in Bristol. That's Cornwall. She'd seen it on the news. Nobody will look it up, she tells herself. Nobody cares.

'Your turn,' Olivia says, pointing to Zara with her drink.

'Dare,' Zara says immediately. She has no truths to tell. She is all lies, these days.

'Get on the roof,' Olivia says, gesturing to the skylights.

'There's no way I can get on the roof!'

'On the roof.'

Zara stares up at it. She'd fall. She'd definitely fall off the roof in the wind and the rain. Break her leg, or worse. She'd look so awkward on the bed, the two girls looking up at her. An unflattering angle. They'd be able to see up her T-shirt. She tucks it into her jeans absent-mindedly.

Her mum would do it. So many times, when she was younger, Zara awoke to her mother's laughter, the clink of wine glasses, music a little too loud, Aidan shushing her. Zara wishes she was like her, but she isn't. She is far more like Aidan. Cautious and thoughtful and scared.

And what would Aidan say? *Don't get on the roof!* His eyebrows would be up, a hand dragging his hair back.

'Truth,' Zara concedes.

'What's your biggest secret?'

Zara puffs air into her cheeks. Olivia goes for the jugular.

'I haven't got one,' she says. 'I haven't really got any.' She smiles benignly. 'Very boring, really.'

'Where's your dad?' Olivia exchanges a glance with Phoebe that tells Zara they have talked about this before.

'He left my mum before I was born,' Zara says truthfully. It is nice to be speaking the truth. Zara's external reality matches her internal self, and it feels satisfyingly tidy, authentic, like a weighty key fitting exactly into an ancient lock.

'Wow.'

'Well, not left,' Zara says. 'He was never with her, really. It was just a . . .' She waves a hand. 'Just a . . . hardly anything at all.'

'Still, imagine – he has a daughter out there who he doesn't know at all.'

'I know, but –' Zara stops herself just in time. She was about to say that she has Aidan. But she doesn't. Not any more. 'My dad's a prick,' she finishes, hoping a swear word will win her some kudos.

'And your mum is . . .'

'A nursery key worker, moved up here for work,' Zara says mechanically.

'You're close?'

'We get on, yeah,' Zara says, again truthfully. 'Mostly. Though we're opposites.' Sometimes, Zara used to think that Poppy and Lauren would have made a much better mother–daughter pairing. Lauren doesn't really care about fashion, it's true, but they have a similar volatile core running through them.

She could tell them about the way her mother has been irritating her these days, and how closed and cold Zara feels, how wrong inside, like she must be totally broken. But then she'd have to tell them why. And nobody knows why.

'You're lucky,' Phoebe says. 'My mum is . . . difficult.'

'Why?' Zara asks.

'Mood swings,' Phoebe says.

Zara knows she is the one with the mood swings. She'll be better tonight. She will. She won't be rude or caustic to her mum.

Phoebe reaches over and opens Olivia's bag of Haribo. Zara looks on enviously. She would never do that. Not without huge amounts of over-thought. Was the bag of sweets for her? Would she look entitled if she opened it? But nothing happens. Zara rolls her shoulders. She wishes she could climb out of her brain, sometimes, and into somebody else's. Into Poppy's, her mother's, Phoebe's.

'You never know which mum you're going to get.' Phoebe drops a fizzy snake into her mouth and puts the bag between the three of them.

It's dark above them, the skylights black, the rain a beaded pattern across them. Zara looks longingly at the beds, all made up, bedtime still hours away.

'My mum's just cold,' Olivia says. She stretches her feet in front of her and points her toes. Her legs are completely shaved. Totally hairless. Not a single ankle hair missed. 'Ice cold.'

'How so?' Phoebe says.

Zara reaches tentatively into the bag and picks up a fried egg sweet. She carefully separates the egg from the white as she listens to them.

'Just doesn't care. Doesn't like me – the real me. Likes it if I get good marks. Achievement, basically. Likes it when I agree with her. But doesn't like the things I say. The things I'm into. Dad's the same. Sort of. He said the other day that I was entitled because I wanted a takeaway.'

Zara swallows. Maybe she's lucky, after all. Her mother's love is so inclusive, it is a trawling net that catches everything. Dogs, cats, strangers on adverts. Everything Zara says to her is considered special. She takes it for granted.

'I do wonder why they had kids,' Phoebe says. 'I mean. I don't know. But I'd like to think I would be *nice* to my child. Make them feel welcome.'

'So it's all hearts and flowers with your mum, is it?' Olivia says to Zara.

'Yeah,' Zara says.

'Oh, well, it's just us two who're fucked up,' Phoebe says, raising her glass of squash to Olivia.

Zara's face is hot. She looks down. She's gone blotchy. She always does when she's nervous. She guesses her cheeks are red, too. Poppy used to use this green-toned concealer on her, on days when Zara knew she was going to blush. School photo day. That sort of thing. 'To avoid you looking like a beacon,' Poppy would say, her fingers feather-soft against Zara's cheeks and temples.

'Next time your mum is mean to you, you call me,' Olivia says to Phoebe. Phoebe's eyes are damp.

Zara is hot with the wanting of it. To shrug off the

shroud of loneliness, of pretence, of lies. To tell them exactly how things are with her mother at the moment. It's been weeks of not fitting in, and now, here she is, finally at the sleepover, and she won't be invited back.

Unless.

She leans forward, elbows on her knees, and leaps.

'Guess what,' she says.

'What?' Phoebe says.

'There's a lot you don't know about me.'

Phoebe picks up another fizzy worm, looking at her curiously. 'Like what?'

'Like . . .' Zara starts.

She thinks of her mum and Aidan and Poppy and Jon, and of every single person who has lost something because of her lie. Harry, the lawyer, whose case fell apart. The jury whose time was wasted. Aidan's mother, who has lost her daughter-in-law. And Jamie himself, of course, whose only advocate told lies instead.

Is ruining all that again worth it? To fit in here?

'I have secrets, like all of us,' Zara says, stalling.

'So tell us one,' Olivia says.

Zara looks up at the window and then down at her hands. No. It isn't worth it. Another betrayal won't make the first lie correct. 'I find it hard to fit in,' she says honestly, though it sounds lame even to her.

Olivia stares at her. 'That's it?' She tilts her head back and laughs, three slow exhalations. '*Ha, ha, ha*. I could have told you that.'

And that's what does it. Olivia's contempt for her truth. Her certainty that Zara is hiding nothing interesting. That she is just nerdy, nobody Zara.

'Actually, there is something else,' she says.

Olivia doesn't even look up. She is fiddling with the Haribo bag.

'You'd better not tell anybody,' Zara adds.

And then she tells them. She tells them every last bit. The murder, the court case, and what happened afterwards. How she was taken into witness protection. Her old name. Her new name. The differences in her dates of birth. And how she is now: cross, unpredictable, moody, scared. So fucking scared.

When she's told them everything, Olivia's mouth parts in slow motion. Phoebe stops chewing. And then all she can hear is the drum of the rain on the skylights, the low murmur of the heating. And the sound of the truth, settling silently like snow on the ground. Flake by flake.

'You're in witness protection,' Olivia breathes.

'Yes,' Zara says. 'So I'm not an ice queen. I'm not . . . I'm just as fucked up as you two. More so.' And, just like that, with the truth out of her chest and her lungs and her mouth and in the ancient bedroom with them, she cries.

Olivia holds her left hand and Phoebe rubs her back, and Zara is drowning in it, this connection, this intimacy, this acceptance.

50

Lauren

Coniston, the Lake District

Six weeks gone

Zara is at a sleepover. Lauren is alone when her phone wakes her.

She must have fallen asleep reading the Next catalogue that dropped through the door the other day. It's splayed open on a page she was about to fold down, a cute Christmas jumper with a pompom snowman on it. It takes her a second to realize that it's late.

She fumbles across the bed for her phone. It's the Ring app that woke her. The video doorbell the protection service installed. It is showing a notification on the lock screen. *Motion detected*, it says.

Her stomach coils into knots immediately. Somebody is outside their house but not ringing their doorbell.

She opens the app. It has never once gone off in the night in all the time they've been here. *View motion?* it asks. Lauren clicks 'yes' and watches as a video plays.

The screen is black at first, but then their security light clicks on, lighting everything from total darkness to grey and white. There's their driveway. There are their bins.

The blackness of the mountains beyond, out of sight. Slowly, a figure looms into view. It's a man. Lauren's chest sparks with anxiety.

He's tall, in a baseball cap that obscures his face, and tracksuit bottoms. He walks slowly up their drive, his eyes to the ground, one hand in his pocket. And then he raises his gaze, his face bleached of features by the security light, and all she can see is that he's slowly scanning the upper windows of their house. After a minute, he seems to see what he's looking for, turns around, and disappears down the drive.

She rushes to the window, draws up the blind, and stares out. The light's gone off. Should she go out? She stares and stares. No. She can't. She's all alone.

She gets her phone and opens the app again and rewatches the footage.

As she watches the stranger leave, there is just something about his walk that is familiar to her. Something about it that seems a little like Jon's.

51

Aidan

Shepherd's Bush, London

Eleven days to go

Aidan wakes in the middle of the night. He's on the sofa. The television is still on. Maybe that's what woke him. A half-drunk cup of tea is at his feet. He reaches to touch it. The ceramic mug is chilled. It must be the early hours.

A rerun of *Countdown* is playing. The numbers round. 100, 25, 6, 7, 3 and 2. Target: 596. His mind immediately starts whirring before he even consciously realizes it. One hundred minus three times six . . .

He blinks. The clock says almost midnight. He would've said four a.m.

Seven times two is fourteen, and add it on.

If he can solve that, he can solve this.

He stares at the television and thinks about Lottie and the Find Girl A meeting.

He knows they went to Truro. He knows they found two elderly people. The hospital had been converted to flats, and Google Street View hadn't caught up. He can't let himself think about that or he will be eaten up by guilt.

They didn't harm them. They didn't harm them. They only frightened them.

What he doesn't know is what is going to happen next. Now that they know he set them up. He was buying time, but they moved so fast, faster than he expected, and now he's running out.

He logs on to his computer and sends Lottie an email. Subject: *Truro*.

Can't sleep, he writes. *Keep thinking about Truro. I know you couldn't get anything on them. That it's better to wait and see through our plan. But I'm so worried it isn't going to work. That they will find L&Z first.*

He's surprised when she replies straight away.

I know, she says. *I lose sleep over it, too. But the nice guys don't finish last. They finish first, in the long game. And that is what we're playing.*

Sleep leaves him like a blanket falling away from his shoulders and tears fill his eyes. Crying at an email from a fucking police officer, what has his life come to?

'Five nine six,' both contestants confirm on the television, and he switches it off. It must have been easy.

He reaches to check his burner phone.

Thirty-nine notifications on Telegram, beginning at seven thirty. Jesus, what's the matter with him? He never sleeps so early. He sits up and rubs at his face. His arms are covered in goosebumps.

The app directs him to the first unread message, but he scrolls down quickly, wanting to read the conclusion first.

Stomach acid burns his throat as he reads the final message. *Outside the house. Going in.*

Aidan's fist is to his mouth. His hand is shaking so much that his lip is being rammed into his new teeth.

He is sitting on the sofa, his feet on the carpet. The messages are time-stamped an hour ago. It will be too late, whatever he does. He can't see. His eyes are misted over with tears, that fist trembling, trembling, trembling against his teeth.

He will read them all and then he will call the police.

He dashes the tears away and wipes his hands on the fabric of the sofa.

7.31 p.m. Kevin: We've found them. Up north. Finn did a reverse-image search and found Lauren on a nursery website uploaded yesterday. @James Thomas ur scrapers aren't performing well enough. Seven of us are going up there now. Anyone else free is welcome to come.

Aidan's heart is in his throat. Of course. He's been so fucking stupid. A dumbo. He was so concerned with faking his own scraper results, he never ran a real one. He could have, and then told Lauren to get anything taken down that showed her. He has been so stupid. And it has cost him everything.

8.07 p.m. Mr G: Sorry not free but wishing you luck hope she gets what she deserves.

8.20 p.m. Shaun: We are free, three of us here, we'll come to you.

8.20 p.m. Kevin: Message me separately m8.

9.10 p.m. Kevin: Just in the back of a van now.

9.21 p.m. Kevin: Speeding on up the motorway.

On and on it goes. Kevin narrating on his own vigilante mission. Aidan's stomach muscles are so tense he feels sick. He scrolls past the messages. Logistics. The journey. Describing what they're going to do to them to silence Zara. They have a knife, a hammer. They're going to barge the door open. Lauren and Zara will be sleeping, and they will surprise them.

At 11.24 p.m., Kevin sent a photograph. His hand, black gloved fingers clutching a knife. It's a proper knife, a knuckle-duster knife with four round finger holes. It's not a kitchen knife. It is a knife for stabbing. The blade double-edged, so sharp Aidan can barely look at it.

Aidan scrolls to the last message again.

Outside the house. Going in.

Lauren might be hiding. Please let her be hiding. He can't call her.

He exits the app and calls 999.

'Please help me,' is the first thing he says to them.

52

Lauren

Coniston, the Lake District

Six weeks gone

Lauren is sitting cross-legged in front of the boiler, the evening after Zara was at the sleepover. She is thinking about last night's video footage. She hasn't told anybody. Aidan would freak out. She can't trust Jon. So who should she tell? The police? And what? It probably wasn't him.

She fiddles with a joint she has discovered inside the boiler. If it wasn't Jon, then she should definitely tell Jon that somebody showed up on the camera.

She has been in this loop for hours.

The joint feels loose, and it tightens as she messes with it. She opens YouTube and follows a tutorial led by a man called Oleh who tells her how to tighten it fully.

Telling people good news is the absolute pleasure of good news, she is thinking. 'I fixed the boiler!' she would say to Aidan, and he would high-five her, and consider her brilliant, a genius, a strong and confident woman. An audience is life, to Lauren.

Anyway. It's after eleven o'clock. The house is double-locked. Zara is already in bed, exhausted from the sleepover last night, and Lauren might just have fixed the boiler.

She releases the taps and the bath runs easily, the hot water lasting and lasting. An inch, three inches, half a foot of hot water. Lauren stares at it in shock. The vapour rises, a miniature water cycle there in her bathroom. Lauren thinks she's never seen something quite as beautiful.

She puts both of her phones on the chair in the bedroom. She used to entertain herself in the bath. Podcasts. YouTube. The *Coronation Street* omnibus, much to Aidan's dry amusement. But tonight, she wants nothing in here. Just this pure, steaming water and herself. Lauren, not Lindsey. She takes her cardigan off. Goosebumps appear over her arms. Next go her jeans, her vest top, her underwear. And then – bliss. Her feet are in, turning red with the water's hot kiss. The rest of her body in the cold air. The exquisite contrast of it, like a July sun in December.

Something jolts her body. It's the door. She stares out at the landing, frowning. She is the sort of person who will dash to open the door, who will welcome an evening visitor 'just dropping by'. Aidan hated it – would put his coat on, pretend to be going out – but she'd open a bottle of wine in the kitchen, light candles, tidy up around them. 'No, no, stay!' she'd say.

But who could be knocking on the door? They don't know anyone. They are completely alone. Zara is reading in her bed. She's probably asleep now. Lauren thinks of the man on the footage last night and, suddenly, the bath feels as cold as it used to run.

Her heartbeat speeds up. It begins whooshing in her ears, as she stands there, naked and vulnerable, the responsible adult who has to decide whether to go downstairs and see.

There it is again. It's definitely a knock. A muffled sort of sound, maybe a gloved hand. Three cordial thumps.

She wraps a dressing gown around her, walks to the top of the stairs and tries to look down without being seen. The frosted glass is dark, unwilling to reveal the identity of the form standing behind it.

Lauren peers over the bannister. Shit. How is she supposed to know what to do? There's danger everywhere, it feels like to her. She sees the form shift outside, an unknown face looking right at her. She wants to reverse back up the stairs and hide under the beds, in the wardrobes. Call 999, wake Zara, smuggle her out the back. She remembers that knife-wielding yob in their garden in Islington and freezes in terror, just staring at the door. This could be it. The figure raises a hand. It's all black. Black arm, black glove. It's waving at her. Tears build in Lauren's throat. She's never been so terrified in her life.

Would somebody really dangerous knock? Would they wave? She tries to reason with herself.

Maybe, she thinks, if they were an enemy pretending to be a friend.

She finds her phone and opens the Ring app.

Jon appears very clearly outside the door, framed in the screen on the app.

She stands still. It's him. Should she answer?

What if he *is* protecting her from something?

'It's me,' he says, a hand through the letter box to hold it open.

'It's so late,' Lauren says back.

337

'I know – you need to open the door.'

Lauren stands in the hallway, frozen. 'Why?' she says eventually, wrapping her dressing gown around herself. Her feet leave damp impressions on the carpet.

'There's been a breach. You're in danger. You need to come.'

Lauren is frozen by fear.

'Look, I . . .' she says. She'd rather risk it. Would rather stay here than go with him. 'No,' she says. 'I . . . no.' But what if he's right?

'What?' Jon says in exasperation. He keeps his hand in the letter box so it doesn't close.

Lauren stares at it, a small chrome rectangle quivering in the night.

'What's going on?'

Something about his low tone invites her confidence. The safety of the door between them. That he isn't forcing his way in.

Everything builds up inside her. Aidan, Zara, that she nearly had her bloody bath and didn't get it, her doubts about him. It all mounts up and spills over. She is unable to keep secrets inside where they belong. Not when she has to lie all day long, too.

'I'm not sure if you are who you say you are,' she says.

'*What?*'

'I'm not sure you're . . . good.'

'What do you want? To see my ID? Call my boss?' he says. He sounds half aghast, half amused.

'Maybe.'

'What's this about?'

'You had a Holloway shirt in your car,' she says in a

rush. 'And you came up on the app – someone that looked like you was outside our house last night . . .'

The letter box sighs. 'Right,' Jon says softly. 'I see. Are you going to let me in?'

'No.'

'It's a Boca Juniors kit,' he says in a resigned tone. 'I play five-a-side in it. Is that alright? Sacha got it for me. Blue and yellow. But not Holloway.'

'Oh.'

'Do you want me to go and get it?'

'No . . .' She pauses. 'And the camera?' she says.

'It was me. Off duty. I was making sure you were safe. You left the windows open a few nights before. I wanted to check you hadn't again.'

'You could have messaged.'

'I just wanted to check. Couldn't sleep, woke in the night worrying. I couldn't text in the small hours. I just wanted to know,' he says. His voice becomes urgent. 'I can't tell you how much you need to come with me now. What do you want – *do* you want to see my official protection service pass?'

Lauren hesitates, her hand on the doorknob, then opens it. She can't – she can't keep this up. This hypervigilance. She's got to trust somebody, in all this. He's had so many opportunities alone with them. She feels he's telling the truth, out there in the cold on the other side of her letter box. She thinks she knows him to be good. She believes him.

'What's happened?' she says as she opens the door, relief rushing through her like white rapids.

'A concerned family member has reported that the

group has this address,' Jon says, his cheeks white from the cold, his eyes darting left and right. 'They're on their way. We have a team here who'll do a sweep and remove any evidence that you've been living here. But you guys need to come. Now.'

'What? Shit.' Lauren says, wrapping her dressing gown around herself.

The panic dissipates, as is often the case during a real emergency. She takes the stairs two at a time, ready to wake Zara.

When they're in the car, later, having thrown as many of their things together as they could, she turns to Jon and says, 'Thank you for understanding. Earlier.'

'It's fine,' Jon says. 'In fact, I'm glad you asked. Means I've trained you well to be suspicious.' He gives a tight little smile.

They're travelling east.

They were found by a bot performing reverse Google Image searches. An old photo of Lauren compared with the latest one on the nursery website. The group systematically went through each hit until they found them. Then they rang the nursery, pretending to be her ex-husband, and asked for her address, said it was a family emergency. Eventually, when they said it was life or death, the nursery gave it. They didn't know any better. They didn't know not to.

Lauren has been told off for allowing a photograph of herself online. There was a cold, serious fury behind Jon's words. The near miss was *very* near. But hopefully the police will catch them, Jon said.

Zara is in the back, in her bed wear – shorts and a T-shirt. She didn't change her clothes. Just packed slowly and shivered on the driveway while Jon put their cases into the boot, then resumed reading *The Time Traveler's Wife* in the car, legs like Bambi's across the back seat. When she looks at Lauren in the mirror, her expression looks weirdly guilty. Lauren would know Zara's guilt anywhere, has parented it for a decade and a half. But why she is feeling guilty now, Lauren doesn't know.

'There are to be no selfies, no website photos, no online footprint of any kind in the new location,' Jon continues.

'Whatever,' Zara says. 'They'll find us eventually anyway.'

'*Zara*,' Lauren says, turning around in the passenger seat to glare at her daughter in shock.

'They will,' Zara says, with a shrug. 'We may as well just accept it.'

'Accept what?'

'That it's over.' She stares insolently out of the window. There is something about the set of her shoulders. She's a ball of teenager anger.

'An attitude like that won't help anyone,' Jon says.

Zara's eyes widen, then close.

Good, Lauren thinks. *Go to sleep.* 'You know Sacha,' she says quietly, looking across at Jon, 'who got you the blue and yellow kit . . .'

'Yes.'

'What happened to her?'

The tail end of autumn goes on outside. Leaves catch on the windscreen. The trees are spindles by the side of the road.

'We were both police,' he says, with a sad smile. 'And she was killed on duty.'

Lauren stares at his profile in the dimness of the car.

'By a burglar who she didn't realize was armed,' he continues. 'I drove straight to her – I was on duty, too, in a different part of the city – but I got there too late.' He stops talking but his hands don't. He rubs at his nose, then seems to want to go on, but turns his hands over, a gesture of defeat, before replacing them on the wheel. It's pointless to keep analysing it, his gesture says.

As Lauren slips into sleep again, she thinks of Jon. He left the police along with his sister, and, unable to protect her, he protects others, instead.

Lauren wakes in the passenger seat. Jon's got the heat up high and her cheeks feel tight with it.

She stares at the rain running down the car windows. Black skies, street lights blurred with drizzle. Lauren misses the bath she almost had.

'We're going to start experimenting with plants,' Jon says quietly to Lauren.

'Plants?' Lauren almost laughs.

'We're going to set up some profiles on social media that the group might think are you. Silly errors. We'll have you "like" Facebook groups that Lauren liked, request to add old family members, and so on.'

'But won't my family think . . .'

Jon shrugs, and Lauren supposes he means it's collateral. More damage, more feelings hurt. More confusion, more family drama, more angst.

'Okay,' she says.

'We'll upload a photo of you to some of them. Make your location clear. We can use twenty or thirty. It will help. We've had some success with them with other clients. So we'll try that.'

Clients, Lauren thinks bitterly. Like they're paying for a personal shopping service, not being kept alive.

'Will they work?'

'Hope so,' Jon says.

Yes. They will try that. It doesn't matter that the first thing – the original witness protection – didn't work. It doesn't matter that they are on to the next, like a second round of chemotherapy after an unsuccessful first. It doesn't mean everything will stop working one day, that they will be found and killed. It doesn't, it doesn't, it doesn't.

Lauren feels her eyelids beginning to droop in the heat of the car, her head lolling to the left. Something about the car is safety to her. The hum of the road beneath them. The heaters on low. The relief of choosing to trust. She'll be so good from now on. No burner phones. No website photos.

She dreams that, this time, the group does find them, and that Zara is frog-marched out of the house, a black hood over her head. As the noose is erected and she – her baby daughter, who Lauren grew in her own body – is placed into it, she wakes up. She checks the back seat to be sure.

When they are safely in their new, bland, army-issue house, a different biscuit tin, a different coffee jar, Lauren gets into another starched bed and pulls the burner phone out.

Let me know you're okay, he's sent.

I'm safe, she sends to Aidan. *Are you?*

She waits for a few seconds. The group are on their case, looking for any crack they can slip through, and she can't do it any more, she just can't. The black hood. The noose. She's got to be good now.

She won't tell him they have moved. If he doesn't know, if even *he* thinks they're in the Lakes, then nobody can find them. Lauren's optimism has finally been rattled. There will be no calls. No texts. No parcels. She adds, a second message, and her last.

We had a near miss but they didn't find us. We need to go back to no contact now x.

Thank God, he replies immediately, at three o'clock in the morning. A second later: *I'm safe, yes. And I understand. Take care x.*

Lauren stares at his final message and wonders where she will be two years from now. There are three options. She lists them on her fingers as she looks out of the dusty bedroom window, at a dead woodlouse on her window sill.

Back at home, the group disbanded. Unlikely.

Safe in protection. Settled in an identity. Ready to leave Aidan in the past, ready to date again, after their promised two years of waiting for the other is up. She can't imagine it.

Or dead.

53

Poppy

Battersea, London

Nine days to go

The balaclava man rings Poppy again. She knows it's him when *No Caller ID* flashes up on her phone. She stands, a rabbit in headlights outside the school gates, cold December mists swirling around her ankles. This is her moment to step in.

'I don't know who told you Truro,' she says as she answers, 'but that was wrong information. They're not there. They never were.'

'Is that right?' the voice says.

'Yeah, so . . . stay away from there.'

'Sure, Poppy Madison. Sure.'

Poppy hangs up before he can say anything else, then switches her phone off. She needs to go inside, but she takes a moment, letting the anxiety dissipate, breathing in the smoky ice-cold air. Breathing out hot breath that looks like icing sugar. In again, out again. Eventually, when even her eyes are cold, she heads into registration.

She worries her way through English and double maths. Later, she taps her pen on the edge of the desk, thinking.

Thinking about what to tell her dad. Nothing, she decides. He isn't telling her anything, after all. How can she trust him to manage the situation when he's making everything worse by his own actions?

She takes her school shoes off and rests her feet in their tights against the radiator. She is thinking about Zara, missing her, wondering if she has been broken or strengthened by what has happened to her.

They were on holiday in France when Zara started her period, only she didn't tell Poppy. On the third night there, she merely took a sanitary towel to the toilet block with them. Poppy saw it, eyes wide: she hadn't started hers yet. 'Is that . . .' she'd said, and Zara had nodded, quickly.

'When . . . ?'

'Recently,' Zara said.

'How do you feel?' Poppy had put her wash bag down in one of the sinks. It was an old campsite, a cheap one – 'character building', Aidan had said, as though holidays should never be fun – and the brick walls were covered with spiderwebs. 'God, I'd hate to start on holiday.'

'I'm fine,' Zara had said, but her eyes were glassy.

'Is it scary?' Poppy had said.

'Yeah.' Zara had disappeared then, into the shower stall, and Poppy was sure she had heard muffled crying.

The next day, Zara didn't swim, despite Lauren's encouragement. Her cheeks reddened the more Lauren tried to make her.

'Zara and I have decided not to swim, this holiday,' Poppy had said from her sun lounger. 'You get a better tan when you just lie in it, and rotate. No uneven bits.'

She'd smiled across the pool at Zara, who'd grinned back over her book. Later that year, when Poppy's period started, a little packet of 'essentials' had appeared in her bedroom, on the bedside table, exactly where she needed them.

Poppy sits there, algebra blurring in front of her, and thinks, too, about her father, and about Lauren. She hopes she is helping, to keep them all safe, in her own misguided way.

Fucking Spirit Day. That is what Poppy is thinking as she browses a horrendous fancy-dress store after school. She's sifting through a shelf of wigs. Red, blue, rainbow-coloured. Quite why, she's not sure. She thought a costume for tomorrow would come to her, in this hour she allotted to looking, but it hasn't yet. Poppy hates fancy dress. She likes to look her best, not her worst.

The brief is 'movie characters'. She walks listlessly through the aisles, picking up cowboy hats and witches' masks.

When her mum first became ill, Poppy enjoyed the challenge of these occasions. Having to deal with things, having to make a World Book Day costume while her mother slept. She enjoyed the adultness of it, like she was trying a lifestyle on for size.

But, these days, years on, it's just a pain. She is jaded now. That's life.

She needs to find something before it gets dark. Although even if she leaves late, she is safe, here, in the centre of Battersea, even if it is slightly grungy, because there are so many people around her. Crimes don't happen in crowds, she tells herself.

She picks up a clown costume. Isn't *IT* about a clown? She checks the price tag. It's cheap enough. Then she sees a movement, just outside the shop. Probably nothing. Something and nothing. She inches behind a rack of Victorian costumes and peers out. Somebody in black is standing outside the shop. But not just standing casually. Standing somehow actively. She feels a white-hot flash of anxiety zip up and down her body.

She knew it would happen. She knew they would find her again. Bad things happen to Poppy Madison. She must have done something to deserve it once.

She reaches for her phone. Should she call the police? She tries to slow her breathing, to calm down. What're they going to do to her, here?

But Poppy knows exactly what they will do. They will wait for her to leave the shop, and then they will threaten her. A strong arm across her chest. Something cool and hard in her back. They will make her walk with them, and if she alerts anyone, they will do something. To them, she is an informant, to be disposed of as soon as the information is extracted.

She only has now, this moment, to act.

She dashes up to the counter, clown costume forgotten. 'Excuse me,' she says to the assistant, a boy only a few years older than her, with braces across his teeth.

He looks at her questioningly.

The man in the dark outfit steps away from the shop frontage, and she sees that he is wearing a Carpetright uniform. He stubs out a cigarette with the toe of his black trainers, and moves on. Poppy's entire back is covered in sweat.

'Nothing,' she says to the shop assistant. 'Never mind.'

She stares and stares outside, but it's okay. She's safe. It's a false alarm. Even so, she gets an Uber home. And she thinks she won't walk anywhere alone again. She can't, not on these side streets after the commuters die out like a river that divides into a hundred streams. She just can't. She'll ask her dad for money for the Ubers.

She won't take the risk.

54

Zara

York, Yorkshire

Six weeks gone

It's an abstract concept to Zara that a section of society
hates her enough to be desperately, violently searching
for her, but she knows it's true. When her mum first told
her they had to move, she thought it was her breach that
had led to the group finding them. But it wasn't. It was
a stupid website photo – her mother not thinking. A coincidence that it happened right after the sleepover.

But nevertheless, Zara can't believe she was so stupid.
To trade her safety for a few minutes' intimacy and understanding. Those feelings may be potent, but they are not a
substitute for being alive.

She needs to be tough in the new place, with everything that's still to come. An ice queen, indeed.

She is scrolling through her phone, now, in the car,
looking back at Phoebe's Instagram as her mother
sleeps in the warm. It's gloriously unlocked, an eye
through the keyhole to her world. There's not a hint
Phoebe misses her. Will she have been told they were
moved, or what?

'The takeaway from this is that you can't relax the rules even for one moment,' Jon had said seriously to her mother as they drove. 'It needs to be better. Or we won't be able to continue to offer protection.' Zara had blushed so fiercely she had begun to sweat.

Two new friends, all that potential, just gone. She will never see them again. It had seemed so important, in that moment beneath the skylights at the sleepover, to be liked and accepted by them. And now – nothing. More evidence that her judgement is wrong. That she is broken inside. That the people who exchange glances about her at school and say, '*Okay*, Sienna,' or the people who ignore her entirely when she speaks – that they're right.

Something bubbles up through her. Frustration, anger, tears. Something negative and horrible is living inside her. This all began with her. It is all her fault.

The list of people they have left behind is growing. The lies and cover-ups will begin again now. They will start to bed down, grow beneath the soil, until somebody – maybe Zara, maybe her mother, maybe somebody else – makes a mistake, and they're pulled out again, their roots shocked and anaemic-looking in the bright sun, just like the lettuces she had planted in the greenhouse where all this began.

Zara stands in the window of her new kitchen.

She spotted what would become their house immediately. She knows the look of army housing now. Plain, identical frontages. Net curtains. Red arm rails. Theirs will be the middle one. She knows it.

Surrounded by two empty houses, like sentries, standing tall, keeping them safe.

She sighed as they approached. Her breath misted the window for just a second, barely perceptible, then faded to nothing. Time to start over.

And now here they are.

New names. Her mother is Leonora. Zara is Suzanne.

They have new neighbours. Zara is surprised that the houses on either side aren't empty, but one isn't.

It's hard to believe it's a normal weekday for these people. Zara watches them from the kitchen window as they go to school. They seem to be a totally normal family unit. The mother is leaving the house in a suit. Sort of shabby and dated-looking. Poppy would have a view on the wide-leg black trousers and ballet flats, Zara thinks to herself, but she likes them. The woman seems like a safe pair of hands.

She allows herself a little reverie at the net-curtained window. She pretends they're here. All of them. Aidan and Poppy. They're late for their totally normal, mundane lives. How Zara would treasure normality, now, if she could grasp it. The boredom of the school day. Pale cheese sandwiches for lunch. No plans for the evening except a book, a shower and bed. These things are bliss to Zara, now. She wants to be bored. To be complacent. To not know her luck.

Her mum is upstairs, unpacking, and so Zara slips out on to the driveway in her socks, still holding the book she was reading in the car on the way here. The tarmac is frozen underfoot, and her feet stick to the frost the way lips stick to ice cubes. Her new neighbour's son is outside. He is about her age, holding a guitar case upright next to him, his hand steadying the top of it. He has mid-brown hair. The 'meet me at McDonald's' haircut that Poppy told her about. He raises his eyebrows and gives her a sort of backwards nod.

She lifts her hand in a wave. 'Just moved in,' she says, gesturing back to the house.

The houses here are pebble-dashed, not grey stone like the Lake District. They're on an estate just outside of the city. Zara knows nothing about York except Bettys Tea Room. She couldn't even have pointed to it on a map.

'I can see that, yeah,' he says, looking at the moving van he no doubt thinks is run by totally normal removals people and not a protection service. 'Where did you come from?'

His accent. Zara stares at him, fascinated. The vowels all bent, but beautifully so, distorted from straight lines into curled wrought iron.

'Bristol,' Zara says.

Same story as for the Lake District. That's been the briefing. Skip the Lake District. It never happened, just like London.

'Yeah? Which school are you joining?'

'I don't know yet,' she says, and the faintest of frowns crosses his features.

He wants to inch towards her, she can tell, but he doesn't want to leave the guitar propped up alone against the car. She takes a step away from him, conscious of her odd socks, taken hastily from the washing airer when they were moved overnight.

'Oh right,' he says. 'Well, I go to Hastings.'

'Is that mixed?'

'Mixed?'

'You know . . . boys and girls.'

'Oh. Yeah. It's full of idiots, to be honest,' he says. 'I go in the music room.' His lip curls up, just a fraction. Dark eyebrows draw down. Like, *why did I say that?* That's the expression that seems to cross his face.

'To practise?' She gestures to the guitar. She likes that. Books and music have a lot in common. Creative endeavour, she supposes.

'Yeah. It's soundproof and warm. Best way to spend break.'

Zara winces. She spent break times in London lost in novels. She tried to make friends in the Lakes, and look. Now what?

'I spend them reading,' she says to him. A way to ward him off, she supposes. Suspicion comes easily to her now. He is not to be trusted. Nobody is.

He tilts his head to the side, appraising her. 'Reading?' he says.

'Yeah.' She waves *The Time Traveler's Wife* at him. 'I like novels.'

'Cool. I like smart people,' he says. 'What's it about?'

'It's a love story,' she says.

He holds eye contact a moment longer than usual. It's like a spotlight is on her.

'I see,' he says quietly. 'Why do you read so much?'

Zara thinks for a second. 'Because I'm anxious,' she says eventually. 'Escapism.'

'I like anxious people, too,' he says. 'Bit of edge.'

Zara's chest fills with liquid pleasure, like she's stepped near to an open fire.

All this time. All this time! She's been trying to mould herself into something cool, something worthwhile, someone other than her nerdy, anxious herself, and failing, failing, failing.

And yet here is the counterpoint to that. It isn't change. It's acceptance. Here is somebody who *likes smart people*. Who *likes anxious people*. Who could like her for herself.

No pretending to be cool. No attending parties when she wants to go to literature clubs, instead. She could be – gloriously, finally – herself. And embrace life all the more because of it, the civil war within her over.

But no. This cannot happen. She thinks of the sleep-over and the website photo and all of the people who want to find her and hurt her. She turns away from him.

'Got to go,' she says coldly.

'Well, if you are at Hastings, knock on Room Eleven in the music block at break or lunch,' he says. He writes his number down on a bit of sheet music with a pen that he pulls out of his pocket. 'Here I am. I'm Dom.' He gives her a genuine smile. Top row of teeth. Straight and white. His nose wrinkles up ever so slightly.

Zara stares at him, still a few feet away, socks slowly dissolving the frost, and takes the paper from him.

But she can't text him. She can't text anybody. Can't let anybody in. No matter how much she wants to.

Dom's mobile number is beautiful to look at. 07900 781187. Such a nice symmetrical number. *I like smart people.*

God, she likes him.

Zara stares at the number and thinks. Maybe she could text. Just . . . if she stays within the parameters. The rules.

She writes her own set down on a note which she'll keep under her pillow.

No confiding.

No hints at secrets.

No intimacy. Keep everything light.

You are Suzanne.

As an afterthought, she adds to the note, right at the bottom. She doesn't know where it comes from, or why, but she writes it anyway.

Don't fall in love.

Zara thinks about it for a few hours, just to be sure. Just to be cautious.

And then she sends a text. She's glad he didn't ask for her number. Partly because she has been issued with a new one in case her old one was breached, and she doesn't yet know it, but also because it seems kind of respectful, to leave it up to her.

This is me, hi, she sends. *Suzanne, your neighbour!*

He pops immediately on to WhatsApp, and she looks at his profile picture. A selfie. Her profile is a cartoon of a bookworm at a rainy window, steaming mug of tea in hand. Anonymous, but normal, too. He won't know that she only has three contacts, including him. Her mother and Jon from the protection service being the others. That's what she likes about WhatsApp. It isn't social media.

Hello there from my bedroom, through the wall, to yours! he sends, with a waving hand emoji.

Bolstered, she begins to type. *So . . . what's it like here? Fill me in!*

He doesn't reply for a while, even though he's read it, but, after a few minutes, a voice memo appears. Zara blinks, surprised, and presses 'play'.

Okay, so, he says, like sending a voice note is totally normal. *Let me fill you in on York. This street is alright – it's pretty quiet. There's countryside not far away, I'll have to show you one of these days . . .*

Zara lies back on her bed and listens to his voice, low and pure and honest, her eyes closed as he teaches her about her new neighbourhood. Later, she gets the courage to send a voice note back, and he reciprocates. They spend the evening that way, as intimate as a phone call, as convenient as a text, with the ability to redraft and start over. To self-edit, as witness protection requires.

Zara is enrolled in Hastings School the next day, once they have had a chance to catch up on sleep and re-buy the things they couldn't bring with them. Their possessions have dwindled so much, but still they lost more. They couldn't take anything that was in the washing machine overnight, halfway through a spin. Gone, too, is Zara's shampoo, lying damp and forgotten in the shower tray back in the Lake District. She hadn't even finished a full bottle. That's how long they lasted there.

She ought to feel nervous, but she doesn't, just knowing Dom is there somewhere. A friendly face in the crowd, a friendly face in Room 11 of the music block. Like she has already got an advantage over York before she's started.

It's break time, towards the end of the winter term. The playground is gilded with frost. A teacher stands nearby, his back to her, watching the students in their hats and scarves walking, talking, laughing. Zara is totally alone, nobody even looking at her. She is invisible, which should be welcome, but it isn't. She's only human.

Cold and bored, she lets herself into the block that says *Music* on it. She finds his room, raises a gloved fist.

And knocks.

Don't fall in love.

That evening, like a little gift to open at the end of the day, a new voice memo arrives.

God, it was so nice to see you this afternoon. I don't know if I'm being way keen here, but I like you, Suzanne Steele. Anyway, let me tell you about my evening. My little sister, Imogen – she's four – literally sucked a reed diffuser, and we had to go to A&E. She's fine, but her breath now smells of fresh linen . . .

55

Aidan

Shepherd's Bush, London

Eight days to go

'James?' Brian says on the phone. 'What's up?'

'I've rented a warehouse in Central,' he says. 'The twentieth of December, remember? Can we all be there to discuss major strategy? Unless we've found her by then.'

'Can't do the twentieth,' Brian says coolly, even though he'd agreed to it on Telegram. 'It's my birthday. The twenty-first, instead?' And then he adds, 'Can you re-book? It's a good idea. It's a good idea to have a group-wide meet. We're two months in and – nothing. Didn't think it would take this long. Surprised your scrapers haven't turned much up.'

'I'll move the booking,' Aidan says.

'Where are the results? You told me it would be easy.'

The hairs on the back of Aidan's neck rise up slowly, like a cold hand sweeping slowly up his spine.

Aidan stammers. 'They're . . . it is harder than I thought. The kid got lucky with the reverse image search.'

'Yeah . . . well, it wasn't them. Was an empty house.'

Aidan sends another grateful *thanks* out into the

universe. 'I'll try to be better on the scrapers,' he says, relief making him feel pathetically grateful.

'Justice,' Brian says quietly. 'That's all we want, isn't it? Luke's been playing games with the homeless people, and everyone is acting like it's murder.'

'Right,' Aidan says tightly.

'It's harmless fun, isn't it? So long as the tramps behave themselves.'

'Yeah.' Aidan swallows bile.

'Innocent until proven guilty, ridiculous, really, isn't it?' he says. 'Anyone can say anything about a young lad, and he'd get tried for it, on the strength of . . . what? Words. That's it. Just words. Just as well he won't be a footballer, now. All because of a little game, is all. A harmless game.'

How strange it is, Aidan is thinking. *The lies we tell ourselves as parents. The self-delusion.*

'Let me know how the scrapers are going. Soon,' Brian says to Aidan.

Aidan is on the phone to his mother that evening, right before bed, tidying up. 'And how's the . . . what you spoke to me about?' she asks tentatively.

'It's fine,' he says.

'Have you stopped?'

He winces as she says it. He can't lie to her. Not so directly.

'No,' he says quietly. 'But it's under control.'

'Aidan,' she says again, using his name with a power only his mother can.

'I know,' he says quickly, blushing, glad she doesn't know the rest of it. The beating. The police. The total

359

disaster that is the scrapers. How many crimes he's probably committing, joining in conspiracies. He closes his eyes and holds the phone tight to his cheek. It's hot, almost like it's his mother's body heat he can feel against his face, here on this cold December night in London.

He opens his eyes and catches his reflection in the window. He momentarily doesn't recognize himself. He's been doing press-ups, and his shoulders are rounded now, his chest a drum. His face is sallow and sunken, beyond tired-looking. His jaw has changed shape. The dentist couldn't make him emergency crowns. He's had to have a temporary denture, ill-fitting new teeth, and his jaw juts out now. He looks like a man who has been running on empty for too long. Somebody who's had a breakdown or been out of work for years. Who's been marooned on a desert island or been sent to prison. He looks like a thug. Somebody who would do anything in desperation. Absolutely anything.

'Stay safe,' his mother says to him. 'Aidan. Please, stay safe.'

56

Zara

York, Yorkshire

Six weeks gone

Dom, in that way of his, sent Zara a calendar invitation last night, with the subject *Bettys and general York tour after school?* She accepted it immediately. The world has cracked open, for Zara. All the things she didn't do because she has been ashamed of her core self have opened up to her. She could do anything. Go to a late-night lecture. Go to Cephalonia to see where *Captain Corelli's Mandolin* was set. Talk freely about what she likes, without shame.

She tells herself she is being cautious, that she is resisting getting close to him. She *is*. But it's a basic human need, isn't it? To be spoken to, to open up. To be touched.

They're sitting opposite each other in the opulence of Bettys now. They had to queue, but Zara has always liked the anticipation of queuing. An emblem of optimism, looking forward to something, literally staring at it with a load of people who feel the same way. She'd said this to Dom, who had laughed. It smells of roasted coffee beans and spices here.

'It's funny to be *live*, and not sending you voice notes,' Dom says, with a smile.

'Why the voice notes?'

He shrugs. 'Just like them. I wanted to chat to you but not . . . you know? Not scare you away.'

Zara stares across the busy restaurant, watching the waiters and waitresses, watching the plates of food and the three-tier afternoon teas being delivered. She wonders if she has ever met somebody who was in witness protection before, without knowing it.

'They're nice,' she says. 'I like them, too.'

Dom smiles at her sincerely across the table. 'So, Suzanne,' he says. 'Suzanne like the Leonard Cohen song.'

'That's me.' Zara smiles tightly. Zara, Girl A, Sienna, Suzanne.

'Were you named after that?'

'Do you know, I've never asked. I doubt it,' Zara adds, when his eyebrows go up. 'Mum's not into music.'

'Not into music,' Dom says, shaking his head slightly like he can't believe it. 'I can't believe you've never asked that.'

'Me neither,' Zara says, and she means it. She would have asked, if she was really called Suzanne. She sips a cappuccino. It has three shots of coffee in it. She's never had one before, but she ordered it without thinking, acting on impulse. She's never done that before, either.

'So what's your story, then, Suzanne-by-the-river?'

'My story?'

'Siblings?'

'None,' Zara says, a wave of sadness moving up through her. She's never thought about that. She's never thought about the future with her stepsister, and now it's gone. Twenty-somethings. Early in their careers, meeting up in London together for drinks, celebrating their thirtieth birthdays together in the same year, moaning when their parents annoyed them . . . all gone. That future, all gone.

'An only child. I thought as much.'

'Did you?'

'Yeah, you're . . . you know. So composed.'

Zara laughs at that. He's right and he's wrong, all at once.

He catches her laugh, and raises his eyebrows, wanting her to share.

But she doesn't. Can't. Something shifts behind her eyes. She can feel it. She's told so many lies now that she can feel the physiological effects of them. When she speaks the truth, she feels light and confident. And when she lies, she feels heavy, like her eyes are black. Cognitive dissonance, is it? When the outside is not the same as the inside?

'Where's your dad?'

'Never met him,' Zara says truthfully. 'You?'

'He's in the army. It's hard. I don't know. He feels like . . . like a very distant uncle.'

Zara picks up a menu on the pretence of ordering some food and stares at it, trying to mask that her eyes are wet. Will Aidan one day become like that? She can't imagine it, her careful, kind stepfather. 'I guess that's natural,' she mumbles.

'Yeah. Maybe. Do you miss having a dad?'

There's a pause. Here she is again, at the crossroads. A whole path in front of her. A whole person will be available to her if she tells the truth. But if she doesn't, she will be safe. And so she can't. She can't jeopardize it again.

'Does it get cold up here, in the winter?' she says. The weather. So benign.

Dom's expression closes down. 'Yeah, a bit,' he says.

They make small talk after that. It's the best way.

She records a voice memo to Dom that evening, in the privacy of the bathroom, away from her mum. In it, she tells him everything. What she did when she saw the crime. Why she did it. That they were taken into protection, then moved again, because of another of her indiscretions. She tells him how lonely she feels, how fucked up, how responsible. And she tells him her secret, too. About the motto, and about her plan. And then, before she presses 'send', she presses 'delete'. She doesn't hear from him. If he saw her recording, he never says.

Zara wakes early the next morning. Six o'clock. Her mother is still sleeping. She sits on her bed, and looks at Dom's WhatsApp profile.

Last seen yesterday at 22.17.

She clicks on his photo and looks into his eyes, wishing she could tell him.

As she does so, a text comes in from him.

When's the next date?

She closes her eyes in relief. She hasn't driven him away: it isn't too late.

57

Lauren

York, Yorkshire

Six weeks gone

Lauren is certain that Zara is falling in love with the boy next door.

She knows all of the moods of her daughter, but this one is new. She realized it last night, over meatballs. Zara was present in body but not in mind. She was staring at her phone and smiling. When she got up from the table, Lauren watched Zara bump into the kitchen bin because she was on her phone, and then not even notice that, either. That's when Lauren knew.

And Lauren is jealous. She is standing outside a nursery, now, before an interview, and she is jealous.

God, she has never once felt jealous of her daughter. Not when she was brand new, one day old, and had an eternity stretching in front of her, when Lauren's time was almost half spent. Not when she looked like a model on holiday in a bikini. She's not ever been jealous – because Zara is an extension of her. She is Lauren's descendant, her successor.

But now she is.

She is jealous because the lies Lauren has to tell are bigger. They won't be subsumed into the past so easily, like Zara's lies. When you're twenty, who you were at sixteen is irrelevant. But Lauren has been Lauren for over forty years. She can't move on.

So, instead, she is standing here, staring at the finger where her engagement and wedding rings used to be. She's lost the tan from the summer entirely, so there's no longer any evidence of them. It never happened, none of it.

Lauren reaches the reception of the nursery. Her lipstick is smeared. Her hair a mess. Later, she is looking forward to eating a Portuguese custard tart on the bus.

The reception has wooden floors, a branded rug with the nursery's name on it. *High Trees*. They're going to ask her competency questions, she is thinking, as the receptionist slides the glass screen back. 'Can I help?' she says, and Lauren thinks: *no, nobody can. Suddenly, I can't recall a time when I helped a difficult child to develop, or I reported a safeguarding concern.* Perhaps she can just tell them the truth. A half-truth. That she really, really needs this job. That she would be good at it. That she will love the children. That there is nothing better, to her, than seeing a three-year-old late talker say, 'Lauren, look!' out of nowhere, as though somebody just turned on the speech part of their brain overnight.

'I have a four-thirty interview,' she says. As she speaks, she smells it. All nurseries smell the same. Poster paints. The plastic smell of lunchboxes: cucumber and bread. She blinks and glances around her. She is home, home amongst these smells and the little starfish hands and feet of the children she will fall in love with. Lauren forgets her frizzy hair, her smudged lipstick.

'Great,' the receptionist says. Her nails click on the keyboard. 'Please can you confirm your name?'

'Leonora,' Lauren tells the receptionist. She glances at herself again, reflected in the glass screen. There is no Lauren any more, she tells herself with her eyes. Lauren is gone.

'This way,' the receptionist says.

Lauren isn't prepared, thought she'd have a few minutes to wait in reception, to calm down, to think of the right answers. She's led, instead, into a back room where two women are waiting for her, their hands folded. It smells of stale tea and chalk. It's heated by a single electric heater, under the table they're sitting at. Both women have their feet on it.

'Leonora? Nice to meet you,' one of the women, who has dip-dyed hair, says.

'And you.' Lauren extends her hand, then sits down in front of them on what appears to be a child's chair. It's lower than she thought it would be, and the surprise jolts her spine.

'So, tell us a bit about you,' the woman says.

Lauren stammers and stumbles her way over an introduction to somebody she doesn't know herself. She's sitting so low, compared to the two women, she feels like she's in *Alice in Wonderland*, like she's shrunk or become distorted. Panic fills her veins. The children's paintings on the wall take on a menacing air, the burnt smell of the heater becomes cloying. The interviewers' eyes look too wide, too prying. Lauren is covered in sweat within minutes.

'I . . .' she says. Where's she from? Bristol? London?

The Lake District? Her mind is a shut-up shop, closed for business. She can't retrieve the current story she's supposed to be telling from the rubble of the lies.

She leaves after the second question. She can't do it. She's not up to it. She's broken.

She goes into the bar a short walk from the nursery and drinks three wines alone. She lingers for hours, drinking moodily, shopping on her phone. Then she buys a cake from a late-night dessert place. She'll eat it all, alone, on the couch, until she feels sick. She finds a taxi rank. She'll treat herself. She can't be bothered to get the bus again, and sit tensed at every stop when people get on.

There's a queue outside the taxi rank, bodies fenced into a small enclosure surrounded with metal railings, and Lauren joins them. A woman's arm presses against hers. Lauren closes her eyes with the pleasure of it, and pretends it's an embrace. She enjoys it so much, that stranger's body heat against hers, that it is the best moment of her day, standing and pretending and watching the black cabs come and go, a traditional, familiar sight. Beetle-shaped. Yellow light on the top.

One arrives for her after twenty minutes, and she collapses tipsily into the seat with her back to the driver, not wanting to look at him. He asks her for her address and she has to look for it on her phone. She's got the street down, but not the postcode. Her voice catches as she reads it off her phone. Another house, another postcode, another name. The driver doesn't make eye contact, and she's glad of it. Maybe she shouldn't have got into this taxi without checking his licence. Maybe he was waiting just for her. Maybe he's dangerous. Maybe, maybe, maybe.

Lauren sits back, drunk, not caring. The disastrous interview is proof she cannot sustain the anxiety of it any longer. *Kill me, then*, she thinks bitterly in the back.

She takes her shoes off and puts her feet up on the seats in front of her. Fuck it. Fuck everyone.

She opens her phone and prepares to do a deep dive on to the internet. Aidan first: nothing. No posts since she left. *Well, good. He should have come*, she thinks angrily. He is miserable without her and she without him.

She goes on to Google Street View and stares at her old house in Islington. She takes a virtual walk down the high street that she loved so much, past the crêpe place she always intended to go to but never quite managed. Past the Starbucks and the bus stops. Past the huge sofa warehouse and the posh estate agents with the double-storey glass frontages. Down into the alleyways where the markets were. She and Zara would laugh at the ridiculous costume jewellery for sale. God, when did Lauren last laugh? The early morning summer sun was warm on their forearms, back in Islington, on the tops of their heads. She can't stand it. She can't stand it.

The taxi takes a corner too fast and Lauren braces herself on the seats. 'Sorry,' the driver calls.

She opens Google Maps again. There she is. That tiny blue dot. She zooms out and out and out, trying to get some perspective. York. England. The UK. Europe. The world. There are seven billion people on this planet. What does it matter that she is in witness protection? That she is missing Aidan?

But she can't get it. It doesn't come. She is solipsistic. The world revolves around her. Her blue dot is at the centre of it, like everyone's.

'Alright, love?' the taxi driver tries again. 'Just up here on the left, is it?'

'Yeah,' Lauren says, though she doesn't know. She ignores him. She slides the burner phone out of her bag.

I wish you were here, she sends to Aidan.

It's a relief, like a blood-letting. The tension in her back and shoulders dissipates. That sentence – *I wish you were here* – is the first truthful thing she has said all day. And she is glad she has said it. To him, to the man that she loves.

She sends a selfie. She is grey and pixellated in the cab, eyes blurry, eyeliner smudged. And she is not alone any more, trying to make boilers work, trying to make new friends, exercising her own judgement over Zara having a boyfriend, over Zara being rude, after a decade of co-parenting.

And that is a life. That is an identity. It isn't paperwork and names and passports. It is other people. Being loved. Being understood. Being witnessed, like every single person needs to be.

She lets herself into the house and she waits and waits and waits in bed for a reply, eating the cake, her eyes closing afterwards for longer and longer periods, but one doesn't come. Aidan is being good, but she isn't able to.

She falls asleep, with the phone in her palm, in the space where his hand ought to be.

58

Poppy

Central London

Eight days to go

Her dad gives a listless yes when Poppy asks if she can bring Emily over. He has no idea, of course, that they plan to use the night to spy on him.

He meets them in a café in central London after school. Poppy knows why: he is her chaperone, since the attack, and he is also taking them on increasingly diverted routes home. He thinks they're being followed, that much is obvious. It's a cold day. Less than five degrees, feels like three, according to her weather app. Her cheeks ache in the freezing air.

Poppy orders a Coke, with a straw: this lipstick was expensive enough (it's the Dior Lip Glow – goes on like a balm and makes her lips look like she's just been kissed). Emily orders a strawberry milkshake, of course.

'We have a little camp bed for you,' Aidan says over his shoulder, to Emily, as they leave.

It's especially impossible, here in Covent Garden, with the ornate balconies and the melodies of the buskers intertwining, to imagine danger. It seems ludicrous that men in balaclavas lurk around the corner when – look – freezing

December blue skies. The hotel across the square is covered in a russet jacket of leaves. There are Christmas lights up on some of the flats nearby. It can't happen here, it just can't.

'Oh, good,' Emily says easily.

Poppy's grateful, but embarrassed, too. She can feel it creeping up her body like warm bathwater. Emily's concerns are the latest ColourPop collection and growing out of her New Balance trainers before she's got a 'season's wear' out of them. Poppy's embarrassed. By everything. By her mother's incontinence pads that arrive in the Tesco online shop. By the camp bed at her father's, his cramped flat, weird routes home to avoid criminals. She's so tired of it. So tired of feeling *other*.

Their lives seem suddenly seedy in the vibrancy of Covent Garden. Her dad strides ahead of them to the Tube, his tread assertively heavy, like he is policeman or bouncer, but Emily hangs back with her.

It won't always be this way, she tells herself. They won't always be frightened they're being followed. She won't always be missing her stepfamily. It won't always be December, be winter. Soon, the spring will come.

The camp bed is set up in the living room. Poppy has said she will take the sofa, to be near Emily, and her dad is too distracted to argue.

It's after eleven. Her dad is in bed, and it's just the two of them in the living room. Poppy likes the strangeness of it. Being able to hear the thrum of the dishwasher, see the blinking light of the Sky Box, being next to the curtains that touch the floor. Like they're in a hotel room, or something.

Emily found some old IKEA candles underneath the sink and has lit four of them along the TV cabinet.

They're drinking the only thing they could find in the cupboard – green tea with mint. The flat still doesn't feel like a home. There are so many things they haven't got. No salt. No sponges to wipe up with. No hand towels. Emily grimaces each time she sips the tea.

Poppy sits on a patch of floor warmed by two pipes crossing, cradling her tea in her hands. Emily's skin looks amazing in the candlelight: nature's highlighter.

'How are we going to do this, then?' Poppy says.

'Where is it?' Emily says in a low voice.

Poppy gives a small, sad shrug. 'In his room, I'd guess,' she says. She doesn't want to be spying on her father. She wants to trust him. But he might be lying to her. And, if he is, someone needs to stop him contacting Lauren, before the group finds them.

Emily fiddles with the string on her tea bag, whirling it around in her drink. 'There's no mint in this,' she says.

'I know.'

'He won't be doing it on his normal phone,' Emily says, and this is why Poppy loves her so much: she actually, genuinely thinks about Poppy's problems, doesn't just pretend she is considering them while waiting to speak herself, or believe that her advice won't be followed, that it isn't her problem.

'Have you noticed anything? A second phone? Weird behaviour?'

Poppy stretches her legs out in front of her and absent-mindedly pulls her socks off. 'I might paint my toenails,' she says. She only did them three days ago, but whatever.

Emily tosses her the nail polish remover and cotton wool.

'No, I haven't,' she says honestly. 'Maybe I'm totally wrong.' Poppy scrubs at her toenail polish with the cotton balls, thinking. 'Let's just look,' she says eventually.

Emily gets to her feet. Poppy stands up and starts searching. The kitchen table is already scattered with their things. Her purse, a set of keys, a few junk flyers for pizzas and political parties. She roots through everything, but she knows it'll be in with him.

'Okay, go for it. Into the bedroom,' Emily says.

Poppy feels suddenly vulnerable, standing there, thinking about the Find Girl A group, the balaclava man, the man's face in the window outside her school.

'Get his bag,' Emily says. 'First. Don't get his iPhone.'

'Okay,' Poppy says.

She walks down the hallway and pauses outside her dad's door. His breathing is even and regular. Poppy inches the door open. Emily hovers in the hallway, saying nothing. Poppy is grateful for the deep carpets that mask the sound of her footsteps. The bag is just a foot or so into the room, right next to the end of his bed. She hooks one finger through the loop at the top and fishes it out.

Together, in the living room, they open the rucksack, the zip sounding like an earthquake in the night.

Her dad is naturally neat. There are no rogue receipts or stale crumbs. Just his wallet, loose in the main section, and his keys in the front pouch. Poppy tips it upside down, but there's nothing else there.

'His iPhone will be on charge by the bed,' Poppy says.

'Yeah. I just don't think he'd use that. He's not an idiot.'

'Yeah.'

'Balaclava man was probably full of shit . . .' Emily says.

Poppy smiles as Emily seamlessly adopts her parlance. Poppy called her attacker balaclava man, and so, too, does Emily.

'. . . and the train ticket was probably nothing. Work, or something. The Truro attack thing could have been a coincidence.' Emily roots around carefully in the bag, even though Poppy is sure it is empty.

Until it vibrates.

Emily starts, staring at Poppy. 'There's a fucking phone in the lining,' she whispers.

Poppy reaches her hand into the rucksack, feeling around.

'It's at the back, there's a rip in the lining,' Emily says. She slides her arm in further, and emerges with a flip phone.

It's glowing: *23.26.*

Poppy should be tired, but isn't remotely. It's otherwise nondescript, except there is a message showing on the front screen.

In Case of Emergency – message.

'It's a burner phone,' Emily says.

The sad sleeping snake is back in Poppy's stomach. She thought he wouldn't be in touch with Lauren. She hoped he wouldn't be. That it would be based on nothing, misunderstandings. But here she is, having found a tiny compartment in her father's weird rucksack, containing the exact thing she was so sure she wouldn't find. And here she is, understanding why he took the phone call on her behalf: because he had things to say. God knows what. He's playing with fire.

Sometimes, it feels to Poppy, there is nobody in her life who has not let her down. She knows that isn't fair to think, but she thinks it anyway. The phone trembles in her hand. Fuck it. Fuck them all.

She holds the phone. The message won't preview, and the phone is locked.

She opens and closes the phone, pressing buttons.

Fingerprint not recognized. Passcode needed, it says.

'Crap,' Emily says, looking over her shoulder.

'I could try my birthdate?' Poppy says, glancing at Emily.

'It'll be unguessable,' she says. 'I mean, what he's doing is basically illegal.'

She's so smart. Poppy is so glad she's here.

'He's not going to use information anybody could guess,' Emily says.

'Shit.'

'Does it say it has fingerprint recognition?' Emily asks.

'Yeah. That's what it says. Fingerprint not recognized – passcode needed.'

It's made to look like an old phone, untraceable, but it is advanced. It is the kind of phone you use for things that need to be kept secret. Illegal things. Affairs. And things Poppy can't even imagine.

'Well . . .' Emily looks to the bedroom. 'I mean . . . how heavy a sleeper is he?'

'Quite, though not at the moment,' Poppy says thoughtfully.

'You could try it and if he wakes up just say . . . I don't know. That it was ringing? You were bringing it to him? God, I mean, he's the one in the wrong here, isn't he?

376

Someone is threatening you because of him. And whatever he told them . . . it isn't working'

'Yes, yes,' Poppy says, feeling bolstered by her friend's kindness and belief.

She rises and goes to the door of her dad's bedroom. He has one arm flung above his hand, the other dangling. Bill is sharing the bed with him, and he wakes, looking at Poppy with one eye open. She ignores him.

It is easy to get a fingerprint. So easy, Poppy is amazed this sort of thing doesn't happen more often.

He stirs, but that's all, and the phone unlocks by magic.

She rushes back into the living room. 'Success,' she says. 'Now, we can't let it lock!'

She sits back down and looks at it. It's defaulted to the home page, the (1) symbol by the text messages glowing red. She leaves it, not knowing what to do about that, and scrolls to the contacts, instead.

There's only one. In Case of Emergency.

She looks up at Emily. 'I think we should read the text,' Emily says. 'Any and all of them.'

Sometimes, Poppy thinks that if she does something late at night, it doesn't really count. It is something that Lauren has told her in that laughing way of hers. 'Calories don't count after ten o'clock,' she once said, inching half a Black Forest gateau out of the fridge, licking a splodge of cream off her finger.

The glow of the screen illuminates a cube of air in front of her face. The rest of the flat is in darkness.

'Can you mark a text unread on this thing?' Poppy says.

Emily googles it and sets the instructions out in front of them on her own phone.

Poppy braces herself, and opens the text.

As she does so, a second comes through. A photograph. A selfie. Poppy stares at it. It's Lauren. Her stepmother. Strong jaw. Slightly crooked nose. Beautiful, happy, sunny Lauren. She zooms in on her features. Streaked eyeliner – she's been crying. It's formed little clear rivulets into her blusher. Poppy can tell a crying selfie from miles away. She scrolls across – is she in a taxi? She can see a driver behind her. And that's where she sees it.

On the taxi driver's satnav: 2 Sunshine Drive, YO5 6GH.

'Fuck,' she says. She shows it wordlessly to Emily.

'Jesus,' Emily says.

Poppy scrolls up through In Case of Emergency right to the beginning. The tentative beginning. Then the banter. Their confessionals. Their love letters.

'Fuck,' she whispers. Emily says nothing, just staring at the texts, then up at her, so Poppy adds, 'We should tell someone.'

Emily reaches for the phone and scrolls down, reading quickly.

'He's protecting her,' Emily says softly. She scrolls to just a few weeks ago, evidently double-checking something, then nods, passing it to Poppy.

She reads it. It's her father all over.

No, don't take the phone out.

Make sure you're with Zara so she doesn't make friends with somebody and disclose.

Remember: no website photos.

Caution, always caution. Poppy closes her eyes. It makes complete sense. Open, social, indiscreet Lauren. The worst person to go into witness protection. Her careful, brave, smart dad. Always doing the right thing. Even when it might seem misguided. He hasn't been reckless. He's been *careful*.

Poppy looks at the rest of the phone. It's anonymous. A blank background image of space. One page of apps. Not much in the photos.

Emily peers over her shoulder and points to a folder. 'Evidence', it is called. It's blurred photos of something, tucked away within the gallery. They're of some sort of messenger Poppy doesn't recognize. *Find Girl A – Underground* is written at the top. In the same folder, a screenshot note made by him: *Meet up 20th December 7.00 p.m.* Then there are screenshots of emails with the police dated throughout November, seemingly arranging for them to meet, though it's not clear why. Another screenshot of another note: *They want to see evidence of conspiracy to murder: forward planning and evidence of weapons.*

'Look,' Emily says. 'Look what he's doing.' She goes back to the photos of the Find Girl A group. There are hundreds of them. 'He's gathering evidence of their plans. And look . . . he's been telling the police.'

Poppy nods slowly. 'I see.'

'He suggested a meeting. Look, Pops. He's going to bust them.'

'Oh my God.'

'In just a few days.' Emily excitedly takes the phone off her. 'The group messages are on a weird app,' she says. 'Telegram.' She finds the app in the folder. As always, Emily is a few steps ahead of her. 'He's joined the group under a fake name. Look at the messages on the right – from this phone. It's James Thomas.'

'Man,' Poppy says, staring at them. 'They're meeting in four days. And the police will be there.'

'Yes.'

'Wow.' And, despite the scary night, the sinister burner phone, Poppy is relieved.

He is the man she thought he is. Her father. He isn't being reckless: he's problem solving, the way he always has. Thank God. Thank God she hasn't lost him.

Emily leans back on her hands. 'What a hero. He's keeping an eye on them, and trying to get them arrested. He's being, like . . . proactive, isn't he? Rather than hiding, like the police suggested.'

Emily gestures for Poppy to uncross her legs, then opens a bottle of nail varnish. 'Purple?' she says.

'Sure.'

Emily begins buffing her toenails as she thinks. 'You can't tell the police. They already know. It's legit.'

'Yeah.'

'All you need to do is wait. And maybe next week . . . maybe it'll all be over.'

'Yeah.' Poppy can't imagine. She feels light as air.

Emily slicks on the first cool stroke of polish. Poppy closes her eyes and leans back against the sofa. Emily paints away in silence. Poppy enjoys the cathartic strokes on her toes. The feeling of a problem shared. Of good advice having been given. Of optimism.

She hears a noise in the bedroom. The creak of the bed. He's just turning over, she tells herself, as she sits completely still, listening.

Emily stops painting and looks up. 'Fuck,' she mouths. They freeze.

A longer creak, and two feet, landing on the wooden floor slightly out of time with each other. Poppy moves as quickly as she can, stuffing the phone down the side of the sofa. She turns it off with her finger so it doesn't make any noise.

Hopefully, he won't notice the rucksack.

'Pops?' her dad says, arriving in the living room.

'We're doing toenails,' Poppy says, gesturing to Emily holding the bottle.

'Right,' he says.

Emily excuses herself to go to the bathroom.

'Can't sleep?' Poppy says.

'Yeah.' He rubs at his beard.

Her upper lip is sweating as she sits there, in her pyjamas, his secret phone down the side of the sofa.

He gets them two glasses of water and sits in the armchair opposite her. 'I miss them,' her dad says. He puts his glass on a coaster on the coffee table and stretches his arms above his head. 'But I think things might get better, you know? I think it'll blow over soon.'

Poppy leans back against the sofa. It's too warm in the living room, the electric radiator in the corner producing steam that rises up into the room like tendrils of hair. She once told her dad that he kept the house too cold and, ever since, he's turned the heating up whenever she comes to stay.

'You think?' she says.

'I really do.'

She can tell he's tired. He would never usually get her hopes up like this. But there it is. Proof. She's seen it on his phone and, if there was any doubt, he's confirmed it. The nightmare is about to end.

'I'm happy on the camp bed, if you two want my bed,' he says sleepily to her. 'I should have said earlier.' He rubs his head. 'Didn't think.'

'No, no,' Poppy says.

Bill pads into the living room. He doesn't like it here. He's been at Hannah's, for a while, but now he's back. She guesses her dad got lonely. Bill looks mournfully out of the sixth-floor window, and then to Poppy. She reaches to pat his head and he nuzzles into her, the way he used to do with Lauren. She hopes her dad is paying him enough attention.

Her dad finishes his water and goes to the sink. He's never been a big talker, not in the way that Lauren is. He is the one who quietly turns the thermostat up, who tries to entrap a vigilante group.

Eventually, he leaves. When Poppy hears his snoring begin, Emily replaces the phone in his bag.

At midnight, they google the address.

York. They're in York. Sunshine Drive.

She knows it, and wishes she didn't, all at the same time.

As she's falling asleep, Bill's chin by her side, she remembers she didn't put the text message back on 'read'. But she's sure he knows where they are. That's the whole point, isn't it?

Sleep overcomes her and, the next morning, it is forgotten.

59

Lauren

York, Yorkshire
Six weeks gone

Lauren is hungover, sitting on the bar stool in the kitchen. They are almost exactly the same as the ones she has at home, in Islington. If she closes her eyes, she can conjure up the feeling of that house. Sunlight on the counter in tiger stripes through the shutters. Bill's dangling jowls resting against her knees. Leathery and warm. The smell of it, only noticeable after holidays: laundry, last night's cooking, dog hair. God, it's almost Christmas. They don't even have a tree.

'I'm going out with Dom,' Zara says. A burst of enthusiasm in the kitchen, like a flower pushing up unexpectedly through pavement.

Lauren feels a heavy sigh brewing within her. Oh, to be sixteen and in love with the boy next door.

'Is that who you were speaking to?' Lauren says.

'Not sure.' Her composure has come back, drawing across her face like a filter.

'What? How can you not be sure?'

'Was I on the phone?'

'I heard you talking.'

'Yeah.'

'To who, then?'

Zara says nothing.

'Where has all this secrecy come from?' Lauren says, anxiety lacing her words like acid. She can disregard her own safety, sit in taxis ill-advisedly and send selfies, but she can't relax the rules for her daughter. Her endangered daughter.

Zara shrugs. She's been less insolent, recently. Happier, but still secretive.

'Look,' Lauren says, 'I get that it's hard. But I don't know why you seem to think that's my fault.' She looks carefully at her daughter's angry little face. 'Because it isn't.'

'Yeah. Sure,' Zara says, and, this time, she isn't angry: she's indifferent.

A funny sort of rage rises up through Lauren. How dare she keep things from her?

They stare at each other for several seconds. Lauren can't see any of herself in Zara, today. Zara is wearing a hat and mittens, hasn't put her coat on yet. She looks like a model.

'If you won't do things my way, I won't help you,' Lauren says. 'I can't help someone who keeps secrets from me.'

'What?'

'We live here,' Lauren gestures around her. 'Together. We're a team.'

'So?'

'I can't do it, Zara. I can't,' Lauren says, thinking of the past few weeks. Feeding Zara chocolate cake for breakfast. Being understanding, understanding, understanding. Letting her go out whenever she wants to. Acting like a kid herself on the burner phone. Her mind circles back even further. Letting her daughter give evidence. Letting her go out alone the weekend after, even though she knew a group wanted to hurt her. God. Lauren needs to grow up. It's time to start parenting.

'It's up to you,' Lauren says.

'Thanks for the understanding,' Zara says sarcastically.

'I do understand,' Lauren says quietly. 'I've left my husband, my stepdaughter, my job, my friends . . . nobody understands better than me.'

Zara stares at her, her eyes two wet pools. 'I know,' she whispers. She drops her gaze. 'I know.'

'I'm not the enemy here,' Lauren says. 'I'm just not. You need to . . . God, Zara. You need to respect me here. Or you can find another ally.'

'Okay,' Zara says.

Lauren sees two distinct tear tracks making their way down Zara's cheeks. Her shoulders sag in defeat.

'What's been going on? Why have you been so . . . so angry with me?'

Zara waves a hand. 'I just . . .'

Lauren waits.

'I feel like there's probably something wrong with me,' she says in a small voice.

'What?'

'Like, I told that lie. And then I don't know . . . I've never been able to fit in. You know?'

Lauren takes a tentative step towards her daughter. 'There is absolutely nothing wrong with you.'

'You would say that.'

'It's the truth. What could be wrong?' She holds on to Zara's long, slim arms. Her skin is still baby soft. 'You're perfection, to me.'

'I like books too much. I'm awkward. Everyone at school is always joking around and I'm so . . . I'm so serious.'

'Serious people who like books aren't worse than chatty, jokey people,' Lauren says. Has she instilled this insecurity in Zara, somehow? In trying to always buoy her up, has she pushed her down? 'I bet Emily Brontë was serious.'

Zara cracks a smile at that.

'I bet she liked books, too,' Lauren adds.

'Probably.'

'I feel like that, you know,' Lauren says. 'I had this interview yesterday and I was a total lunatic in it. We all feel awkward sometimes. We *all* feel like we don't fit in. It's part of being human.'

'Is it?' Zara says, her eyes fixed on her mother's, like she's just told her something amazing.

'Absolutely. I feel like it every day.'

'Every day?'

'Every day.'

Lauren ascends the stairs later. She turns the wrong way — already, her muscles have memorized their first house's layout.

She starts the bath running. The water clatters out of the hot tap, steaming within just a few seconds, and she watches it, hoping it'll hold, even though it's a different bath. A different house. As she turns to go and investigate which of her bath oils made it across here with her, she sees something on the edge of the bath. A bottle of Radox Stress Relief. A Post-it note next to it.

Here's to York – Jon.

Tears fill her eyes.

She dumps a quarter of the bottle in and watches the water turn a bright aquamarine. She fetches a towel and removes her clothes, then gets in. Warm feet. Goosebumps everywhere else, like she is outside, wild and free, the cool wind on her skin, the hot sun just reaching her feet, like she's stepped out on to a patio half in shade, half in light.

She adds a little cold, then sinks down into the water as she fills it. She closes her eyes, thinking nothing, her mind a bicycle wheel slowing down, down, down.

Her burner phone is in a drawer, the ill-advised text to Aidan gone unresponded to.

She thinks of their near miss, and of Zara's smile when Dom WhatsApps her. It is here, safe in the warm water, that she can finally consider it. She is wounded by Aidan's silence, but could she also be free? Could she . . . could she try to grow up, and move on?

The longer they stay, the deeper their roots grow, and the more pain they would experience if they returned home. If Zara could somehow move back to London, and discard Suzanne, and be Zara again, would she? She would right now – but what about next week, next month? Soon, there will come a tipping point, where here feels more like home than London.

And what about herself?

She's been in denial, thinking this'll end, thinking she

can fix it. But she has been offered a new identity, on the state. The gold-standard last resort. It is not the kind of problem that will suddenly fix itself. They have to try, here, in York, and make it home. She has to accept the hand she's been dealt, stop trying to rebel against it like a child. She'll never not love Aidan, but she has to move forwards, not backwards.

She submerges her ears beneath the water, the steam tickling them, and blanks her mind.

After half an hour, she hears Zara's voice outside. And then the boy's voice, too. Just broken, a brand-new man's voice in a boy's body.

She can't make out what they're saying, but she can tell the tone of it. Happy, excited. Interrupting each other constantly and enthusiastically. Finally. She's coming out of herself. Her shy daughter who's always felt like she isn't enough. Lauren momentarily wonders who Zara had been on the phone to. She'll try to ask again, later. Baby steps.

The melodies of Zara and Dom's voices mingle as Lauren closes her eyes, letting the steam heat her shoulders, wiggling her toes against the side of the bath. *If Zara is happy*, Lauren is thinking, *then I am, too*. Zara could be happy here. She could settle here. And so could Lauren. For Zara. Happiness by proxy.

60

Aidan

Shepherd's Bush, London

Two days to go

Aidan turns on Lauren's old coffee machine. The top is dusty. He puts a tea pod in that went out of date in 2014. He thinks of all of the times Lauren must have made coffee in the early days of their relationship. Did she press it, this button here, faded from her fingerprints, and think of him?

He strokes the button slowly, thinking. The day after tomorrow is the day of the meeting. And so, in two days, she will be in his arms again. His Lauren.

He's nervous, but he's optimistic, too, his stomach fizzing with it. He feels like he's had three coffees and a bag of sweets. He's jittery, shifting his weight from foot to foot as his mug fills with tea.

Right. Think.

The police. Lottie. She wanted an update today. He finds her and presses 'call'.

'It's all on for the day after tomorrow,' he says to her. 'They should all be there. It's a group-wide meet. I've asked everybody to bring all of the information they have, so there should be evidence. If not the weapons themselves.'

'Good. I'm plugging away here. I know it might not feel like it, but I'm lining it all up.'

'Good. Is it . . . are you getting grief?'

Lottie hesitates. 'A bit,' she says. 'It isn't . . . orthodox, what we're doing. And you know, I'm junior here.'

'I know. Sorry,' Aidan says.

'No worries. Look, I told you – I'd do the same thing for my babies.'

Aidan stares into his tea. She's so young, and with two babies already, and this volatile career of hers. What's behind it all? he wonders.

'What'll happen if it goes wrong?' he says.

'It won't go wrong.'

'I mean, to you. Why are you . . . why are you putting it all on the line for me?'

Lottie appears to think for a second. 'You know,' she says. 'I just always wanted to do the right thing, from when I was a child, even.'

Aidan's mouth twists into an ironic smile. He takes a gulp of tea. 'You sound like my stepdaughter,' he says softly.

Lottie laughs, a small, sad laugh. 'I always was quite . . . I don't know. Anti-establishment. Right?'

'A classic young person. Bet you vote for Jeremy Corbyn. Just you wait.'

Lottie chuckles. 'We'll see. I always wanted to tackle gang culture,' she says. 'People who get caught up in it, and can't escape.'

'Maybe you will work with gangs,' he says.

'But I already am.'

'Yeah?'

'The Find Girl A group might be middle class,' she says. 'Footballers. Football fans. But they are a gang.'

Aidan sits in silence. They *are*. He thinks of the way Brian riles them up. Mob rule. Of their form of vigilante justice. Of Goodbye Mr X leaving the group and getting his arm broken. It's all gang culture. And he's right in the middle of it. He's joined a gang.

'A gang,' he echoes softly. 'Yeah.'

'But we'll get them.'

'Have you told your team?' he asks.

'Had to, after your . . . your injury. My superior doesn't like the idea of you being in the group. But to me it's the only way.'

'Are you in trouble?'

'No. But . . . well, I think I might have to leave if we don't get a conviction. I've forced a few hands. Called in a few favours.'

'*What?*'

'I mean it,' Lottie says. 'I believe in it. Plugging away, doing the right thing, playing the long game. That's the kind of officer I am. Want to be.'

'Wow,' Aidan says, glad he has this woman on side, this beacon of hope on the horizon of the dark dawn.

'Have they any idea?' she asks.

'Who I am? No. I don't think so.'

'I'm just thinking of double bluffs,' she says.

Aidan briefly thinks of Brian's suspicion, of the two blokes who beat him up, one of whom might have been at the last meeting, but doesn't voice it. 'No, nobody suspects,' he says.

Aidan reconfirms the address to her. It's written on a Post-it note he keeps on his desk, and his hand is trembling as he holds it. He tries to stop it, but he can't. Soon, soon. Lauren will be back in his bed, warm skin sticky on his, and he will finally relax.

'Even the ones we can't convict will be witnesses,' Lottie says to him. She seems to be thinking aloud.

'Good.'

'How advanced is their plan, would you say?' Aidan can hear as she shifts the mouthpiece. She becomes louder.

'They're intermittently trying to find her. They never say too much about what will happen when they do. But the implications are clear. And those pensioners in Truro. They had a knife . . . the police there fingerprinted the house, didn't they? And I'll be able to testify —' he swallows, thinking about Zara having done this exact thing, '— about the group.'

'I know,' she says. 'Okay. Right. Good.'

He sips his tea, enjoying the bitter taste of the tannin.

'You'll be there, I assume,' she says. 'I'll have to arrest you, too. Otherwise they'll know it was you.'

'You're smart,' Aidan says.

Lottie laughs. 'I try. Leave it with me,' she says. 'I'll call you in the morning. Let me know if anything changes.'

They pause, both saying nothing. Aidan owes this woman so much. How can he ever thank her — a bunch of flowers, a box of chocolates? They all seem trite.

'Okay. What are . . . what're your kids called?' he says, wanting to prolong the call. To see a chink in her armour.

'Katie and Siân. My whole world,' she says sincerely.

He hangs up and sips his tea slowly, thinking. He's

thinking of parenthood and how parents are at the centre of all this chaos. Aidan, Lottie, Lauren, Brian. All doing the best for their kids, however misguided.

Next, he reconfirms the meeting place and time with the group. Asks them to bring all of the information they have, again, trying not to labour the point. It's read by everybody except Brian and another member. Aidan navigates to their contact details and sees Brian's online. So is the other man. But he's not responding to him. His mind scans over the last few weeks. Brian's insistence on the scrapers. His suspicion. What if they've rumbled him? What if he is discussing him with the other member right now?

He opens his text messages, thinking about whether to tell Lauren, to give her a hint, but then he closes them again. He shouldn't have told Poppy what he did the other night. It'll get her hopes up. It's cruel. It's cruel when there's so much at stake, and so much that could go wrong. And it's cruel for her, specifically. She has suffered so much.

But wait. Was that . . . he opens the texts again. Lauren's sent a selfie. The other night, shortly before midnight. He must have missed it. He opens it. She's in a car, looking at the camera. She's so beautiful, and so sad, his wife who can't stay away from him. He smiles back at her selfie, until Brian writes back on Telegram, distracting him.

Sounds like a big day, he says.

Aidan swallows. He opens Brian's contact and types. *All okay?* he says.

Yeah, mate, looking forward to seeing you, Brian writes.

Aidan leaves it there. Anything else would reveal too

much. He has to trust. He has to relax. He has to believe that he might be able to pull it off. Doubts won't help at this stage.

He takes the tea over to the sofa and puts his feet up, feeling the anticipation of the relief he might experience when it's all over. He allows himself a reverie on the couch. Lauren and Zara are here, no, not here, back in their sunny Islington house, together, under their own names, and they're safe. They're making pancakes. Buying Christmas presents. The worst autumn of their lives forgotten. A bullet dodged.

61

Zara

York, Yorkshire

Seven weeks gone

Dom hasn't gone off her at all. Quite the opposite, in fact. It's the end of another walk with Dom, and Zara doesn't want to leave him, not yet. It's early evening, but their walk's finished. They're back home, standing at the seam of their two terraces. Dom's fingers are on the dark brown putty between the bricks. He is unconsciously moving his fingertips over it. He has neat fingernails. Short. Perfect circles.

He told her, in that northern accent of his, that he is 'actually utterly rubbish' at the guitar. He talks fast, but with big pauses while he thinks. Short staccato bursts. He doesn't seem to have any pretensions about him. He has named no obscure bands. He doesn't have a particular niche interest. He told her he enjoys biology – 'I like animals and plants' – and she wanted to tell him so badly about her lettuces, but she didn't. She has been good. Zara has been erased, Suzanne in her place. Sienna barely exist-ing, like a firework that never went off, the gunpowder never there in the first place. She almost misses her, that life, even though she was miserable there for the entire time. That's nostalgia for you, she guesses. Everything is enjoyable if it's a memory.

His feet are only a few inches from hers, down there on the frosted pavement, and that must mean they're standing close to each other. Zara looks at him, his face a pale amber in the street light.

'We could sit out, for a bit,' Dom offers. He gestures to the steps outside their houses, separated by a metal rail.

'It's so cold,' Zara says, but she sits down to show him that she wants to stay. The frost seeps immediately through her jeans.

He sits next to her, on the other side of the handrail. It runs above them, between their heads. A kind of separation.

Zara wants to lean into him, like a needy animal, and tell him how scared she is. She wants to tell him how it feels to be pursued by a justice group, to be *wanted*, to be in danger. She wants to tell him how closeted she feels, how closed away, her emotions dulled and flattened by the protection service. How every single sentence requires forethought, and so how everything is fake.

'It's pretty early days, Suzanne-by-the-river, but I think you're kind of cool,' he says.

Zara roots around for something she can say.

'Same. Look,' she says, 'there's a lecture on next week, about this novel I read. I know it's nerdy . . .'

'If you're there, I'm there,' Dom says, and the sun comes out on Zara's life, just like that.

'Settled in yet?' he says after a few minutes.

'I feel like I'm in a holiday home.'

Dom laughs. 'Some holiday home,' he says, but then his expression becomes set again. 'As a serial mover, let me tell you that this is absolutely normal. It takes three months to feel at home,' he says. 'I go through all the stages each time. First, I'm really good, like it's the New Year or something and I've decided to change all my habits. But then, after a while, I relax, let my room go to ruin. And it's only then that I start to feel at home.'

'That's it,' she says, thinking. She needs to bond with the house, the town, and with herself, Suzanne, too. 'I keep thinking about my old life. Old me. Missing it all.' And there it is. It's easy, with him, to find some truths amongst the lies. You just have to search for them.

Dom nods and sits forward again. He's left two starfishes in the frost. Zara stares at him, and thinks: *I could love those hands of his.* The thought surprises her. It arrives fully formed in her mind. Same as she wrote on the Post-it. *Don't fall in love.* Except, this time, the thought is: *I could love him.* She's never thought anything like it before, but she thinks it again as she looks at him. *I could love him.*

The future unfurls in front of them, the past irrelevant, like disappearing contrails in the sky.

'So what's the first song you'll teach me – on the guitar?' she says, shifting imperceptibly closer to him. She never would have asked such a question a few months ago. She would never tease, be too afraid to. But now she isn't. Because he likes her for who she is.

'Ha, hmm. "Three Blind Mice"?' he says.

Their laughs ring out in the night. High and low, commingling like their warm breath in the cold December air. Zara, wet bottom, cold hands, doesn't ever want to leave.

Here, in York, over a year after she witnessed the crime, she has found happiness, just a speck of it. At last. As Dom reaches forward to kiss her, his lips as soft as candy-floss, she lets him: she lets him in. And that's the first step. The first step to *here* being home, and London being somewhere she never wants to return to.

But, sadly, she must.

The phone rings exactly when Zara expects it to. She is sitting on her bed. Her mother is out. This is it.

'Zara, Harry from the Crown Prosecution Service here,' a voice says. 'Can you talk?' Harry. Zara hasn't seen him since the trial. But she has spoken to him. Many times.

'Yes, yes,' Zara says, staring at the nondescript walls, the cheap wardrobe, the dusty mirror. It's not a home yet. She thinks about what Dom said about settling in.

'We're working hard over here. We're ready, now, for your list of names. And the date has been set for the trial: end of February.'

'Okay,' Zara says, taking a deep breath.

This is why she has to return. And this is why things are going to get worse.

But she is ready for it. Whatever it entails.

62

Aidan

Holloway FC, London
Two days to go

Aidan goes up on to the roof terrace to think. He tries to map it out logically. In the end, he goes and gets a paper and pen. He finds a floral stationery set Lauren left right in the back of a cupboard, the first page bearing an old shopping list of hers – *curry paste, something LOVELY to put in the bath, something for A for when he comes – beer, or nice tea??* – and his heart just about rolls over in his chest. He gently pulls the list out, being careful not to rip it, and puts it in his pocket.

He turns to a new page of the notebook and writes one word: *Mal.*

Luke was dropped but Mal, who never served time, is still a player, yet not at the meeting nor in the group. Why?

What if he could find Mal, and speak to him, and – if he isn't interested in the group – get him to talk?

It's time, he has realized. It is time to take the information that he has about the cover-up, and do something with it.

*

Aidan stands, finally, at Holloway FC, where it all began, watching the training. Back and forth, back and forth, dribbling around cones. Mal is tall and wiry, a deft touch. Aidan watches, waiting for his moment. Mists swirl around the pitch, only noticeable from a distance. Aidan stares at his own trainers. They're probably steeped in it, too, winter's freezing steam, only it's invisible.

His moment arrives when they leave the training ground.

'Mal.' Aidan catches up with him.

Mal dismisses his fellow footballers with a nod. 'Can I help you?'

'I'm the one from Facebook Messenger,' Aidan says. 'Mr A.'

They stand alone in the cold. Aidan feels strangely vulnerable, out here on the training field, the bleachers behind them, and nobody around. It's dark – isn't it always dark in December? – and the fog gathers around the floodlights.

'I want to talk about that night,' Aidan says.

He knows it's dangerous to be here. Mal could easily place him as Zara's father from the public gallery. He's taken his glasses off, has got his beard, and all he can do is hope that Mal doesn't connect him to Aidan. He meets his eyes, and doesn't see any recognition. Aidan is fairly nondescript, and the public gallery was pretty far from the dock.

Mal immediately leads him inside, into an empty changing room that's open. Blue and yellow, garish gloss paint, pristine benches lining the walls. It's cold down here, like a church or a tomb, and Aidan shivers as he realizes they're totally alone.

'What's going on?' Mal says.

'I know what you were doing,' Aidan says 'I know about the deaths, and the cover up.'

Mal's skin changes colour. Aidan has never really seen anybody pale before, but he recognizes it immediately. His lips turn winter-sky white. 'You've been told,' he says, to Aidan's surprise.

There is something dangerous about Mal's expression. Something that says they're headed somewhere from which they can never return. Aidan hopes he's imagining it, and begins to negotiate.

It's hard to believe that darkness exists when it's so light like this. A bright Nando's restaurant. His beautiful daughter in front of him, sipping an Indian nectar tea and waiting for her lemon and herb chicken.

'The art foundation is almost this year,' she says. 'On January the first, I'll be able to say it's this year.'

Aidan smiles sincerely at his daughter. Aged three, she taught him to appreciate everything. The specific blue of the sky in the springtime. The march of a line of ants down the pavement. Aged seven, she taught him optimism, that Monday mornings were equally as exciting as Saturday nights, the weekdays as full of adventure as the weekend. And now, as a teenager, she is teaching him something else. The art of looking forward to a new year, not bemoaning another year lost, zipped by in double time.

'And then art school,' he says.

'Art school,' Poppy echoes, her smile so wide her eyes crinkle shut. 'And then . . .'

'And then I'll be front and centre of your fashion show.'

'Sorry – front row is reserved for A-listers,' she says, smiling at him as she sips her tea. 'The frow.'

It's the first time they've spoken like this for a while. In a normal way. A happy way. It's the first time since Lauren left. Or maybe since Zara saw the murder. Aidan is aware in a dim, hidden part of his mind that *this* is the right path to follow. Leaving his family in protection, ceasing meddling, moving on.

'Anyway,' she says. 'I can't talk about it. Honestly, I can't. It makes my stomach hurt with excitement.'

'You'll never work a day in your life, if you love your job,' Aidan says. He misses his father, suddenly. He misses a man saying this stuff to him.

'I know,' Poppy says, so secure in the notion of doing what you love that it isn't even a revelation to her. 'I honestly can't wait.'

'What will Emily do?'

Poppy blinks, surprised. 'She wants to do HR! Always has. Likes people. She'll be good at it. She gives me good advice.' Poppy looks at him, her expression suddenly serious.

'Will you stay in touch?'

'Of course we will,' Poppy says, as if it's that simple. And maybe it is. She plays with the string of the tea bag.

'Nicer than detox tea?' Aidan says wryly.

'You look like you're on the detox – not me,' Poppy says, appraising him levelly, finally saying what she'd noticed before.

'Don't you worry about me, Pops,' Aidan says.

'You got new teeth.'

He says nothing.

Their chicken arrives. Poppy ignores the waiter, look
ing at him earnestly.

'Everything is going to be fine,' he says.

'Yeah?' she says.

No false hope, no false hope. But – fuck it.

'Yeah,' Aidan says sincerely to her. He brings his beer to
meet her tea cup. 'We're going to be fine,' he says. 'Trust me.'

Poppy gives him a strange look, a look he can't read. A
knowing look.

But it can't be.

63

Zara

York, Yorkshire

Seven weeks gone

Zara doesn't know how she has managed to keep six calls with Harry a secret from her mother, but she has. On each one, she has described a different homeless person to Harry, and he has gone off to interview them. Sometimes they talk to him, and sometimes they don't. It has been Anna's turn, this week. He is building a new case. This time, the defendants aren't Luke and Mal. It's all of Holloway FC.

'Did she speak to you?' Zara says quietly, sitting on her bed.

'No. Afraid not.'

'She was let down by the police, before,' Zara explains. 'She left an abusive relationship and the CPS . . . you . . . they . . .' Zara rolls her eyes at her over-thinking, 'they let her down.'

'I thought as much,' Harry says. 'Still, we have your evidence about what she told you. It's hearsay, but it'll still work.'

'Me, the known liar,' Zara says.

She says something like this during each phone call

with him. Harry has spoken to five other homeless people about the hazing in their community by Holloway FC, but Zara is at the centre of it. She is the one who pulls all the strands together. And she's a discredited witness.

Zara went to visit Jamie's friend, Anna, the weekend after the trial, all those weeks ago. She went to apologize. To give her condolences. To talk about their mutual lost friend.

'It's not the first time, and it won't be the last,' Anna had slurred. Zara had averted her eyes from the can of alcohol in her hand and concentrated on what she was saying.

In a cold and dark underpass, Anna told her everything the homeless community knew. Her information was meandering and confusing – government conspiracies about aliens wound up with the truth – but certain points came up again and again. That youth players from Holloway FC were in the habit of baiting homeless people as part of their initiations. And that, sometimes, it went wrong.

Once Anna had told her everything – that it was common for footballers during initiations to pick on them, to taunt them, to piss on them – she went straight to the police before going home, even though she felt it was hopeless. She'd got the evidence of what she knew in her gut to be true – that Luke and Mal were monsters – two days too late.

The police didn't believe her, so she called Harry and they met up. She told him to look up the dates of youth team footballers' birthdays and correlate them with crimes against homeless people. He said he would, but that he'd have to do it on the side, that it would take weeks.

And then.

And then. The wheels turned too quickly, and she was

grabbed in the street. And it was decided they would be taken into protection.

She overheard her mother and Aidan talking. About how their lives were ruined by Zara testifying.

And so on the eve of leaving, she called Harry. Told him to keep in touch, that she'd testify, but only if her mother wasn't told. He wasn't supposed to do that – apparently, he needed parental consent – but he broke the rules for her.

And here she is, the star witness in yet another pending trial. A bigger one. A greater one. A conspiracy. A discredited witness, yes, but people believe her. Because there is evidence.

'They can't talk about the previous trial,' Harry tells her patiently, again. 'And, even if they do, your lie makes sense, now. You sensed contempt, for Jamie, and you were right to. Because of what Anna told you after the trial.'

'Maybe,' Zara says doubtfully. If she hadn't lied . . . imagine. But then, would Anna have told her the real story? That none of the homeless people wanted the police to find out, because they feared repercussions from the club? Maybe not. And then Harry would never have found all the evidence. The birthdays and the attacks.

'Anyway, I've got three more homeless people who reported abuse on footballers' birthdays. So that's six.'

'Good. Good,' Zara says. 'I'm glad.'

Each week, he uncovers more and more. Each time, they speak on the burner phone he gave her that day.

And then what, after it's done? Who knows. Who knows what the future holds for Zara, for Sienna, for Suzanne. Perhaps she could leave for ever. She's seen enough homeless people to know she could get by.

64

Aidan

Croydon, Greater London

Tomorrow

Brian has called an emergency Find Girl A meeting.

Everything feels like it's falling apart. The entrapment meeting is tomorrow, the twenty-first. When Brian called the new meeting, Aidan panicked, and tried to rally Lottie, but she insisted on keeping their entrapment plan in place. That is when she has the staff to arrest, she said. Only half the group could make today, and Aidan doesn't know whether they have their burner phones with them. It's better to wait. It's better to be fully prepared.

Aidan left work in the middle of the afternoon to be here, in the warehouse in Croydon.

'Thanks for coming, those who could,' Brian says. 'I'm afraid we need to up our game.'

'What's happened?' one of the players says.

'Somebody was contacting Mal on Facebook. They started to harass him about the initiation. There's a leak. Mal spoke to his uncle, who's a cop, who did some digging. For a fee, obviously. There's an undercover investigation going on into all the initiations around homeless people.'

Aidan's jaw slackens in shock.

'God,' Luke says, almost to himself.

'And Zara is going to testify.'

A hot flash moves up and down Aidan's body, which he tries to conceal. She's testifying?

His mouth is dry as he works it through. How could that be? Does Lauren know? Why is she doing it? And what then – afterwards?

And finally. And finally. The last piece of the puzzle falls into place.

This.

This is why Zara is in witness protection.

Because she is the most important witness in unmasking a cover-up. And she needs protecting. She is valuable.

'We need to find her,' Brian says. 'And, now, there's too much at stake. Everyone will go down for it. She can't be silenced. We need to kill her.'

65

Poppy

Battersea, London

Tomorrow

It is December the twentieth.

It is finally here. The day it all ends.

The Find Girl A group is meeting this evening, according to her dad's texts. And – so far – nothing has happened. Poppy feels that curdled combination of nervous and hopeful. *Please, please, please, just go well*, she is thinking. Let the meet go ahead. Let the arrests happen. And let her family come home to her. She squirms with the anticipation of it.

Emily has gone to the cinema after school with a few of their friends, but Poppy can't bear to. She wants to be at home, near a phone, for when it happens. She wants to hear it ring, and see that it's her dad, and know that this will all be over.

She brings up the Uber app on her phone as she waits outside the school gates. She's later than she wanted to be – she got carried away chatting, she felt so light and hopeful and free.

The sky is still a pale blue-grey, but the sun has set, and the school has emptied. She calls for an Uber and watches it crawl towards her on the silent street. She inches back inside the school gates as she waits. The breeze is cold against her legs.

By tomorrow, Zara will be here with her. They could camp out in the garden come summer. They could go shopping in Camden together. Cook a three-course meal for their parents, bickering over who's making the most mess, Bill eating scraps of food off the floor . . .

Your ride has had to cancel, Uber says, and Poppy dismisses the alert and searches for another.

She looks around her. There are people dotted here and there. It's not yet completely dark. And it's ten minutes. Down a high street. Totally safe, really.

And besides. Poppy wants to live her life. To walk down a street in Battersea, London, the capital of the UK and of the world, and feel the winter wind against her face and see the Christmas lights of the shops spilling on to the pavements, and smell the roasted chestnuts, and arrive at home, pink-cheeked and full of optimism.

Poppy decides, on the day that almost everything is going to be sorted, to take the risk. She cancels her Uber request, closes the app, and begins to walk.

66

Zara

York, Yorkshire

Seven weeks gone

Zara has fallen in love. She used to idly wonder how you would know. She would google what it would feel like, rationalizing that 'being in love' was just thoughts and hormones. She'd asked her mother, once, who had said, 'Oh, believe me, you'll know,' but Zara hadn't thought she would.

But she does.

And it isn't just thoughts, or hormones, or pure biology.

She stands now, waiting at the school gates, and thinks about what love is rather than what it isn't. It is smiling so hard at a text message that even her ears hurt. It is replaying and replaying each moment spent together, each kiss, the pass of his hand over hers. It is time running heavy without him. It is two people who combine to form a reaction, something that simmers and bubbles beyond themselves. It is chemistry. Zara doesn't care about homework. She doesn't care about reading or making friends. Zara doesn't even care about witness protection.

She is about to see him now, and time feels like lightning. So quick and hot and full of tension. He rounds the corner, and there he is. Hair that's longer on top, shorter on the sides. Dimples. Guitar case.

She stares at her feet on the bleak December grass, beaded with dew that's already begun to freeze white. Two weeks ago, she was afraid she would never go home again. And, now, she is afraid that she *will*.

But then what, after the trial? Zara doesn't know. She was prepared to go it alone, let her mother go back to London . . . but, now, Zara has somebody she must keep with her, no matter what.

He raises his hand in a wave that looks so casual she wonders if he could really feel the same as she does, but she knows he does: he tells her so.

'I'm so late – I got talking,' he says. His expression is sunny and untroubled.

'Don't worry,' she says, smiling up at him.

'Thought you might have gone,' he says, kissing her. Cold skin. Woodsmoke. Warm lips.

She prolongs the kiss, another thing she once would have been afraid to do, scared to give too much of herself too quickly. But now, the anxiety, the insecurity are small parts of her brain, and Zara, true Zara, is the rest.

'I'd never go without you,' she says back, intending it to sound light-hearted, but it comes out so seriously he stops and looks at her. And she can't possibly mean these words she has spoken to him, but she does. And that's another thing that love is. Love is lies, sometimes, but she means them. She wants to mean them.

'Good,' he says, one end of his mouth lifting, the other turning downwards.

Inside, privately, Zara calls it his ironic smile. She has all sorts of words for the things that he does, because they elicit such strong feelings in her that she feels they ought to be named.

'Good,' he says again, softer this time. He goes to say something more, but he stops himself.

And she's glad he does. She can't tell him. She will just *be*, just be here, instead, suspended in time with him, the rest of the world not really seeming to matter at all.

He kisses her again and she surrenders to it.

If I die tonight, Zara is thinking, as their bodies press together, *I will die happy*.

67

Poppy

Poppy's on her road when it happens.

It's dark. Windows are illuminating, one by one, as people get home. Street lamps are reflected in the bonnets of shiny cars.

And then.

And then.

His hot breath at her neck.

The brush of wool. A balaclava. A word in her ear: *Poppy.*

And then.

And then.

The thing she knew would happen. The thing she's been waiting for, all this time, convincing herself it wasn't going to happen. A cold knife at her throat. She can feel its sharpness even though it hasn't yet sliced into her. The pressure of it makes her skin yield, the muscles and tendons parting, hiding behind each other like hostages.

'Your daddy's a liar,' the man says.

Poppy can't turn around to look at him.

414

She can't turn around. The knife feels like a great pressure on her throat, disproportionately heavy because of the damage it could do.

'He said he wasn't in touch – and you know what? He is.'

'No, I . . .'

'So you know what I think, Poppy? He knows where they are, and I think you do, too. How can we trust a word he says if he sends us to Truro when they aren't there? But, Poppy, we can trust you. You said they weren't at Truro.'

'He wasn't lying.'

'You *liar*,' the balaclava man screams in Poppy's ear.

Her whole body responds in shock, arms jerking out to the side like a starfish. The man's body is so tense against Poppy's back and the knife digs further into her neck and she closes her eyes and thinks: *please, just kill me. Let it be over.*

'I've been patient but I'm going to ask you one time, Poppy. And you're going to tell me. And you know what's going to happen if you don't?'

'No,' Poppy whispers.

Think. Think. How can she get away?

'I'm going to slash this knife across your throat. Unless you tell me. Right now. Where they are.'

Poppy opens her eyes, looking at the rows of houses, wondering if she could scream. Wondering what would happen. But this man with the balaclava over his face and his gloved hands would pull the knife tight across her throat, run away and let her bleed to death. She knows it.

What time is it? Just after five. The meeting will happen

in just a couple of hours. And this guy will go to it, with the information she gives him now.

It will happen before they can get to Lauren and Zara. The group will be arrested before they even set out.

'Okay?' he says.

Poppy's entire body is trembling. It feels like there are a thousand birds in her ribcage. Her arms and legs are swarms of moths. She is not a solid human being but a shaking, frightened animal. If she doesn't say, he will slit her throat. She can tell because of all sorts of things she didn't even know she had radar for. The confident way he holds the knife. The force of his arm around her upper body. Even his tone of voice.

She could lie again. She blinks, looking up at the black sky.

Her entire body chills as she thinks it through: he might already know where they are. He might know the general area. And so, if she lies, he will kill her. He's a millimetre away from doing so.

'Okay, Poppy?'

'Okay.'

She's going to have to tell him. She's worked it all through, the way her father would. The knife tightens against her throat. Poppy feels fear sweep across her. Her face is sweating. Her trousers are wet. She closes her eyes. Oh, God. She has wet herself. She has wet herself in terror.

'On three. One . . .'

Poppy thinks of all the things she loves about her step-sister. Her careful attention to detail. Her chronic shyness.

'Two . . .'

The way she handed these boys over to the police so ruthlessly, so correctly, it turns out. Because they are criminals.

'Three . . .'

The way, when her dad and Lauren first got together, they sat up late at night playing *Candy Crush* on their phones and not speaking, not knowing what to say to these new family members. But they got to know each other. Even through those silences. They merged, like spices slowly cooking together. They adopted each other. Skipped over deep talks and straight into family life: Zara telling Poppy that flower crowns made her look mad. Poppy telling Zara that if she was going to pluck her eyebrows she needed to do it more evenly, the middle was too thin.

'Okay?' the man in the balaclava says.

'York,' Poppy says, sacrificing that beautiful stepsister of hers to save herself. 'Their address is 2 Sunshine Drive. York.'

68

Aidan

Shepherd's Bush, London

Tomorrow

Zara is going to testify.

Lottie doesn't know. Does she? She can't. Why would she be helping him, if there was an official investigation?

So it must be covert, Aidan thinks. A secret even within the police, save for a small team, because the more people who know, the more chance it would be leaked to somebody before the evidence can be gathered. Aidan watched a show on it once. A Chinese wall was set up within the police, but even then, there was a leak, and a load of drug dealers got rid of every last shred of evidence, and no arrests were made.

He sits and tries to think. His brain feels like sludge these days. He's not eating enough.

If he tells her what he knows, she will call off the meeting. His only shot. She wouldn't jeopardize a covert op. Not even Lottie breaks that many rules.

And then he would be left with – what? Hiding from the group, if he left it. And waiting. Waiting for the slow wheels of the justice system to turn.

No. The Find Girl A meeting must go ahead. He'll tell them he has more results from his scrapers. Maybe even a lead. To make them come.

And then he will tell Lottie afterwards. His entrapment evidence can be added into the covert op.

Once he's made his mind up, he decides to try and eat. He cooks chips with nothing else and reads the Telegram app, standing by the light of the oven.

Confirmed sighting in Edinburgh, a woman called Sacha wrote in there very late last night.

And, just now, Kevin said: *Firm lead on York*. If the leads amounted to nothing, he said, they would regroup at the meeting tomorrow and come up with a new plan.

Aidan looks out of the window. Lauren and Zara are in the Lake District. Safe. Undiscovered.

Everything is coming together.

Aidan sits on the sofa in his wife's old flat, puts his socked feet up on the table, and considers what to do. He stares at the December sky. The people in the flat exactly opposite have already got their tree up, a family affair, no colour scheme, too much tinsel and chaos and ornaments made by children. He likes to look at it.

He thinks about what his own tree will look like in Islington when everybody is back together. It'll be a top-of-the-range Douglas fir, lugged home by Lauren, smiling manically as she pulls it through the door after her. 'I've travelled long and far with this,' she will say, gesturing grandly to it.

There is nothing more he can do, he decides. He is prepared enough.

Instead, he does what he often does in these moments, these idle moments in the spaces between life. He calls his most favourite person in the world, his daughter, Poppy, to chat.

She answers on the first ring, which makes him laugh.

'How are you?' he says, but he is not prepared for the answer. Not at all.

69

Poppy

Battersea, London

Tomorrow

It has taken all of Poppy's strength not to call her father. She arrived home, limbs still shaking, and was sick in the downstairs toilet. She heard her mother shouting hello from upstairs, but she ignored her, wiping her mouth with toilet roll and looking at herself in the mirror that's always hung crooked above the sink. She reached out to straighten it.

If she called him, he wouldn't attend the meeting. And then, the group would go to York. So she has instead changed her jeans, washing them in the sink in the bathroom in secret, and then paced her bedroom, biting the skin around her fingernails, even though she swore she'd stop doing that.

And now. The call comes exactly when Poppy expects it. Just after seven. Something pleasurable moves up her body. Heat. Nerves. Happiness. Fear. All mixed together.

She escapes outside into their tiny garden. Her mum is having another good day today. Poppy thought she wouldn't be, when she called down from upstairs to her, but she is.

She's cleaning, capitalizing on good health in the frantic way the chronically ill do: she is cleaning out their wardrobes. Bin bags line the hallway. It smells of polish and open windows up there.

'How are you?' her dad says.

He sounds relaxed. The air around him is completely silent. She expected him to be out, the city winds in the speaker of his phone. She expected him to be stressed, harassed, excited. Nervous.

'Okay. Pretty quiet. What news have you?' she says.

He laughs softly. 'News?'

'Well, do you . . . has anything happened?'

'No?'

Poppy's heart speeds up. She starts to pace around the paving slabs. 'I thought . . . I thought you were busy tonight.'

'Busy?'

She stares at the wall of the house. She can still feel the knife against her skin. Cold and sharp.

'I thought you were meeting the Find Girl A group tonight,' she says.

There's a stunned pause that seems to throb down the line like a bass beat, a sound wave.

'What?' he says eventually.

'I saw on your phone.'

'My phone?'

'Your second phone,' she says softly. But there is no time for explanations. There is no time for self-preservation. Poppy looks up at her house, her lovely old Victorian home, and feels white-hot panic rush up through her again. What if she's condemned them to death? She should have lied. Sacrificed herself. She's so selfish, so fucking selfish.

'What? It's tomorrow,' her dad says faintly, eventually.

The edges of Poppy's vision go black, like a solar eclipse. Spidery tendrils seem to come off the blackness. She blinks, trying to make it go back to normal. Shock, it's just shock. How could she get the wrong day?

They will be going to York. They will be heading to their exact address, and all because of Poppy. She stares up at the light of her mum's bedroom, watches her shadowy form moving to and fro, bending over, sorting out jeans and jumpers, and her eyes fill with tears. Her life as she knows it is ending, here, tonight.

'You looked at my phone?' he adds, but he says it mildly, gently.

'Dad . . .' she says.

God, why won't her vision go back to normal? She sits on a garden chair that is freezing against the backs of her thighs, her eyes closed.

'Something very bad has happened,' she says. Saliva fills her mouth. She is going to be sick again.

'What?' her dad says.

She starts to whimper. A great Catherine wheel of fear has started up in her chest. She can't think straight.

'Pops?' he says.

'They're going to die,' she says.

'*What?*'

'I got threatened again. They said they knew you were in touch with Lauren.'

'When?' her dad says sharply.

'Just now. The man in the balaclava again. But I thought you were going to get them arrested tonight . . .'

'What did you tell them?' her dad says, and he doesn't

sound angry. His voice is so soft and still and quiet, like this conversation they are having is the most important of his life.

'I saw you were arranging a meeting. I thought it was safe.' The shock has worn off and Poppy feels tears in her throat. 'I'm so sorry.'

'Poppy.'

'They put a knife to my throat. Dad,' she says. 'They would have killed me. I told them they're in York two hours ago.'

'But they're not in York,' he says, his voice a warm caramel gloop of relief. He laughs. 'It's fine, Pops!'

Poppy's eyes flash open, and the blackness has gone, and she can see completely clearly now. 'No?'

'No!' he says, his voice full of laughter and sunshine. 'They've been in the Lake District all this time.'

'She sent you a selfie with her address on it,' Poppy says. 'In the taxi.'

'What?' Aidan shouts. She can hear him scrambling for his burner phone to check. 'No,' he says. 'No, no, no.'

She sits up on the garden chair like a rabbit who's heard gunshots.

She has sent people to murder her stepsister and stepmother. She has sentenced them to death. She is so angry at herself, she could kick the wall. Stupid, selfish Poppy Madison.

The reality is so awful that Poppy is not defensive. She doesn't explain herself. She doesn't say anything at all, except, 'They've gone there. After them. I gave them their street address.' Now she has said it, it sounds mad. She wants to explain about the blade. About the feeling of it

424

nudging her neck muscles out of the way. Of the balaclava man's hot breath at her ear, of the survival instinct it is impossible to suppress, but she doesn't. There's no time, anyway. And it's pointless. It's so pointless in the face of everything. She stares up at the house and – it feels like – into the past, before everything changed.

'Okay,' he says, sounding like a robot. 'I have to get off the line now, Pops, and I need to call 999. You take care and I'll be in touch soon, sweetheart, okay?'

70

Aidan

The M1, northbound

Tomorrow

Poppy. A rage bubbles up through him.

He calls Lottie. She gasps, and that sound is the worst thing to him: confirmation of her worry. She tells him she will personally ensure the police in York send a team to Lauren's address. Two Sunshine Drive. It's right there in the background of the selfie, just like Poppy said it was. If only he had looked more closely, like he had when she sent him photos in the early weeks. If only Poppy had told him. If only, if only, if only.

Next, he calls 999. The operator seems perplexed by the backstory, the vast context, the crossed wires, but says they will dispatch somebody. Then, and only then, he calls Lauren. Her burner phone rings out. He closes his eyes. She's doing exactly what she should: being good. Fuck's sake. His hands form fists by his side. He needs a private plane. A helicopter. To be able to teleport. To go back in time.

Desperate, he calls the protection service. He has to google their number, reaches a hotline. He presses 'four' for *other enquiries* and waits. He tells the operator, Sophie, their backstory.

'Two Sunshine Drive,' she reads out. 'We'll be sure to get in touch should we have any news from there. Thank you, Aidan.'

'Will you do it right away?' he says.

A frown communicates its way down the phone line in her tone of voice. 'I'm surprised you know so much about the group's intentions – and your wife's location,' she says.

'You need to be going *now*. Dispatching someone. They've found them. Look, I need her number. She was called Lauren Starling, please look her up on your systems and give me her number.' God, how come he doesn't know her new name?

'There is no way I can reveal the telephone number or any contact details of somebody who is in protection,' she says. 'But rest assured, we will look into this for you.'

Aidan feels his face fill with blood. Hot, red rage. 'Am I speaking to a human or a fucking automated machine?' he shouts, louder than he's ever shouted before. And then he presses the big, angry red 'end call' button, then throws his phone across the room.

He might be too late. He might already be too late.

Maybe Lauren isn't not answering because she's being good, but because she's . . . he can't bear to think about it. She's hiding. She's bound and gagged. She's got a gun to her temple. She's dead. She's dead, she's dead, she's dead.

He kicks the wall furiously, then throws the coffee machine on to the floor. Its fucking stupid plastic parts skid everywhere like kids' toys, and he kicks those, too. It's all his fucking fault. In trying to protect his family, he has condemned them, sentenced them to death. If he had never been in touch with Lauren, Poppy would never have seen.

He can't stand here and do nothing, waiting for the protection service to call Lauren's other phone that – even now, even fucking now! – he's not allowed the number of. Waiting for the York police. Waiting for Lottie. Waiting for a train, buying a ticket. He can't wait any longer. He leaves his flat and gets in his car.

He takes the roads too fast, his foot to the floor on the motorway. He will be too late, he knows, but he doesn't care, not any more. He might be too late, but he will be there.

With his wife. Where he belongs. Where he has always belonged.

71

Lauren

York, Yorkshire
Tomorrow

At first, Lauren thinks she awakes to cooking.

Aidan?

She is still in the before, where they live in Islington, where they have trained themselves to sleep through the sounds of London's sirens, where Aidan makes cooked breakfasts.

No, they're in the Lake District.

No. They're in York.

But they're okay. They're happier. It's taken a while, but they're happier.

She thinks of something she could do today. The sort of things she hasn't done for a while. She could go out and buy chrysanthemums. Late autumn flowers. Put a couple of bunches around the house. It's a small thing, but it's a start. Buy a couple of Christmas presents for Zara.

But who's cooking?

She turns over, sniffs the air, then drifts back into her dream. She's hot. She dreams of ovens and sunshine and hot baths. Sweat vaporizes between her skin and the duvet.

She's naked, she still sleeps naked, the way she always has, since Aidan.

She turns over a couple of times, then accepts that she's waking up.

She opens her eyes, expecting a dim room, hazy in the early morning light. But it isn't gloomy or dark. It is orange. It's orange just at the edges, around the door frame. Like the wood is shining. She tilts her head, studying it. Is the sun up already? But no, it's dark out of the window.

The realization sweeps over her like she has walked into a cold fog. Her entire body freezes in terror.

That's not the sun. Nobody's cooking.

Their house is on fire.

The bathroom is a bonfire at the end of the hallway. It is so enormous and hot that it has eaten the door. The walls are burning and embers are being spat out on to the stairs. The air itself seems to be on fire, hot little dust motes and pops and flashes. There's no way out. There's no way through. Lauren can easily see that it's already spread to Zara's room. Black smoke hangs over everything. Lauren's throat is hot and sore with it.

Somewhere, though she is hardly aware of it, a smoke alarm sirens out, their family's swan song. She runs, still naked, back into her room and grabs her phone. She dials 999. They tell her to plug the gaps in her door frame with towels, with wet clothes. Anything she can find. They will be there soon. They ask her who else is in the house, and she tells them Zara.

She hasn't forgotten their new names. It isn't a slip of

the tongue. She doesn't care any more. Because she knows this is them, that they have come for them. And she knows, too, that they will have thought this through: they have managed to find two people in witness protection. They will ensure they kill them.

She's told to 'stay put' by the 999 operator. She tells them she will. They ask if she wants to stay on the line, and she says that she doesn't. She wonders if the operator will think about her, later tonight, when he goes home and tells his partner that he couldn't help a woman who died in a fire with her daughter. She wonders about the stories the papers will run. About the Find Girl A group and how many different methods the department for person protection tried, and how none of them worked. She wonders if they will recover the burner phones or trace her stupid letter to Hannah and conclude that her breaches led the group to them. She thinks of the text the other night, the selfie to Aidan, and thinks maybe they did.

She thinks about Hannah as she pulls on a dressing gown. She thinks about the niece or nephew that she will never meet. First steps, first day of school, first Christmas play. Bouncing a fat baby on her knees on its first birthday.

She fumbles with the hot door handle to Zara's bedroom. Her grip slips on it, and it brands her hand, a large blister forming immediately. She thinks about how they never had a true, fair shot at this, not from the moment Zara stood in that playing field over a year ago and saw the murder. Because it was a murder. Maybe not of Jamie, but of them. Of Lauren and Zara. They are being murdered, here, in York, by the people who say they are innocent.

She takes one last look behind her at her room. She could ease open the window. She could fit right out, in her dressing gown. Save herself.

But this isn't what parenthood means to Lauren. It never has been. She has put Zara before herself for Zara's entire life. Sleep sacrificed. No drinks out. Lovely handbags replaced with changing bags. Her breasts sucked and saggy. Her stomach distended. Her conversation poor, limited to whether Zara enjoyed bananas and the dry skin she used to get on her feet that they couldn't get to clear up. She's done school plays when she should have been working. Carried her when her arms were aching with the effort. Shared plates of food with her. Shared beds. Shared Aidan. Shared a life, up here in York. Given up everything to keep her safe.

She wrenches open the door. A wall of heat hits her. She feels her skin curling as she steps into it. But she can't give up. She must save Zara. She must find Girl A, her precious Girl A. She must find her, and save her, though she knows she can't, though she knows she is dying here.

She takes one step, two, into the flames. It doesn't hurt, not immediately. She is existing in the moment between injury and pain, just a few seconds, just a few seconds more.

Zara is sleeping on her back, in that way she always did, one arm flung above her head. Lauren reaches for her. She shakes her shoulder, but she doesn't move. She's not sleeping, Lauren realizes. She's unconscious.

Lauren's skin is burning and blistering now. She coughs into her hand, and her palm comes away black. The door frame behind her has been subsumed into flames. There's no way out. She puts a palm to the window, and the glass feels molten. She comes away scorched.

The die was cast right from the beginning. They had no chance. Lauren is tired as she thinks of it. Her eyes are heavy, like she's been injected with a general anaesthetic. She can't keep them open. Leaden limbs. Black coughs. Burnt hands. She kneels on the bed next to Zara, then lies down next to her, her body curling protectively around Zara's like it has a thousand times before.

She closes her eyes, just for a second. She'll get her strength back. Her breathing is becoming laboured, burnt breaths coming in little gasps.

She closes her eyes for a moment longer. She needs to get Zara out. She needs to keep her . . . keep her safe.

Her body relaxes into unconsciousness. It's a tidal wave she can't fight. Her skin becomes even hotter, as the flames burst into the room.

For a second she feels pain. And then she feels nothing except love. Motherly love.

72

Aidan

A lay-by, the A1, northbound
Today

Aidan's phone jolts him from his intense, angry thoughts. He's been driving too fast, zigzagging across the traffic. Doing eighty, ninety, one hundred miles per hour. It's late. There's not much traffic. Just the blur of taillights in the distance. It feels good to be doing something. He will just drive and, for sure, something will await him, but, for now, he doesn't know what. He is changing gear fluidly. Spotting things up ahead in good time and dodging them. He is not human, not thinking, merely a predatory animal on the chase.

But now his phone is ringing. He drives too quickly into a lay-by off an A-road outside York, wanting to concentrate. His tyres kick up gravel as he tries to stop. He comes to a finish near to a shut-up lorry that apparently usually serves *tea, coffee, hot chocolate + kebabs!!!*

He takes his phone and answers.

'Aidan, it's Jon, from the department for protection here.'

'Hello,' Aidan says. 'I'm on my way up to York, I'm almost here.'

'I thought so,' Jon says.

Aidan doesn't ask how he knows.

'I can explain what's gone on. Are you there?' Aidan says. 'In York?'

'Come to . . . come to the hospital, okay Aidan? York Hospital? I'll meet you there. A&E.'

'Okay. Are they . . . are they okay?' Aidan says, wishing he was looking at Jon, now, that he could gather clues and pick over them. But he isn't.

There is nothing. Just the black night all around him, cars whizzing by, a shut-up van in front of him.

'Come to the hospital. A&E. I'll see you there.'

The fluorescent strip lights are too bright for the small hours. They cast Jon's skin in a kind of yellow glow. Sick-looking, jaundiced. Eerie. Aidan is relieved when he is led into a side room. Dimly lit. Two pink sofas, not quite enough to seat three people, too large for two. Old-fashioned lampshades, also pink. Pull cords that are segmented, string and white plastic beads. Aidan stares at them.

'Where are they?'

'Aidan, sit down.'

'Where are they?'

'The Find Girl A group found out Lauren and Zara's newest address a few hours ago,' Jon says, reaching out to press Aidan's shoulder so that he sits.

There's a box of tissues on the brown table in front of

them. Jon nudges it towards Aidan with his foot – unconsciously, Aidan thinks – as he crosses his legs. He's put on a suit with trainers. Dressed in haste, illogically: Aidan hopes it means he cares.

'Yes. I know. I . . . me and Lauren . . . we –' Aidan says.

Jon holds up a hand that seems to silence Aidan with no effort at all. The words simply stop like a tap turned off.

'A 999 call was made by Lauren at ten o'clock tonight.' Jon leans forwards, elbows on his thighs. Feet in those trainers turned slightly outwards. 'You also made one at almost exactly the same time.'

Aidan's mouth twists with the irony of it. Apart but together. Separated and alone but connected, too. By telephones and shared goals and by love.

'A fire engine, ambulance and police were dispatched as soon as possible.'

Aidan stares at the pull cords and wonders at all Jon's detail. He knows rationally that this conversation is groundwork. Procedures were followed. *We did everything we could.* Liability disclaiming. And yet. And yet. There is hope. Now. Still.

'They attended on the scene and a fire had taken over the whole of the house.' Jon rubs his hand across his chin. The beginnings of ginger stubble are poking through.

Aidan braces himself as Jon reaches the point. He knows, but he is still staring at the speck of hope. As tiny as those segments on the pull cords. *Maybe it won't be both of them. Maybe they are merely injured. Maybe, maybe, maybe.*

'Two bodies were recovered from the scene. We believe them to be Lauren and Zara. We are so very sorry, Aidan, that this has failed: that we have failed you. We will be undertaking a thorough investigation . . .'

Jon's sentence continues as Aidan's world ends. One world streaming out into the room in front of them like ribbons, one cut off, amputated. Stopped. And it's all over.

Aidan's hands are shaking as he brings them to his mouth. His face is wet with tears and drool and snot. He doesn't care. They are gone. His beautiful wife and step-child. They are gone. He did everything he could to save them. He thinks about fire and flames and heat and his babies, his most precious people, the loves of his life, burning, incinerating, dying, ending, right there in the smoke, being cremated, before he could say goodbye.

Later

73

Aidan

Islington, London

February, the following year

After the funerals, and after the arrests, and after fucking Christmas, which cycled around even though it was inappropriate, *wrong*, it is February, and Aidan is standing with Bill Gates outside the Old Bailey.

Zara's evidence will be read out posthumously, at the trial of the players, coaches and members of Holloway FC for the murder and abuse of many homeless people.

The double murder of Zara and Lauren was dropped by the Crown Prosecution Service three weeks ago. Aidan took the call, said he understood, then excused himself to go into the work toilets to be sick.

The entrapment meeting never happened, of course. The fire – a home-made firebomb posted through Lauren's letter box – was so 'successful', as the police put it, there wasn't enough evidence as to who started it. Each group member gave the others alibis, and, in the aftermath of the fire, they ditched their burner phones. The forensics were poor because of the intensity of the flames, and, on one bleak early January day, Aidan got the call to say there would be no prosecutions.

The department said they would concentrate on the wider conspiracy, with Zara's evidence read out to the court. She had given many statements in writing over the course of her weeks in protection, by email, unknown to anybody.

Zara's statements would be given more weight, not less, Aidan discovered. A small and poignant piece of law: that the dying have less reason to lie. And Zara knew she would be found, eventually, because of what she knew. She kept reams of notes about it: about what she feared was coming for her, and about what she knew.

She is the only person in the world who could connect the murder of Jamie, where she heard the motto shouted, to the murder of Bertha, where Anna – who won't testify – heard it. She is the key that unlocks the dates of attacks on homeless people occurring on footballers' birthdays. Zara is at the centre of the cover-up.

Her evidence will be read out in the Old Bailey and, hopefully, Luke, Brian and the rest of the group will go down for the murder of Jamie and Bertha, and the abuse of many others, as they should have months ago. The police got Mal acquitted of his role in the club's murders in exchange for his knowledge – precisely what Aidan thought he'd agreed with Mal himself when he met him. An especially dirty deal with the police, considering Mal double-crossed Aidan and tipped the group off. His loyalties seem to lie nowhere.

Aidan used to think grief would be like entering a fug, a temporary hole, but he is just as painfully conscious as he once was, only in immense pain, too, and expected to work and commute and put away laundry, the same as everybody else.

He is widowed. His remaining daughter has been diagnosed with PTSD and, it turns out, a whole host of anger issues which she is working through with a therapist named Betty.

His mother never said *I told you so*. Never once laid the blame in his lap that he had caused their deaths. She has been only nice. 'It'll get easier,' she said again to him, last Thursday, when he took Poppy to the shop. 'I lived through it – and I know.' She had held his hand in hers, and brought it to her chest.

Poppy had asked if Brenda stocked any shampoo other than 'this cheap apple-scented monstrosity', and that had made them laugh, just a little.

And now, here he is, standing alone in the winter sun, hoping for convictions. He's meeting Harry and his matcha-green tongue soon.

It's not an outcome that will do anything to undo what has happened. But it is an ending, nevertheless. Justice. A sad conclusion that will allow them all to move on, a conclusion Aidan has pushed for with all the determination of a man who has lost everything, and has only the truth to uncover.

Lottie left the police. They met in a draughty Starbucks in the City on a weekend, when it's like a ghost town. Steamed-up windows. Cold air blowing in with the automatic doors. The comforting whirr of the coffee machine. She told him she had quit after her second sip of a latte.

'I couldn't do it any more, not after what happened to you,' she said, eyes on him. 'You did everything right, and you lost. That is not justice or law enforcement, Aidan. They kept a covert op from me and sent you off to the slaughterhouse.'

'You left for me.'

She shrugged then. A small, sad shrug. 'I'm a rule breaker. I don't belong in an institution that adheres to the rules above everything else.'

'What'll you do?'

'Be a mum, for now,' she said. 'Parenting is all about doing the right thing, no matter what, isn't it?'

'Yeah,' he said. Because, even though it's another loss, it's a gain, too. For him. An ally. A friend. Finding meaning in meaningless tragedy.

'And then?'

'I think I might work with gangs,' she said thoughtfully. 'Not against them. Prevention is better than cure.'

He raised his coffee up to her, at that.

And so here he is, two failed court cases behind them: Luke's, and the arsonists'.

And now here it is. Another attempt.

The final one.

Luke, Brian and many members of the club are convicted of the double murder of Jamie and Bertha, and many counts of assault, at the end of a five-week trial.

It was Luke's idea to begin the initiations when he was only twelve. He is sentenced to twenty-two years without parole. Brian is given twelve years. The sinewy man, eight. Lesser members of the group, four. It's one of the biggest trials of the year, covered on all the national news channels.

Aidan should feel relief, but he is numb. He doesn't feel anything any more.

Still, the day after the jury returns the verdict, he goes to see his mother and they drink coffee together and he manages a smile or two.

He's got rid of his iPhone, and his burner phone.

They did so much damage, he wants to live without them.

Epilogue

Aidan lets himself into the Islington house after his weekly visit to Brenda. The *For Sale* sign is up.

Poppy is coming over for a takeaway later and a drive. They're not taking pleasure in these things, but they are doing them. Poppy's therapist said she should try to go with the day, and not with the mood, and that makes sense to Aidan. So he will keep making cups of tea. Keep changing the sheets. Loading the dishwasher. Walking Bill Gates. Going to work. Until something shifts internally.

Maybe it never will.

A parcel is lying on his hallway floor, pushed in through the letter box and dropped. It's a jiffy bag. No postmark. He stops dead in his hallway and stares at it.

No. Please no. Not the group. Let the peace continue, even amid the grief.

He opens it. It's small but weighty. Inside is bubble wrap.

He opens that, and there it is. A burner phone. Wrapped in a note secured with elastic bands.

His hands shake as he pulls the note out and flattens it on the kitchen counter. Before he reads it, he rushes to the front door and locks it, then closes the shutters.

Then he returns to it. Chest full of helium and hope.

Keep in touch. L. xx

He stares and stares at the piece of paper, slightly tufty and ripped at its edges. Then he turns on the phone. One contact: In Case of Emergency.

He texts ICE, not knowing who he is texting, not knowing if it's a trap, or a joke, or a game.

The phone rings immediately.

'It's me,' she says.

And, oh my God. It *is* her. It is her voice, it is her voice, it is her voice.

'I'm so sorry. I'm so sorry . . . we had to wait until the group broke down and Luke got convicted and it was definitely, definitely safe. I'm so, so sorry. We're alive. We're alive. I'm so sorry. I'm so, so sorry I had to let you believe it, too. It was the last resort. The only way to keep us safe. I've been so fucking lonely! I've been having two baths a day! Eating so many cakes, I've got so fat!' She prattles on, his ebullient wife. Not allowing him time for it to sink in. Not giving him space. She rumbles on like a freight train, like she always has. Months. She's been dead for months.

'What . . .' he says, but he can't think. Can hardly speak.

He sat in the hospital and was told she was dead. He attended her funeral. And yet. And yet. Here is her voice, big and beautiful and true.

'The person protection service faked our deaths. It was the only way to keep us safe. Apparently, it was always their plan if the group found us for a second time. Zara was going to testify at the new trial but they thought if the

448

case wasn't successful, she would be in even more danger. So they faked our deaths. We've been in Scotland since December.'

'I can't . . .' Aidan stands in the kitchen where two minutes ago he was a widower, and stares at the wall. 'You're both fine?'

His mind skitters over the facts. No doctor ever told him they were dead. The protection service arranged the funeral. He never saw the bodies – they were too damaged, he was told. No wonder the court case fell apart against the arsonists, there were no bodies. There was no proof. He never saw a pathologist or a nurse or a funeral director. He saw a death certificate, but Jon gave it to him. Faked. All faked.

Fuck.

They're alive.

They're alive!

Could it be?

It could. It *is*. He's on the phone to her.

He tilts his head back. A slice of March sunlight from the edge of the shutters illuminates him.

'We're fine. We get asthma if we exercise. That's all. They got us out.'

'Is this safe?' Aidan says.

'Yes. The members of the group who aren't in jail have disbanded . . . properly disbanded. Tell me everything,' she says.

'Poppy is looking forward to the art foundation,' he says woodenly.

'Oh my God,' she says. 'Zara has chosen all artsy A-levels.'

A-levels. Aidan shakes his head. His body still feels like they're dead. A heavy, sad weight in his stomach. How can this be? How can they be talking about fucking A-levels?

Lauren is about to say something. Aidan can still tell, can still read her so easily. He waits for a beat.

'We can come back,' she says. 'Now that they're all inside. Aidan?'

Aidan turns to the window at this precise moment, the moment he is given everything he ever fucking wanted, and blinks. 'To London?' he says.

'Yes. Well, maybe we could go . . . nearer to Poppy. Wherever you are,' she says, 'I can be.'

'When?' Aidan says.

'Now. Now. Now. Zara will bring a boy . . . he'll probably have a heart attack. He thinks she's dead, too. He's our next phone call.'

'A boy?'

'She met this boy called Dom. Family moves around a lot anyway. He might come with us. I think we should let him. Once he recovers from the shock.'

Bill Gates pads into the living room and barks.

'Is that Bill?' Lauren says, her voice deliciously warm in his ear.

'Yeah,' Aidan says, dumbstruck, punch-drunk. So fucking lucky he can't even see straight. 'You want me to put him on?'

'If he can fit me in around his meetings,' Lauren says, and she laughs so loudly Aidan has to move the phone away from his ear.

*

She comes home a week later.

'We're free,' she says as she gets into bed next to him for the first time in months. 'We're free.'

He slides his hand down her arm, and reaches for her hand.

Their fingers interlock, under the duvet, as they always did. As if no time has passed at all.

Author's note

It turns out, witness protection is not a very easy subject to research, for obvious reasons. While I have endeavoured to find out how it works, there are many blanks I have been unable to fill in, due to the UK's protection service not wishing to reveal their secrets to me (quite reasonably), so necessitating the use of quite a lot of artistic licence and some common sense. I hope it was believable despite basically having . . . made it up.

Acknowledgements

There is something rather wonderful about writing the acknowledgements section of a book. It's like tidying up the bottles and the glasses after a good party. Novelists mark the passing of the years by which book they were writing, and 2019 will always be *How to Disappear*, for me, and for all the people who assisted.

Firstly to my agents Felicity Blunt and Lucy Morris. I have rarely met two smarter women. I am honoured to have you steering the ship of my career, reading draft after draft of this book, always tweaking, always asking clever questions, always highlighting the lines that are me at my best, and asking very kindly for the rest of the manuscript to be so! I was a lesser writer before you two. Really, I was.

Secondly to my wonderful editor Maxine Hitchcock, who lets me write books with two parallel narratives, with nineteen narrators, and now, too, a conspiracy book! Whatever I do, she is on board. To everybody on the Michael Joseph team, especially Rebecca Hilsdon, Olivia Thomas, Jen Porter, Grace Long, Shân Morley-Jones, sales and marketing and art. I am one of very few authors who can say that their every book since day one has been a bestseller, and it is because of the MJ dream team.

Writing a book about witness protection is something of a tricky thing, and the following people have helped enormously. Imran Mahmood, who, when I asked him whether the initial concept worked, said 'absolutely'. Muhammed Hafiz, my very kind post-office helper, on postmarking rules. Dalbir Kaur, who gave me the quite frankly wonderful guide dog story. To Jane Gosden and all at HMP High Down (including the very wonderful restaurant The Clink), who gave me a brilliant tour and let me ask lots of weird questions about how footballers would fare if in prison on remand. To Ian Foster for the football help, and Jade Deacon too. To Emma at Bodmin Agents, and Phil and Tin Johnson at JJ Associates – both of their help was invaluable on finding people who don't want to be found.

And finally, of course, to my friends and family. To Holly, Lia and Lucy for the sanity-saving best friendships. To Claire Douglas, Beth O'Leary and G X Todd too, for the WhatsApps, word-count tallies and lols. I have to say, there is nothing like befriending writers and asking them research questions. The answers you get are so vivid. The voice notes and the smell of cucumber sandwiches all belong to Lia.

This novel would be truly different without my father. I came up with the idea one autumn night in 2018 while he was over and we were boiling potatoes together, the clammy smell steaming up my kitchen. He turned to me and, even though I was actually planning a different novel, said, 'You have to write this.' He's helped me take it through various guises – it started life with Zara having been sent into protection because she was a released offender, if you can believe that. Then followed an extremely wooden draft where Aidan knew about the Find Girl A group, but did nothing to assist it. Aidan was finally born one day playing chess with my father where he said, 'So Aidan: is it that he takes too much care?' Those ten words changed this book. After he left, I thought, yes, yes, yes, Aidan would infiltrate the group, and this novel was changed for ever.

And finally, thanks, as ever, to David. This one's a stone cold love story, and you're the only man I've ever loved. It could only ever be dedicated to you.

The new book from

GILLIAN McALLISTER

COMING 2021

Read on for a sneak peek . . .

BRITISH MAN MISSING IN VERONA

A MAJOR search is underway in the hills just outside Verona, Italy as British National, William McGovern, 31, is still missing after forty-eight hours.

The Italian Carabinieri have confirmed today that McGovern is an ex-pat, living and working in Verona, where he disappeared. He has not been seen since the evening of Sunday, 6 July.

The Polizia di Stato are calling for any sightings of McGovern who stands at six feet one inch, is slim, with dark hair and glasses. He was wearing a white T-shirt and blue jeans on the evening of his disappearance.

The Carabinieri have today employed cadaver dogs to comb the local area.

The search continues.

Forty-eight hours earlier

Cathy

Cathy only answers the phone call that comes in the middle of the night because she is awake, online shopping. Two fake trailing plants, reduced from twenty pounds to ten. Irresistible. They will arrive while she's still here in Verona, a little insurance policy against the post-holiday blues.

Frannie. Slide to answer. Cathy's eyes flick to the top of the screen. It's 1.25 a.m. The room is completely dark around the blue bubble of light the phone creates. Cathy knows that beyond the phone lies a pine chest of drawers, a stone floor and a still-damp blue bikini dangling off a chair, but she can't see them. All she can see is her sister, calling her in the small hours. Calling Cathy because she knows Cathy will be alone, because Cathy is always alone.

She sits up in the bed and swipes to answer. The sheet falls away from her. She's wearing pyjamas, even in the Italian heat. It seems somehow wrong to sleep naked. That particular luxury, for Cathy, is reserved for the future, she hopes, with some as yet unknown man.

'Help me, please help me,' Frannie shouts as soon as Cathy answers. Electricity shoots across Cathy's chest and down her arms.

'What? What?' Cathy says. Sweat forms on her upper lip and between her breasts.

'Please help me,' Frannie says.

'Where are you? Are you safe?'

'Please come. I'm on the road. Turn right off the track road and then left. Half a mile, tops,' Frannie garbles.

Cathy waits. Waiting for Frannie to start making sense.

'It's him. The man from the market,' Frannie says, and then rings off.

Him.

Shit.

Cathy gets out of bed and starts scrambling around for clothes to throw on over her vest and shorts. She finds a pair of pink shorts she bought in Verona a couple of days ago and pulls them on, the price tag scratching against her lower back.

Why didn't she stay on the line? Cathy tries to call back, but it rings out.

Cathy rams her feet into her dusty flip-flops and grabs her bag. As she leaves the silent villa, not thinking to wake anyone, the closing of the large wooden door sounds like a gunshot in the night. The outskirts of Verona are completely black at this hour. Even after a week and a half, Cathy still isn't used to it. Struggling to see her own feet as she walks. The total power of the moonlight a shifting, eerie white-blue light that beams through the window.

The only other light comes from her bedroom window in the house behind her. It projects a neat rectangle of light on to the patio. And then: nothing, like she might be at the edge of the world without knowing it. The world has no horizon. It smells of cooked hay and rose bushes.

Frannie is scared. Cathy is sure of it. She tries to call her again, but this time it goes to voicemail. Maybe she is exaggerating. Cathy hopes so. She's always enjoyed the drama of Frannie's hyperbole; the way she tells a great story. 'There were literally fifty dogs in the waiting room today,' she once said. She's the receptionist at their family veterinary practice. She had refused to concede when Cathy pushed her. 'Yeah, *actually* fifty,' she'd said, and Cathy had thrown her head back and laughed. 'They must have had to sit some behind the reception desk,' she'd said, while Frannie nodded, eyes gleaming.

She sprints, the long, tough grasses whipping and snapping around her ankles like snakes, muttering pointless prayers out loud. Please be okay. Please don't be hurt, or frightened. As she reaches the end of the drive, she turns and sees headlights in the distance. She can only see it because of the deep Verona dark.

It must be their hire car, a Land Rover none of them likes driving. 'It feels like a fucking *bus*,' Joe had said on the first day.

She breaks into a proper run down the road. Right and then left, just like Frannie said.

Cathy's pace slows when she sees the silhouettes. She would know them anywhere: her siblings. Joe, standing by the Land Rover, his hands on his hips. And Frannie, kneeling down, her hair and long limbs illuminated by the headlights. She is so beautiful, has always been so. A wide nose. Cat eyes. A mane of dark, shiny hair.

Why is she on the floor? Cathy stares, then takes a breath, just one. She breathes it out as slowly as she can. This is . . . she stares at the shadows and the lights. Something has happened. A sweep of fear covers her shoulders. She starts to go cold. It's not from fear exactly. It's from knowledge. Knowing that – if she walks forwards – something is going to happen. A light breeze flutters Cathy's hair across her face. She tucks it behind her ears, breathes again, and walks forward.

Joe has evidently just arrived too, from his villa, and he walks across the lights, in and out of shadow, like a flickering bulb. Cathy wraps her arms around her middle. The bad feeling settles over her, like she is being watched, as she stares at them, as yet unseen.

She turns the torch from her phone on and shines it along the pale, dusty ground in front of her. Around her are the smells of Verona: dry heat, parched grass. It's been the hottest July on record. Cathy's family have had to buy after-sun most days. They've been through bottles and bottles of it. All of her clothes are oily at their hems. She can hear only the car's engine and the crickets. Otherwise, silence.

Cathy moves towards them and sweeps the torch slowly towards where Frannie is kneeling. And that's when she sees it.

Frannie is leaning over something. Cathy stops walking, but can't stop staring at Frannie. She has something – a T-shirt? – in her hands. As Frannie stands up, Cathy realizes Frannie's taken her own top off, that she's in just her bra.

She is in the dead centre of the two pools of headlights,

lit up like an actor on a stage. In the glare of the lights, it's clear that her hands are bloodied. She lifts them up. Red drips run down her wrists. Her stomach is streaked with the blood. It's dried, burgundy, the colour of red wine. She is a terrible tableau. Nausea rises up through Cathy. 'Fucking hell,' she whispers to nobody.

Joe is leaning over her now. Frannie extends her hands to Cathy and shouts: 'Help me.' A single plea that sets something off in Cathy. Something deep, familial, some thing protective rises up through her. It brings back when Frannie fell off a swing on to her back when she was three, when she choked on a sweet and Cathy thumped her hard between her shoulder blades and she coughed it right up. The first time Frannie went out as a teenager and Cathy waited up for her even though their mother had gone to bed. She still remembers it now: the ticking of the grandfather clock in their hallway, the hum of the fridge. And the relief as Frannie's key turned in the lock. And, of course, it reminds her of Rosie.

Cathy runs to Frannie. The headlights are a Venn diagram of light, a portrait of her sister, and a body lying at her feet.

Joe

What the fuck, what the fuck, what the fuck, Joe is thinking as he arrives in front of the car and stares at his sister. She is kneeling on the ground. He can see each individual knot of her spine, illuminated in the headlights in alternating patterns of shade and light. She's too skinny. Always has been.

'What . . .' he says, but his sentence ends there, like a

match that fails to strike. He can't believe what he's seeing. A body. 'What the fuck!' he whispers. 'What the fuck!'

'Help me!' Frannie shouts over her shoulder to him. In the distance, he can see the pinprick of Cathy's torch. Thank God, he thinks. She'll know what to do.

'I hit him,' Frannie screams to both of them. 'I hit him with the car.' Cathy's torch beam wavers as she runs towards them, leaving tracks in the night air like a sparkler. 'It's the man from the market.'

'What?' Joe says. He can't stop looking at the man lying underneath her. He's totally wrong looking. His skin both bloodied and waxy.

Frannie shouted at this man earlier today. He lit a cigarette up in the market and blew smoke all over her baby, Paul, who she was holding on her hip. Joe and Cathy had intervened, talked her down, but an Italian *carabinieri* – policeman – had seen and moved them on. His gaze was judgemental and unforgiving, a hand passing subtly over some weapon attached to his belt. 'Let's not cause trouble here, on this nice day,' he had said, looking at Frannie.

Joe approaches Frannie, even though he doesn't want to. Her face is blood-stained, streaked with tears and snot, too. He wants to turn away from it, run back to his villa, and to Lydia. Away from this – this grotesque mess.

It feels like he's walking through water that won't part in front of him. He tries to step forward, but he can't. He forces himself to look at the person lying on the ground. Tall, slim – his hip bones are visible. Frannie's lifted his shirt up. His torso is bleeding. His glasses are cracked.

He's very obviously dead.

Their family are almost all vets, including Joe and

Cathy, and death is obvious to vets. It's the blood. It's the quantity of the blood. Pints and pints of it. He gets his phone out as Cathy has and shines his torch across the road. The blood shimmers back, like petrol. There's so much blood. Joe tries not to gag. It smells fetid, both metallic and rotten, like just-turning food.

He turns to look at his sister, in a begging position on the road. Her nose ring shines in the light from his torch. 'What the fuck's gone on?' he says.

'I hit him – I hit him.'

'I can't – *how?*'

'Please help me,' she says, gesturing frantically to the body.

Joe kneels down next to it. Cathy joins him, but she's just looking, silently. He wishes he had her cool head. He and Cathy recently operated together on a Labrador and she spent at least a minute, after they'd opened him up, just looking. Not rushing. Just gathering information, in that way that Cathy does.

'Frannie,' he says, the words forming and exploding out of him like a cough.

'I hit him on his side,' she says, gesturing. 'It was my fault. It was my fault. It's the man from the market.'

'Shit,' Joe says. '*Shit.*'

'Please help me,' Frannie says. 'Please help – if we try to stem the bleeding, we . . . we just need to stop the bleeding, then he'll be okay, he'll be okay.'

Joe glances sharply at Cathy. She's the smartest of all of them, and he can see that she knows exactly what he knows.

'Hold your T-shirt to the wound,' Cathy says. 'Tight as you can.' Her face is inscrutable. 'You've called someone?'

Her voice is clipped but as she raises her phone to gesture, Joe sees the beam of her torch zig-zag across the body, leaving a shaky trail of light which fades to blackness after a second or two. Straggly-lined evidence of her panic.

Cathy moves towards the body. Her long, thick hair is piled on the top of her head. She is a less beautiful version of Frannie. Thicker set. Features slightly distorted somehow, or perhaps they only look so compared to Frannie's.

Cathy peers at the body. Joe can only just make out her face beyond the light of her torch. 'That's a lacerating wound,' she says. 'He's bleeding a lot for something like that.' She reaches to take his pulse.

'He'll be okay, won't he?' Frannie says.

'How fast were you going?' Joe says. He thinks he's going to be sick. Sweat has broken out across his forehead and his stomach is rolling over and over like a rough ocean. He's fine with blood usually. But this is – it's panic. His sister has hit somebody and there's blood everywhere. And now – now it's his problem too. He's got to fix it for her. His sister who wasn't always the youngest sibling, but is now.

'Barely,' Frannie says, but Joe's forgotten what he asked.

'Have you called an ambulance?' Cathy says to Frannie, kneeling over the body.

'Has he got a pulse?' Frannie asks.

'How have you not taken a pulse?' Joe says. He leans over, his hands on his thighs, breathing heavily. Stomach acid sloshes up his oesophagus. Get it together, he tells himself.

Cathy is starting CPR, though she must surely know it to be pointless. He takes the heart while she straightens the head. They've done it a thousand times before on animals. The body is cool beneath his fingertips. He darts a look at Cathy, who doesn't meet his gaze. He stares back down at it in the gloom. A man, his jeans and T-shirt dirty, blood circling beneath him. Four cuts on his arms, one oozing a small amount of blood. A bump already appearing on his forehead.

What are they going to do? She'll go to prison. Joe's stomach lurches at the thought of it.

His mind turns immediately to Frannie's son, Paul. Twelve months old, and he looks just like Joe. They laugh about it, compared baby photos of the two of them. The same heavy brow, dark features. Paul has the beginnings of Joe's Roman nose. Paul, innocent Paul, who loves cheese sandwiches, party rings, and his mother. What the fuck are they going to do?

The ground blurs beneath Joe. He's going to faint. A few minutes ago, he was sleeping off another day of sun. And now this. A body. No pulse. His culpable sister. He pumps at the man's chest, his fingers just a few inches from this stranger's heart.

'What happened?' Cathy says, checking and opening the man's airway, a quick finger swabbing around his mouth.

'I was on the wrong side of the road,' Frannie says. She drops her head towards the body like a condemned woman. Joe stares at her, aghast. Cathy closes her eyes.

'Shit,' Joe says softly. He looks at Frannie. Then at the body.

He knows the man is dead. But what he hasn't quite wrapped his head around is that that means his sister is a killer.